Table of Contents

1	7
2	18
3	27
4	33
5	40
6	47
7	54
8	63
9	71
10	83
11	89
12	97
13	103
14	110
15	116
16	121
17	131
18	138

19	144
20	149
21	157
22	162
23	166
24	172
25	180
26	188
27	194
28	202
29	208
30	217
31	220
32	228
33	233
34	241
35	248
36	253
37	262
38	269
39	275

40   282

41   288

42   293

43   301

44   308

45   316

Historical Note   321

FT
Pbk

1

Sparks flew and the screech of tortured metal set teeth on edge. There was a brief respite as armourer's mate Abel Grist raised the cutlass from his grinding wheel and tested the edge with his leathery thumb.

Watching sailors and marines waited expectantly. But Grist shook his head. In his expert opinion, the blade was not yet sharp enough to disembowel a Frenchman. So he pressed the metal to the grindstone and worked the foot-pedal again.

The on-lookers winced as another stream of sparks spewed forth.

There was nothing like a boat action in the offing to encourage all involved to seek a keen edge to bayonets, cutlasses, half pikes and boarding axes. And the horny-handed armourer's mate was happy to oblige them.

But in a wooden-walled frigate, with a magazine full of powder, this was a job for the open deck. Not the best workspace with a strong westerly breeze ruffling Grist's straggly greying hair.

A few more turns and he took his hand from the wheel to brush away a wisp from his eyes and test the blade again.

Finally satisfied, he handed the cutlass to a waiting seaman who accepted it gingerly and ran his own thumb down the blade.

'You reckon 'tis sharp enough then, Abel?'

Grist sneered gap-toothed at the doubter and growled: 'Give it back 'ere.'

Grabbing it, he held one of his own side whiskers – known in the service as buggers' grips – across the blade and snipped it in two with a flick of his wrist.

Then, smirking happily at this proof of his expertise, he handed the cutlass back and told his audience: 'You could shave a dozy mouse with that and the little bleeder wouldn't wake up!'

*

Attached to the squadron blockading the port of Le Havre, the frigate HMS *Phryne* had been firmly under the scrutiny of the admiral for some weeks. So, to avoid the danger of missing an order or summons, the captain had despatched a midshipman assumed guilty of being behind a series of annoying gunroom pranks into the rigging with a glass to keep an eye out for flag signals.

After many an hour of boredom the youngster almost fell from his lofty perch when he spotted the frigate's number being run up, summoning his captain on board the flagship.

George Phillips, captain of *Phryne*, called for his coxswain and his steward hurried him into his best uniform as the barge was being lowered.

A proud Welshman from Pembrokeshire with prematurely iron-grey hair, a florid complexion hinting at his enjoyment of good brandy, and the beginnings of a paunch due to lack of exercise rather than fine dining, he clambered a trifle clumsily down into the boat, nodding to the coxswain who growled: 'Dip oars.'

As he was rowed across through a slight swell, Phillips pondered possible reasons for the summons. Some misdemeanour, missed instruction or perceived laggardly station-holding perhaps? Always possible causes for a dressing-down on blockade duty.

But no, Vice Admiral Sir Ethelbert Leng was no nit-picker. More than likely this would mean orders for a brief detachment to carry out some task or other – normal use of a frigate – and *Phryne* was known for being the speediest in the squadron.

Piped over the side and greeted with all the formality due to a post captain, Phillips was escorted straight to the admiral's extensive quarters, aft on the upper deck.

'Come in, my boy.' Leng gripped his hand warmly and bade him sit. His captains were all 'my boys' to him although he was only a few years older than most of them.

'You'll take a glass of something?' Phillips suspected he needed to keep a clear head for whatever was to come, but welcomed a brandy, telling himself that it would be prudent to sip rather than his usual gulp – and to decline refills if offered.

Perhaps in part because of his diminutive stature and his years of being overlooked in favour of larger boys at school and later as a midshipman, the admiral had applied himself assiduously, climbed the ranks, led like his contemporary Nelson in a number of daring actions – although unlike him had managed to retain all his body parts – and now clearly enjoyed playing head boy at sea.

Small wonder, the one-time schoolboy fag and dogsbody was now God to all in his world, saving only his superiors at the Admiralty. But out of earshot among his fellow officers throughout the navy, his rapid rise and still youthful looks had earned him the affectionate nickname of the Boy Wonder. If he knew of it he no doubt considered it a mite less embarrassing than Ethel, the inevitable nickname of his schooldays for a small weedy boy cruelly christened Ethelbert.

Phillips stole a glance around the admiral's apartment – luxurious and enormous compared to his own not insignificant quarters in the frigate, but then everything in his world appeared miniscule compared to a ship of the line. 'Perhaps one day ...' he told himself.

After a few pleasantries and enquiries as to the state of *Phryne*, the admiral got quickly down to brass tacks, as was his wont. He indicated a chart of the Normandy coast laid out on his desk and unclasped his hands to indicate a point that Phillips took to be somewhere to the north.

'I have a task for you, my boy. You're to be let out of school, as it were – off the hook, eh?'

Phillips was relieved. He had been right – there was no misdemeanour to be chastised, but there was a chance to break the monotony of the present service.

Leng took a swig of his brandy and motioned his steward to replenish his visitors' already near empty glass. 'None of us enjoy blockade duty, do we? But just occasionally I get a chance to give one of my frigate boys a few days off ...'

'Most grateful, sir. Should I make notes?' The steward approached, rolling slightly with the swell, and somewhat reluctantly Phillips waved away the flat-bottomed decanter.

The admiral appeared not to have noted the abstemious gesture and shook his head. 'Notes? No need. You'll have written orders. Now, draw up your chair and take a closer look at the chart.' They both pulled up closer to the desk and Leng pointed out the small harbour of St Valery-en-Caux nestling in a break in the otherwise sheer Normandy cliffs to the north.

'Caux means chalk, you know,' he explained. 'You only have to see the cliffs to know that there's plenty of it in Normandy. In normal times this St Valery is merely a tin-pot fishing port and boatyard. But, of course, in wartime any usable harbour with repair facilities on the Channel coast has been pressed into military service and is deserving of our attention.'

Phillips nodded. 'I know the coast there, sir. So, may I ask if this St Valery is now of particular interest?'

'It is indeed. As of this very morning I have reliable intelligence indicating that a most troublesome French privateer is lurking there.'

Phillips was all attention. Armed vessels of that kind, owned and officered by private persons, were given commissions, known as letters of marque, from the French government to prey on British merchant shipping. And the Royal Navy regarded them as little better than licensed pirates.

The admiral tapped a document on his desk. 'A royalist sympathiser, already known to us, came on board from a fishing boat at first light with a first-hand report claiming that this particular privateer has been putting to sea once or twice a month with a large crew to cruise off Hampshire, Sussex and Kent intent on seizing small unarmed coastal vessels—'

'What type of vessel is it, sir?'

'We don't know exactly – our royalist friend is a landsman after all. But from what he tells us she's two-masted, mounting up to a dozen guns and well manned.'

'What we might call a gun brig, sir?'

'That's about the size of it. If so, she'll have a shallow draught and won't be too stable in the open sea but'll be fast and manoeuvrable enough to overtake and overwhelm easy prey around the Channel coast.'

Phillips got the picture. Such a raider could fairly easily avoid British men-of-war and a shot from one of her guns across the deck of a coaster would invariably be enough to convince the skipper that immediate surrender was not only wise but inevitable.

The familiar pattern in such cases would be that once the attackers had boarded, anyone who resisted would either be killed or thrown overboard. Those who cooperated would be allowed to make their way ashore by dinghy or makeshift raft.

The fact that the brig was heavily manned meant that a prize crew could be put on board the captured coaster to sail it to one of the

Normandy ports, leaving the privateer to continue the hunt. These predators were a menace, deeply damaging to British coastal commerce.

All this was well known to those who had sailed the Channel in these post-revolution years. The admiral did not need to elucidate further.

'Do we know the name of this privateer, sir?'

'We do indeed. She rejoices in the suitably revolutionary name of *Égalité*, and in the past few weeks St Valery's shipwrights, carpenters and riggers have been helping the crew make good some minor storm damage. According to our informer the victuallers are even now busy replenishing her and in a few days she'll be ready for the next foray along the English coast'.

'But you have other plans for her, sir?'

The admiral smiled broadly. 'Indeed I do! And that, my dear boy, is where you and Phryne come in ... and I need hardly remind you that if you cut her out successfully there will be a favourable mention in the Gazette – and prize money.'

This time Captain Phillips did not wave the decanter away.

*

Back on board *Phryne*, Phillips called for the master, first lieutenant and lieutenant of marines to outline the mission and formulate plans.

Brandishing his written orders, he told them: 'We're to look into the harbour of St Valery-en-Caux and ...' He screwed up his eyes and recited: '... and taking all measures consistent with the safety of your, that is my, ship, destroy or cut out the privateer currently reported to be under repair there ... etcetera, utmost despatch ... etcetera, etcetera. You get the picture?'

They got the picture – and throughout the day the frigate had headed north and then east along the Normandy coast towards Dieppe.

The opportunity to escape the boring routine of blockade had come as a welcome relief. Every frigate captain – and all those who served under him – aspired to be well out from under the penetrating gaze of the flagship and to be given an opportunity to cruise independently, with a chance of winning glory and capturing prizes. Preferably both.

This was a specific mission rather than a freelance hunting expedition. But, as the admiral had indicated, the possibility of reward was strong.

Once away from the squadron, the captain's sense of freedom was shared by everyone on board, from the quarterdeck to the lowliest newly-pressed landsman.

And although only those the captain had summoned yet knew in any detail where they were bound or why, there was a buzz unknown in the confined atmosphere of blockade duty. For the few members of the ship's company who had ever attended one, it was indeed like being let out of school early.

*

Night was falling as the ship passed the small fishing town of Étretat, framed by its strange door-like cliff formations – unmistakeable landmarks for mariners.

There was little need for caution. Without her tell-tale white ensign, *Phryne* was instead falsely flying a French tricolour at the masthead – an acceptable *ruse de guerre*.

It was hoped coast-watchers and gunners manning shore batteries would assume the 32-gun frigate to be French, as indeed she was. She had struck her colours two years earlier to a superior British force in the Mediterranean and been duly pressed into King George's service.

In inky darkness just before the end of the middle watch the prevailing westerlies brought Phryne close to her destination.

Men who spent much of their waking hours moaning and muttering about their lot were cheerful enough now. And orders cascaded throughout the ship to prepare for a possible cutting-out raid heightened the level of excitement.

So many seamen volunteered to man the boats that lots had to be drawn. Those who pulled marked wooden chips from a leathern bucket appeared cheerful, if a little thoughtful.

Those whose tokens were blank affected huge disappointment in front of their shipmates, but some were privately relieved – a foray on a hostile, reputedly heavily-defended, shore was a daunting prospect. In any case, all would share the prize money whether or not they were chosen for the boat parties.

Of the men selected, those who could, slept. But by midnight, start of the middle watch, all were wide awake and already preparing for action.

The raiding parties were fed, blackened one another's faces with some hilarity, and confided in their pigtail mates how their possessions were to be disbursed should they fail to return. And for once most had money they had not yet had a chance to waste on strong drink and weak women.

Before joining the Le Havre blockade Phryne had done well for prize money on a cruise along the northern Mediterranean coast, taking several rich French merchantmen and sending them into Gibraltar with prize crews aboard.

The second lieutenant, Oliver Anson, who was to command one of the boats on the raid, had himself taken in a coaster with a cargo of leather goods worth a good deal of money, and before sailing he had drawn 20 guineas of his entitlement in gold from the prize agent on the Rock.

Now, as they sailed along the Normandy coast, he took an old, well-worn uniform jacket from his sea chest and busied himself unstitching some of the seams. The task completed, he secreted guinea and half guinea coins in the gaps in the lining and set about sewing them up again.

It would not make sense to risk damaging his best white-lapelled blue coat, white waistcoat, breeches and stockings on a mission like this; the old jacket and a scruffy pair of trousers better suited to a tramp would suffice.

Lieutenant McKenzie of the marines watched the needlework fascinated, remarking to Anson: 'As a Scot I commend your prudence, but your money will be safe enough on board, y'know.'

Anson grinned. 'Good point. But where I go, it goes.'

'So you are by way of thinking that if the raid goes wrong you'll be able to pay your way home, eh?'

Anson nodded: 'Something like that.'

*

Captain Phillips had spent the earlier part of the night with the master, somewhat anxiously checking and re-checking the frigate's position. Josiah Tutt, the affable, grizzled senior warrant officer whose job it was to supervise the vessel's pilotage, was an old Channel hand and had already consulted his charts, books and pilot notes.

'What do'you know of this St Valery, Mr Tutt?'

'Well sir, it appears there's tidal streams that run across the entrance at something like two-and-a-half knots on the flood and a little less on the ebb.'

Phillips shrugged. 'That shouldn't trouble our boat crews too much?'

Tutt checked his notes. 'The tidal streams are somewhat complicated on the flood because there's a counter-current, but part of the eddy runs into the harbour. So no, well-oared and heavily laden, our boats shouldn't have a problem. Well, leastways, not with the currents.'

'What about towing the privateer out?'

'That'll have to be on the ebb.'

'And high tide is …?'

The master consulted his tables. 'Just after dawn, sir.'

'Perfect. So if we get our timing right and all goes well, the boats will be able to land the men high up on the slipway and have a little help from the eddy when they row into the harbour?'

'Exactly, sir – and it should help them getting out on the ebb.'

Phillips was satisfied it could be done. 'Capital. Now, master, just make sure the officers and coxswains know about this tidal stuff. Timing will be of the essence.'

He had not needed to spell that out. If the boats were lowered away too early there would be too far to row before dawn. Too late, and they would miss high tide and most certainly be spotted by watchers ashore. And the cutting-out party could only rely on having an hour either side of high tide during which they could be certain there would be sufficient depth to tow the privateer out of the inner harbour.

*

As the middle watch ended at four o'clock the boat parties were called to the main gun-deck to be briefed on the mission.

Stumbling about in the flickering lantern light they joshed and ribbed one another to break the tension and hide jittery nerves until bosun Taylor's bark silenced them: 'Cap'n present!'

Phillips made his way to one of the 18-pounders, put a foot on the gun carriage and leaned back against the barrel. A lantern swinging nearby lit his face intermittently as he readied himself for the exhortation expected of him.

Every man's eyes were on him and only the slaps of the waves and creaks and squeaks of the ship's timbers broke the silence.

'Well, boys …' He looked slowly around the expectant faces. They were his boys at a moment like this, men on more formal occasions, and lubbers when they got it wrong or when the loneliness of command soured him. 'Yes, my brave boys, at last we've a chance to strike a blow for old England!'

He paused to allow them a ragged cheer and smiled good-naturedly on hearing an unmistakeably fellow-Welshman at the back ask: 'And Wales too, eh sir?'

'Most certainly for Wales, boy. And Scotland and Ireland too!' He knew the Paddies and Scots, who hated being lumped in with the English, would like that.

The buzz of laughter was cut short by the bosun tapping his rattan cane on the cannon and the captain's upheld hand. 'Now this is serious, boys. There's a privateer lurking in the harbour of a place called St Valery—'

'Saint 'oo?' queried a voice from the gloom.

Bosun Taylor banged his cane fiercely and shrilled: 'Hold yer tongue when the cap'n's speaking!'

Phillips smiled benevolently. He knew how to work his audience. 'For the benefit of that man who's obviously spent too much time working the guns and has addled his hearing, the port is Saint Valery ...'

His riposte provoked nervous laughter and he paused for effect.

'Yes lads, it's a place called St Valery-en-Caux. That's where we're bound. This poxy privateer's been causing mayhem on our coast, capturing unarmed merchantmen and feeding their crews to the fishes. Now he's holed up and we've a chance to give these cowardly Frogs some of their own medicine.'

He looked round at the sea of expectant faces picked out intermittently by the swinging lantern. 'So, we're going to cut this privateer out. Are you up for it, lads?'

A chorus of muted cheers and 'aye ayes' greeted his call to arms.

And there were more cheers, and louder, when he added: 'If we pull this off there'll be prize money, boys – and likely there'll be lots of it!'

In his case there most certainly would be plenty – thanks to the Admiralty's patently unfair system of doling out the proceeds from the sale of a captured enemy vessel. It would be divided into eighths and then shared out according to rank rather than risk.

Sceptics could well have queried the fairness of a scale dictating that in a case such as this the admiral commanding the fleet would receive an eighth although hundreds of miles away from the shot, smoke, blood and guts. The captain's share was to be two eighths, although in this instance he would be remaining on board the *Phryne*. And a lucky captain could make thousands.

Fair enough that the next ranking officers would share an eighth and the two levels further down the food chain would also each split an eighth.

Less acceptable, in some lower deck eyes, was that the lowliest seaman or marine risking his life on a dicey raid would receive a mere fraction of the rest of the ship's company share of two eighths. Divided so many times over, it was often barely enough for a good run ashore.

But if there were any such sceptics aboard they wisely held their peace in public, saving their muttering for their hammocks.

Phillips was not one for long speeches. 'Now, listen up to the first lieutenant who'll tell you what you're to do, boys. I'd like to be with you, but someone's got to mind the shop while you're enjoying your run ashore ...' He paused to let the nervous laughter subside and added: 'I know you'll do your duty.'

Every member of the cutting-out party knew the captain meant what he said. He had proved himself to them often enough.

They nodded and muttered their assent and Phillips strode away, back to his charts.

*

For Lieutenant John Howard the raid was a golden opportunity, and his eagerness to crack on was infectious.

In allowing him to lead the expedition, the captain of the *Phryne* was doing his first lieutenant a supreme favour. Success could mean an honourable mention in the Gazette and almost instant promotion, not to mention a decent share of the prize money the privateer would fetch once safely alongside in Portsmouth or Chatham.

Certainly failure could mean death, maiming, or kicking his heels as a prisoner of the French until he could be exchanged. But the rare opportunity for advancement outweighed the risks and any naval officer worth his salt would have been eager to lead the raid. Howard, scion of a noble family, was no exception.

Supported by McKenzie of the marines, Lieutenant Anson and young Midshipmen Lampard and Foxe, he briefed the boat parties on what lay ahead.

The three boats would be launched two hours before dawn, and, with extra boarding crews and marines aboard, would be towed nearer the objective. An hour before first light the boats would cast off, slip round the slight headland to the west of St Valery and row hard for the mole – a long, high, man-made stone jetty jutting out into the Channel and sheltering the small natural harbour.

The plan was for the boats to land Howard, McKenzie with his marines and a dozen of the seamen on the slipway at the opening of the inlet used by St Valery's fishermen. The raiders were to deal with any sentries and make their way swiftly down the mole.

Once in the inner harbour, where the privateer was believed to be lurking, it would be down to the marines to take in the name of King George and enable the seamen with them to get on board and prepare for sailing.

Anson and the two midshipmen were to stay with *Phryne's* boats which, after dropping the raiding party on the mole, were to row like hell straight for the privateer, hopefully arriving immediately after she had been taken, and tow her out before the French woke up to what was happening.

2

Westward, back to Fecamp, and east towards Dieppe, stretched a wall of off-white chalk cliffs known as *les falaises* to the French, broken here only by the inlet and harbour of St Valery-en-Caux. Inland lay the Pays de Caux – the land of chalk.

To an attacking force the gap, the only route inland, was the maritime equivalent of a breached citadel wall. But this entry port had been formed by the battering of nature, not siege guns. And, given the good fortune of surprise, the *Phryne's* boat crews would not have as formidable a task as a forlorn hope about to assault a heavily-defended breach.

There would be batteries on either side of the inlet, and watchers enough. But in the hour before dawn the boat crews, appearing suddenly and silently on the mole from the shelter of a bulge in the cliffs shown on the captain's chart as the Falaise d'Aval, had every chance of achieving complete surprise.

Phillips had no precise intelligence about the shore batteries guarding St Valery, but elsewhere the French were known to have 24-pounders or even 32-pound monsters commanding entry to their harbours, and capable of blasting out of the water anything that could float. They would be well protected behind embrasures 5ft thick and 8ft high, and behind them would be furnaces for heating shot – a frightening proposition for men in a wooden warship unable to elevate their own guns enough to counter them.

*

At zero hour a tot of rum was issued to each member of the cutting-out party and the boats were lowered.

Twenty seamen and ten marines clambered into the launch. A dozen sailors and four marines manned the smaller jolly boat, and ten seamen and six more marines scrambled into the cutter. With the officers and midshipmen, there were 67 in all – a third of the complement of the *Phryne*.

There was some confusion in the pre-dawn darkness as men struggled to reach their appointed places, but there would be time enough to sort themselves out as the frigate towed the boats nearer the objective.

When Phillips judged it close enough, and in silence lest bosun's pipes and shouted orders carried ashore, canvas was lowered and *Phryne* hove to, rocking gently in the slight swell.

Topmen remained aloft along the yards ready to cast off the gaskets and let the sails fall when the time came to follow the boats, and gun crews gathered to man the starboard battery.

Phillips had taken every possible precaution and it was now down to the cutting-out party – and good fortune.

From the launch, Lieutenant Howard waited for the expected low shout from the ship: 'Ahoy boats. Cast off!'

Tow ropes were abandoned and with a wave of Howard's second-best bicorn hat and to hissed orders of 'Dip oars, give way together,' the boats pulled slowly away from the frigate.

The oarsmen were fit and, with only a couple of miles to row and a westerly breeze pushing them on, they made good progress towards the Falaise d'Aval despite an increasingly choppy sea.

Greased sacking muffled the rowlocks, but they still squeaked and cracked noisily. And however carefully the rowers slid their blades into the water they could not avoid splashing.

Pock-faced bosun's mate Duff exchanged a pained look with the young officer commanding the cutter and snarled venomously at the worst offender: 'Stop squeakin' yer effing oar, Robson!'

'Bollocks!' The response was just loud enough to provoke a stifled guffaw from those nearest the offending rower.

Duff, feared on board for his fierce dedication to his disciplinarian role, hissed: 'If ye're answerin' back, y'pile of shite, I'll have ye!'

Notorious though he was for his cheek, Robson was ever careful to play the innocent when it mattered. 'Not me, mate. I just said it's me rowlocks. I canna help it. I allus seem t'draw a squeaky whore. I mean oar!'

Duff's muttered oath and piercing glare cut short the boat's crew's half-suppressed chuckles. He growled: 'Ye're doing it on purpose you pillock. Cut it out or ye'll be the death of us all.'

Robson knew when to toe the line. But he provoked more sniggers with his Tyneside-accented: 'Whey-aye aye, man!'

Within the hearing of an officer – and Lieutenant Anson was a clergyman's son to boot – the bosun's mate had learned to refine his profanities and abuse. But his retort was none the less forceful: 'Cut the effing crap or I'll stick yer effing oar up yer effing arse meself, yer effing cretin!'

'Amen t'that,' muttered Robson, provoking Duff to spit again with venom: 'Button yer lip!'

His fierce stare swept the rowers. 'Next one of you dozy scum to make a noise'll get a whack for breakfast.'

Being 'started' by a bosun's mate with a rope's end was no picnic. If disregarded, Duff's threats were known to be backed by action. And so the cutter carved its way through the waves, now somewhat quieter, if not squeak-free.

Squatting in the stern among a half-dozen grappling hooks and listening to the banter, Lieutenant Anson could not stop the ghost of a smile tugging at his blackened features.

Glimpsed when the cloud cover gave way briefly to moonlight, the Normandy coast to starboard was lined with seemingly sheer chalk cliffs, fortress-like and forbidding.

In those occasional brighter moments Anson looked over the raiding force as they closed on their objective.

The dark shapes of the two other boats lay to larboard, the three linked loosely with ropes to avoid becoming separated by St Valery's tidal currents in the pre-dawn gloom.

There was just enough light for Anson to make out the red-coated marines clutching blackened muskets and his seamen, pistols in their belts and armed with their newly-sharpened cutlasses, half pikes, axes and tomahawks, crouching in the thwarts between the oarsmen.

The seamen may have been chosen by lot, but there would have been enough volunteers to man three more boats if need be. By tradition, no-one ever dared ask the marines. They were always assumed to have volunteered en bloc – by sacred right.

Faces were camouflaged with burnt cork and the seamen wore white armbands for identification ashore. The red jackets of the marines were unmistakeably British.

If in doubt as to friend or foe, the password was easy enough to remember – the name of their ship, pronounced by all on the lower deck as 'Fry-nee'.

Muskets and pistols that had not been loaded until the men were in the boat for fear of accidental discharges while clambering down the ship's side, were now charged and checked over and over again, their priming carefully protected from spray by hats or cupped hands.

Edged weapons were fingered nervously as the seamen carrying them reassured themselves that Abel Grist had done his work well and they were ready for business.

It was time to give the French a painful wake-up call.

*

Soon after the boats had pulled away from the frigate they had attracted the unwelcome attention of screeching seagulls.

Howard willed the launch on, concerned that the ravenous gulls following the little flotilla in the hope of a meal, just as they no doubt always followed the local fishing boats, would put sentries on the *qui vive*.

'God-damned creatures,' he mouthed at the cackling ghost-like shapes wheeling above. 'Damn their eyes!'

His coxswain, close enough to pick up the muttered oaths, misinterpreted the target of Howard's ire and hissed at the oarsmen: 'Row, ye buggers, row!'

With the launch in the lead, the little flotilla at last reached the end of the mole and pulled for the slipway.

Crouched in the stern of the cutter, Lieutenant Anson scanned the shoreline anxiously. Surely someone would spot them approaching.

And in the jolly boat Midshipman Lampard, only 15 and still with choirboy looks but already a promising seaman keen to prove himself in action, was earnestly urging his oarsmen on.

The boats approached the sloped landing place used by St Valery's crabbers and lobstermen and the launch was first to touch, keel scraping on the granite blocks of the slipway.

Howard, determined to be seen to lead by example and unconsciously observing the ancient naval tradition – senior officer last in, first out – jumped but lost his footing on the greasy, seaweed-covered slipway and sprawled awkwardly into the water, twisting his ankle and dropping his sword as he fell. It was an ill omen.

Helped by a wild-eyed, tomahawk-wielding sail-maker's mate, he climbed painfully to his feet, scrabbled to find his sword, muttered 'Thankee Coppins,' and hopped on.

The rest of the marines and sailors making up the mole party followed Howard and Lieutenant McKenzie into the water and up the slipway.

As planned, Anson and the two midshipmen remained with the boats' crews, ready to pull away as soon as the shore party had disembarked. Then, as the shore party raced down the mole to board *Égalité*, they were to row flat out for the inlet and the privateer's berth alongside the harbour walls.

From their briefing they knew that the tidal inlet curved to the right, bordered by typically-Norman timber-framed and red-painted houses. A blue flare was to signal that the ship had been taken by the shore party and the rowers were to spurt the last few yards, turn under *Égalité's* bows and secure the tow ropes that were to be thrown down. Then it would be a case of pulling like devils for the open sea. No blue light would mean the boats' crews would need to clamber aboard and help the shore party overwhelm the ship. Hence the grappling irons in the thwarts.

The prevailing westerly would be of no help in bringing the privateer out, so the attackers would need to rely on muscle power and the ebbing tide until she was clear of the harbour.

Once clear of the mole, they would get her under way while *Phryne* swooped in to provide protective fire and recover the boats before sailing clear of the shore batteries.

If all went well, first light should see the frigate and her prize setting a course for Portsmouth.

It was a simple enough plan and if it worked it would be an excellent morning's work. Everything depended on achieving surprise – and on swift and determined action. But if the alarm was raised too soon and the mole party became bogged down ashore, or if the enemy batteries came into action, it could so easily end in disaster.

*

Ashore, through a powerful glass from an observation post atop Falaise d'Amont to the east of the harbour, the frigate's arrival had been noted. It was still too dark for the French lookout to identify the ship as friend or foe, but he played safe.

Messengers had been despatched to alert the shore batteries and the infantry battalion that had been bivouacked around St Valery for the past few days.

It was better to be safe than sorry, and when a second messenger arrived with news that boats had been seen leaving the warship, the French infantry colonel ordered a company down into the harbour.

Half took up positions in the town and the inner harbour, and the rest set off at a trot down the mole.

*

As Lieutenant Howard hopped up the slipway, dark-jacketed figures could be seen approaching from the port. French infantrymen!

The sickening realisation hit him. The enemy had been alerted. Surprise was lost.

He paused for a moment debating whether to press on or beat a hasty retreat before the boats pulled away for the inner harbour. Without the boats his party would be trapped.

A shouted *'Qui en va?'* followed closely by the crack of a musket gave him the answer.

He turned and shouted: 'Hold the boats men. The Frogs are waiting for us!' And he discharged his pistol towards the shadowy figures.

Fire was returned immediately and a dozen musket balls buzzed angrily by – one felling the seaman who had helped Howard when he stumbled.

Lieutenant McKenzie bellowed to his marines: 'Fire boys, fire!' and a ragged volley sent the leading Frenchmen scuttling for cover.

Howard was now in no doubt whatsoever that the mission had failed before it had begun. The only sensible course of action was to withdraw to the boats. Anything else would be suicidal.

More and more Frenchmen were reaching the scene and musket balls splattered the stonework around the slipway.

But McKenzie's marines were reloading, kneeling to make less of a target, and returning fire.

Above the rattle of musketry, Howard's voice was as strong and clear as if he were on the quarter-deck. 'Marines form a rearguard, the rest back to the boats!'

But in the limited pre-dawn light there was nothing but confusion on the slipway. And as more Frenchmen joined their comrades, their rate of fire steadily increased.

A marine fell and two more seamen went down, their blood blossoming out in the wavelets washing the slipway. Those who had just jumped ashore pressed forward, some colliding with those heading back to the boats.

Still in the cutter, ready to lead the boat assault on the privateer, Lieutenant Anson knew instinctively that a critical moment had been reached. With more of the enemy concentrating at the end of the mole, the slipway had become a death-trap. It was vital to re-embark everyone immediately, and to achieve that he needed to buy time.

He clutched Duff's shoulder, shouting in his ear: 'Take charge and get them aboard!' and leapt for the slipway.

Above the din he yelled: 'Get the wounded back in the boats!' and splashed through the steadily rising water now covering half the slipway to where Howard was struggling to keep his footing.

Anson grabbed the first lieutenant's arm. 'You're hurt. Go and get the boats away or all will be lost. McKenzie and I will cover you!'

Howard, as the senior officer, made as if to argue the point, but knew Anson was right, shrugged in resignation and hopped for the launch.

McKenzie was at the head of the slipway encouraging his marines and Anson splashed to his side shouting: 'We need to hold them for a few minutes!'

A musket ball whined between them, making both flinch. This was not a time for shilly-shallying. For the marines, attack was reckoned to be the best form of defence. Without hesitation McKenzie, already hoarse from shouting, croaked: 'Steady lads. Fix bayonets!' There was an almost instant clash of metal on metal as bayonets were locked home.

'Ready? Charge!' And, to the astonishment of the nearest Frenchmen, a dozen red-jacketed marines led by two sword-wielding officers appeared out of the gloom, steel-tipped muskets to the fore.

The nearest Frenchmen turned tail and scuttled for cover, pursued for a few yards by the red English devils who knelt, fired, re-loaded and, at McKenzie's order, retreated backwards down the slipway.

Anson glanced back at the boats. The charge had bought the raiding party precious minutes. In the rapidly improving light he could see that most of the other Phrynes, including several wounded, were back on board. To his front the French infantrymen, their numbers growing by the minute, could now see how few faced them and began to push forward again to shouts of *'Allez, allez!'*

Gripping McKenzie's arm, Anson urged him: 'Time to go, Ned!'

McKenzie called his men back and Anson gathered the handful of sailors still on the slipway.

A sudden searing pain in his leg made him stagger. He stumbled for a couple of steps, wincing – and instantly realised that, slowed down as he was, he was too far from the boats to make it back quickly. And if he held up the withdrawal all would be lost.

The crackle of French musketry continued as the surviving marines and sailors struggled across the slimy slipway to wade the last few steps and fling themselves into the boats.

Musket balls whining around them, the rowers began pulling on their oars, desperate to get clear.

Whoops from excited French infantrymen, agonised cries of the wounded and the desperate calls for a helping hand from those not yet embarked, added to the confusion and chaos.

But above the din, the first lieutenant could be heard shouting: 'Back lads, quick as you can!'

McKenzie, now beside the jolly boat, was urging each of his men as they made it back to the boats: 'Reload and fire at will!'

Further back down the mole, more Frenchmen were being hurried forward by their officers and sergeants with cries of *'En avant!'*

Despite the burning pain in his leg, Anson, now the last officer ashore, joined a lightly wounded marine corporal who was rallying the few men left on the slipway. The joker Robson was at his side muttering cheerfully: 'Reet hot work this!'

Anson switched his sword to his left hand, pulled a pistol from his belt and fired towards the nearest Frenchmen, some in the act of kneeling and firing, others reloading.

With no hope of reloading himself, he turned the pistol to use as a club. But the Frenchmen showed no inclination to close for the moment. It was sufficient for them to pick off the raiders with musketry from a distance of no more than ten yards, a range which rendered their weapons –

normally only effective for volley firing against a close-ranked enemy – accurate enough for this work.

To fight on would be suicidal. Anson dropped his pistol and, helped by Robson, limped down the slipway.

But as they neared the boats a French musket ball struck the Tynesider in the head, exited with a clout of blood, bone and brain, and felled Anson.

A marine stooped, decided that the lieutenant was a goner, and made for the last boat, a ball piercing his scarlet jacket and searing his arm as he flung himself aboard.

The first lieutenant shouted at him: 'Where's Mr Anson?'

'He's dead, sorr, shot through the 'ead!'

Howard nodded. This was not the time for inquests. Instead he turned his attention to the living and urged the boats' crews: 'Pull, damn you, pull!' And to two dazed and slightly wounded sailors he growled: 'Give a hand at the oars. But keep low!'

Two more men were hit as the launch pulled away after the other boats. And as more Frenchmen reached the end of the mole it seemed they would be able to pick off the rest of the escaping raiders almost at will.

But in the improving light the unfolding disaster had been witnessed through a glass from *Phryne*. The frigate had crammed on canvas, followed the boats round the Failaise d'Aval and was now preparing to recover the cutting-out party. A sighting shot from one of her 18-pounders struck the mole, splintering stonework and scattering the leading Frenchmen.

It was followed by another, and another, forcing the infantrymen to take cover and reducing the level of musketry directed against the escaping boats to a few, desultory, poorly-aimed balls.

As was the time-honoured custom of the sea, Captain Phillips had hoisted *Phryne's* true colours before going into action, so it would not be long before the shore batteries returned fire.

The oarsmen pulled hard and within minutes were safe on the seaward side of the frigate.

And as soon as they were secured, *Phryne* altered course nor'east, standing away from the mole as the first ball from the shore batteries splashed into her rapidly-increasing wake.

3

Pacing the quarterdeck as *Phryne* left the cliff walls of Normandy far behind, Captain Phillips counted the cost. There would be no glory, no rapid promotion for Howard – and no prize money.

Instead, they were without the second lieutenant, confirmed dead on the mole, and two marines and three seamen who had been seen to fall during the action and were now missing – prisoners, if not dead.

Two more had been killed at their oars during the escape and been brought back rolling bloodily in the bilges to await a proper burial at sea, and several more were wounded, including one who would lose an arm.

This had been a bloody and wasteful business – all to no avail because *Égalité* would now complete her repairs and replenishment without further disturbance and live to cause more mischief another day.

It was time now for still more distasteful tasks. The captain returned to his cabin, flung down his hat and drew paper, pen and ink from his desk. There was a report to write to Admiral Leng, and a more difficult letter to Lieutenant Anson's father – and him a parson to boot. That would require more than the usual platitudes.

*

On the mole, where but a short while earlier there had been frenetic activity and the din of battle, all was now strangely quiet apart from the groans of the wounded.

Once the retreating boats had pulled out of musket range from the mole, *Phryne* had ceased firing and slowly French infantrymen emerged from cover and advanced warily to check the wounded and search the English dead for valuables and souvenirs.

Not all were dead. Corporal Tom Hoover, his red jacket darkened by his own blood, lay back with his shoulders propped up against the stonework where he had dragged himself out of the water lapping the slipway.

There was something about the way the wounded but clearly unafraid and menacing corporal of marines stared at the Frenchmen that encouraged most to by-pass him.

Nevertheless, two were not put off searching the pockets of the nearby sailor with the shattered skull. Drawing a blank, they rolled him aside and turned their attention to the body of the naval officer sprawled beneath him. But they turned in alarm on hearing the wounded corporal growl: 'Get back you heathens! *Allez*, or by God I'll skin you alive!'

He had raised himself to a sitting position, bayonet in hand.

One of the body-searching Frenchmen picked up his musket and stepped towards the corporal swinging it like a club. There was no mistaking his intention – to smash this impudent marine's skull.

But a French officer who had observed the drama unfold stepped forward, waved off the musket-swinger and addressed the wounded man in excellent English. 'You are a brave man, but it would not be sensible to continue the battle. You are on the losing side and if you do not submit my men will kill you, just as you have killed their comrades.' He indicated the sprawled bodies of several blue-jacketed Frenchmen.

Hoover nodded and turned the bayonet hilt towards the officer, who took it and handed it straight to the would-be executioner. *'Souvenir d'une petite victoire.'* The man took it, sneered triumphantly at the wounded marine and moved away.

The French officer, gentlemanly of manners like those of the old regime rather than the newly-elevated types of the new republican order, shrugged and told Hoover: 'It is for the best.'

After a while two horse-drawn carts arrived on the mole and a party of soldiers began throwing the bodies – French and English – into one and lifting the half dozen wounded into the other.

The bloodlust had cooled. And the presence of the French lieutenant who had saved Hoover from death by musket butt ensured that he and a diminutive foretopman called Fagg, now crippled with a broken ankle and apparently the only other survivor from the *Phryne* party left ashore, were helped into the second cart no more roughly than the French wounded.

*

How do you break the news to a proud father that the son he imagines to be a budding Howe or Rodney is dead? And how do you explain that the life of the young naval officer for whom his family had such high hopes has been squandered in a useless, aborted raid that would not rate a single line in the history books?

Pacing his cabin in *Phryne*, Captain Phillips pondered the wording of the letter he must write.

At least he could say that his second lieutenant had died bravely for his country, even if the cutting-out expedition had been so singularly unsuccessful. But then, how was he to have known that French infantry were there in force? So much for the quality of the intelligence from the admiral's tame French royalist spy.

The attackers had been overwhelmed almost as soon as they set foot on the mole. From the survivors, the captain had learned that Anson was among the first to be wounded – in the leg – and then felled by a French musket ball through the head as he led a small rearguard trying to give the others time to regain the boats.

To Phillips, it was a huge relief that so many of the Phrynes had made it back to the boats and escaped under the frigate's protective fire.

It was something of a miracle, made possible only by over-excited Frenchmen failing to press home their advantage in the half light on the mole, and the shore batteries coming into action so late and so ineffectively.

If Phillips were to be totally honest, he would have to admit that his second lieutenant had been no Howe or Rodney. In truth, despite being a distant kinsman of the circumnavigator Commodore George Anson, the young man had not been the ablest of seamen; a poor grasp of mathematics hampered his navigational skills; and he had been perhaps a little too familiar with the men.

But maybe, having grown accustomed to enduring the loneliness of command, this was the natural judgement of any captain of almost every junior officer. Stiff by nature, Phillips had tried hard not to envy confident, relaxed young officers like Anson.

A comfortable upbringing as second son of a wealthy churchman and extraordinary luck with prize money did not endear officers like him to Phillips, even though a large share of such riches came the captain's way.

The achievement of post command had been a long hard ride for the captain. By comparison, advancement in the service seemed like a stroll for officers like Anson, especially anyone with a famous naval name, even if that kinship was many times removed.

Nonetheless, whatever the captain's opinion of his second lieutenant, now was not the time to be mealy-mouthed. Now was the moment to be generous with his praise for an officer who had laid down his life for King and country: a hero.

He would be missed, certainly. There would be glum faces on the lower deck this night as news of his loss, and of the other casualties, spread – and the promise of prize money evaporated. The gunroom, too, would miss Anson's wit and cheerful optimism. His unswerving sense of duty and natural courage would be a loss to the navy, but such qualities were hardly in short supply in a service in which hundreds of young officers were chasing promotion and a command of their own.

Now there would be one less thirsting for advancement that seemed to promise so much, but for many – Phillips included – could so easily become more like a poisoned chalice.

Finally satisfied that he knew the line to take, Phillips sat, dipped his pen and began scratching:

'To the Revd Anson
The Rectory
Hardres Minnis
Near Canterbury
Kent
Dear Sir

It grieves me to have to inform you that your son Lieutenant Oliver Anson has been killed in action during an attack against the French at St Valery-en-Caux in Normandy. He was my trusted second lieutenant, a gallant, efficient and resourceful officer whom I had marked out as being worthy of further, early advancement, and I have no doubt that had he lived he would have achieved high rank and afforded his country valuable service. Sadly, that is not to be.

In brief, the circumstances of his death are these: he had volunteered, as I had come to expect of him, to take part in a boat attack aimed at cutting out a French privateer that had been harrying our coastal shipping. His party made a successful landing on the French coast, but the alarm was raised and a large party of French infantry bivouacked nearby forced them to withdraw. It was whilst fighting a gallant rearguard action that he and a number of others were cut down.

I am, Sir, only too acutely aware of the pain this sad intelligence will bring to the family that your son revered above all else but God and his duty. There is but one consolation: his was a hero's end in keeping with the best traditions of the service and of his illustrious kinsman. In breaking the sad news to his mother, brothers and sisters, you can with certainty assure them that he not only died bravely at the head of his men, but that he did not suffer. Before withdrawing, his companions satisfied themselves that he had been struck in the head by an enemy musket ball and had clearly expired instantaneously. They were loath to leave his body where he fell, but were forced by superior numbers to make good their withdrawal rather than suffer further casualties. However, despite their national animosity towards England, I am confident that the French will recognise gallant foes as we do, and will give your son and his fellows a decent Christian burial. The personal effects he left on board will be forwarded when we next reach a home port.

I am, sir, your obedient servant

George Phillips, Captain, Royal Navy.'

Then, remembering that the recipient was a clergyman, he added a postscript:

'The entire ship's company will remember your son and his grieving family in our prayers on board HMS Phryne on Sunday.'

After sealing the letter ready for the mails that would be passed to the next Dover-bound vessel encountered, and calling for the first lieutenant to ensure that the ship would be rigged for church on Sunday, Phillips sent for the ship's muster roll.

In addition to basic information about each member of the ship's company, capital letters had to be inserted alongside the name of anyone who left, indicating what had happened to them, such as D for Discharged and R for Run, meaning deserted.

Against the name of Oliver Anson, Second Lieutenant, he wrote DD – the navy's laconic shorthand for Discharged Dead.

*

At the end of the mole the wounded were unloaded from the cart and stretchered into a stone building that reeked of fish. Fagg was laid unceremoniously on his back beside the French casualties. He grinned at Corporal Hoover: 'S'pose we're prisoners of the Frogs now, eh?'

The marine had brushed aside an orderly and, clutching his wounded left shoulder, seated himself on a fish crate by the door. 'Guess so.'

'I just 'ope they feed us with summink better'n frogs' legs and all that other crap they eat.'

Hoover shrugged. 'At least we're still here.'

The two had only known one another by sight on board, but must now team up since there were no others.

A surgeon arrived with two more orderlies and began examining the wounded, French first.

Outside, the infantry officer who had persuaded Hoover to surrender his bayonet, returned with a sergeant armed with a notebook and the precious stub of a pencil – imports of English graphite having been interrupted by war.

The sergeant called to two passing soldiers and gestured to them to pull the bodies off the other cart and lay them outside the makeshift casualty station.

Once the French dead were lined up on their final parade he began identifying and listing them, all members of his company.

Watching him at work, the officer glanced at Hoover and said quietly: 'So young. Seven more mothers will soon be weeping for their sons. Not exactly a glorious death, but they fell defending France nevertheless.'

Hoover nodded. It gave him no pleasure to see young men cut down, friend or foe.

The list of French casualties complete, the sergeant indicated the dead Englishmen and asked: *'Et les Rosbifs?'* The officer pondered for a moment whether he should try to identify the enemy fallen, but dismissed the idea with a shake of his head. Their ship would know who had been lost.

However, perhaps he should at least see if the dead English officer was carrying any identification or indeed any papers of interest for intelligence purposes. So he ordered the sergeant to extricate the officer from the English dead on the cart and search him.

The sergeant grabbed Anson's ankles, pulled his body to the back of the cart and, studiously avoiding looking at his blood, bone and brain-splattered head, began going through his pockets.

But to his astonishment the corpse stirred and groaned and the Frenchman started back in alarm exclaiming: *'Mon dieu, il vive!'*

4

The raiding party survivors were treated with the same rough care as the French casualties but even here revolutionary *égalité* gave way to the privileges of rank and the English officer was assessed first.

A pitcher of water thrown over Anson washed away the worst of the gore and skull fragments that had splattered him when the joker Robson was struck by the musket ball, and the shock of the drenching brought him back to consciousness briefly before he drifted away again.

The surgeon tutted over a triangular flap of skin that had been gouged out above the English lieutenant's left eye by a piece of flying bone, pulled it back into place with a pair of tweezers he had first cleaned with spit and a rub on his jacket, and deftly stitched the wound. While the surgeon was at work his orderly cleaned and bandaged the gory furrow that had been ploughed in Anson's thigh by another musket ball.

The two other English casualties awaited their turn after the French wounded had been assessed and treated.

Sam Fagg had been brought down by a ricocheting musket ball that had broken his ankle. The torn flesh was cleaned up by the orderly and the fracture splinted by the surgeon. It hurt like hell but at least the bleeding had stopped. The surgeon told him in broken English that he must keep off it for at least six weeks.

Corporal Hoover's shoulder was painful but not too serious. The ball that felled him had also been partially spent. Once the uniform fragments had been fished out of the wound all should be well, though no doubt the bruising would be spectacular.

The garlic-breathed orderly who helped him remove his jacket and shirt got to work with tweezers probing the hole in the marine's shoulder just below the collar bone, first for the musket ball and then the small pieces of scarlet cloth that had been punched into the wound.

With some of the French wounded watching, the marine endured the ordeal in silence, only an occasional wince recording the pain necessarily being inflicted. The torture over, his left arm was put in a sling to avoid shoulder movement.

All three prisoners were then left to rest on straw-filled mattresses along with the French wounded who totally ignored them, muttering only occasionally among themselves.

On board the frigate, marines tended to keep aloof from the seamen they regarded as lesser mortals, but here, with no-one else to talk to, Fagg attempted to cross that barrier by asking: 'You're from Amerikey, ain't yer?'

Hoover nodded. 'Was once.'

'Thought you lot was agin us?'

'Some are, some ain't.'

'So what are y'now, 'merican or English?'

'I'm a marine.'

There was no answer to that and Fagg shrugged and lapsed into silence.

After a few hours all the wounded were fed with bread, soup and watered wine. Fagg examined his bowl for snail shells. Finding none, he tasted the soup gingerly and announced with obvious relief, 'Onion, thank gawd. Not snails or bleedin' frogs.'

When he had wolfed his own ration he crawled across to the half-conscious officer and spooned some of the soup into his mouth, muttering: 'Surprising how 'ungry these 'ere early mornin' larks make yer innit, sir?'

Hoover, chewing on a lump of bread, raised his eyebrows heavenwards. Some lark …

The officer lapsed into unconsciousness again and Fagg did his best to make him more comfortable by removing his sea boots. As he eased the right one off he felt Anson's dirk, still tucked inside.

He turned conspiratorially to Hoover: 'Blimey, look at this mate. They've missed 'is little sword thingey.'

'Dirk – it's his dirk,' muttered Hoover. 'And don't wave it about – they'll all want one.'

'Yeah,' Fagg nodded. And looking round to make sure none of the Frenchmen were watching, he secreted the weapon in his own shirt.

*

They passed the rest of the day dozing in silence, not wishing to draw attention to themselves, and trying to avoid movement that would trigger pain from their injuries. Anson still appeared semi-comatose.

The only breaks came with meals – more soup, bread and a kind of fish stew – and the struggle to cope with the bucket supplied for calls of nature.

With night came the sleep of exhaustion accompanied by a chorus of Anglo-French snores, groans and still less musical sounds from the wounded in the temporary sick bay with its overpowering odour of fish.

*

After they had spent two days and nights in the fish hall, the French surgeon adjudged the English casualties fit enough to travel. He explained to Hoover and Fagg that they were to be sent to the citadel at Arras, maybe a week by wagon. 'From there, *peut-etre* ...' He shrugged, searching for the English word. 'Perhaps ... yes, perhaps to a prison for navy men.'

Indicating a wizened commissariat corporal and a youngster with a vacant stare, the doctor assured the prisoners: 'These imbeciles 'ave been ordered not to mistreat you. Your officer is not bad hurt. It look bad but it is just a surface wound. No ball in 'ead. And his leg? *C'est la meme chose*, not bad.'

Fagg was still concerned. 'So 'e'll live will 'e, monsewer?'

The doctor, who shared the Englishman's habit of dropping aitches, shrugged. 'Of course. He will 'ave a sore 'ead for some days, but you are all young and strong ...'

He gesticulated at the filthy makeshift sick bay. 'All will 'ave a better chance anywhere than 'ere.'

And as further reassurance, he added: 'These guards will 'ave rations for you and papers for billeting *en route*. It will not be a race, but what you English say, a long 'aul.'

*

A long haul it was. Orderlies carried the English officer to a wagon hitched to two docile carthorses, laid him on a pile of grain sacks and hay and helped Fagg and Hoover aboard.

An elderly wagoner watched proceedings and when all were embarked he clicked his tongue, flicked his whip, and they were off at a gentle pace.

At first they followed the coast road north, busy with both military and civilian traffic, and in mid-afternoon reached the port of Dieppe. Leaving the simpleton on guard while the wagoner fed and watered the horses, the be-whiskered old soldier disappeared into a fishermen's drinking den.

After a while he emerged, wiping his moustaches with his cuff, and resumed his seat on a sack of horse feed in the back of the wagon, feet hanging over the backboard.

'All right for some,' Fagg muttered. 'The old sweat smells like a bleedin' brewery. Me, I'd give me left bollock fer a tot right now.'

Eventually satisfied that his horses were ready to roll, the wagoner clicked, flicked, and they were off again.

But now, on reaching the outskirts of the port, he took a road that led away from the coast and headed into the Normandy countryside.

'We're 'eading nor-east, I reckon,' Fagg suggested.

Corporal Hoover grimaced as he eased his shoulder and adjusted the sling. 'We're going away from the coast, that's for sure.'

The wagon climbed slowly up a long incline, eventually reaching undulating fields and woods. The soil here was reddish, brick-earth perhaps.

The two French soldiers guarding them were sprawled on sacks at the back of the wagon, cradling their muskets and dozing in the warm sunshine. They appeared to speak no English and took no interest in their prisoners' desultory conversation.

Their only communication with the wagon driver was when the older of the two, the whiskery veteran, called for a halt and climbed down to relieve himself against a tree. Adjusting his breeches, he remounted, called '*Allez*', and on they rumbled.

Fagg had already dubbed the hairy veteran 'Whiskers' – and his feeble-minded sidekick 'Simple Simon'.

After a while Hoover pulled himself across to the young officer. A bloodied bandage round the temple covered the wound inflicted when the musket ball exited Robson's head.

'Mister Anson, sir, can you hear me?' But there was no response.

Although now conscious, albeit with a pounding head, the officer feigned sleep – determined to keep quiet in case the guards were listening. Escape would be easier if they thought him incapable.

'How is he?' Fagg asked.

'Sure looks a mess. But those French loblolly boys didn't seem to think he was about to snuff it, did they?'

Anson had noted both his fellow-prisoners on board *Phryne*. As an American, Hoover had stood out. Sailors from the new world, pressed or volunteers of necessity, were not unusual in His Majesty's navy. But Americans happy to wear a redcoat uniform were rare. To do so, willingly, almost certainly made him a loyalist, which indeed Hoover was. However far from home, the marines did not care where you came from. They were his family now. And, as a corporal, he had already won respect on board for his quiet courage, skill at arms and immaculate turn-out.

Fagg was altogether a different kettle of fish – a stocky, chirpy, confident foretopman dragged up in the seamier streets of Chatham, where survival depended on a quick wit and nimble feet. On board he was one of the elite able seamen whose part of ship was the most perilous. They had to be fit, alert and courageous to ascend to the tops in a blow and had to have the stamina to endure long stints as look-outs from the mastheads. Ashore or afloat he was an expert scrounger and, without a word of French, had already managed to wheedle a fill of tobacco from the whiskery corporal for his clay pipe that had survived the raid, battered but still smokable.

In moments of wakefulness, Anson told himself he could not have chosen two better companions for the escape he was already certain he would attempt.

As the day wore on the cart passed occasional wayside inns, timber-framed farmhouses and barns with high-pitched roofs. From time to time church spires could be seen in the distance.

At times they were on a dead flat plain. Then the country undulated again, making the horses labour slowly on the up-slopes, pushing on marginally faster downhill.

The trundling, swaying motion made Anson drift in and out of sleep and consciousness. In his dreams he was ratting again as he had hunted for vermin as a child with a terrier called Jack in the outbuildings at the back of the rectory and in the huge tithe barn near the church. Or he was re-living his time as a midshipman, attempting to complete impossible tasks ordered by a succession of villainous superior officers.

His efforts to set his dreams off on a more satisfying tack, by recalling the charms of various females as he lay half awake, never seemed to work. The minute he drifted off he was chasing rats or dashing aloft again rather than resting his head on a soft and ample bosom.

Vivid while dreamed, the images and incidents were elusive and soon faded in moments of wakefulness.

Drained from the sheer physical effort they had put into the abortive raid and the shock of their wounds, Fagg and Hoover sprawled as comfortably as possible in the wagon and they, too, lapsed into an exhausted sleep.

A sudden jolt when the iron-shod wheels hit a particularly deep rut jerked both back into full consciousness and Fagg took the opportunity to check the officer again.

Lieutenant Anson lay on grain sacks between hay bales the French had placed either side of him to prevent his apparently near-lifeless body from rolling with the ship-like motions of the wagon as it negotiated the pitted road like a man-of-war crossing a stormy Bay of Biscay.

Fagg lifted the blood-soaked bandage to examine the officer's head-wound, but could deduce little. 'Still too much blood in 'is 'air to see anyfink,' he told Hoover. 'Soon as this 'ere bleedin' wagon stops for long enuff I'll try washin' the blood orf.'

Hoover nodded. 'Hope he makes it. He's the best of the *Phryne* bunch.'

'He is that,' Fagg agreed. 'Always had a word fer us – and 'e knew our names. Like you wasn't just a number, know what I mean?' Fagg reflected for a moment. 'Mind you, that ain't necessarily a good fing. Sometimes 'tis better t'be … what's it called … anonymouse.'

He shook his head sagely. 'Nah, it don't always pay to 'ave yer name on everyone's lips. Meself, I've got out of more'n a few scrapes by bein' anonymouse.' And he leaned back against one of the hay bales contemplating the undoubted wisdom of his last remark.

Darkness fell before the French corporal woke up to the fact that they needed somewhere to harbour up for the night. They trundled along for a while in faint moonlight as he looked for a wayside auberge. But none appeared.

Finally he spotted a small farmhouse with adjoining barn and the driver urged the horses off the road and down a track towards it.

Whiskers dismounted and rapped at the door of the shabby, single-storey house. A hoary old peasant appeared and, after much gesticulation, what the prisoners guessed was some sort of billeting ticket changed hands and the wagon was driven into the barn.

The driver unhitched the horses and he and the peasant fetched buckets of water and armfuls of hay.

Whiskers fished a sack of rations from the front of the wagon and a few coins encouraged their host to produce a flagon of what proved to be rough cider.

The French corporal swigged long and hard before passing it on and although Fagg treated it with great suspicion, Hoover reassured him: 'It's more'n likely safer than the local water.'

Fagg gulped some down, wiped his mouth with his sleeve and announced: 'Ain't all that bad for a Froggie drink, long as y'don't fink too much abaht what's in it.'

Bread and cheese were produced from the ration sack and they settled down for a restless night on their make-shift hay beds, sleep frequently interrupted by creepy-crawlies, the rustling of rats, the hoots of owls – and the screams of amorous foxes.

It was something of a relief to set off on the road again next day, ploughing steadily on with only occasional farm and military traffic to break the monotony.

5

Stunned disbelief greeted the arrival of Captain Phillips' letter at Hardres Minnis rectory.

Distraught, Anson's mother swooned and took to her chaise longue in a despair only a parent can know on losing a child.

HMS *Phryne* had fallen in with a Sheerness-bound sloop two days after the abortive raid, so the news had not been long delayed.

The Reverend Thomas Anson was himself used to dealing with death as an inevitable part of his calling. But he, too, was dreadfully grieved at the loss of his second, but secretly favourite, son – the son he had encouraged into the navy out of admiration for his distant kinsman.

Commodore George Anson's heroic endurance of extreme hardships while circumnavigating the globe in HMS *Centurion* half a century before – losing two of his accompanying ships and all but a third of his men, yet trumping it all by capturing a Spanish treasure galleon – was the stuff of legends. The hero's subsequent rise to become an admiral, First Sea Lord and reformer of the navy, made his name renowned throughout the service and the country.

Being himself the eldest son of a clergyman, Thomas Anson had been given the martyred Becket's Christian name, and to his own intense disappointment had been destined from birth not for the navy but to follow his father's footsteps into a career in the church.

Like his father, he was a great one for lumbering his male offspring with the names of his heroes and made sure that his own first son Augustine, pointedly named after the saint who brought Christianity to England, likewise followed him into the church as family custom required.

So it was, vicariously, that the rector's own frustrated seafaring dreams were acted out through his second son. To have called him George after the famous Anson would in his view have been too obvious, so he named him Oliver after another character from history that he rather surprisingly admired – the Lord Protector, Cromwell.

The rector had enjoyed young Oliver's occasional ink-splotched letters and even rarer home visits. But all along he had been fully aware of the fact that life at sea was at best precarious. The possibilities of death by enemy action, disease and natural disaster were ever-present threats in the navy. The war with France magnified the dangers.

So the loss of his son was a terrible blow, but not an unimaginable surprise.

And, of course, there was the third son, young Abraham. He was named not after the Biblical patriarch, but to honour General James Wolfe's famous – if personally fatal – taking of the Heights of Abraham in Canada during the Seven Years' War.

Wolfe Anson, the rector had reluctantly conceded, would have been a little too much to swallow. So the youngest son rejoiced under the name of the battlefield rather than the victor. And it suited the rector if most of his parishioners assumed that the boy was named after the biblical patriarch.

Abraham, still at school, was pre-destined to go into the army. There had not been a soldier in the family since great uncle Hannibal Anson, who, rather than crossing the Alps with elephants like his namesake, had been thrown from a howdah when tiger-hunting in Uttar-Pradesh while serving with the East India Company Army and been trampled to death by one.

At the news of Oliver's death, the rector comforted his daughters. But although mightily upset, neither Elizabeth nor Anne could feel close to a brother they had seen so infrequently since he left to become a midshipman at the age of 13. His last brief visit had been during the Nore mutiny, and then he had suddenly upped and left for service in the Mediterranean.

Their brother's life as a naval officer was so remote from theirs. The rambling rectory, its extensive grounds cared for by several gardeners, and the houses of a familiar circle of what passed locally for society were the extent of their world.

Life for them was a round of church-going and related activity, such as the flower arranging rota, and harassing the sick and poor with well-meant but condescending, uninvited visits.

Their creative diversions included embroidery, painting insipid floral watercolours and devouring romantic novels. They were much looking forward to reading one that was currently being written by a Miss Jane Austen, whom they had met during a visit to nearby Godmersham House.

Calling upon neighbouring, similarly as-yet-unattached young women and engaging in endless speculation about the perceived merits or shortcomings of potential husbands to be found within a ten-mile radius was undoubtedly their favourite pastime.

In a strange way their brother's death would draw not unwelcome attention to them, and both would bask – demurely of course – in this unfamiliar limelight. Any lingering sorrow was lessened by their father's assurance: 'He has died a quick but honourable death. That is our comfort. And now we must honour him and put his soul to rest.'

Eldest brother Augustine drove out from Canterbury and 14-year-old Abraham had been sent for from school and came post haste. They were told: 'There can be no funeral without a body, so we will place a marble plaque in the church and dedicate it at a memorial service. Without such a service your mother will never rest easy.'

Augustine Anson was still basking in the glory of his new role at the cathedral as a minor canon and Six Preacher, an ancient office that gave him lodgings in the precincts in return for preaching on nominated holy days, plus 20 more sermons elsewhere. He agreed: 'We must invite the squirarchy, the members of parliament of course, selected churchmen – certainly the dean and archdeacon ...'

He fingered his chin. 'Why not invite the archdeacon? Why not indeed? Oh, and perhaps some navy people or someone from the army. Our family's contribution to the war with France and our great sacrifice must not be allowed to go unnoticed.'

*

As his family prepared to honour him as a dead hero, the object of their mourning was still very much alive and heading for a French prison. His fellow-prisoners took turns at feeding him and Hoover helped him into the bushes when nature called during periods of consciousness.

Several more uncomfortable nights, in wayside barns and hour after hour of boredom as the horses slowly but surely pulled the wagon further away from the coast, passed without incident.

Then, at a crossroads, a pair of mounted gendarmes called them to a halt. While one examined the papers Whiskers offered, quizzing him aggressively, the other looked the wounded prisoners over haughtily.

Simple Simon did his best to look alert, but Hoover noted that the young soldier's hands gripping his musket were shaking. It was evidently unwise to incur the wrath of a gendarme whether you were on the same side or not.

Finally satisfied, the gendarmes waved the wagon on. Out of earshot Hoover heard Whiskers mutter: '*Cochons!*'

On the fifth day the wagon with its motley and dishevelled crew trundled into a small village dominated by a twin-spired, slate-roofed church. Scattered around the tree-lined central square were stone-built houses, flaking doors and windows shuttered for the afternoon doze. To the right was an inn. A weather-beaten sign with a crude painting of a seaman identified it as the Auberge du Marin.

The French corporal called a halt and the driver jerked on his reins, bringing the wagon to a lurching stop. Fagg and Hoover stretched aching muscles and their French escorts jumped down.

Anson awoke, looked up at the sign and muttered: 'The Sailor's Inn, how appropriate.' Fagg jerked his head and leaned over one of the hay bales to find himself staring into the officer's no longer dazed eyes.

'Welcome back Mr Anson, sir,' he grinned. 'Feelin' better?'

Anson gave a slight nod. 'Don't make it too obvious,' he whispered. 'Let the Frogs think I'm on my last legs.'

Fagg caught on right away and put a finger to his lips. 'Aye aye, sir, mum's the word.' And, as an afterthought, he whispered: 'I've got yer little sword thingey tucked in me shirt.'

'Good man. Hang on to it 'til we're alone.'

With the Frenchmen out of earshot, Anson caught Fagg's attention again and whispered: 'We must convince these idiots that we need to rest up here for a few days and then disappear and make our way home.'

Hoover was listening in. 'We're with you there, sir,' he said, clearly surprised that the officer was not half as badly hurt as he had been making out. Fagg nodded: 'Just give us the word.'

The Auberge du Marin took up most of one side of the square. The sprawling, ramshackle building was clearly the result of various haphazard extensions in the past and Hoover noted that it looked like it could do with more than a lick of paint and the close attention of a roofer.

Beside the front door, the inn's large-bellied proprietor could be observed urinating nonchalantly against the wall. Otherwise the square was empty.

The French corporal surveyed the inn keenly. Scenting alcohol, he stirred himself and approached the patron to negotiate.

Relieved, the inn-keeper shook himself, adjusted his clothing and held out his now free right hand to shake with Whiskers. Business was slow and the newcomers promised custom.

The prisoners waited as the corporal, clutching his sheaf of papers, disappeared into the inn with the patron to sort out billeting arrangements.

Eventually the old sweat emerged, wiping his now wine-sodden droopy moustaches on his sleeve, leaving a red stain on his cuff. He beckoned and announced: '*Nous sommes ici.*'

Fagg nodded to Hoover. 'Orl right, yankee, let's get the orficer on board and into 'is 'ammock.'

But it was Whiskers and his simpleton comrade who, with surprising gentleness, carried Anson into the inn and laid him on an old couch in the low-ceilinged bar.

A young woman appeared, took in the scene, and fetched a pitcher of red wine. Whiskers, leaning proprietorially on the bar, poured himself a generous measure and pushed the jug towards the grizzled wagon-driver. Simple Simon patiently awaited his turn.

Anson, lethargic through loss of blood and enduring mile after mile in the swaying, creaking cart, watched through half-closed eyes, apparently totally indifferent to what was going on. His lank black hair was still spikey and reddened with dried blood.

The woman produced a second pitcher of wine and an earthenware mug. She tutted at Anson's blood-stained face, poured some wine and handed him the mug.

'*Prisonniers?*'

Anson nodded.

'*Anglais?*'

He nodded again and motioned for her to pass the mug to Fagg, who protested: 'Arter you sir—'

Anson shook his head. 'You first. As they say, thy need is greater than mine. Anyway I've already got a headache. And if you drink first I'll know if it's poisoned.'

Fagg grinned. 'Most thoughtful, sir!' He sipped gingerly but after the first mouthful registered approval. 'It ain't 'alf bad for Froggie drink. Gonna try it, lobster?'

The American turned up his nose at being addressed by the mildly insulting nickname sailors gave their red-coated soldier shipmates. 'Just don't go abusin' the marines, Jack Tar. Could be the last thing you say afore I rip out your tongue,' he muttered good-naturedly as he accepted the proferred mug.

Having witnessed the English officer's unselfish gesture, the woman had disappeared, returning with a small glass. She poured wine from the pitcher and handed it to him. '*Vin*,' she said softly. 'Wine, not poison.'

He smiled and took a sip. '*Merci, mademoiselle.*'

'*Madame.*'

Anson corrected himself. '*Merci, madame.*'

Whiskers and the patron were deep in negotiation in, to Anson, unintelligible French. The first pitcher of wine was already empty and the French corporal commandeered the prisoners' jug for consumption in the service of the Republic.

From his sheaf of documents he produced some voucher-like papers which Anson guessed the innkeeper would be able to redeem for services rendered. Simple Simon fetched the sack containing provisions from the cart and that, too, was handed over.

Having made their deal, Whiskers and the patron shook hands on it.

There was more unintelligible gabble which seemed to concern where the prisoners would be billeted and, with his bayonet, Simple Simon encouraged them to rise until Fagg told him to 'Bugger orf!' so fiercely that he jumped back fearfully.

The patron led Whiskers and the prisoners to a dilapidated outhouse and indicated a pile of straw. As he passed the younger Frenchman, Fagg hissed 'Boo!' making the simpleton jump again.

Helped to the outhouse by Hoover, Anson took in the scene, gave the patron a look normally reserved for idle back-sliders, and shook his head. '*Non!*'

'*Non? Pourqoui non?*'

'*Chambres. Vous avez chambres.*' The golden coin that had appeared as if by magic between Anson's index finger and thumb forestalled further debate. Realising there could be more gold wherever this had come from, the patron took the coin and muttered a response.

'What's 'e say, sir?' asked Fagg.

Anson shrugged. 'He says now he has rooms.'

Famished, they sat at a small, wine-stained table in the bar, stomachs grumbling as tantalising cooking smells wafted in from the adjacent kitchen.

Fagg drummed his fingers on the table. 'I could eat a 'orse.'

'And you more'n likely will,' observed Hoover.

The meat, when it came, did indeed have a bluish tinge. But they wolfed it down just as voraciously as if it had been choice beefsteak.

6

The first night at the inn turned into two, then three. Whiskers was, as Fagg aptly put it, 'Like a pig in shite,' quaffing the rough red wine with the innkeeper and dozing in between bouts. His side-kick appeared content to sit on the front step, whittling pieces of wood into strange soldier-like figures.

The enforced rest with plain but wholesome food was helping the Phrynes to recover their health and strength.

Soon after their arrival, madame had insisted on confiscating their blood-, sweat- and dirt-stained clothes and laundering and mending them.

She had also bathed Anson's head, washing the congealed blood from his hair and removing the stitches from the livid v-shaped scar above his left eye.

Examining the wound carefully, she told him: '*Il fait bon.*' Gently, she tried to wash off the scattering of blackened impregnations beside his right eye, but he reached out to stop her and then she understood. These were old powder burns.

Sitting in lukewarm water in an old metal bath, Anson examined the wound that had caused the searing pain in his left leg. Again, it was probably the work of a musket ball that had ploughed a surface furrow without damaging bone or muscle. And it, too, was clean and healing well.

When she fetched more warm water, madame lingered a little longer than was necessary and he sensed she was appraising his lean, muscular body. But when he looked up at her she dropped her gaze, appearing not to pay any attention to his nakedness.

Over the next few days she remained caring but subdued and serious; an unhappy marriage, Anson supposed.

Far younger than the fat, balding, uncouth innkeeper, she was dark-haired, with clear skin and a full figure, but by no means overweight. Small wonder – she was constantly on the move, cooking, waiting at tables, fetching drinks and laundering, as well as caring for the wounded Englishmen.

Anson used the lengthening stay at the auberge to get to know his fellow-prisoners a little better. Corporal Hoover intrigued him. Rebellious seamen could easily be kept under control by the navy's draconian disciplinary code, fiercely emphasised by the rope's end and enforced by the lash. But the marines were buffers between officers and the lower deck, and total loyalty was demanded of them. The scarlet jacket was not something the average son of a now-independent United States would aspire to.

Hoover was happy to confirm what the officer had already deduced. His family were loyalists and after his father was killed fighting alongside the British at the Battle of Brandywine in Pennsylvania his mother had brought him and his sisters over to England.

They had sailed into Portsmouth and his mother, an accomplished needlewoman, opened a tailoring shop and settled there. Hoover confessed: 'She wanted me to go into the business and I did for a while, but I guess measuring, cutting and stitching just wasn't for me, so when I was old enough I joined the marines.'

What he did not add was that although loyalty to the British crown had been instilled in him from birth, part of his heart was nevertheless with the new country.

He was strangely proud of the fact that the former colonists had won their independence and created a new order in which, according to the Declaration, 'all men are equal … endowed by their Creator with certain unalienable rights, and among those are life, liberty and the pursuit of happiness …'

It was a fine aspiration, and although it was as yet too soon, some day, when the wounds had healed and there were no longer 'rebels' nor 'loyalists' but simply Americans, he would return.

His accent, which sometimes resulted in him being mistaken for an East Anglian, betrayed to the careful listener his New England upbringing. It was perhaps the due emphasis he gave to each syllable in a word, a habit attributable to the custom at his childhood school for pupils to read words aloud together as one class.

In England he had learned from bitter experience that most people deemed all Americans to be rebels. So it was easier to let people assume he was from Norfolk, Suffolk, Cambridgeshire or Essex than to be quizzed about why an American would be willing to put on the scarlet jacket so hated by most of the former colonists.

Having been brought up in the new world where blasphemy, slander, cursing, lying, railing, reviling, scolding, swearing and threatening were all punishable offences, Hoover was looked upon by his fellow Phrynes as an upright man, unlike most of his whoring, hard-drinking shipmates.

He was fit, hard and dependable, a textbook marine.

Fagg was chalk and cheese different. The son of a Chatham dockyard matey, he had grown up amid the jumble of ale- and whore-houses, chandleries and tailors' shops that had leeched off the navy for many a decade.

The hard school of the dockyard town's mean streets had sharpened him into a wiry, chirpy, cheeky chancer – an ace procurer of whatever was required to make life bearable, be it an extra tot on board or a willing floozy ashore. A good man for a situation like this, Anson told himself.

Corporal Hoover's shoulder was healing well, but Fagg's ankle caused some concern. He had made himself primitive crutches and hopped around wisecracking like a cheerful stork, but it could be weeks before he was able to put any weight on it.

All three needed to be fit to travel if they were to take the opportunity to escape from their lackadaisical guards before they reached prison.

For Anson there would be no advancement, glory or honour being cooped up for what could turn out to be years. In his thinking, there was no question of sitting out the war. Escape was a necessity, and sewn into the lining of his coat was the wherewithal.

It was the 20 guineas of his entitlement drawn from the prize agent in Gibraltar that he had sewn carefully into separate hidden mini pockets behind the buttons in the inner lining of his old naval uniform jacket before they set off on the St Valery raid.

All he had to do to free a coin was to unpick a few stitches at the top of each pocket and work it free. In this way he had been able to produce the guinea that had secured them as if by magic proper rooms at the auberge. That it bore King George's head meant nothing to the patron. Gold was gold.

Anson was acutely aware that to make their escape with a reasonable chance of success it was absolutely necessary that they should go no further inland. Every mile they rumbled away from the coast would have to be retraced if they were to escape. And each extra mile on the road dodging gendarmes or cavalry patrols would present greater dangers of recapture.

If they could ensure that the inn was the end of the line, successful escape remained a real possibility. For him it was not a matter of if they would attempt it, but when.

An unspoken bargain was struck with Whiskers – drink for recovery time. Every time the Frenchman showed signs of moving on, Anson indicated that the wounds he and the others had suffered on the mole were far worse than they were – and ordered more wine.

To the inn's handful of regular drinkers Anson's head-wound looked far worse than it was. Yellow and purple bruising now covered his left temple and the bandage that he allowed to slip down over his left eye when others were about hinted at unseen disfigurement.

Fagg played his part well, having mastered dumb insolence and swinging the lead during the 12 years he had inhabited His Majesty's upper rigging and lower decks. On board ship, when it came to making the most of a strain or knock to win light duties, he was a past master.

His ankle was genuinely painful, but he made it seem ten times worse. Every time he put his foot to the floor he winced and groaned so convincingly that even the patron or Whiskers would give him a hand.

Hoover's shoulder wound hurt less when his arm was supported by a sling, but it ached dully and, Fagg told him, made him even more cack-handed than your average marine.

Theoretically they could overpower their two guards, one boozy the other dozy, on any lonely stretch of road after leaving the inn. The elderly peasant driving the two-horse wagon was unlikely to give any trouble.

But, whichever way Anson decided to make the attempt, it was vital to win time to get over the worst of their wounds and gather their strength before making a move.

And meanwhile, life at the auberge was pleasant enough.

*

After a few days, a toddler tottered unsteadily into Anson's room closely followed by Madame Thérèse who apologised, picked him up and made to leave.

'*Votre fils?*'

She nodded. '*Il cherche son père—*'

Anson pointed downwards, '*Le patron?*'

For the first time since the prisoners' arrival she laughed. '*Non, non – le patron est mon père!*'

Strangely bucked to discover that the landlord was her father, and pushing his fractured French to the limit, he learned that her husband was dead. They had grown up in the village where his widowed mother lived on the other side of the square. When the recruiters came and the drums beat he had been desperate to enlist. It had been accepted that they would marry eventually. Now it had become urgent. They had pledged themselves in the village church, and three days later he went off to war.

Within the year, with little Thierry at her breast, news had come that her husband had been cut in half by an Austrian cannonball at Lodi in Italy.

So madame – Thérèse – was a widow.

That night she came to dress his wounds which were healing well. She lingered beyond all necessity, smoothing his hair back from his scar and fussing with his bandage.

And she pretended not to notice as he began to fondle her, until he took her in his arms and pressed his lips to hers. Then she showed she was aware.

*

It was another reason to stall Whiskers for a few more days, and keeping up a steady supply of red wine saw to that.

While the French corporal succumbed to copious amounts of wine next evening and his simpleton side-kick's attention was captured by Fagg, who was attempting to teach him how to tie knots, Anson quietly talked escape with Hoover.

'From what I can deduce we've travelled more or less due eastward from the coast.'

Hoover nodded. 'Reckon that's about right, sir. But where's this place?'

'It's just a tinpot village of no account. I judge we're well to the north of Paris, somewhere around a place called Amiens if I've heard correctly.' He gestured to the bar where a few locals were boozing and making idle small talk.

'I've quizzed Whiskers here and he tells me he's under orders to take us to Arras but then we may be sent on to Verdun, where they keep most of the naval prisoners.'

'Where's that?'

'A prison fortress beyond Reims. I think it's in the province of Lorraine, well out of our way. It would be inconvenient to say the least if we ended up there.'

The marine looked around to make sure no one was eavesdropping. 'So, sir, do you plan to make a run soon?'

Anson thought for a moment. 'I've got to try it. But there's no need for you to come.'

Hoover frowned. 'Why wouldn't I?'

'Because you're an American. You can tell the French you were pressed by the British, and wait out for a ship home to the States.'

The marine smiled and shook his head. 'England's my home now and I'm not quitting. Thanks for offering, but I'll stick with you, sir. I could be stranded among the snail-scoffers for years, and even if I got to America I wouldn't get much of a welcome, being a loyalist's son.'

It was the answer Anson wanted. 'Good man. I was pretty sure that's what you'd say.' He raised his glass to the marine and took a sip. 'Now that's settled, this is my plan. As I see it, we mustn't let Whiskers here take us any further away from the coast.'

As if on cue, their moustachioed escort emitted a gross, ear-piercing snore that made every head in the place turn. The two exchanged a grin and Anson confided: 'It's plain we could slip away whenever we wish, but we need to be as fit as possible to make it to the coast.'

He frowned. 'It's not going to be easy. We'll have to live rough, travel only at night and lay up during the day. And I'll need to plan it carefully so we don't stir up an ants' nest when we make the break.'

Hoover turned to make sure Fagg was still occupying the younger Frenchman who was tying his fourth granny knot, much to his tutor's frustration. '*Non, non*, you cretin! Left over right, then right over left. *Droit* over *gauche. Regardez*? Look, 'ere I go agin.' His fingers flew and a perfect reef knot appeared. Simple Simon studied it and looked down at his own failed effort, perplexed.

Fagg winked at the marine and encouraged his pupil to try again. 'Come along now, 'ave another go. *Gauche* over *droit, droit* over *gauche*. Simple, ain't it? Leastways, you are at any rate, ain't yer?' Simple Simon wagged his head enthusiastically and tried again.

Anson continued to outline his plan. 'So we need to lay up here for a few more days, recover somewhat, and get together what we need for the run.'

'Will we head back for the Normandy coast?'

The officer shrugged. 'That would be easiest, but maybe too obvious I think. From what I can tell we've gone past Amiens so we could head for St Omer, by-pass the town and continue north to the Channel ports.'

Hoover could not help looking quizzical.

'Yes, I know it's a bit further than the Normandy coast – maybe 80 or 90 miles – but it's through Picardy where it's likely to be pretty quiet. The coast roads will be buzzing if the alarm's raised. But I don't think the Frogs'll be expecting us to head north. If we make it to the Channel ports and manage to get a boat of some sort we'll have only a short passage to the Kent coast. But then Normandy is nearer. It's a toss-up.'

Hoover looked thoughtful and far from confident.

Anson saw the doubt in his face, but shrugged it off. 'Trust me – whether it's Normandy or the Channel Ports, we'll make it!'

That night Thérèse again slipped into Anson's room after the inn settled down for the night. There had been a need.

7

And then, suddenly, it was over.

A military messenger stopped by to feed and rest his horse in the inn's stables, and accepted an invitation to join the patron, the guards and wagoner for supper. They sat at the big table and the landlord called for Thérèse, who appeared with a pitcher of wine and took orders for the meal.

Fagg whispered behind his hand to Hoover who got up and nonchalantly strolled outside. The Frenchmen took no notice – too intent on the exchange of news over their wine.

Anson was sprawled in a corner seat, feigning sleep but straining to follow the rapid French of the diners. As far as he could make out, the galloper was passing on rumours of some major action against *'les Anglais'*. And, from his hushed tones and hostile glances at the prisoners, it had clearly not gone well – for the French.

Thérèse reappeared with a bowl of what smelt like onion soup and was ladling it out when the door burst open and Hoover stumbled in shouting, 'Monsewer, your horse has scarpered!'

The Frenchmen looked up, startled, and the patron demanded: *'Qu'est-ce que c'est?'*

Anson, somewhat taken aback himself, tried to explain, *'Il dit que votre cheval est disparu ...'*

'Disparu?' The messenger panicked, jumped up and made for the door, closely followed by the other Frenchmen, and they ran to the stables shouting.

'Heh, heh!' Fagg laughed as he hopped across to where the messenger had been sitting and pulled his satchel from the back of his chair. 'Keep cave lobster, whilst I just see what's in this Froggy's handbag.'

'Relax. You'll have plenty of time. Guess his horse will have made off quite a-ways. I gave its aft end a hell of a smack when I let it out.'

'Good man. Now, let's 'ave a look.' Fagg opened the satchel and pulled out a bundle of documents. 'Borin' – all in Frog-speak I reckon. Don't know why they don't learn to speak English like what we do.'

He undid the flapped pocket on the inside of the satchel. 'Hello, this is a bit more interestin' – just what you need, Mr Anson. A map.'

Anson leapt out of his seat. 'Let's have it. By heavens, it's a map of the whole region!'

'Where's that?'

'Here, you idiot! Everywhere from here to the Channel coast …'

Fagg, who was now helping himself to the messenger's bowl of onion soup, pretended to be more miffed than he was. 'Oh, so I'm a idiot now? I thought that was a blinking clever trick getting the lobster to make that messenger bloke's horse go walkies and nicking his handbag—'

Anson caught on to the diversionary ploy. 'Yes, yes, it was very clever.' He spread the map on the table. 'Now, let me concentrate. We may only have a few minutes.'

From his look-out post beside the half-open door, Hoover reassured him: 'You'll have plenty longer than that, sir. After the slap I gave that pony he'll be halfway to Paris by now.'

'Why not go and give them a helping hand?'

Hoover smiled knowingly and set off to join the hunt, closely followed by hop-along Fagg. Anson knew that with the kind of help they had in mind the messenger's horse could stay at large for some time.

Without the necessary materials it was not possible to make a copy, so he studied the map carefully, noting the positions of the major towns. He knew roughly where the auberge was in relation to them and with his finger traced the route south west, back towards the Normandy coast, and then the way north via St Omer to the Channel ports.

Thanks to the map it was now obvious to him what their escape route should be and he committed the important features to memory.

Outside, shouting erupted as the English prisoners joined efforts to catch the horse which had been driven back into the main square by a passing farmer. From the French and Anglo-Saxon oaths, Anson could picture the chaos his apparently innocent companions were causing and the map and papers were back in the satchel long before the door was flung open and the perspiring horse-herders returned, still arguing volubly as to whose fault it had been – and who the saviours of the situation were.

The patron called for Thérèse to bring more wine and he and his fellow diners returned to their now luke-warm soup – or, in the case of the messenger, what was left of it.

When they were alone, Anson confided in Hoover and Fagg. 'From what I could make out listening to what the messenger told the others, there's been a major battle involving the English.'

Hoover nodded. 'And as we've got no troops on the Continent right now it could only have been at sea?'

'That's right – a fleet action. Perhaps Nelson.'

'Why 'im, sir?' asked Fagg.

'He's been hunting Admiral Brueys' ships for months. While we were blockading Le Havre we were warned the French had at least a dozen ships of the line at sea.'

'D'you reckon Nelson's found 'em?'

'Seems likely. Whatever's happened, Whiskers is looking jittery. He won't be able to hang about here any longer, and the further we go from the coast the more difficult it will be for us to escape, especially once word spreads of a naval defeat.'

Fagg scratched his head. 'So, if we've seen orf the Frogs …?'

'English sailors will be in season.' Although he was sure no Frenchman was in earshot, Anson lowered his voice. 'It's time to make a move.'

Whiskers, had indeed sensed that word of English prisoners being holed up at the Auberge du Marin would spread via the galloper, and next morning he went into a huddle with the innkeeper.

Nights on the wine at the English officer's expense were all well and good, but clearly the realisation had hit him that trouble could be looming unless he delivered his charges to Arras very soon.

Broken axles, lame horses or sick prisoners would excuse some delay. But all good things must come to an end, and the messenger's appearance had convinced him the time had come. He sought out the English officer and announced that it was time to be off.

Anson knew that the Frenchman had no choice and it was pointless to argue. But Arras did not fit in with his plans. It was time for the parting of the ways, but for the coast and England, not a French prison. He could not ignore the war and his duty.

The desire to escape overwhelmed everything else. The war could last for years and kicking his heels as a prisoner would mean wasted opportunities. Contemporaries, even juniors, would be winning glory and promotion over his head.

He thanked God he had not given his parole, trading his word not to escape for restricted freedom and the possibility of exchange at some future date. That would have meant loss of honour if he escaped, and sitting it out waiting for exchange was not an option for an ambitious officer.

There was no question: escape before they reached prison was an absolute necessity.

Getting away from their dozy guards would not be a problem. The difficulty would be the journey back to the coast across hostile enemy country – and crossing the Channel.

It was easy to persuade the newly-righteous Whiskers to go along with his proposal that they stay for one last night – a farewell supper with flowing wine. So what if they delayed just a little longer for a morning departure and slept off the wine in the wagon as they headed further inland?

*

Thérèse was busy in the kitchen serving up what Fagg dubbed 'the last supper'. He and Hoover were charged with ensuring that their guards, the wagoner and the patron drank themselves insensible. And to finance that, Anson produced another golden guinea and called for the best wine.

As the meal progressed, Fagg used skills that smacked of a recruiter ensnaring yokels: proposing toasts in appalling slurred Anglo-French, constantly topping up his victims and appearing to be getting steadily more drunk himself while remaining more or less sober.

Anson liked a drink but needed a clear head. He slipped away to his room after the meal complaining of a headache and needing to sleep it off before the onward journey.

Soon afterwards, Hoover, who had also put on a show of drinking while staying sober as a Methodist, rose unsteadily to answer a call of nature in the outside privy.

The Frenchmen, by now singing the new Republican anthem, conducted by the wily Fagg, did not notice that the American failed to return. He was busy in the stable behind the inn.

Thérèse came to Anson's room and they lay in each other's arms, speaking in whispers to a background of drunken singing. He did not need to spell out what was afoot. She had read the signs.

'Now you forget me?'

He shook his head. 'I will return when peace comes.'

'Promise?'

She could not see that he had crossed his fingers. 'I promise.'

Eventually the raucous singing tailed off and the inn fell silent.

In the early hours floorboards creaked. Anson, already awake, acknowledged a theatrical cough from Hoover in the passageway with a hissed 'Wait!'

He dressed hurriedly and gave Thérèse a package and whispered instructions. They clung together for one last time, and then he was gone.

Outside, Fagg and Hoover, now dressed in some of the patron's cast-offs Thérèse had found for them, were waiting with the wagon. They clambered aboard and, with the marine at the reins, slowly left the square and headed back down the road towards the coast.

As Anson turned to look once more at the moonlit inn and fix it in his memory, he glimpsed a face at an upper window and raised his hand in a sad farewell salute.

Fagg chortled: 'I got them Froggies drunk alright! Snorin' like pigs they are. They'll 'ave terrible 'eads come morning!' Then in the moonlight he caught the officer's desolate expression, understood, and fell silent.

*

Through the night they continued coast-bound and just before dawn abandoned the wagon at another auberge near crossroads Anson had noted on the way inland 15 or so miles down the road. It would be unwise to draw attention to themselves by continuing on the main road in daylight.

Hoover tied the horses to a rail and they set off on foot, Fagg supporting his game leg with the makeshift crutches he had made at the inn.

Anson held up his hand for a halt when they reached the finger post pointing four ways – back towards Arras, south to Amiens, west to Dieppe, and north to St Omer. He stared up at it for a few minutes before confirming the decision he had made while studying the map back at the Auberge du Marin – and turned north.

As soon as it became light they would hole up somewhere close to the road and rest until nightfall.

Fagg and Hoover exchanged a knowing glance. So it was to be the Channel ports. And the short sea route home.

*

Back at the inn, Thérèse spent a sleepless, tearful night rehearsing her instructions. When the carousers came to she was to give the corporal back his written orders that had been issued to him at St Valery-en-Caux and borrowed from his pocket by Fagg during the last drunken supper.

Thanks to an ink-stained cork whittled painstakingly by Hoover it was now stamped '*Reçu Arras*' – Received Arras – over a florid, totally illegible signature. It was a convincing enough receipt for the English naval prisoners that would surely pass muster with all who had never seen the real thing – even supposing such an item existed. And it should get the bemused Whiskers off the hook.

As dawn broke, the escapers left the road and crawled into a thicket to rest up until nightfall.

They shared supplies Thérèse had given them and Anson told the others: 'Tonight we'll need to by-pass St Omer and head for the Channel ports.' An insect buzzed his ear and he slapped it away. 'If we make it there and manage to get a boat of some sort we'll have only a short passage to the Kent coast.'

Far from the sea, his tattered dark naval jacket could pass muster and in the inn-keeper's cast-offs his companions made plausible peasants, except for one thing. The officer stared at Fagg. 'It'll have to go.'

'What've I done now? What's gotta go?'

'The pigtail. It's a dead give-away. How many French peasants have you seen with pigtails?'

Fagg was stricken. 'Well I, well … not a lot, but then I've been growin' this 'ere pigtail pretty well ever since I joined …'

On board, and ashore in the naval ports come to that, the length of your pigtail showed you had got some service in, and Fagg reckoned his had been one of the best in *Phryne*.

But Anson knew he was right and was not to be denied. 'Off!' he said, handing him his dirk.

Reluctantly Fagg took the blade, held the pigtail in his left hand and sawed away at it with his right. Once cut, he threw it into the undergrowth and shook what remained of his hair free.

Hoover looked on appreciatively and teased: 'Lovely – just like some gal I met in Portsmouth one time …' But then he caught Anson's eye, felt for his own short queue of plaited hair and held his hand out for the dirk.

They spent an uncomfortable day dozing and fending off voracious insects, and late in the evening emerged from the thicket and set off again on foot.

It was not long before Anson noticed that even after covering only a mile or two Fagg was having increasing difficulty with his ankle.

'How's it holding up?'

'Perfick sir, jest the odd twinge when I puts it down ockered like,' he lied.

They must be all of 60 miles from the coast and it was already becoming clear that Fagg would not be able to go much further on foot. They struggled on at a snail's pace, with Anson and Hoover taking turns to support the crippled Fagg and resting every few hundred yards. This must be the main Amiens–St Omer road, but to their relief it was traffic-free.

Towards dawn they saw the outline of a barn which lay down a rough track. A nod from Anson sent Hoover off to reconnoitre while he and Fagg hid in a roadside ditch.

Soundlessly the marine melted into the shadows to check the barn. After ten long minutes he slid into the ditch beside the others to report. 'All clear. Not a soul about.'

Nevertheless they entered the barn cautiously and in the growing light made out piles of what appeared to be recently-harvested turnips. A crude ladder led up to an open loft area full of hay.

Anson indicated the far end of the barn and then the loft, whispering: 'Heads down there, beds up there.' Fagg hopped off to relieve himself in the far corner.

Cautiously Anson mounted the ladder and, after checking all was clear, he beckoned the others to follow. From the open loft they would be able to keep an eye on the barn doors.

Although he did his best to disguise it, Fagg had a lot of trouble negotiating the ladder rungs. It was increasingly obvious that his ankle could no longer bear weight. But nothing was said.

They breakfasted on bread, hard-boiled eggs and one of the bottles of wine Thérèse had given them in a sack along with a large chunk of cheese and some apples when they had left the inn. If they could find water they could eke out these supplies for a few days.

In the loft they burrowed into the hay and tried to get some sleep. Hoover was soon snoring gently, but Fagg was restless. Unable at first to find a comfortable position for his throbbing ankle, he muttered as he rubbed his itchy eyes: 'I 'ate 'ay. Bleedin' stuff gets right up me nose …' But eventually he too drifted off.

Anson took even longer to succumb to fatigue. He realised now that it had been a major tactical error to abandon the wagon – or at least both horses. Round and round in his head went the realisation that Fagg would never make it to the coast without help. They could not have covered more than five or six miles during the night and it was clear that Fagg would not be able to walk, or hop, for another six let alone 60.

There was a simple choice. He could be left to his fate, or they had to find him some sort of transport. Leaving him to be recaptured by the French had some merit. The chances were that he would be given some medical treatment. But there was no guarantee and Anson dismissed that option.

They had stuck together so far and they must see it through together. Not least, if Fagg fell back into French hands the Arras receipt would almost certainly be revealed as a forgery. He could not even be sure that he had used the correct French wording. And if Fagg was retaken the trail would inevitably lead back to the Auberge du Marin – and make trouble for Thérèse and her father, not to mention Whiskers, his young side-kick and the wagoner.

All could be deemed responsible for aiding and abetting enemy escapers. No bounds what the punishment would be, but the French had a reputation for seizing any opportunity to exercise Madame Guillotine. No, they must push on for the coast together. And that meant finding and stealing or borrowing a horse – and a cart.

Anson dozed, returning over and over again to the problem in moments of consciousness. Finally, exhausted, he too fell into a deep sleep.

*

Mid-morning, back at the auberge, the revellers were slowly coming round. Only the patron had made it to bed and now he was dipping his frowzy head in a bowl of water in a vain attempt to wash away the ravages of Bacchus.

The wagoner was on his back under the table, mouth lolling open, grunting like a litter of pigs at feeding time, his nasal passages emitting a shrill whistling noise between snores.

Corporal Whiskers, who had slept where he sat, head cradled in his folded arms on the bottle-littered bar counter, staggered to the door to relieve himself. On the step he found the sprawling, groaning body of the youngster lying in his own vomit. And, having relieved himself against the wall of the inn, the corporal returned, drew a bucket of water from the well and threw it over his spluttering side-kick.

It would be a while before Thérèse could tell them what had happened, explain how the English officer had arranged to give them money and the protection of the prisoner receipt, and then send them off on foot to the village inn some miles back down the road to retrieve the borrowed wagon and horses.

8

Anson awoke suddenly. Someone was opening the barn doors. He shook Hoover and Fagg, and as they stirred he put his finger to his lips and indicated the door. Both understood immediately and Fagg scrabbled for his crutches. Then they lay still, hidden in the hay.

A man dressed in muddy, weathered working clothes came in and began filling hessian sacks from the piled root crops, apparently completely unaware that he was being watched. He carried a sack out of the barn and returned for another.

As the farmer went out for the second time, Anson whispered: 'He must be loading a cart, and that means ...' Hoover nodded, '... a horse.'

In the half light of the barn the escapers had no idea of the time, but instinct told Anson it must be near evening and the farmer was about his nightly chores. After carrying out half a dozen bags, he returned and approached the ladder.

Fagg muttered: 'Blurry 'ell! Why don't 'e bugger orf 'ome!'

They pulled more hay over themselves and froze as the farmer climbed the ladder. Oblivious to their presence, he took a pitchfork that was leaning against the wall and speared a pile of hay with it.

Anson steeled himself to leap up and confront the man if the pitchfork came too close. But the farmer merely pitched the hay down to the foot of the ladder, pierced more and threw it down until satisfied he had enough. He swung his leg over the loft edge and slowly descended the ladder, pitchfork in his left hand.

Itchy-eyed, Fagg stifled an almost overwhelming urge to sneeze, as down below the farmer pitched up a forkful of hay and carried it outside, returning for more until the pile had gone. Then he shut the barn doors and the fugitives heard the sounds of a horse-drawn cart moving off.

Anson signed to Hoover to follow and the American hurried down the ladder.

*

In the barn, the half light faded to darkness. The door creaked. A sudden chink of moonlight and a figure entered, stage-whispering the password of the aborted raid on the mole, '*Phryne.*' It was Hoover.

Anson helped Fagg down the ladder and they made their way outside gingerly. Hoover reported: 'He lives about half a mile farther down the track and the stable's in another barn attached to the farmhouse. He's fed the horse and put it t'bed. His cart's in the lean-to next to the stable. I could hitch him up again – no problem. But there's dogs ...'

Brushing hay from his jacket, Anson deliberated. The thought of making off with a peasant farmer's only horse bothered him. Even in an enemy country it went against the grain. Then there was the practical problem of the dogs. And if their barking alerted the farmer, he would have to be dealt with too.

'A change of plan,' he told the others. 'We're escaping prisoners, not horse thieves, and we're not at war with the peasants. We'll get ourselves down the road a bit and see if we can find an easier lift.'

*

Fagg was clearly in pain and was no longer trying to disguise it. His crutches and sheer determination were the only things that were keeping him going. His usual chatter and quips had gone, and, apart from wincing every time his foot touched the ground, he was silent now.

Drizzle turned to a downpour but they hurried on, soaked through. Hoover lent Fagg his shoulder and they hobbled awkwardly down the track after Anson as if they were taking part in a village sports three-legged race.

They came upon the main road again suddenly and Anson beckoned the others to join him crouching under a tree that offered partial shelter. The ordeal of movement over for the time being, Fagg could not resist commenting with feeling: 'Effin' bleedin' country!'

They lay, slumped close together against the tree trunk, rain dripping on and off them. Anson whispered: 'We'll rest awhile and see what comes along.'

But when at last they did hear hooves there were too many of them. Hoover crawled around from the blind side of the tree and in the moonlight made out a troop of cavalry heading north. When the horsemen had disappeared into the rain and gloom, Fagg voiced what all three feared: 'D'you reckon they're arter us?'

Anson considered the possibility but dismissed it. 'Too soon. There's no way the guards will report our escape while they've got a chance of getting away with that forged Arras receipt.'

Fagg nodded. 'And I'll bet Whiskers is still drunk from all that van rouge 'e put away. Bottles and bottles of it …'

The rain eased and stopped. Now it just dripped from every tree, branch and twig. They lay, wet and shivering. An hour or more went by and the road remained empty.

After weighing up the options, Anson rose stiffly, motioned to the others to wait where they lay, and set off back down the farm track.

Hoover whispered: 'What d'you reckon he's up to?'

Fagg shrugged. 'Orf to murder the farmer and steal 'is 'oss, I 'ope.' He reached for the sack. 'So 'e won't miss a sip or two of this here van rouge, will 'e?'

*

Anson made no attempt to conceal himself or stay quiet as he approached the farm buildings, and the dogs erupted in a broadside of excited barking that could be heard by his fellow escapers down by the road.

He rapped at the farmhouse door, sending the chained dogs into an even greater frenzy.

A light flared upstairs and after much muttering within and barking without, shutters creaked open and a night-capped head appeared. So did what looked to Anson like the business end of some kind of ancient fowling piece.

'*Bon soir, monsieur*,' he said, moving into the square of light below the window. It was clearly important to take the initiative if this relationship was to get off on the right foot.

The farmer growled thickly: '*Où êst vous, et qu'est-ce que vous voulez?*'

Anson had prepared his response. '*Je suis un ami, monsieur. Excusez-moi de vous dérangé, mais j'ai un problème.*'

'*Problème?*'

'*Oui, je suis un officier Flamanque au servis de France en route la côte à rendezvous avec mon bateau.*' A Flemish background would excuse his poor French and make him a plausible ally.

The response was garbled but Anson could make out various *sacrés* and *merdes* – and what appeared to be a suggestion that he should *allez* off and find his boat. If not, the farmer would first fire his shotgun at this disturber of the peace before *setting les chiens* on him. *Les chiens* dutifully backed his words with a further volley of barking.

'*Pardonnez moi, monsieur, mais j'ai besoin de votre assistance et j'ai beaucoup d'argent.*' And in case the message had not got through he added, '*D'or!*' and to prove it held up a golden guinea that glinted in the light of the lantern the farmer was now holding out of the window.

Anson had calculated correctly that peasant farmers did not see much if any gold in a year, or even a lifetime.

After much banging about inside the farmhouse the top half of the ground-level, stable-style door creaked open on rusty hinges and the farmer – still in nightshirt and nightcap – held up the lantern to examine the mysterious, unkempt nocturnal visitor who came seeking aid and offering gold.

As a precaution he held his rusty weapon by the barrel in his left hand.

Anson could understand the man's caution, confronted as he was by a wild-looking foreigner. But he guessed the farmer would be in the greater danger if he attempted to fire his elderly gun.

The farmer held his lantern closer and stared at the gold coin Anson held out to him. Satisfied it was real, he nodded and motioned his visitor inside. The dogs at last subsided.

Inside the large flag-stoned kitchen, the farmer, as hairy and weather-beaten a son of the soil as Anson had ever seen, indicated a bench and plonked the lantern down on a much-stained table which bore the rings of a hundred bottles.

Hesitating for a moment, the man decided his visitor offered no immediate threat and laid the ancient shotgun down. He filled a crude pitcher from a cask in the corner and poured some of the contents into two pots.

Anson sipped the rough red wine and opened negotiations by placing the glinting coin in the farmer's calloused hand.

The Frenchman held it close to the light in his open palm for a moment before closing it tightly in his fist. It didn't matter to him that there was the face of some foreign king on it. Just as the patron at the Auberge du

Marin had concluded, gold was gold, and a rare sight for a peasant farmer.

In his halting grammar school French, aided by appropriate gestures, Anson repeated his claim that he was Flemish, from Zeebrugge, and an officer in the French Navy.

The pots were filled, and emptied, again. The wine was not for a dainty palate, and it was strong. Anson soon felt a warm glow and struggled not to slur his words as he embarked on his story.

He and two of his matelots had been in hospital recovering from wounds sustained in a fight with the English *cochons*. Now they were on their way north to rejoin their ship, but the wagon taking them had shed a wheel. In haste not to miss the rendezvous they had continued on foot.

The farmer refilled the pots and Anson struggled on, his French coming back to him more fluently thanks to the wine. Now, he explained, one of his matelots was lame, his injury making it impossible to continue one more step. And with much gesticulation he painted a picture of all three, still not fully recovered from their wounds, being too exhausted to continue on foot.

The farmer appeared to have understood, but remained silent, his tanned and deeply-furrowed whiskery features deadpan.

Anson took another slurp of wine and made his bid. If the farmer would provide food and drink for the journey and take them to St Omer in his cart they could find military transport to take them from there to Calais and their ship. He would be given another two pieces of gold now, but they had to leave '*immédiatement!*' Otherwise, they would miss their ship. And on their safe arrival at St Omer he would receive three more such gold coins.

The farmer stared back, still silent. Anson asked earnestly, would he do it '*pour la France?*'

At last, after querying the financial arrangement, the man nodded. '*Oui, pour la France!*' Anson managed to stutter that such patriotism deserved its reward – and handed over the agreed advance of two guineas.

The Frenchman examined the coins closely and, satisfied, mounted a rickety wooden ladder that did duty as a staircase. There was a muttered conversation with his wife who sounded querulous at first, but her tone softened when, Anson assumed, she was handed the gold coins for safekeeping.

The farmer descended, now dressed in the same muddy working clothes he had been wearing when he almost stumbled on the escapers in the hay loft. He gathered bread and cheese and took down a ham from among several hanging from the beams, filled a large stone bottle from the wine barrel and pulled on an oilskin topcoat and hat.

Outside it was again raining steadily. The dozing dogs stirred, rattled their chains and set up a desultory token barking as the farmer tacked up the horse and harnessed it to the cart.

Exploring the ramshackle outbuildings, Anson came upon an old tarpaulin sheet and gestured that they should take it as a makeshift shelter for the cart. The farmer shrugged his agreement and helped throw it over and prop it up with an old wooden saw bench. Anson pointed to the well-head beside the barn door and the farmer nodded. He produced a large cask and, while he worked the handle pulling up bucketfuls of water, Anson filled the barrel – and several more stone bottles he found beside the back door.

The Englishman led the way back down the track on foot and, when they reached the main road, he called softly: 'Your carriage awaits.'

Fagg and Hoover emerged from the gloom and soon, much to their relief, all three were in the cart making themselves as comfortable as possible on a rough bed of straw under the tarpaulin – and heading north.

Anson whispered: 'We're supposed to be Flemish, so just keep your mouths shut, pretend to sleep and leave any talking to me.' For the exhausted pair it was an easy order to obey. Pretence was not necessary. And it was not long before he himself succumbed to the rhythmic swaying of the cart.

*

He awoke to daylight – the heavy horse still plodding steadily along an empty road. Anson reflected that a lot of water had passed under the bridge since the failed cutting-out raid not much more than a fortnight since, but it seemed far longer.

Although there was still a steady drizzle, Fagg and Hoover had emerged from under the tarpaulin sheet, but were obeying the last order and keeping quiet. When Anson pointed to Fagg's ankle and raised an enquiring eyebrow the response was a thumbs-up.

Whenever occasional travellers on horseback and the odd farm cart approached, the escapers ducked back under the tarpaulin. The only military traffic they encountered was a line of commissariat wagons heading south, but the accompanying soldiery – collars turned up and heads down against the rain – ignored their cart, no doubt assuming this was merely a lone peasant off to market.

Mid-morning and again late afternoon, the farmer stopped to water, feed and rest the horse, and after a while they continued clip-clopping and creaking northwards.

In the early evening the pace and noise changed, awaking the dozing escapers. It had stopped raining at last and the farmer had pulled off the road into the shelter of a copse of trees where they could not be easily seen from the road.

The passengers got down, stretching aching limbs, and relieved themselves in the bushes while the Frenchman unhitched the horse, gave it water from a pail and left it to graze.

'*Il est fatigué,*' he grumbled. '*Moi aussi.*'

Anson nodded. The man must be kept on side. Surreptitiously he teased another guinea from its hiding place in the lining of his jacket and handed it over. '*Pour manger.*' It was important to conserve the remains of what they had brought from the auberge in case they could obtain nothing else later.

Magically, the farmer's attitude turned from taciturn to friendly. He examined the coin carefully before tucking it into his pocket with the ghost of a grin and doled out chunks of gammon, bread, cheese and more of the rough red wine.

They rested up overnight, dozing for a few hours.

Back on the road early next morning, Anson thought it wise now to keep a lookout lest they were caught unawares by passing gendarmes or chanced upon more military traffic.

He took the first watch himself while the others dozed, but nothing untoward occurred other than occasional encounters with other farm traffic.

A shake woke the catnapping Hoover with a start. Anson signed that it was his turn and the marine took over the watcher's role. They pulled off the road for a makeshift meal and to rest the horse before setting off again towards St Omer.

For mile after mile there was nothing to report as the horse clip-clopped slowly along pulling the creaking, lurching cart.

But then, late in the afternoon, ahead of them on one long straight stretch, Hoover spotted two stationary wagons and what looked like two blue-coated figures apparently giving the first of them a going-over.

He put his hand on the dozing officer's shoulder. Alert in an instant, Anson raised his eyebrows questioningly. The marine gestured down the road. A blue-coated figure was now on one of the wagons, looking under a tarpaulin. The other appeared to be questioning the driver. Gendarmes?

'Shit!' Anson stirred the sleeping Fagg with his foot and, as he came to, put a finger to his lips, and called softly to the farmer: '*Arrêt ici, s'il vous plait.*' A tug at the reins and the cart halted.

Checking that the gendarmes were still fully occupied searching the other vehicles, the prisoners gathered their rolled-up coats and the sack of food, and disembarked, Fagg easing himself down with the aid of his crutches.

There was a whispered exchange and more gold coins and the remains of the ham, cheese and bread changed hands, drawing a full-sized grin from the farmer who immediately set about turning horse and cart back towards home.

The escapers hurried into the bushes beside the road. 'I've given him an extra guinea on condition he goes straight home and tells no one about us because we're on secret business for France,' Anson told the others. But as they set off into the woods the retreating farmer called softly: '*Bonne chance, Anglais!*'

Anson winced. So much for posing as Flemish allies. The wretched man must have known they were English all along.

9

What passed for the county set gathered outside the parish church to attend the memorial service for the late lamented Lieutenant Oliver Anson, RN.

The invitation letters had been penned by his elder brother, Augustine, or Gussie as his naval brother had always called him to his intense annoyance.

He had been jealous of his younger sibling's adventurous life at sea almost to a degree of hatred. So it was with some only thinly-disguised enthusiasm that he organised the service on behalf of their grieving family.

A brother fallen fighting for King and country was more useful in death than life to an ambitious young cleric, so Gussie had made sure that what he called 'the right society' was invited.

His invitation had smacked of blackmail. Distance precluded many, but who of those unfortunate enough to live within half a day's journey could ignore a call to honour the sacrifice of a hero such as this? Any who responded with a 'much regret unable' would be made to feel unpatriotic, and their absence would be noticed – and remembered.

And so the ivy-covered, flint-walled, 12th century church dedicated to Saints Cosmos and Damian, pioneer makers of prosthetic limbs, was full to mark Lieutenant Anson's passing.

Everyone who was anyone was there, from minor gentry and squirarchy to the navy, including officers from the dead hero's ship, red-coated representatives from Canterbury and Dover garrisons, a goodly sprinkling from the church, and land-owners and farmers from the neighbourhood.

The navy was there in no lesser personage than Captain Phillips of HMS *Phryne*, temporarily berthed at Chatham. Immaculate in post captain's best fig, his jacket heavily edged with gold braid, he attracted every eye.

He was accompanied by the first lieutenant, John Howard, a particular friend of the late Lieutenant Anson, and by Lieutenant McKenzie of the marines, resplendent in scarlet jacket that contrasted sharply with his magpie-uniformed naval colleagues. His left arm, struck by a French musket ball in the boat pulling away from the mole at St Valery-en-Caux, was still supported by a black sling.

Captain Phillips was somewhat taken aback when, on arrival, he was presented by Augustine Anson with a monumental mason's hefty bill for work done on the memorial about to be unveiled. As he opened his mouth to query it, he was told sharply: 'The plaque is in the name of his brother officers. That's you, is it not?'

The rector himself, apparently completely unaware of his eldest son's barefaced effrontery, welcomed Phillips warmly.

The captain expressed his condolences and asked: 'I gathered from your late son, sir, that you are related in some degree to the great circumnavigator?'

'Yes, but distant, I fear. And you, sir, are one of the Pembrokeshire Philipps, I assume?'

'I am, indeed, from that glorious county of Pembrokeshire, sir, but a Phillips with two 'l's with a single 'p' at the end. Not to be confused with one 'l' and two final 'p's. They are the ones with the money who live in castles.'

The squire – portly, ruddy-faced Sir Oswald Brax – was as ever, loud and prominent, arriving in the family carriage with minutes to spare before the mourners filed into the church.

As owner of the area's largest estate, he held the advowson – the right to nominate a rector who met his criteria: a cheery, hunting cleric, Tory of course, who kept a good table, a well-stocked cellar, and would not go around prophesying doom and spreading gloom among the peasantry.

Parson Anson the elder fitted the bill admirably, although he did tend to get carried away of a Sunday and rant against the ranters. But fair enough in an age when non-conformist sects were constantly hovering like hungry wolves around the edge of your flock trying to make off with easily-persuadable yokels.

In the Brax family pew, ornately-carved in an otherwise largely austere boxed-seated nave, was the squire's plump, extravagantly-attired wife, envied by most because of her position in society and imagined lifestyle, but to be pitied if they only knew of her husband's private peccadillos.

Next to her sat their three daughters, Charlotte, Jane and Isobel, aged 20-something, 18 and 14 respectively, and youngest son William, at 16 not quite forceful enough to defy his father like his elder brother George. The latter had chosen to ignore the memorial service and was elsewhere, either destroying some kind of wildlife with gun or hounds, playing with the local yeomanry troop, drinking and gambling at his Canterbury club, or hunting a softer species of game among the housemaids at Brax Hall. Like father, like son.

The church was well represented by the archdeacon and Gussie's fellow minor canons, as well as assorted rectors, vicars and curates from nearby parishes. The archdeacon, a decent though thoroughly unworldly man more interested in antiquarian than spiritual pursuits, had been flattered to be invited to conduct the service, give the address and dedicate a memorial tablet to a naval hero from such a respected Anglican family. Centre stage, he felt a little of the reflected glory.

The principal farmers were there with their wives, in Sunday best but awkward among so many clerics and their pinch-faced womenfolk, smugly superior in their bespoke mourning dresses. And at the back of the church a score of rectory servants and labourers, given the morning off to attend, shuffled in to pay their respects – more to keep in with the living rather than honouring a dead hero they had scarcely seen this past decade.

The Anson family – whey-faced father, weeping mother and daughters, Gussie with a carefully-contrived fixed expression of saintly piety, and younger son Abraham, proud to be a hero's brother – filed in last and took their places at the front.

'I am the resurrection and the life, and all that believeth in me shall inherit eternal life,' droned the archdeacon, not altogether convincingly. And so the service began. Words, meant to be of comfort and reassurance of heaven's many mansions, were punctuated by robust hymns specially chosen.

It had pleased the family to introduce a nautical theme with 'Oh God our help in ages past … Our Shelter from the stormy blast.' And the verse about time bearing all its sons away to 'fly forgotten, as a dream' brought a tear to the eyes of most mothers present.

The congregation was suitably stirred and impressed by Gussie's reading from Psalms Chapter 107:

'They that go down to the sea in ships, that do business in great waters; These see the works of the Lord, and his wonders of the deep.'

But when he reached the line about storm-tossed sailors who 'reel to and fro, and stagger like a drunken man ...' Howard and McKenzie exchanged a glance and stifled grins. Both recalled happier times reeling and staggering with their deceased shipmate.

Came the eulogy, and Captain Phillips strode forward. He placed his notes on the lectern, and gripped it firmly as if clinging to the yardarm in a gale. Clearing his throat, he took a quick look round at the assembled mourners and, a shade less confidently than when on his own quarterdeck, proceeded to state the praises of his fallen lieutenant.

'It was,' he said, 'for King and country that this bold young officer fell on an alien shore. He had shown great promise in his chosen profession, was well respected, and, indeed, well liked by every officer and man in HMS *Phryne*, and had died a hero's death, bravely rallying his men against overwhelming odds to allow others to reach the boats and safety.'

It was standard fare for grieving relatives and on this occasion had the merit of being largely true. Only Howard heard McKenzie's muttered: 'And all for a foolhardy mission doomed from the start ...'

A few more platitudes and the eulogy was over. Augustine Anson left the family pew and ushered Captain Phillips to a space between two stained glass windows, one featuring an odd-looking green-clad Virgin Mary and child, where a white ensign hung.

From the pulpit, the archdeacon delivered a blessing as the captain tugged at the cord attached to the ensign. The pegs holding it gave way and it fell, revealing a marble tablet but enveloping its unveiler, who quickly pulled it off his head to avoid further embarrassment.

The memorial was surmounted by a scroll and a relief of a warship under sail, and the simple inscription was supported by various nautical symbols: a cannon, compass rose and fouled anchor. It read:

'Erected by his brother officers in affectionate memory of Lieutenant Oliver Anson, Royal Navy, second son of the Reverend Thomas Anson DD, Rector of this Parish, who fell in action at St Valery-en-Caux in Normandy, Anno Dom. 1798.'

It was, all agreed, a fitting tribute to a fine young man – truly a local hero.

*

Still very much alive, if a shadow of his normal self, the object of their memorialising was pondering what to do next.

Minutes after abandoning the cart it became clear that there was no hope of Fagg getting far on foot. With his splinted leg bent at the knee to avoid any risk of grounding it, he hopped awkwardly, alternately putting his weight on his crude crutches. The effort involved was considerable.

Anson observed him apprehensively. 'How is it?'

Fagg paused in mid-hop, glad of a chance to lean on his crutches. 'A bit dot an' carry, like they say, sir, but I'll make it.'

'And pigs might fly. Here, put your arm round my shoulder and we'll try it three-legged again.'

They set off shoulder to shoulder with Hoover in close attendance, protesting: 'Let me give him a hand while you navigate, sir.'

'You'll get your turn soon enough,' panted Anson. 'The priority now is to get well away from the road. Then we can rest up. I reckon we're still some miles south of St Omer, and if we keep the road on our right we shouldn't get lost.'

They staggered off deeper into the wood, with Hoover now scouting ahead, holding one of Fagg's crutches like a musket, which he dearly wished it was.

Fagg grumbled: 'I wish to Gawd there was a bleedin' river to float down. I 'ate all these bleedin' woods an' fields. Ain't bleedin' natural.'

Anson supposed the countryside would not suit a Chatham guttersnipe like Fagg. Back alleys were his natural environment ashore.

'If Gawd 'ad meant us t'go cross-country 'e'd 'ave issued us with bleedin' wheels or 'ooves, so he would. Will I be chuffed to see Boologny and the sea!'

Anson corrected him. 'Not Boulogne. That'll be too full of uniforms. No, our course is for Gravelines.'

Hoover asked. 'Gravelines, where's that?'

'To the north east of Bolougne, between Calais and Dunkirk. English smugglers use it.'

'So we'll stand a better chance of getting a boat from there than we would from Calais or Boulogne?'

'Correct – or anywhere else for that matter.'

'And it's still only 30 miles or so to cross the Channel instead of hundreds from the Normandy coast?'

'Exactly.' Anson was determined to keep morale up by maintaining a confident attitude, born more out of wishful thinking than certainty.

All they had to do for now was skirt inhabited places and avoid human contact. It would be if and when they neared the coast that their real problems would begin.

Anson's dark blue jacket could be taken by country bumpkins for a French infantryman's uniform and his fractured French for the Fleming he reckoned he had already successfully passed himself off as – until he recalled the farmer's farewell when he had dropped them off.

Lank-haired, unshaven, and in the innkeeper's cast-offs Thérèse had given them, Fagg and Hoover could pass for French peasants – until they opened their mouths. True, Fagg could now order drinks and curse like a Frenchman, but with an accent that shrieked of the mean streets of Chatham and of the lower deck.

Hoover, naturally reserved, spoke only when he had something to say. He had no intention of speaking any French whatsoever. If the Frogs wanted to speak to him they had best learn the King's English.

The marine seemed tireless. Whenever a halt was called he took it on himself, without orders, to find the best cover, reconnoitre the surrounding area and hunt for water, berries, nuts and anything else drinkable or edible that he came across.

Anson, having noted the marine's fieldcraft skills, was content to leave their security to him. It had become blindingly obvious to Anson that with Fagg's ankle as it was they could only make a few miles a day and at that rate it would take a month of Sundays to reach the coast.

There was only one alternative. Anson judged they were now fairly close to St Omer. If he was right and they could skirt the town undetected they should hit the river that flowed all the way down to Gravelines on the coast.

*

By nightfall they had reached what Anson hoped was the northern end of the wood. Through the trees they could see the outline of a road. They crawled forward and lay up near a straight stretch to observe the traffic, but there was none save a solitary horseman who trotted past, unaware that he was being watched. Slung over his shoulder was a leather satchel. Another official messenger, perhaps?

Cloudless, the night sky soon glittered with stars. Anson sought the Big Dipper and with his index finger drew an imaginary line through the stars Merak and Dubhe, moved it upwards five times that distance to Ursa Minor – and with it pinpointed Polaris, the Pole star. He stood facing it, and confirmed: 'This is north.'

With virtually no traffic, he reckoned taking to the road again was worth the risk. Even with Fagg's game leg they would be able to make better progress than through the woods, and could scuttle into the ditch beside the road if they met any other nocturnal travellers.

Emerging from the trees, they set off up the road. It was a struggle, with Anson and Hoover taking turns to support their injured comrade who was coping manfully with the aid of his crutches.

Anson estimated they were perhaps five, at most ten, miles south of St Omer and wondered if Fagg would be able to keep up this sort of pace. Hopping along was hard enough for him, and adding that to sleeping rough without proper food, the odds appeared to be stacked against them.

Progress became slower and slower, and it was to the relief of all three when the emerging dawn forced them to seek a suitable wooded area where they could leave the road and hide up again until nightfall.

*

Waking from a brief doze, Anson focussed on his two companions sitting beside him. Fagg looked nervous. 'Sir?'

Anson blinked and rubbed his eyes. 'What is it? Trouble?'

'Not exackly, sir. But while you was sleeping, well, we 'ad a meetin' …'

Schooled as he was in naval discipline, and conscious that it was not long since he had been tangled up in the Spithead and Nore mutinies, Anson had a deep distrust of lower deck meetings. 'A meeting?'

'Yeah, well we what-you-call mulled it over like, y'know—'

Hoover came to Fagg's aid. 'We kind of talked through how we're fixed, sir.'

'And?'

A magpie fluttered down into the clearing and, spooked by the unexpected sight of humans in its bailiwick, skittered away squawking.

Fagg touched his temple in superstitious salute to the bird – a precautionary Kentish custom – and tried again. 'Well sir, t'cut a long story short, we reckon you'd stand a better chance on yer own, escapin' like.'

'Why?'

Hoover cut in. 'The fact is, sir, that you speak French – and Fagg here can't help it with his leg and all, but he slows you down.'

'So what are you proposing, that we should leave him behind?'

'No, sir. Sam and I will stay together. We'll try our luck in slow time.'

Anson pursed his lips. 'We'll take our chances together, and that's that.'

'But like 'e said, sir, I'll slow yer down. On yer own you could get back to the navy that much quicker.' Fagg rested his case.

'That's true enough, sir,' Hoover added. 'On your own, wearing a blue jacket and speakin' French, well, you'd make it sure enough. But with the two of us along, why, we'd be sure to finish up in that prison place.'

Case made, they awaited the officer's response. Anson smiled. 'Your consideration for me is touching. Or maybe you want to get me back into the war that much sooner?'

They grinned.

'Well, whatever your motives, let's get a couple of things straight. We may not be on board ship, but this is still the navy. And allow me to remind you of what Captain Phillips was fond of telling us – that the navy is not a democracy. I make the decisions here. And get it into your thick heads that we are going to make it together. There's no question of anyone going it alone. We'll stay together and we'll make it back to England together. That's final. Understood?'

Fagg and Hoover exchanged a relieved glance. 'Well, we tried, sir,' the marine muttered philosophically, 'but we're glad you think that way.'

And Fagg nodded. 'Yeah, stick together it is, sir – an' I'll try not t'slow yer down.'

Suddenly they froze. Someone, something, was rustling in the nearby undergrowth.

Anson raised himself stiffly on an elbow. Sleeping in the open was taking its toll.

A sheepdog appeared and barked at the fugitives, teeth bared. 'Here boy,' Anson called softly and held out a crust of bread. But the animal was not to be enticed.

Fagg swore quietly. 'Bleedin' hanimal. Don't let 'im near me. I 'ate the effin' fings!'

The dog was unimpressed and came closer, barking fiercely. Hoover reached for his stick and the dog turned its attention to him. He raised the stick but before he could strike, a whistle stopped the dog in its tracks. The escapers froze.

Giving Hoover a final threatening snarl, the dog turned and dashed back to his unseen owner who could be heard admonishing the creature for running off.

'Phew,' muttered Hoover, 'that was awful close.'

The three exchanged relieved glances. 'Bleedin' shepherd must 'ave thought Fido was arter a rabbit or somefink,' whispered Fagg. 'Picked up our scent, like. It ain't hardly surprising when you fink about it. We must smell a bit by now.'

'You can say that again,' Hoover agreed.

'Met some girl when I come ashore down at Portsmouth one time. She said I niffed a bit so I told her as I had a barf reg'lar every month whether I needed it or not ... And d'you know what she said?'

Hoover sighed. 'I don't doubt you're gonna tell us, again.'

'Yeah, she give me the evil eye and she said: "I 'ope the month's nearly up." Cheeky cow!'

Anson's eyebrows went skywards. Whatever, he knew they must break their rule about laying up in daylight. They needed to quit this place – just in case the dog's owner had spotted them or had his suspicions roused enough to report strangers hiding in the woods.

They struggled to their feet and set off as quietly as possible deeper into the wood, following Hoover's example by walking – in Fagg's case hopping – through brackish puddles in an attempt to disguise their scent lest the dog returned to track them.

The marine came to a fallen tree and, judging that they were now far enough from the road, he beckoned them forward calling softly: 'Good spot to harbour up. Plenty of cover.'

Fagg collapsed gratefully among the grounded branches, greedily refilling his lungs and gently massaging his throbbing ankle. They could not have covered more than a few hundred yards.

He already looked totally done in and Anson touched him on the shoulder reassuringly. 'I reckon that's quite enough footslogging. We'll have to find some transport.'

Hoover offered: 'Will I go and see what I can find, sir?'

The officer nodded. 'Do that, but take care – and bring us back a couple of beefsteaks and a bottle of wine while you're at it.' He fished in his jacket for a coin and passed it to Hoover. 'And remember, we're not thieves.'

The marine grinned, stuck up his thumb and disappeared into the bushes.

*

At the rectory the sherry, good wine of suspect origin – as was invariably the case in smuggling territory around the Kent coast – and a cold collation of meat and cheese platters fuelled conversation.

Avoiding the gentry's tipples, the farmers stuck to the small beer, as even otherwise abstaining non-conformists rightly regarded the local water as too dangerous to drink, unboiled.

Even without a body to bury, the feeling was that Lieutenant Anson had been laid to rest satisfactorily and a cheerier atmosphere prevailed, as almost always after a funeral or memorial service.

Clerics, naval and military mourners, and the farmers formed separate cliques. Lesser mortals had shuffled away as soon as the service ended and were already back at work.

Squire Brax held forth to Captain Phillips and the assorted colonels from nearby garrisons about the evils of the new-fangled income tax that was being introduced to finance the war. He urged them: 'Put the wretched Froggies back in their boxes as soon as you like and put an end to this damned iniquitous tax!'

'It is, we are led to believe, a purely temporary measure, sir,' Phillips countered reassuringly.

'Thank the Lord for that!' grunted Brax, adding after a moment's reflection, 'temporary maybe, but it wouldn't surprise me if once begun we'll never see an end to it in our lifetimes.'

And, pandering to Phillips, he added: 'You navy people have got the right idea. Don't know why we need an army at all. I say the best way to keep the lid on everything is the good old English way of building a damned great fleet and letting the Frogs do what they ruddy well please as long as they stick to their own side of the Channel, don't you think?'

The colonels, clearly reluctant to take issue with him on an occasion such as this, gradually moved away and involved themselves in less inflammatory conversations elsewhere.

Augustine Anson used the occasion to ingratiate himself further with the archdeacon and his hawk-nosed daughter.

In truth, if forced to give an honest opinion, the archdeacon would have had to confess that he had never warmed to the man, regarding him as something of a Pharisee who observed the tenets of the church and rules of society, yet in reality was chiefly concerned about his own advancement and outward appearances. But since Augustine Anson showed every sign of climbing further up the ecclesiastical ladder, he would make a useful catch for Rachel, who was no beauty nor in first flush.

Abraham, the youngest Anson brother, the squire's son William, and the other young men quizzed Lieutenants Howard and McKenzie about life at sea, and among themselves the farmers discussed corn prices, which had risen as ever in wartime.

The older womenfolk who classed themselves as quality surrounded the dead hero's mother, oozing sympathy. Then, as such social gatherings providing for the exchange of information were few and far between, the talk turned to important matters such as possible matrimonial alliances for sons and daughters.

The daughters commented on one another's dresses and eyed the uniformed male contingent speculatively.

The farmers' wives, large and small, critiqued their betters' fashions – and discussed the marriage prospects of their own offspring.

As ever, servants were assumed – quite erroneously – to see and hear nothing. But in a lull between topping up glasses, George Beer, the rectory butler-cum-steward, observed to old Maggie, the cook: 'If you ask me, I'd say Master Oliver is well off out of it all.'

'You shouldn't say such 'orrible fings, George Beer.'

'Don't mean no harm by it. If he weren't dead he'd have been married off three times already today, to that there archdeacon's daughter with the unfortunate face or to one of squire's flibbertigibbet daughters. Mind you, Farmer Finn's girl might have suited. Good pair of child-bearin' hips she has. As it is, that nasty piece of work Gussie is one of the few choices left round here. And who'd want him, the pompous prig?'

Maggie shrugged. There was no arguing with that.

Wherever his body lay, Lieutenant Anson had been laid to rest in the minds of shipmates, family and neighbours.

10

Hoover skirted the edge of the wood, now fringed by nettle and thistle-dotted meadows, until he saw a cluster of farm buildings a cable's length away.

Apart from the smoke rising from its solitary chimney, the long low farmhouse with barn attached had a neglected look and the yard beside it was littered with old pieces of equipment, a dunghill, woodpile and patches of nettles.

Slipping back under cover of the trees, he watched for activity. For a while there was none, but eventually a fat peasant woman emerged from the farmhouse and waddled with a bowl in one hand and bucket in the other towards an ark-shaped chicken house. She threw the bowl's contents into the fenced run, poured water from the pail into some kind of drinking trough, and knelt at the back of the ark to open a hinged flap.

Hoover muttered: 'Collecting the eggs. Wish I'd got there first …'

The woman placed the eggs carefully in the bowl, picked it and the bucket up, and wobbled over to her stable-style back door, the top half of which was hanging open. She hesitated, as if remembering another chore, put down the bowl and bucket, and headed for the barn entrance.

The marine tensed, sensing an opportunity. After a moment or two he heard the sound of chopping from the outbuilding. She was cutting firewood.

Hoover was up and running full pelt across the stretch of meadow, a wine bottle in each hand like some drinker rousted from an alehouse by the press gang.

At the back door he stopped, breathing heavily, to assure himself that the woman was still busy and that there was no one else about. Satisfied that he had a few minutes, he tilted the half full bucket to fill the wine bottles. Then he scooped up three of the half dozen eggs into his hat and flitted back across the meadow into the cover of the trees, where he froze, gasping from the effort.

The sound of chopping ceased, and in the rapidly fading light he saw the woman emerge, pushing a wheelbarrow loaded with kindling and logs. She stopped at the back door, tipped the logs and firewood out of the barrow, and wheeled it back empty – Hoover guessed ready for tomorrow's fuel. He watched her go back to the house where she picked up the egg bowl and stared at it for a moment. She clearly felt sure she had collected more eggs than the few that remained, but shrugged and went inside.

Hoover saw his chance, emerged from the trees and entered the barn, placed the coin the officer had given him on the chopping block where she was bound to find it, and quickly wheeled the barrow away into the trees.

Back at their hiding place, the marine's arrival pushing a wheelbarrow provoked some mirth, and louder laughter when he told them how he had come by it – and at what cost.

Anson commented somewhat ruefully: 'Must be the world's most expensive wheelbarrow ...'

They each cracked an egg and ate it raw, and as soon as the light began to fade, Anson and Hoover helped Fagg into the barrow, his legs for'ard and arms dangling either side. He grinned cheerfully: 'I feel like a hupturned tortoise.'

Hoover grabbed the handles. 'Permission to shove off, sir?'

Anson nodded. 'Let's go.' And the marine lifted the handles, leaned forward and gave the barrow a shove.

It was surprisingly easy. Fagg was no fatty, and whoever invented wheelbarrows knew what he was about. But whoever made this one had built in an annoying squeak. Every time the wheel turned, it squeaked. Over potholes or on the level, it squeaked.

After weaving through the trees for a few hundred yards Hoover dropped the handles and scooped up a handful of mud from a puddle. He smeared it around the wheel pin, cleaned his hand with grass and resumed his place between the shafts.

His passenger clucked appreciatively. 'Well done, Dobbin, we'll make a cart'orse of ye yet.' Hoover grimaced. Had he been a swearing man, his response might well have referred to shoving the wheelbarrow up somewhere it couldn't possibly fit. But he resisted the temptation.

For a few turns of the wheel there was blissful silence. Then the squeak returned, slight at first but soon as loud, if not louder, than before.

'Effing Frogs! Can't even build a barrer proper,' observed Fagg. 'That bleedin' squeak'll drive us all nuts afore the night's out.'

Hoover grunted and pushed on. And Anson resolved to acquire some grease at the earliest opportunity.

In the increasing gloom, he took a turn between the shafts while Hoover scouted ahead, beckoning the barrow on when satisfied all was clear, and showing the flat of his hand in a stop motion if any noise or movement ahead gave the slightest cause for concern.

As he pushed, Anson considered the situation. Now that they had the barrow and could move Fagg along at a reasonable pace, there was no question of abandoning it and attempting to find their way round St Omer, especially because of the marshy ground that lay all around.

No, they were going to have to take the risk, take to the road, brazen it out and wheel their way straight through the town to find the river.

*

Ahead, on higher ground, lay St Omer, its great square-towered cathedral dominating the skyline, and just before they reached the outskirts, Anson motioned Hoover to push the barrow into some bushes beside the road.

He helped Fagg out of the barrow. 'We'll attract attention with you in that thing, so you'll have to do some more hopping.'

Fagg knuckled his forehead. 'Aye aye, sir.'

'Now, we'll put our kit in the barrow and collect some wood to cover it. That'll make it look as if we're going back into the town with firewood.'

Five minutes later they set off again, Anson pushing the wood-filled barrow, Hoover walking beside him with a bundle over his shoulder, and Fagg hopping along on his crutches some distance behind.

Scruffily dressed with unkempt hair and some days' growth of stubble, they looked every inch French peasants as they made their way slowly past the old walls and into the town. The few people still about were traders bringing their unsold goods away from the town square in carts and barrows from the day's market, and no notice was taken of them.

All was going well until, as they passed through the market debris where a lone dog was gnawing on some discarded offal, Anson and Hoover heard a sudden cry and crash behind and turned to see Fagg sprawled on the road. He had taken a heavy tumble.

85

They looked around, but in the semi-darkness they could see no one close enough to have noticed, so Hoover wheeled the barrow back to where Fagg had fallen.

He was sitting now, groaning and massaging his leg. 'Sorry sir, I took a tumble on these bleeding cobbles and me ankle's givin' me gip agin ...'

There was only one thing for it. Anson looked around to make sure they weren't being watched and tipped the wood out of the barrow. He helped Fagg climb aboard again and once more they set off, Hoover now bringing up at the rear carrying their kit.

With the light load of wood the wheel had barely squeaked, but Fagg's weight set it off squealing with every turn and Anson cursed under his breath. They could hardly fail to draw unwelcome attention to themselves now.

Hoover broke step to join a scruffy dog rummaging among the market detritus, Anson presumed in search of anything edible. Fagg urged the marine: 'See if ye can find summat to eat – me stomach's grumbling somefink terrible.' But he might have been less enthusiastic if he had known that the food sold at the market that day had included fresh frogs and snails from the nearby marshes.

The marine waved the dog away with a heavy stick he had kept from those they had tipped from the barrow. He grabbed at whatever the mongrel had been chewing and caught up with the others in triumph.

Anson was unimpressed. 'A bone's not much use to us.' Hoover shook his head. 'It ain't a bone, sir. Leastways it is but it's got a heap of smelly old gristle and fat on it.'

'That damned squeaky wheel—'

'Yeah!' Hoover set to work greasing the axle and when he had finished Anson gave the barrow a shove and they were off again, mercifully squeak-free.

They had passed through the middle of town unmolested and were heading through the northern outskirts when a group of young men swigging from bottles emerged from a side street, spotted them and approached jeering and laughing.

Anson decided the best thing to do was to take the initiative. '*Prenez garde garçons! Mon ami est ivre ... tres, tres ivre – et fou. Derangé!*' Drunk and mad should keep them at a distance. To emphasise, he put his finger to his forehead in what he hoped was the international sign for having a very large screw loose.

Fagg, arms and legs hanging akimbo over the sides of the barrow, had caught on fast and did his best to imitate a drunken madman, tongue lolling out and eyes rolling. He had seen enough cases during his naval service to be convincing.

The revellers made to gather round, maybe to have a little fun, but Anson casually revealed the dirk in his belt and Hoover approached hefting his stick. Scar-face with a blade, a soldierly-looking man with a cudgel and a drunken maniac were clearly somewhat off-putting and the youths drew back, shouting insults from a safe distance. Anson took the barrow handles and set off again, flanked by Hoover, stick now over his shoulder.

Once out of earshot, Anson muttered: 'A close run thing, that ... and they may yet follow, or report us, so let's get the hell out of here before they attract the watchmen.'

They made it to the northern outskirts without further incident and as they descended towards the marshes the moonlight picked out the silvery thread of a watercourse.

'Thank Gawd,' Fagg murmured, 'water, at bleedin' last.'

Anson recalled the map he had studied back at the auberge. This, he deduced, must be a branch of the River Aa, navigable at least for large barges all the way to Gravelines.

'Is that the river we want, sir?'

'Yes, it's the Aa ...'

'The what?' Fagg queried.

'The River Aa. It's spelt with a double 'a'...'

'Daft name for a river. 'Ow d'you say it, Ay Ah or Arrh?'

'No, I think they pronounce it Ah-ah.'

'Well I'll be buggered! Funny lot these Frogs.'

However it was pronounced, Anson felt an enormous sense of relief at being so close to the element they were most comfortable with – water – and, beside it, a rickety wooden jetty.

They hid up in a clump of trees near the water's edge where they could keep an eye on it, and, exhausted from the journey and lack of food, they dozed for some hours until Hoover woke to the sound of approaching voices. He gave the other two a shake and pointed to the jetty.

There was just enough moonlight for them to pick out an approaching boat. This, Anson knew, was a flat-bottomed craft known as a *bacôve* used by the people who farmed around the Audomarois marshes to move their produce.

It was being propelled punt-like towards the jetty by a man with a pole and, as it touched, his companion stepped ashore clutching the painter and tied it up to a post.

Anson couldn't help himself mouthing: 'So there is a God!' and pulled a wry face as he thought how disapproving his father would have been to hear him say it.

He put his finger to his lips, whispering: 'No tongue: all eyes: be silent!' Neither of his companions was familiar with Shakespeare's *Tempest*, but they got the message nevertheless.

The boat was loaded with sacks of fresh vegetables. The watchers could see cauliflowers, carrots, artichokes and endives spilling out – most likely being brought in for the coming day's market.

With clearly no idea that they were being watched, the two Frenchmen set off up the hill into the town, no doubt to seek an early-morning drink before returning to unload their produce.

Anson picked up a piece of chalk from the river bank, whispered: 'Right, let's go,' and they emerged from their hiding place and clambered onto the jetty. There was not much room in the boat, so they man-handled most of the sacks ashore.

He paused for a moment to chalk something on the barrow and placed a tied-up piece of rag from his tattered shirt in it before stepping aboard. Last in, first out. Then he untied the rope and Hoover took up the pole and pushed off.

Looking back, they could see the piled sacks of vegetables and the abandoned wheelbarrow, standing forlorn beside them. As the jetty faded from sight, Fagg observed: 'Thank Gawd we've seen the last of that bleedin' squeaky fing. Them Frogs is going to get a terrible surprise when they find their boat's turned into a barrer!'

11

Hoover's shoulder was beginning to ache, so Anson took over at the pole. The going was easy. Through trial and error, he found that all he had to do was stand with one foot forward on the thwarts and plunge the pole into the water ahead.

Leaning forward provided enough pressure to send the *bacôve* surging ahead and by pulling the pole out and repeating the manoeuvre their progress was rapid. It was the perfect craft for the canalised river – and the surrounding water-logged marshland.

Dawn saw them already some miles down-river. All they had seen so far was a horse-drawn barge heading to St Omer. The man plodding beside the horse took no notice of them, but Anson was becoming concerned. During the day they could easily come across others who might recognise the *bacôve*, but not its crew, so it was necessary to keep a low profile.

A few miles ahead a minor tributary branched off to the left and a little way down it they could see a large tree overhanging the water. It was an ideal place to harbour up and Anson poled the *bacôve* towards it. They used the low branches to pull the boat against the bank and made fast to a partly exposed root. Here, there was a good chance that they would not be spotted from passing craft and they could rest up for the day.

Ravenous, they breakfasted on the last remains of the food the farmer had given them: bread, now rock hard, a lump of cheese that they carefully split into three, and raw cauliflower and carrots from the vegetable sacks left on board.

Anson tried an artichoke heart and offered the others endives, but Fagg pulled a face and declined. 'More French muck! Never 'eard of a hendive and ain't gonna try one now …'

As the morning wore on they heard more river traffic but their leafy canopy made it near impossible to see – or be seen. Anson lay back on a sack and through a gap in the branches could see a pair of buzzards circling high overhead, mewing as they hunted.

A commotion nearby alarmed them but it turned out to be a few head of cattle coming down the bank to drink from the steam. Dragonflies hovered over the water and a sudden splash made them start in time to see the dazzle of a kingfisher emerging with a small silvery fish in its beak.

During the afternoon Hoover crept ashore to reconnoitre, returning to report seeing nothing but a few grazing sheep on the tussocks of grass in the higher areas of the marshes – and very little traffic on the main waterway.

There was a fishing line in the *bacôve* and Fagg borrowed the dirk to fashion a crude rod from a branch of the tree, but, despite baiting with worms dug out of the bank, he caught nothing in the sluggish stream.

Finally, by early evening, Anson judged it safe enough to venture out from their hiding place. He poled the boat back down to the main waterway and set off north, now expertly plunging the pole in and propelling the *bacôve* forward in powerful surges.

Herons fished from the banks and all was peaceful apart from the croaking of frogs, provoking Fagg to mutter: 'Them bleedin' creatures are gonna give me nightmares fer years to come ...'

As it grew dark they passed the ruins of an abbey but saw no signs of life, and the watery moonlight was enough to enable Anson to avoid steering into the banks.

After a few hours of uninterrupted progress, with Hoover, his shoulder now rested, taking turns with the pole, the marshes began to give way to sand dunes and they saw lights ahead: Gravelines.

They pulled in to the bank, abandoned the boat, and pushed it out to drift in the waterway where it was sure to be found and hopefully returned to its owner.

And, looking like scarecrows in their torn and filthy clothes, they approached the massive star-shaped fortifications dominating the small town at the mouth of the Aa where it flowed into the North Sea.

*

For the escapers, the first priority was to go to ground until they could reconnoitre the port.

The darkness was both friend and enemy. They could move around without making themselves too conspicuous, but it was going to be difficult to find somewhere safe to hole up.

They entered the town via a narrow lane and, approaching the harbour, came upon what appeared to be an open-fronted building smelling strongly of fish. Was this where the local fishermen brought their catches to sell?

There was just enough moonlight for Anson to make out a pile of wooden crates and casks at the back of the building and he shepherded the other two behind them, throwing off his naval jacket and whispering: 'Stay put while I look around.'

In his scruffy state Anson reckoned he could pass for a common sailor without much problem. He completed his disguise with a hat – similar to the woollen caps many French boatmen wore – fashioned from one of his own holey stockings during the wagon journey.

'Will I do?'

Fagg could not hide his amusement. 'You don't look much like a navy orficer in that 'at, sir. More like a dog's brekfust.'

The least favourite possibility, now, was to steal a boat and sail or row it to England. To Anson the hazards were self-evident. If the French were worth their salt, security would be tight. Oars and sails might well have been removed from boats overnight and there could be military patrols in the harbour area.

But this was Gravelines and there was another possibility. Anson, like any naval officer who had seen service at the North Sea corner of the English Channel, was well aware of the port's reputation. He knew it suited the French to treat it almost as a free port.

Gold was needed to pay neutral countries for war material, so a blind eye was turned to English smugglers bringing them guineas in exchange for contraband wines and spirits. It was well known that the smugglers even brought over the latest English newspapers, an invaluable source of intelligence for the French.

He kept to the shadows, stopping every few steps to look and listen. Fifty yards further down the quayside a buzz of noise was coming from a building with a pool of light showing at its open door. A fishermen's drinking den?

From the lane behind him came marching feet and a swinging lantern. A patrol. Suppose they stopped and questioned him?

There was no time to consider. Anson strode out towards the pool of light and ducked through the open door as nonchalantly as he could for someone whose heart was thumping wildly and who felt as conspicuous as a bishop in a bordello.

The patrol carried on past, no doubt assuming he was just another fisherman going for a nightcap or two. And, to Anson's relief, no-one in the crowded, ill-lit drinking hole appeared to take any notice of his entry.

Guttering candles revealed a crowd of drinkers through the pipe-smoke fug. Drinks were being dispensed by a heavily-tattooed, scar-faced, broken-nosed man who looked as if he had spent most of his life fishing and brawling, which indeed he had. Providing assistance and a lady's touch, was a blowsy female – his wife perhaps – who matched him for ill looks, lacking only the broken nose, illustrated skin and scars.

Anson realised to his annoyance that he had no money on him. He had left what remained in his jacket with the others – and in any event presenting a gold coin for cheap wine or beer in a den like this would have been a certain give-away, drawing unwelcome attention to him. A Flemish sailor with gold? Never happen …

But being without a drink in a drinking den would also look suspicious.

While Anson was wondering what to do one of the drinkers went outside, presumably to urinate into the harbour.

Anson turned, snatched up the man's abandoned pot and moved quickly to the back of the room where he found a free end of a wooden bench, sat down and hunched himself over his drink.

He saw the urinator return, look around for his drink and mouth curses at those around him before giving up the hunt and going up to the patron for a fresh one.

Then, through the buzz of noise, Anson heard the unmistakeable tones of an Englishman – and a Man of Kent at that – speaking excruciatingly bad French.

*

Back in the fish hall, Fagg and Hoover were lying low. They had heard the patrol march past and silently willed Anson to evade capture.

Fagg whispered: 'Gawd knows what'll 'appen if 'e gets caught. There's no way I can make a run for it with this blasted ankle.'

Hoover was optimistic. 'He won't get caught. He's too fly for that. Anyways, he can speak some Frog, and dressed like he is, well, he looks pretty much like a fisherman.'

'Smells like one an' all.'

The American turned up his nose, 'And he ain't the only one. Must be about time for that monthly bath of yourn?'

Fagg gave him a disdainful stare and felt in his pocket for the stub that remained of his clay pipe. 'S'pose we gotta sit tight an' hope he comes back for us. I'm dying for a smoke.'

'And you probably will die if you light up that pipe, so let's button our lips and keep quiet like he told us 'til he comes back.'

*

The Englishman was clearly totally at ease among the French maritime flotsam congregated in the quayside drinking den. He was tall and wiry with a sharp, handy look about him.

He was dressed in similar fashion to the French fishermen – a drooping woollen hat, faded and stained jacket that might once have been blue, and baggy trousers tucked into calf-high boots that looked to have seen plenty of sea service. His left ear sported a gold earring – as was the custom with fishermen – to fund his funeral should he one day be washed up dead on some foreign shore.

That small part of his face that was not hidden by a gingery full set beard was heavily tanned.

Anson sat, head down, nursing his stolen drink and biding his time.

The English fisherman was in deep discussion with a Frenchman, a landsman by his dress. Over the hubbub of the drinking hole, Anson could just about make out talk of a cargo to be loaded aboard the Englishman's lugger – and what he thought was some haggling over a price. A smuggler arranging a run, no doubt.

Agreement apparently having been reached, the Frenchman called for more drinks and the smuggler patted his shoulder in a familiar way, muttered something in his ear and went outside, evidently to relieve himself.

Anson waited for a few moments, then slipped out after him as unobtrusively as possible and crept up behind the man as he urinated into the harbour.

'When are you sailing friend?'

The smuggler started, spun round and stared at Anson. 'Who's arsking?'

'Just a fellow countryman who's looking for a berth home.'

The man pulled back his coat to reveal the butt of a pistol tucked into his wide leather belt.

Anson raised his left leg slightly and tapped the hilt of the dirk partly hidden in his boot. 'No need to worry, friend. I mean no harm. Just looking for a passage home – and I can pay my way.'

The smuggler looked Anson over. 'Can you now? What wiv, fish?' The disguise had clearly worked.

'No, with gold.'

He had the stranger's full attention. 'Let's see it.'

'It's with my two ...' He had been about to say men, but hesitated and said, '... my two friends.'

The man's hand went to his pistol butt and he looked around suspiciously. Reassured that they were alone on the quayside, he demanded: 'Who are yer and where's these friends o' yourn?'

'They're waiting, nearby.'

'And who are you?' the man insisted.

'I told you, a fellow countryman seeking a passage home, and I can pay with gold. You don't need to know more. And since when were smugglers so particular who or what they carry?'

The stranger did not argue the case. 'I'm a fisherman and what if I does a bit of free tradin' on the side? Everybody does. And in my line of business you 'as to be careful.'

Anson wanted to close the deal before anyone else appeared. 'Your business is your business friend, and will be forgotten as soon as we step ashore in Kent. I'll give you two guineas when we're aboard your boat and four more when we reach England safely.'

'Each?' The fisherman-smuggler had the confidence of a gambler convinced he was holding all the cards.

'I'll not haggle. You'll get two when we're on board and clear of the harbour. Four more when we're safely ashore the other side. That's final, there's no more.'

'And supposin' I says no, 'tis not enough for the risk involved? You may smell like one but you don't talk like no fishin' man and if you're escapers like I think ye are then the Frenchies'll be grateful to get yer back—'

In a flash Anson stooped, drew the dirk from its scabbard in his boot and pricked the smuggler's Adam's apple with it. And with his left hand he grabbed the pistol from the astonished man's belt.

'This,' he whispered menacingly, twisting the dirk to draw a spot of blood, 'is what I'll do if you choose not to cooperate, you traitorous dog. I'll rip your throat out. Then I'll push you in the harbour so you can bleed to death and drown at the same time. And then I'll take your miserable boat anyway and sail it back to England myself, for free.'

It was a bluff. Anson had no idea which was the smuggler's boat, nor where it was berthed. But the pressure of the dirk on the man's throat was enough.

'Awright mate. Steady now, steady. I was only 'aving a little joke. I wouldn't turn yer in.'

'You don't make jokes with me, friend. I've killed men for less. Now, take me to your boat.'

The smuggler protested. 'They're expectin' me back in there.' He nodded nervously towards the drinking den. 'I'll take yer right enough, but I've got to go back in and clinch a deal furst.'

'What deal?'

'Stuff I'm taking t'other side.'

'Contraband?'

'Let's say just a cargo, and can ye take that knife orf me throat? It's diggin' in me.'

'When's it being loaded?'

'Take that blessed blade outta me throat and I'll tell yer.'

Anson relaxed the dirk a fraction. 'So, when's it loading?'

'Some time tomorrow. It ain't bin agreed yet. That's why I've got to go back in there.' He took a half step back towards the drinking den.

'No, not yet. First take me to your boat, now!' And to emphasise the point he raised the dirk blade and slashed it across the smuggler's cheek, marking him with a deep scratch that instantly bled into his beard.

The man's hand flew to his cheek and he cried angrily: 'Bugger me! What did yer do that for y'bastard? I'll kill yer fer that!'

'No, you'll keep your mouth shut and you'll take me to your boat. Now! Any nonsense and it'll be your eye next.'

As a midshipman, Anson had been in a boarding party that had taken on a much bigger enemy crew and won – despite absurd odds. The lessons of the value of audacity and surprise had left their mark on him. Having seized the initiative, and gained the upper hand, he intended to keep it.

The smuggler continued to mutter and whinge, but held his tongue after the dirk swished again inches from his face.

'Your boat,' Anson commanded, and the smuggler set off reluctantly, shuffling along the quay.

Anson stopped him, and with his left hand pulled the man's arm over his shoulders, and put his right arm around him with the dirk turned back inside his coat, the point against his ribcage.

'Go!' he ordered, and the pair stumbled off looking like two drunks propping one another up as they rolled away from the drinking den.

Their route to the smuggler's boat took them past the fish market where Fagg and Hoover were hidden.

Anson halted his captive and, after looking round to make sure there were no patrols near, called out to his fellow escapers to join him.

They emerged from the shadows, the marine supporting Fagg in exactly the same way as Anson was linked to the smuggler.

'Who the 'ell are they?'

Anson snapped: 'Keep silent! Just take us to your boat.' And off they went along the quayside like competitors in some bizarre nocturnal drunkards' race.

Unmolested, they reached what Anson instantly recognised as a Deal lugger, tied up to a bollard. She was two-masted, indicating a small crew, and was typical of the type favoured by Kentish boatmen who used them to service ships sheltering in the Downs, for fishing – and other less worthy but lucrative activities.

Their shallow draught made them ideal for negotiating the ever-treacherous ships' graveyard of the Goodwin Sands, and for beaching in the absence of a harbour. There was a small forepeak cabin and crudely painted in blue on the lugger's prow was her name, Ginny May.

12

Anson noted that the upper side of each of the lugger's two sails was attached to a spar – a traveller – that could be hoisted up the mast by a halyard. The lower ends of the sails were held by ropes, easily adjustable.

With the halyard attached near one end of the yard he could see that, when lifted, most of the sail would lie fore or aft of the mast. This rig would be no problem to work, once clear of the harbour. It would be simpler to handle than a square sail, and would enable them to sail close to the wind.

'Is this it?'

The smuggler grunted an affirmative and Anson let go of him, pushing him on board with the dirk at his back.

Anson scrambled after him and Hoover helped Fagg board.

'How many crew?'

'Two and a boy.'

'As well as you?'

The skipper nodded sullenly.

'Where are they?'

'One's on board, asleep on watch agin more'n likely. The others'll still be ashore, pissed as coots by now on account of we ain't sailing 'til tomorrow.'

Anson corrected him. 'You weren't sailing until tomorrow, but you are now.'

Hoover found the watchman, a beardless young lad, fast asleep with an empty wine bottle beside him. There was no need to secure him – the wine had already done the trick.

The marine found some spare rope and bound the protesting skipper's wrists.

Fagg took the dirk and pistol and watched over him as Anson and Hoover searched the lugger.

In the tiny cabin they found a musket, various knives, an axe, and several clubs or bats that Anson recognised as weapons favoured by

Kentish smugglers to deter Revenue men and nosey parkers. There were nets on board and hooked lines. But he guessed the fishing gear was more for show, disguising the true role of the free trader.

The smuggler protested: 'What the 'ell are ye doin'? I can't sort out the cargo tied up like this, and ye can't sail without me and me crew.'

Anson found a piece of sacking ready to gag him, just in case a patrol chanced by.

'Don't fret friend. We'll sail on the tide, and we don't need you – nor your cargo.'

'But what about me crew? You can't leave 'em 'ere.'

'If they turn up in time they're welcome to take passage. If not, they can stay and drink themselves stupid until you return for them – after we've got back to England.'

The gag reduced the smuggler's protests to grunts.

Hoover expertly re-primed the smuggler's pistol that Anson had confiscated on the quay. 'If you wanted a job done properly,' he muttered, 'do it yourself.' Satisfied that there was now no fear of a misfire, he handed it back to Fagg who was watching over the skipper, the dirk still at the ready.

Next, Hoover loaded and primed the musket. It was a weapon totally familiar to him, a shorter-barrelled sea service version of the Army's Brown Bess.

Anson warned: 'If the other crewmen come back before we sail we must take them without shooting.'

Fagg and Hoover nodded. A shot would raise Cain and surely bring a patrol running. No, blades and the bats would do the necessary.

An hour passed and the trussed-up smuggler appeared to have fallen asleep – thanks, no doubt, to the drink he had put away earlier.

Anson was watching the steadily rising tide that was now bumping the line of fishing boats against the quayside where they were berthed.

A low whistle from Hoover. Two figures had emerged from another drinking den and headed towards the line of boats. Predictably, they appeared the worse for drink, staggering as they approached the Ginny May.

Anson signalled Fagg to stay low.

Sure enough, the men stopped next to the boat and drunkenly half climbed, half fell on board, giggling inanely – the taller of them still clutching a bottle from which he took a long draught. When he lowered the bottle from his lips there was a blade at his throat and the shock of it made him choke on the spirit he had just swigged.

Anson emerged from the shadows swinging one of the bats and the other crewman gaped and stared, terrified as a rabbit confronted by a stoat.

Recovering some of his wits, the taller man slurred: 'Steady mates. We won't give no trouble. What d'ye want?' And holding out the bottle he offered: 'Here y'are, 'ave a swig.'

Like any Kentish smuggler, no doubt he had seen what damage a batman could do to anyone interfering with the landing of contraband during a run.

Hoover snatched the bottle, dropped it overboard and searched him, pulling a knife from his waistband. Anson swished the bat in front of the other prisoner who hurriedly reached into his smock and dropped a cudgel on the deck.

Although drunk, the crewmen were not so far gone that they couldn't take in the scene – their skipper bloody-faced and tied up, and the three well-armed strangers clearly in control of the lugger.

Anson made the situation clear. 'We're sailing on the tide. If you do as you're told you'll come to no harm, and there'll be grog for you when we land on the other side. If you don't play straight I'll kill you and throw you overboard. Choose now!'

They knuckled their foreheads. However unkempt he might look, there was no questioning his authority. 'Anyfink you says, master.' And the smaller crewman echoed: 'Aye, us'll play straight yer worship.'

Anson smacked the business end of the bat into the palm of his left hand several times. It stung, and that was only a tap. God alone knew what damage a determined blow could do. Break an arm or leg? Crack a skull? No question.

The two crewmen were clearly impressed and he had their complete attention. 'Now lads, I want you to go about your normal duties and make ready to sail. But quiet as mice, right?'

More knuckling of foreheads. They might be drunk, but they must know their way around the Ginny May blindfolded. Although he and Fagg were experienced seamen, Anson was not familiar with handling luggers and needed their help to clear the port without drawing unwelcome attention.

The tide had risen fast and was on the turn. Looking over the side, Hoover saw the outline of a small dinghy tied up next to the Ginny May. This must be the lugger's boat for harbour work.

He pointed it out to Anson and made a rowing motion.

The officer nodded, looked down to gauge the state of the tide and put up both hands, fingers extended indicating ten minutes.

Anson waited, watching to see the tide abate. Finally satisfied that it had turned, he climbed over the side, lowered himself into the dinghy, untied it and threw the rope to Hoover who made it fast to the lugger's prow.

He cast off from the bollard, pushed against the harbour wall to get the Ginny May moving and called softly: 'Take her away.'

In the dinghy Anson pulled on the oars, clumsily at first until he struck a rhythm, and to his relief the lugger began to move slowly away from the quayside.

At last they cleared the harbour and Anson secured the dinghy and clambered back aboard the lugger. He ordered the inebriated crewmen to raise the fore and aft sails, and they headed north-west for the Kent coast – and home.

*

During the night, once clear of the French coast, Anson freed the surly skipper and allowed the crewmen to sleep off their excesses.

The skipper snatched at the hardtack biscuit and cheese Hoover offered him and sat munching morosely, muttering when he thought his unwelcome passengers were listening: 'Fuckin' pirates!' But he offered no trouble.

The drunken youth came to in the early hours, stared uncomprehendingly at the interlopers and turned to throw up the previous night's booze over the side. His older companions remained comatose.

Precise navigation on a cloudy night was impossible and first light found them a few miles off Dungeness in a slight swell. It was farther west than Anson had wished, but no matter.

There had been no encounters with other vessels, foe or friend. Now all that remained was to get ashore.

Anson roused the crew and ran the Ginny May before the prevailing westerly, no more than a breeze now, down the familiar coast past Dymchurch and Seagate. The skipper, sprawled with his back to the mast, took no part but followed Anson's confident handling of the vessel and crew with close interest.

Off Hythe, Anson went to him and handed him a piece of cloth tied with string. It clinked. 'Your money, as I think we agreed, though I admit it was rather a one-sided bargain.'

The smuggler fingered its contents through the cloth, fiddled the string loose and tipped six golden guineas into his cupped palm. A look of genuine astonishment replaced his scowl and he stared at the gold coins, clearly hardly able to believe these 'fuckin' pirates' would keep their bargain once they had reached their goal still holding all the weapons.

Notwithstanding his amazement, he quickly stuffed the coins into his pocket. No sense giving his crew false expectations.

Anson smiled at the skipper's surprise. 'Now, I believe, we're quits.'

The smuggler fingered his wounded cheek, the deep scratch now crusted with dark dried blood. 'I still owe yer for this,' he said ruefully. 'And this 'ere money ain't nuffink to what I'd 'ave got for a full cargo.'

'Come now, no hard feelings. You've helped three of old England's sons of the sea to live to fight the Frenchies another day. Ain't that a happy thought?'

The skipper scowled. 'Navy men – I blurry knew it! Stitched up by the fuckin' navy!'

Anson squatted beside him. 'Now friend, we'll go ashore in Wear Bay.' The skipper showed surprise at this indication of local knowledge, but said nothing.

They were now off Folkestone, which had grown from a fishing village clustered around its man-made harbour to a small town with a church and some gentrified housing perched atop the grass-covered downs. It was a place Anson knew well. He had been at school there.

The headland of Copt Point was fast coming up on their larboard.

Hoover removed the flints from the musket and pistol, went aft and hauled the dinghy, which had been towing behind, up close.

Anson stirred the skipper with his foot. 'Now, just as a precaution, you're going to accompany us ashore. In fact, you can row.'

The man grimaced in disgust, but struggled to his feet.

'Once you've dropped us off you'll be free to sail away wherever you like, back to Gravelines for that cargo of yours for all I care.'

The Ginny May stood into Wear Bay and Anson ordered sails to be taken in and the small kedge anchor to be lowered. It caught, sufficient to hold and steady the lugger.

The crewmen, now much recovered from their excesses of the night before, helped the three escapers and their reluctant ferryman down into the dinghy. Although unwilling, the skipper did not need telling that this was the only way he would be sure of getting his boat back.

It was cramped in the dinghy, but they were only 50 yards or so offshore. As he worked the oars, the smuggler grumbled: 'What if we gets taken by the Revenue now, and what will ye tell the navy as to 'ow ye got back? Ye'll drop me in it, I'll be bound.'

'No need to worry, friend. You're just honest fishermen going about your lawful business, ain't you? Picked up us poor escaped sailors drifting in a dinghy in the Channel and brought us home out of love for King and country, didn't you?'

For once the smuggler managed a half smile. 'So I did, didn't I?'

The dinghy crunched on shingle and Anson stepped into the water and held it steady while Hoover helped Fagg, still clutching his makeshift crutches, to disembark. They waded ashore and Anson turned to dismiss the smuggler, but he was already pulling back towards the Ginny May.

They were safely ashore back in England at last – and free.

13

At Dover, the naval captain greeted Anson and his companions with some suspicion. Small wonder – their clothes were filthy and in tatters. They were exhausted, unshaven, dirty, and gave off a strong smell of fish – and worse. All three, weakened by lack of proper food and living rough in all weathers, had hacking coughs.

The port officer motioned Fagg and Hoover to remain outside and led Anson into his office. Leaving him standing, he heard the story of their capture and escape in silence except for the squeak of his pen as he made occasional notes.

Anson kept it brief: how all three were wounded during the abortive cutting-out raid at St Valery, eventually escaping while en route to Arras and making their way, not without difficulty, to the coast.

He ended with a sanitised version of their Channel crossing and was taken aback when the captain laid down his pen, gave him a searching stare and demanded coldly: 'You broke your parole?'

'No, sir, I did not break parole.'

'How is that, when it is customary to honour it?'

'I was not in a position to give it or withhold it, sir. I was wounded, unconscious.'

'But surely when you had recovered sufficiently?'

'No, sir. By the time I had recovered my senses we were already heading for Arras in the back of a wagon driven by a peasant and guarded by two extremely dozy French soldiers. I doubt they knew what parole was.'

The captain remained sceptical. 'Enquiries will be made. Meanwhile, go and get yourself and your men cleaned up and report back to me when you are decent. You are a disgrace to the navy in that state.'

'But we have no other kit. Everything was left aboard *Phryne*. And we have no money. What's more, as you have seen, sir, one of my men needs medical attention to his ankle. Also, we have not eaten properly for days.'

The captain relented somewhat. 'Very well, I will instruct my purser to advance you sufficient to see you through. No doubt he can also rustle up a change of clothes from slops if the mood takes him, although getting anything out of the hammock-counters is akin to squeezing blood from a stone.'

*

The purser, a cheery, chubby soul grown fat on the perks of his office, proved more accommodating than forecast, although Anson had to sign and sign again for what they received.

They repaired to a dockside inn where the gnarled, heavily-tattooed and obviously ex-navy landlord took kindly to them when he heard they had just escaped from France.

He led them to a pump in the inn's backyard and, while they stripped and washed, he fetched a razor so that they could scythe off the worst of their whiskers.

Cleaned up, they donned their rough issue shirts and trousers and returned to the bar-room where they devoured cold Romney Marsh mutton with boiled potatoes, cheese and porter. It was, Fagg observed: 'The fust square meal what we've 'ad since that there auberge – and not a bleedin' snail or frog's leg in sight, thank Gawd.'

Replete, they sat back to sip from their mugs of ale, relishing the familiar Kentish voices around them and the freedom to drop their guard and truly relax for the first time in weeks.

*

On his return to the port captain's office, Anson was greeted more warmly. On the desk lay a copy of the Kentish Gazette.

'My dear boy! Why didn't you tell me? You're the fellow who's supposed to be dead, aren't you?'

'I suppose they could well have believed that in Phryne—'

'Not only in Phryne, my boy, your family too.' He picked up the Gazette. 'Here's a report of your memorial service!'

Anson was again taken aback. 'Memorial?'

The captain guffawed. 'It'll be like reading about your own funeral, what!'

He passed Anson the newspaper. Too startled to take it all in, he registered the key phrases of the report. '… son of the rector … killed in raid on French coast … memorial service in his father's parish church in the absence of a body to bury …'

Anson, nonplussed, could only mutter: 'Good grief!'

'Rich, ain't it?' the captain chortled. 'They've even unveiled a plaque in your memory – but here you are, large as life! You'll give 'em quite a shock when you turn up on your father's doorstep!'

'I must get home and set matters to rights, sir.'

'Of course, of course, my dear fellow. But there are a few formalities to observe first. Paperwork you know, the curse of the landlocked seaman. And I've sent for a surgeon-wallah to give you and your men the once-over. Wouldn't do to send you off unsound of wind or limb, would it?'

Anson could not disguise a sigh, but submitted without argument. Truth be told, he was too dog-weary to protest.

As an afterthought the captain asked: 'By the by, are you by any chance related to the Anson?'

Anson shrugged. It was a question he had answered so many times since he joined the navy. 'Merely a distant kinsman, I'm afraid, sir, many times removed.'

A surgeon's mate, breathing rum fumes that could have put a passing fly to sleep, examined the three. Good food and rest would cure their coughs, he said, but he expressed concern at the state of Fagg's ankle. 'Otherwise, I'm of the opinion that your wounds are mending surprisingly well considering the lack of professional treatment.'

Anson had smiled at that. He would far rather have been treated by Madame Thérèse than by some half-drunken, jumped-up loblolly boy, any day.

However, despite the intake of alcohol that had turned his pitted nose a shade of purple, the man seemed to know what he was doing and advised that they should be sent to the naval hospital along the coast at Deal for treatment and recuperation.

But Anson was adamant that he would not go himself. The port captain agreed that as his home was near he must go forthwith and show them that the report of his death was premature. 'In any event, sir, I'll surely receive better treatment in a parsonage infested by a parcel of female relatives with time on their hands than I would in any hospital.'

The captain acknowledged the sense of that, said he would write directly informing the Admiralty of all the circumstances, and added: '*Phryne* was in Chatham just recently, did you know?' Then after a moment's thought, 'No, of course you wouldn't have known, would you? Anyway, I'll let your captain know the glad tidings, although no doubt you will have been replaced by now, being presumed dead and all …'

That had not occurred to Anson before, and if he had thought about it at all he would have assumed that he would be reinstated automatically. Whatever, he was too bone weary to worry about that now.

Once dismissed, he divided up the remainder of the money advanced by the purser between his two companions, who, although reluctant, accepted with gratitude. And he embarrassed both by shaking them warmly by the hand and wishing them Godspeed to hospital and full recovery.

'If we don't go back to the old *Phryne*, will you send fer us when you get yer own ship, sir?' Fagg asked, almost shyly.

'That I will, never fear.'

*

Within the hour Anson was in a carrier's cart, drawn by a fit young gelding, trundling along the flinty track, gradually ascending the hill and passing the castle as it left the coast.

Twice a week, Hezekiah Dale served the villages along the old Roman road from Dover to Canterbury and back, changing course as required to outlying villages along the way, carrying mail, packages and occasional passengers.

But Hezekiah, perched up front wearing his tall, pointed, home-made felt hat, had seldom carried a more unusual passenger – a bedraggled, hatless naval man with a clearly recent livid v-shaped scar on his forehead.

The carrier had agreed to divert off the main road for a few miles to take his passenger to Hardres Minnis.

A mile or two out of Dover, he turned to look at his dozing passenger and observed: 'You look like you bin in the wars, squire.'

Thanks to his years of travel, Hezikiah regarded himself as being far more worldly wise than his country cousins. Why, unlike all those who never strayed more than a few miles from their native village, he'd been pretty well everywhere. That is, everywhere from Dover to Canterbury and back, and just about every village and hamlet either side of Watling Street.

Anson came to with a start, imagining for a moment that he was back in Normandy and a prisoner in the wagon heading for Arras. But no, he reassured himself, he was home – in the North Downs.

'In the wars? That I have,' he acknowledged. 'And I'll be obliged if you'll make a small diversion to the rectory when you get to Hardres Minnis.'

Hezekiah could tell an 'orficer' from a common sailor when he heard one. 'Gladly, yer worship. I s'pose a gennelman like you 'as got the wherewithal t'pay?'

'I haven't a sou, nor a penny piece. Nothing but what I stand up in. But I'm sure that my father the rector will be only too happy to stump up the necessary for me.'

The carter nodded knowingly. 'Ah, I've heard about you – s'posed t'be dead ain't yer? Cash on delivery's fair enough for a churchman's son.'

Hezekiah liked a yarn. It helped to pass the all-too-familiar miles. 'So 'ow did yer come by that there battered 'ead?' he ventured. 'Battle at sea, were it?'

But Anson was not in the mood. 'Something of the sort,' was all he'd say, stretching back against a pile of sacks and ending the conversation by closing his eyes.

He well knew that news such as his, imparted to a carrier, would spread like pox from a bum-boat harpy. And, having learned at Dover that he had been reported dead, he wanted his family to hear of his resurrection from Lazarus himself, as it were, before the whole countryside knew.

Now that he was on home soil, the exhausted Anson at last allowed himself to relax his guard and drift into dream-filled sleep, shaking himself awake from time to time and only relaxing again on confirming this was England, and Kent – not France.

*

He was oblivious to the change of direction when Hezekiah turned off at the finger post that led after a few miles to the series of upland commons that stretched to Hardres Minnis and the rectory.

Anson awoke from confused dreams that had seemed real but escaped memory the moment he opened his eyes. All around now were the North Downs' heathlands, divided by historic ownership into this, that or the other Minnis, an old Kentish name for largely infertile land that the Lord – of the local manor rather than the Almighty – did not want.

These manorial commons were left for the local small-holders and peasants to graze their sheep, cattle, pigs and geese, and gather firewood, furze and bracken for animal bedding, by ancient right. But the soil remained firmly in the ownership of the lord of the manor, in this case the local squire.

Fully awake now, Anson looked about him with interest and affection. It was on these commons that he had played as a boy, making camps in the bracken and stalking, or being stalked, by the village urchins.

In his newly-published history of Kent, Edward Hasted had described it as 'a wild hilly country, mostly situated on high ground and exceedingly healthy. The soil is but barren, consisting of an unfertile red earth, intermixed with quantities of flints. On the north and east sides it is covered with woods … along the whole length of it interspersed with houses and cottages, many of which are built on the middle of it, with fields and orchards taken out of it and inclosed around them, which form altogether a not uncommon and not unpleasant scene … The inhabitants of them,' he had asserted, were 'as rude and wild as the country they live in'.

It was a description, had they been aware of it, that the commoners could not honestly have disputed.

Over the home straight, Anson became aware that his appearance was creating intense interest among the handful of graziers and yokels they encountered, shy and insular though they were.

Nothing more than a startled look and a touched forelock in his direction or an 'Arternoon Zac' was passed. But Anson knew that although he had been home so infrequently that his was not a well-known face, the local peasantry were wily enough to put two and two together.

One, bolder than the rest called: 'What y'got there, carter? A drunk what's lost 'is way 'ome?'

Hezikiah was offended, and tugged on the reins. 'T'ain't no drunk, 'tis the parson's son, 'ome from the wars.' The incredulous smallholder shook his head. 'Well I'm flummuxed. He's dead, ain't he? Leastways, they 'eld a great big service fer 'im not a week since.'

'It's 'im awlright, but 'e's only harf dead.'

'Course they didn't bury 'im,' the yokel recalled. 'Well, ye can't 'ave a fun'ral wivout a body, like, so they just memorialised 'im.'

Hezikiah nodded sagely. 'What they calls a memorium service, weren't it?'

'That's roight. Such hexpense, wiv 'arf the county there – and harchbishops, gen'rals, hadmirals and whatnot. An' they stuck a notice up in the church, writ in marble.'

'So what did that say? I mean they couldn't say 'ere lies wot's-'is-name, could they?'

Anson's eyebrows rose heavenwards, but he kept his peace.

The smallholder grinned. 'I seen it and I can read orlright, though not to understand it loik. It give 'is name an' all, wiv carved ships and stuff. Such a hexpence. They'll be a suckin' o' teef up the rect'ry when you shows up wiv 'im, aloive-loik. Wouldn't surprise me if parson didn't put the tythe up ter pay fer it all.'

Hezekiah snorted dismissively. 'More likely parson'll give me a guinea fer bringin' his boy back from the dead.'

Spurred on by the thought, he touched his horse's rump with his whip and the Lazurus journey continued.

It was inevitable that by the time the cart turned out of Lymingham Street – a hamlet of some two dozen cottages and an alehouse half a mile from home – some unseen miracle of local communication had occurred.

Figures were to be seen in the carriageway leading from the rough highway up to the rectory. A parcel of females, Anson surmised.

Then a mounted figure detached itself from the others and approached at a canter. In a moment Anson, still sprawled weak and exhausted on the sacks, was gazing up into the eyes of the Reverend Thomas Anson, rector of Hardres Minnis.

'The Lord be praised! Oliver, is it really you?'

14

Several days passed before Anson felt up to joining the family at breakfast. At first, physically and mentally exhausted, he had kept to his room, enduring daily calls by genial Doctor Hambrook and too-frequent visits from his parents and excited sisters, answering their many questions in monosyllables.

Away from those who had shared his ordeal, and away from the familiar brotherhood of the navy, he was, according to his mother's concerned comment to the rector 'Too quiet – quite mumchance'.

At least the medical man's recommendation of lots of thick chicken soup and plenty of rest seemed to be doing the trick as far as his general health was concerned. But for some time he remained almost in a reverie, his thoughts constantly going back to the raid, the sojourn at the Auberge du Marin and the escape.

Consulting with his sisters, his mother decided the very thing to shake him out of his brown study was a dinner party. 'But,' she warned, 'we must wait for the right moment to propose it.'

*

Today he woke feeling refreshed and a little more like his normal self than he had since the boats pulled away from *Phryne* off the Normandy coast. He felt well enough to go through his sea chest that the ship had forwarded from Chatham following his reported death.

All the clothing had gone – sold on board to his brother officers, as was the custom in such cases. But his sextant, telescope and a few personal items and papers, including his commission, were there – as was his red leather-bound diary.

He had kept this personal log ever since his early days as a midshipman and, seeing it now, he realised that during the escape he had missed the daily routine of recording location, weather and any significant events. No flowery prose – just brief notes.

Opening it, he read the last entry:

'At sea, Normandy coast in sight. Weather fair, sea calm. Preparing for cutting out expedition against privateer, St Valery-en-Caux.'

That note had been written a mere few weeks ago, yet so much had gone unrecorded since then, so he wrote:

'Raid failed. Wounded, captured, escaped, returned to England.'

Anson dated and blotted it, satisfied that his log was now up to date.

At Dover, he had learned of the great sea battle that had brought a sudden end to the sojourn at the Auberge du Marin. After a four-month sea hunt Nelson had trapped the French fleet in Aboukir Bay off the coast of Alexandria and inflicted a crushing defeat, destroying or capturing nearly all the French ships.

The French flagship *L'Orient*, pride of their navy, had blown up and many men had been lost – including the aristocratic fleet commander Vice Admiral Francois Paul, Compte de Brueys d'Aigailliers.

And Napoleon was marooned ashore in Egypt, his army cut off from all communication with France, and now without hope of being able to dominate the region.

There was still elation in England, where the invasion threat had receded as a result of the victory that was being called the Battle of the Nile, but Anson was dejected that he had missed such an action. The fact that his old ship had not been involved at Aboukir was no comfort.

His father attempted to cheer him. 'It may have been on a smaller stage, but you were involved in an honourable operation against the French.'

But Anson was not to be consoled. 'There's precious little honour in grovelling after privateers and getting myself captured while our navy was engaged in the greatest fleet action since Copenhagen. Now I know what Shakespeare meant when he put those words into Henry V's mouth before Agincourt – that gentlemen abed in England would feel themselves accursed that they were not with the band of brothers for the battle. And now I could be stuck ashore for the foreseeable future.'

The rector suggested soothingly: 'Can you not do some lobbying at the Admiralty?'

'I'll be going as soon as I'm fit enough, but I've no friends there, no interest, and I fear I'll be lucky to be re-appointed to *Phryne*, or to get any sort of sea-going appointment. Even if I do it'll doubtless be something like a storeship.'

He was on his second tack round the shrubbery after breakfast when the crunch of hooves and the grate of iron-shod wheels on the gravel driveway heralded a visitor.

A chaise pulled by a pair of smart black geldings hove into sight and halted a few yards from him. From the back of the house young Alfred the stable lad came running and held the horses as the black-clad arrival climbed down.

The newcomer stared long and hard at Anson. 'Good God, so it really is you! He that was lost is found again. Surely a miracle ...'

Heavy sarcasm was a speciality of Augustine Anson, minor canon at Canterbury Cathedral, particularly – as it had always been – when addressing his younger brother Oliver, their father's favourite son.

Before the younger Anson could think of a suitable response, Augustine added, 'Delivered by the carrier like a sack of coals I hear. And I thought we'd laid you to rest with that extremely costly memorial tablet.'

'My time had obviously not come, Gussie.'

Augustine winced. He had never been able to hide how much he hated that nickname, convinced that it was used only to provoke him.

Unable to disguise his annoyance at the turn of events, and smarting, as ever, from the knowledge that Oliver received a £100 a year from their father to supplement his naval pay, he could not resist further sarcasm. 'So life really does imitate art! The return of the prodigal. I'll tell cook to fetch another fatted calf ...'

Oliver ignored him. As far as he was concerned Gussie was a self-righteous prig who observed rules to the letter but in reality was mostly concerned with his own image, social standing – and getting more than his share of everything that was going.

But he had to smile when Augustine remonstrated with him for returning alive. 'You really have placed me in an extremely embarrassing situation. I organised a memorial service worthy of an admiral. For goodness' sake, the archdeacon himself was there – and half the incumbents for miles around. How am I going to tell them you weren't dead at all, and are walking round large as life? It's outrageous!'

'Remiss of me I'm sure, Gussie. Another time I'll ask the French to send a special messenger to let you know I'm temporarily detained and unable to travel – so there's no need to go to the trouble of organising a wake.'

Ever one to get the last word, Augustine retorted sharply: 'I've told you a thousand times not to call me by that childish nickname. You do it on purpose to annoy me and after your miraculous reappearance all I will say is that I now accept that it's true – the devil really does look after his own!'

*

Later, alone with Augustine, the rector raised a delicate issue. 'We must remove the memorial tablet.'

'More expense! Why not cover it with a curtain and alter the date of death when the time comes?'

'Augustine! Your cynicism is not even faintly amusing. If your mother had heard you ... and do not forget that you pressured his brother officers to foot most of the bill, did you not?'

Then the satisfying thought struck him. 'In any event, your brother's return from the dead is a kind of resurrection, is it not?'

*

At breakfast next day, Mrs Anson announced: 'We are inviting the cream of local society to dine at the rectory on Friday week – something of a welcome home for you, dear.'

Anson looked up from reading an account in the Kentish Gazette of a yeomanry exercise and pulled a face. 'Sorry mother, I find I have arranged to visit my tailor in Chatham that very day.'

Mrs Anson huffed. 'Nonsense! You have clearly just dreamed that up. I blame your unsociability on all the time you have spent with uncouth men in the navy. Of course you must be here. All three of the Brax girls will be coming and I cannot make up my mind which of them is most taken with you after seeing you at church on Sunday. And the Bumsteads have a very pretty daughter.'

It was no secret that the rector and his wife would like to marry off their sailor son, preferably to a wealthy heiress – and they already had a number of conveniently local possibles in mind.

Anson wrinkled his nose in distaste. 'Stop matchmaking this instant mother, else I'll most certainly find urgent business elsewhere.'

But she ploughed on: 'You must get a new best uniform, and I imagine I'll seat you between Charlotte and Jane ...' These were the two eldest

Brax girls, both likely to bring substantial dowries to a marriage bed. Besides, she had privately reasoned, coarse and bovine though Squire Brax was, he had the advowson of this and several adjoining parishes giving him the power to appoint the rector, and as such he would best be kept on-side through a linked bloodline.

Anson grimaced again. Being caught between two broadsides was a dangerous business, but then, the invitation did promise light relief from the usual confined atmosphere at the rectory. And, he privately acknowledged, he had noticed how attractive the Brax girls were.

The Reverend Anson defined the planned event: 'A celebration, yes. Well, perhaps more of a thanksgiving.'

The reaction of the Anson daughters was enthusiastic. 'It will be divine father,' gushed Anne. And Elizabeth was emphatic: 'We shall simply have to have new dresses!'

But their re-born brother was not at all keen. 'I enjoy a party as much as anyone. Howsoever, the last thing I require is to be the prize exhibit for a parcel of yokels to come and gape at.'

Mrs Anson tutted: 'Sir Oswald and Lady Brax are not yokels. He's lord of the manor and sits in Parliament. And Mr Bumstead's an honourable – and he's captain of the yeomanry.'

Her husband corrected her: 'Colonel dear. He's colonel of the yeomanry.'

'Yes, well, he's whatever they call the one in charge,' she acknowledged.

Anson grunted and muttered: 'A parcel of jumped-up yokels then.'

Elizabeth kicked him under the table and immediately winced in case she had struck a wounded limb.

Anne admonished him. 'They are not yokels – they're society!'

Having left at the age of 12 to join the navy as a midshipman he had spent so long away, with only rare home leave, that he barely knew those who passed locally for 'society'.

Nor did he wish to be exposed to cross-examination about his experiences or asked for his learned opinion on how long the war was likely to last and suchlike matters.

His father persisted. 'Your modesty is commendable Oliver, but you must understand that these, er, yokels you denigrate were a great comfort to your mother and I when you were reported dead. They were solicitous enough to attend your memorial service—'

'And they do have some very pretty daughters,' his mother offered.

Anson was not averse to meeting pretty daughters. 'Fair enough. I can see I'm out-gunned and out-manoeuvred. If they had the decency to come to the service to see me off, we'll do the decent thing. I'll make my number with them and give 'em a drink or two.'

His capitulation was enthusiastically received, and after he had excused himself to go for another limp around the large well-kept rectory gardens, his family set about planning the great event.

His mother rang a silver bell for a maid.

'Let's make a list. Pen and paper please, Mary. You can clear away later. We have work to do!'

She smiled triumphantly at her husband and daughters. 'So the Braxes and the Bumsteads must come. Now, who else has pretty daughters?'

Her husband muttered: 'Only the quality mind. No pretty church mice, if you please.'

'I do hope he meets someone he likes,' mused Mrs Anson. 'It's high time he settled down and now he's home for a while there's absolutely no excuse for him to remain single.'

Having cornered her son, Mrs Anson reminded her husband that it was the custom nowadays for a liveried footman to be stationed behind each diner. 'A trifle presumptuous perhaps, but rather charming.'

The Rector looked doubtful. 'We've only Beer and Jeapes presentable enough, but I suppose we could ask Squire Brax to bring his two proper footmen and more if we need them. But the rest would be some of his keepers and tenants' lads that he dresses up in the nearest-fitting livery.'

The Reverend Anson clenched his hands and pondered, frowning, chin resting on his thumbs – an unconscious but regular habit of his when deep in thought – until a happy idea struck him. His eyebrows soared and the frown disappeared. 'Of course, Oliver must be able to call upon a Jolly Jack Tar. Dressed up in his best uniform, pigtail and all, why, it'd be the very thing to create a naval atmosphere!'

Mrs Anson raised a gloved hand. 'Excellent! And rather than risk a bowl of soup down our backs, I'll ask Augustine to bring some servants from the cathedral precincts …'

15

A few more days' convalescing and Anson felt up to travelling to London. His father insisted on taking him to Canterbury, and it was a relief to join the mail coach there and be away from the cloying confines of the rectory and his mollycoddling family.

During a stop at the Bull in Rochester to exchange horses and allow passengers time to eat and stretch their legs, he walked into Chatham and called on his naval tailor who kept clients' measurements on file and was able to fulfil orders without their physical presence.

Anson collected a new bicorn hat to replace the one lost on the mole at St Valery, and the new uniform he had ordered by post on arrival home.

It fitted, although somewhat loosely. The tailor, anxious not to accept blame for incorrect cutting, observed: 'Better too large than too small. Most of my gentlemen put a few pounds on between uniforms, but you've lost more than a few since you called here last, Mr Anson. May I suggest a diet of beefsteaks and mutton for a few weeks? Then it'll be a perfect fit.'

Bouncing around in the coach, Anson pondered the request his father had put to him on the drive into Canterbury for a smart sailor to act as a footman for the dinner party he had allowed himself to be nagged into.

A smart sailor to wait at table? These landsmen had no idea and would be horrified at the reality.

Anson imagined a piratical character in a tarred hat, stained pea jacket, patched trousers and greased sea boots, poking his oar into the dinner conversation, peering down the ladies' cleavages, chewing and spitting 'baccy, and smiled at the thought.

A dandyish, rather effeminate man with a heart-shaped patch on his cheek sitting opposite caught the smile he supposed was for him and winked archly in return, to Anson's greater amusement. He was not that kind of sailor. And to avoid being drawn into an unwanted conversation he leaned back, closed his eyes and feigned sleep.

Arriving at Charing Cross, he grabbed his bag before the dandy could importune him and marched the short distance to the Ship and Shovel, a hostelry frequented by navy men in the warren of lanes off Whitehall, just a brisk walk from the Admiralty, and took a room.

At supper, he fell in with a fellow naval officer, one Commander Amos Armstrong, some years his senior, who also had an appointment at the Admiralty next day.

Armstrong poured an extra glass from his already half empty wine bottle and introduced himself as the unfortunate officer in command of a Sussex coast signal station.

'A good number?' asked Anson.

'Damned if it is!' Armstrong was vehement. 'Trouble is, everyone assumes it's a comfortable berth compared to a man-of-war. But I tell you, it's a nightmare job.'

He gulped back a mouthful of wine. 'When I first arrived I found the station in a ruinous state – a filthy and wretched place. Took me a month of Sundays to get it shipshape. I've a midshipman – a disagreeable moonfaced child I've had to leave in charge of the station, God forgive me! There are two lower deck simpletons laughingly described as signalmen, and two dragoons – one to be sent off with despatches when anything significant occurs.'

'Not an easy berth then?'

Armstrong frowned and shook his head. 'Absolutely not. I have the strictest orders to be on the lookout by day and by night, the French coast being so close that you can damned near see it without a glass on a clear day ...'

'So you'd be among the first to spot invasion barges,' Anson observed.

'That's if my eyes haven't given up the ghost by then. The utmost vigilance is demanded. Whenever the wind blows strong from westward, merchantmen take shelter under Dungeness, and the French privateers are sure to come over and attempt to pick off one or more of them before our men-of-war can regain their station off Beachy Head and scare them off.'

He picked up the wine bottle, held it up to check the level and signalled the landlord for another.

'Same agin, sir?'

Armstrong nodded. 'Same again indeed, mine host. Your wine tastes well enough but there ain't much in your bottles and it's damned expensive stuff to boot.'

Being so close to the Admiralty, the landlord was used to naval officers' banter and countered good-naturedly: 'If you navy men'd stop blockading the Frogs we could get it cheaper. And I can assure you gennelmen that the bottles come ready corked, so if there ain't enough in 'em that's down to the Frenchies.'

'Good point well brought out,' Armstrong conceded and topped up both glasses with the remains of the first bottle, observing to Anson: 'Remarkable, ain't it? Even your London landlords openly admit they're selling smuggled drink. So much for our blockades ...'

'Do you have to keep a look out for smugglers, too?'

'Ironic, ain't it? We have to be on watch constantly in case of smugglers being on the coast, and for prisoners-of-war making their escape. If we spot anything queer like that, we're supposed to signal a warning to the next station up the line and send a dragoon off to report to the nearest military.'

'So there's no such thing as being off watch?'

Armstrong shook his head. 'There's no relaxation from duty except in a thick fog, which will sometimes last for ten days at a time. Bliss!'

'What can you do at such times?'

'Nothing but walk the cliffs and seashore, as long as I watch my footing. But such times are rare. I tell you, *mon vieux*, anyone who says a signal station's an easy berth fit for old worn-out officers could not be more wrong. Mind you, I soon will be worn-out if I'm forced to stay there much longer.'

Most recently accustomed as he was to the rigours of life afloat, Anson was sceptical.

Noting his questioning look, Armstrong assured him: 'Yes, I know all about sea service and how hard that can be. But without fear of contradiction, I can safely say I've suffered more from anxiety at my signal station than ever I did on board a man-of-war. When your watch is over at sea you can catch some rest—'

'True,' Anson had to agree.

'But at a signal station you're watch-on, stop-on, and woe betide you if you fail to spot an enemy sail or are sluggish at relaying a signal. It's like having a testicle permanently in the mangle – the same effect as catching a finger in it, but a damned sight more painful!'

Anson queried: 'But surely not everyone finds it so, er, uncomfortable, and not all who want the post are accepted. I've heard it said that a one-eyed officer unfit for active service applied to Admiralty for a signal station appointment but was refused.'

'That's correct, their Lordships told him that for such a post he would need two eyes …'

Armstrong poured another glass. 'Aye, and damned good eyes at that! Not only d'you need good eyes, but strong nerves are a must. In the sou'west gales I've been astonished that the signal house roof hasn't blown away, we're in such an elevated situation.

'I well remember one dreadful gale blowing our chimney down on to the roof, the fire blew out of the stoves and the glass out of the window frames.'

Anson raised his eyebrows.

'What I'm telling you is gospel. You couldn't stand upright in it. It was a night as black as Erebus and rained so hard that it swept everything away, including our garden, leaving nothing but the bare rock behind. I'd sooner face a storm in the Bay of Biscay any time.'

'So you're here to seek a different appointment?'

'Me, among many. I'd take any sea-going post offered. Even command of a hulk would be preferable!'

Anson nodded sympathetically and made a mental note that if on the morrow he was offered a signal station appointment he would decline it smartly.

His companion warned him off accepting any post with the Sea Fencibles. 'It's a poisoned chalice, only one step better than the impress.'

Anson had heard of the Sea Fencibles. The name came from defencible, and they were a part-time force of fishermen and boatmen commanded by naval officers for local coastal defence, especially against invasion.

Armstrong warned: 'The men are totally unreliable, no doubt smugglers to a man, and they only join to get a protection from being pressed into the proper navy. They're a scruffy, drunken lot, impossible to discipline and train – and sure to melt away at the first sign of danger. When their Lordships offer someone a Sea Fencible appointment he can be sure his career is over. It's the end of the line. There's no honour in it, no hope of prize money – and no one's ever going to obtain promotion commanding a bunch of scallywags like that.'

It was sobering stuff, and Anson told himself that on the morrow he would take neither job and accept nothing but a sea-going appointment.

The wine level sank steadily as they talked of other things: Nelson's defeat of the French at Aboukir; and of old ships and mutual acquaintances.

The French foray into Egypt and the loss of their fleet had clearly lessened the invasion threat, but Armstong drew attention to a framed engraving, hung on the wall by the patriotic landlord, showing French soldiers and a priest preparing to embark for England. The wording on their flag read: *'Vengeance et le Bon Bier et Bon Beouf de Angleterre'.*

Anson was amused at the verses under the cartoon:
'With lanthern jaws, and croaking gut,
See how the halfstarv'd Frenchmen strut,
And call us English Dogs!
But soon we'll teach these bragging Foes,
That Beef & Beer give heavier blows,
Than Soup & Roasted Frogs.
The Priests inflam'd with riotous hopes,
Prepare their Axes, Wheels and Ropes,
To bend the Stiff-nek'd sinner.
But should they sink in coming over,
Old Nick may fish 'twixt France and Dover,
And catch a glorious Dinner.'

It was good morale-raising stuff that his father would enjoy, and Anson resolved to repair to Robinson's the publishers in Paternoster Row to seek out a copy after his interview at the Admiralty on the morrow.

The remains of a third bottle of red vanished over the cheese, and Armstrong pressed two large brandies on him before Anson insisted on calling a halt to the convivial evening.

Weaving slightly, he made his way to bed and to sleep disturbed by dreams of struggling to hold down the roof of a wind-battered, cliff-top signal hut as starving Frenchmen led by axe-wielding priests streamed ashore.

16

He looked in vain for Armstrong at breakfast and, despite a dull throb behind his eyes, managed a hearty plate of bacon and eggs before setting off to learn his future.

It was but a short walk from the Ship and Shovel to the Admiralty in Whitehall.

For minnows like him, the centre of the navy's worldwide web was always spoken of with some awe and it was with trepidation that Anson crossed the cobbled courtyard.

He was conscious that he was following in the footsteps of the great and good of the navy – and that here his immediate and, indeed, long-term future would be decided.

Heading for the main door framed by four imposing pillars, he hesitated for a moment debating whether or not to remove his hat, decided he should do so, and entered the hallowed building.

Inside the large, square, high-ceilinged entrance hall, with arched corridors to left and right, his eyes were drawn first to the large, fire-less fireplace and to an impressive six-sided candelabra hanging from the centre of the ceiling, a three-anchor badge above each face and topped with a crown.

Below were three curious, heavily-padded, black leather armchairs, built with wide hoods. One was occupied by a be-whiskered porter, sheltering from the draughts from the regularly opening doors.

Anson was amused to see that the man's feet were ensconced in a drawer which slid out from under the chair, and his head was shielded by the seat hood.

Knowing of the tyrannical reputation of the Admiralty's messengers and porters, feared by anyone below flag rank, it was hardly surprising that they were indulged with custom-built seats to protect them from the elements.

A second man, clearly the porter of the watch, hovered expectantly. Hat now stowed under his left arm, Anson cleared his throat nervously and announced his name and business.

The haughty porter looked him up and down, sniffed, and directed him to the second door on the left which led into a small waiting room.

This was the most hated room in the Admiralty – a limbo where unemployed officers awaited their fate, both the refuge and torture chamber for lost naval souls washed up, each hoped only temporarily, on shore.

It was a place of hope for a new ship and the promise of promotion, glory and prize money. But, more often than not, it was a place of shattered dreams leading to no new appointment, nor any prospect of escaping the ignominy of half pay – half life. A naval officer without a ship was like a cavalryman without a horse, a shepherd without sheep.

Among those already there was Armstrong, who greeted Anson with a wry smile and indicated a chair he had saved for him. But despite the wine-assisted chatter of the night before, neither felt much like making small talk and they soon lapsed into brooding silence, each awaiting his fate.

Written on the wall was a verse that summed up their feelings:

'In sore affliction, tried by God's commune
Of patience, Job, the great example stands,
But in these days, a trial more severe
Had been Job's lot if God had sent him here.'

One by one a succession of officers entered, cheerily greeted anyone they knew, made a bit of small talk, exchanged gossip – and then themselves lapsed into silence. It was as if they felt telling one another their aspirations might bring bad luck. And, like most sailors, jobless half-pay officers were particularly susceptible to ill omens.

A bolder officer who went to the door and accosted a porter, demanding to know when he would be seen, was swiftly made aware that he was no longer on the quarterdeck and slunk back, tail between his legs.

Eventually, first one and then another of the supplicants was collected and marched off to an unknown fate.

Each time the door opened, Armstrong exchanged a questioning look with Anson, who shrugged in reply, and the clock seemed to move slower and slower.

Anson turned over recent events in his mind: making ready on board *Phryne* for the raid on Saint Valery-en-Caux; the desperate fight on the mole; trundling along in the wagon on the way to the Auberge du Marin; Thérèse's embraces; and the escape.

So it was with a start that he registered his name being called, and he leapt to his feet and followed the porter, eager to learn his destiny.

Yet to be called himself, Armstrong gave Anson another wry smile and mouthed, '*Bon chance, mon vieux!*'

*

'First and foremost sir, I should like to go back to *Phryne*.'

Captain Wallis shook his head slowly back and forth. In his post he was resigned to young officers requesting the impossible.

Anson hesitated at the clear rebuff, but pressed his point regardless. 'And if it cannot be *Phryne* I should very much like to be appointed to another frigate.'

Wallis, sharp-featured and balding, blocked Anson's plea with a raised hand. 'I much regret I am unable to offer you anything of the kind—'

'But why can I not return to my ship, sir?' Anson persisted. The captain shook his head. He could guess exactly how a keen young officer must feel on being deprived of his rightful ship without any immediate chance of another. To your true seaman it was akin to losing a mistress without having a wife to fall back on.

He sighed. 'Look here, Anson, you must forget *Phryne*. You were presumed dead, seen and reported dead, and your old appointment has been filled. Let me remind you that we are at war. We cannot chop and change at the whim of every officer who thinks he deserves this, that or the other.'

'But—'

Wallis again raised his hand to silence Anson. 'But me no buts, d'you hear? I sympathise with you. It's most unfortunate, but there's no going back. Accept that and look ahead.'

Anson blinked and twitched his mouth in reluctant resignation. 'So is there no chance, sir, of another frigate?'

Captain Wallis again shook his head. 'Not a cat's chance in hell. I'm bedevilled with half-pay officers seeking ships. You join a long queue, I'm afraid, and there's a good few of them in the waiting room again today. And some of them have …'

He stopped himself from saying that many of those on the beach awaiting appointments did not lack interest – that naval euphemism for influential friends in positions of power – and instead added '… some of them have, shall we say, priority.'

'So, sir, what can I have?'

Wallis sighed. 'Alternative employments for an officer in your situation are few. There's here at Admiralty of course – highly suitable for an officer who enjoys sailing a desk and is partial to the social scene in town. Daresay I could find you an appointment here.'

Anson pulled a face but the captain appeared not to notice. 'It's also a berth in which you can be noticed and set yourself up, provided you pin your flag to the right rising star.'

Every officer knew all about the effect such interest could have on promotion prospects. The lack of it prevented many a first-class, sea-going officer from getting the ship or promotion he deserved, hence the popular wardroom toast to 'a bloody war or a sickly season'. Those with well-placed interest did not have to wait for dead men's shoes.

'By the by,' Wallis asked, 'does your surname indicate a kinship with the Anson?'

Anson was well used to the question and shook his head with resignation. 'I'm afraid that in all honesty it's a distant kinship, many times removed. But of course all in my family, especially my father, are most proud of the great Anson's circumnavigation and capture of the Spanish treasure galleon.'

'Your father is a parson, is he not?'

'He is indeed, sir, but a would-be sailor.'

'So you sail in his place?'

Anson considered the thought and agreed: 'Yes, I suppose I am fulfilling my father's naval ambitions.'

He had never really thought of it this way before, but suddenly it was crystal clear. His grandfather, as rural dean, had obviously pushed his only son into the church, and eventually used his own influence to shoehorn him into the living of Hardres-with-Farthingham.

Likewise, in his turn, as firstborn son Gussie had been predestined for the church. And so Oliver, as second son, was actively encouraged to join the navy as a midshipman at the age of 12, although he had not needed pushing.

And now he could understood why, vicariously – an apt choice of word, he thought – his father followed his naval career with such close interest, quizzing him in the greatest detail whenever he returned to the rectory.

Captain Wallis returned to the question of Anson's employment. 'Well, would Admiralty suit? Such a surname as yours would be no hindrance here.'

'No, sir. Most kind of you to suggest it and I'm quite sure the Admiralty would be an excellent place for some fellows, but I should hate to be cooped up, pen- pushing.'

Wallis appeared to miss the unintentional slight and nodded: 'Well then, there's the dockyards. Chatham, or Sheerness, perhaps? I'd advise Chatham. It's nearer your home and Sheerness really is the arsehole of the world.'

'It would still be pen-pushing—'

'There's the impress service of course. Vital work if we're to keep the navy fully manned, but somehow I don't think you're cut out for that.' Distaste had registered on Anson's face. No, the thought of leading a gang of bully boys to press unwilling men was abhorrent.

'Well, then there's a signal station. Important work that, too, keeping an eye out for the French.'

Anson shuddered at the thought of what Armstrong had described over last night's supper – a watch-on, stop-on, stress-filled life, looking out for few-and-far-between signals, ship movements and the comings and goings of smugglers.

'So is there really nothing for me at sea at all, sir?'

Captain Wallis shook his head vigorously. But he had clearly taken a liking to this young officer and had a card up his sleeve. Convinced he had read his man well, he had deliberately chosen to save it 'til last. Face a man with options you know he'll reject, was his philosophy, and then the probability must be that he'll jump at the one you want him to take.

'Very well, Anson. We have now exhausted every possibility except one. I have the ideal appointment for you. It's not at sea, of course, but it's beside the sea and your local knowledge will be of the utmost value. You will be in command of men, quite possibly in action. Oh, and there will be minimal pen-pushing.'

Wallis tapped a docket on his desk. 'I've been reading up on you, and I can tell you that your services during the Nore affair have stood you in good stead.'

Anson's mind flashed back to a confrontation with mutineers the year before when his life, and much more, had hung in the balance. 'Thank you, sir. It was a trying time with a more satisfactory outcome that we could have expected at the height of it.'

The captain smiled. 'You did well and their Lordships are aware. Nevertheless, although at present I am not in a position to offer you a ship, there is something that you might find equally challenging.'

He opened the docket. 'Since the Nore business, by something of a miracle you have played a part in a successful frigate cruise taking prizes in the Med, survived your reported death in Normandy and escaped from France. So I would say that makes you a lucky officer, and we will need lucky officers when the Frogs invade—'

'Surely after Aboukir there's no way they can invade, sir?'

'It was indeed a great victory for Nelson and his band of brothers – and would that I had been there instead of being cooped up in this ...'

Lost for the right word, Wallis coughed drily and continued. 'I'll grant you they'll not attempt it for a while. They're not ready. And Aboukir has certainly bought us time to put our defences in order.'

Anson nodded. He had heard similar comments from officers in the gossip-ridden waiting room.

Captain Wallis's fingers found the British Isles on the large globe beside his desk. 'The French have suffered a major setback, but their objective has surely not changed, and by hook or crook they intend to defeat us here in these islands. To avoid that, we'll need to continue to frustrate and blockade them forever and a day.

'Mark my words, before long they'll be building invasion barges in every port from Cherbourg to Zeebrugge and beyond. All they'll need is for our Channel fleet to be lured away or otherwise off station, a fair wind – and they'll be over here forcing us all to eat frogs' legs.'

'You really believe they'll invade, sir?'

'I say not if they'll attempt an invasion, but when, and we'll need lucky officers to frustrate their landings.'

Anson was ahead of him, and Armstrong's warning about life with the Sea Fencibles came back to haunt him. 'Not fencibles, sir?' Anson's disappointment was written all over his face.

'Why not? Has some kind person put you off them?'

Anson held his tongue.

'Don't tell me!' Captain Wallis nodded knowingly. 'It'll be Armstrong, I'll warrant. Always here at the least excuse, pleading for a ship. No doubt you've heard him wittering away in the waiting room. I saw the wretched man there earlier—'

'I did have occasion to discuss possible appointments with Armstrong over supper last night, sir, and it's true he was dismissive of service with the Sea Fencibles.'

Wallis shook his head and sighed. 'Armstrong, just as I thought. He's a good enough fellow, but itching and bitching to get back to sea. However, I can assure you not all fencible and signal station appointments are as wearisome as he finds his.'

Anson was still overcome with disappointment at having his hopes of a sea-going post dashed, and said nothing.

'You are from Kent, and familiar with the coast – the invasion coast?'

Anson could but agree. Sea-mad, he had learned his small-boat handling out of the fishing port of Folkestone and knew the coast well from the North Foreland to Rye.

'The Channel has been a useful defensive ditch for many a year, but it's not guaranteed to stop an enemy invading successfully. The Romans managed it well enough, albeit second time around. The Normans and Dutch weren't put off, and the French are a damned sight better equipped to do it now. If only they can win control of the narrowest strip, between Dover and the Marshes and Calais-Boulogne for a day or two, I'm convinced they'll try it.'

Anson did not agree. 'But surely the Channel Fleet'll never let them take control, sir.'

'Maybe, maybe not, but the weather might interfere to their advantage. It did, in reverse, for the Spanish Armada. We forget the lessons of history at our peril. The Spaniards had plans to land at Dungeness, create a beachhead, bring troops across from the Netherlands and march on London – and with better luck they might well have made it.' Every naval officer knew of the Great Wind that blew Philip of Spain's would-be invaders to destruction – with a good deal of help from Drake's fireships.

Captain Wallis warmed to his argument. 'With some clever manoeuvring, like a break-out from one of their blockaded bases, and the right wind – or better for them no wind – and the French could wrong-foot our ships. That could leave the way clear for their invasion barges to cross, rowing all the way if necessary.'

Anson saw the point. 'Given a reasonable sea state, and with our ships off-station, they could row across in a few hours?'

'Just so, and once across the Channel they could regroup before we could gather enough soldiery to strike a decisive blow against them. We may have a great number of men under arms in the south east corner – regulars, militia and volunteers – but they are spread wide and it would be difficult to concentrate enough of them to oppose a landing when we don't know where the Frogs will come ashore.'

'Nor when, of course,' Anson ventured.

'Exactly, so we have to have a plan to hit them before they land. And if the Channel Fleet is off-station for whatever reason, we are left with the Sea Fencibles …'

Captain Wallis sat back in his chair, cupping his chin with his hand, and studied the earnest young officer expectantly awaiting a decision on his future. It was clear that the scenario was beginning to interest Anson, but pressurizing him was almost certain to be counter-productive. The role he was being offered required a keen volunteer – not a pressed man.

'We have been overly successful in raising Sea Fencibles, particularly on the Kent coast. I would like to think this is due to a clamour to serve King and country, but I fear it has more to do with the protection they obtain against proper naval service,' Wallis confided.

Like every serving naval officer, Anson was aware of this dodge enthusiastically seized upon by seafarers in the coastal towns. By joining the fencibles, they qualified for a certificate exempting them from being pressed into the navy proper.

And a part-time – and paid – role based ashore was infinitely preferable to infinite service in a man-of-war. Small wonder men who feared the press gangs were eager to sign up with the fencibles.

Wallis explained: 'There is already a Sea Fencible detachment down at Seagate that has something of a chequered history. The company was formed under a Lieutenant Crispin who appears to have left under a cloud, and it's apparently now being run by his bosun. We want you to take over.' He paused for effect, but Anson showed no reaction.

'The district captain, one Captain Hoare, will brief you about that little local difficulty. He tells me that many of the original recruits have, shall we say, melted away. But no doubt you'll soon fetch 'em back. All you need tell 'em is that it's Sea Fencibles or a man-of-war. Fear of the press is a pretty good recruiting device!'

Anson could but agree.

'The present bosun is somewhat suspect following the Crispin affair,' Wallis warned, 'so you will need your own senior rates. Proper navy men you can rely on.'

Anson's mind went immediately to his fellow escapers. Their loyalty to him, personally, and their reliability in a tight corner was proven beyond doubt – and this could be his opportunity to repay them.

'Think it over while I check something.' Wallis rose, opened the door to his outer office and spoke quietly to one of the clerks. Anson could only ascertain that he was asking about the movements of some other officer and when he would be in Dover.

Although he was not happy with what the captain had told him, Anson already knew he would have to accept the fencible appointment. Clearly he could not have what he wanted – above all a return to *Phryne* – but then, being in the front line facing an invasion could be a whole lot better than skulking in a dockyard, pen-pushing in the Admiralty rabbit warren, or worst of all, unemployed and sitting the war out on half pay.

Wallis returned, remained standing beside his desk, and gave Anson a friendly smile. 'Well, my boy? Do you need more time to think it over? You are due more leave to get over your ordeal in France—'

'No, sir. I would much prefer matters to be sorted out straight away ... and I'd like to accept the Seagate appointment.'

'Bravo! Good man! I'm quite certain none of us will regret it. By the by, now you've accepted it I should explain that there is, shall we say, an extra dimension to this appointment—'

'Extra?'

'Yes, but I am not at liberty to tell you more. That's the province of Commodore Home Popham. So this is what I want you to do – go home and rest up for another couple of weeks. Then I want you to get yourself to Dover to meet him while he's there to see the progress on some, let us say, special craft.'

'I am intrigued, sir. May I ask—?'

Wallis interrupted him. 'Trust me, Anson. I know things that you do not – yet – and let me tell you that if you'd already seen what's afoot down there and heard what Home Popham has to say, then I am confident that you would not just have been agreeing, you'd have been biting our hands off to accept this commission.'

Anson had heard of this Home Popham, known in the navy as 'a damned cunning fellow'. The description had been given to him not in a derogatory sense but out of admiration for his ability to think outside normal parameters – and for his inventiveness, particularly regarding signal codes.

Before Anson could ask more, Wallis walked over to the door, held out his hand and, nodding vigorously, repeated: 'Yes, biting our hands off …'

The interview was clearly over and Anson was instructed to return next day to collect his orders and a letter of introduction to present to Home Popham at Dover a fortnight hence.

On the way out of the building, Anson put his head around the waiting room door. Armstrong was still there with a few other hopefuls. He looked up expectantly. 'Was I right?'

Anson nodded. 'No sea-going appointments to be had, apparently. It's to be the fencibles, based down at Seagate.'

Armstrong nodded sympathetically. 'I regret I cannot wish you joy of it, *mon vieux*. But never mind, they say worse things happen at sea!'

17

Anson returned to the Ship and Shovel to extend his stay for another night, which he achieved without difficulty. That evening, as he settled in a corner of the bar to peruse a copy of *The Times* over a glass of sherry, a shadow loomed over him. 'Armstrong! A successful visit to the corridors of power, I trust?'

''Fraid not, *mon vieux*. For some unaccountable reason their Lordships declined to see me in person. And, finally, after an extremely long period of contemplating my own navel, some jumped-up junior captain condescended to see me – only to tell me how bloody lucky I am – excuse my Anglo-Saxon – to have a job at all. Seemed to think my signal station is some kind of sinecure. Cheek of the devil!'

Remembering Armstrong's diatribe of the night before, Anson ventured: 'I've no doubt you explained the facts of signal station life to him?'

Armstrong held up his hands in mock surrender. 'I tried, *mon vieux*, believe me I tried. But to no avail. He made it crystal clear that I will not get another job this side of Armageddon, so that's that.'

'Ah well, allow me to start drowning your sorrows with a drink—'

'Good idea. I think we both need to do a night's-worth of sorrow-drowning – you faced with a dreaded Sea Fencible appointment and me stuck firmly at my signal station. We'll have a quick one here and then set a course for brighter lights to seek members of the fair sex who might need cutting out!'

Anson bowed to the inevitable, fully aware that the night's sport would once again leave him with the very devil of a headache.

*

Sure enough, the dull pain behind his eyes was there once more when he awoke next morning, but a long lie in and a good breakfast set him up for his return to the Admiralty.

His fellow-reveller was nowhere to be seen, but the run ashore with Armstrong among the hostelries of London had sealed their friendship, and alcoholic oaths had been made to keep in touch – and give aid to one another should the need arise.

This time, Anson was not kept waiting by the Admiralty flunkeys. As soon as he announced himself he was shepherded by a porter to Captain Wallis's outer office where he was handed his commission and the letter of introduction to Home Popham.

But as he made to leave, the clerk asked him to wait for a moment and he was summoned into the inner sanctum.

Wallis looked faintly embarrassed. 'Your predecessor at the Seagate detachment was mentioned, er, in passing so to speak ...'

'That I recall, sir. Is there something more I should know?'

'The thing is, Anson, that he's missing, we know not where, nor why.'

Anson registered a puzzled frown. 'I'm afraid I don't understand, sir.'

'No more do we. The fact is that he's disappeared and although nothing can be proved it is suspected that the detachment's bosun may have had something to do with it. Apparently Lieutenant Crispin had complained to the divisional captain that something was wrong and that he was investigating. Then silence.'

'So am I to investigate his disappearance?'

'Not to the point where it interferes with training up the detachment and trialling the new craft. If he turns up again, which seems unlikely, you'll have to hand him over to the divisional captain. And you may need to replace the present bosun if you find the present one suspect.'

'With one of my own choice, sir?'

'Of course. In view of the special relationship you will have with Home Popham, just do whatever you think fit.'

'Through the divisional captain?'

Wallis frowned. 'To be honest with you, Captain Hoare is, well, a bit of a fop. He's keener on the social round than he is on navy business. Do him the courtesy of keeping him informed about the routine – the manning, training and suchlike. But in reality you will be reporting discreetly to Home Popham – and taking your instructions from him.'

'Might that not cause difficulties, sir?'

'Maybe, maybe, but Home Popham and I will back you up as long as you get the detachment sorted out and get the job done.'

Anson wondered if there were still more skeletons in the cupboard, but thought it wiser not to voice further concerns. However, before leaving

Wallis's office, he managed to stutter a request which the captain, clearly somewhat embarrassed by the revelations he had just made and anxious to get on with the other business of the day, impatiently granted with a dismissive wave. 'Yes, yes. Dictate a note to my clerk and it shall be done.'

He left London a happier man. It had been obvious that his need for recovery time would keep him ashore for a while, but he had at least avoided a sedentary post, or worse, no job at all. As he had seen in the Admiralty waiting room, there were plenty of unemployed half-pay officers around, washed up on the beach, missing the opportunities of war. And he had just avoided becoming one of them.

In his pocket, he carried orders instructing him 'to take command of a volunteer force of Sea Fencibles effectually preventing the landing of an enemy in this country'. His task was to protect the coastal strip 'from Folkestone exclusive to Dymchurch inclusive' with Seagate at its centre.

The vellum document added: 'We require and direct you to repair forthwith to Seagate, and take upon you the command of all such men as may from time to time enrol themselves within the said district for the defence of the coast.'

He also carried a sealed letter addressed to Commodore Home Popham, and another that he had himself dictated to one of the clerks. Now duly signed, sealed and official, it was a request to the naval hospital at Deal that Captain Wallis had been only too willing to support for the officer about to take command of the Sea Fencibles of Seagate.

Having endured quite enough bouncing around in coaches on his way to London, Anson had resolved to go back by sea and caught the Margate hoy, one of the sloop-rigged, single-masted coasting vessels that carried passengers and freight to and from the capital from all around the North Kent and East Anglian coast.

After a swift, incident-free, passage he hired a post-chaise to Deal where he asked to be set down outside the naval hospital in the East Barracks, made his number with the officer commanding to explain his business, and was shown around.

Anson was impressed by what he saw. The Deal hospital was no match for the two great home station naval hospitals at Haslar and Plymouth, but it was sufficient for its role of servicing the warships using the Downs anchorage.

Clearly great strides had been made in the treatment of the navy's sick and hurt, as they were euphemistically known, and Anson knew only too well how important good treatment and care was in a service where more men were lost to disease and accidents than ever perished in battle.

He found the two objects of his mission sitting on a bench wearing drab hospital uniforms and supping mugs of ale. A pair of navy-issue crutches leant against the wall.

Both men were astonished to see Anson and made to rise, but he signalled them to remain seated.

'Didn't expect to see you 'ere Mr Anson, sir,' said Fagg, removing the foully smoking clay pipe that had been clenched between his teeth. 'Come to be mucked about some more by these sawbones? There's plenty of 'em 'ere and they'll take a knife to yer as soon as look at yer.'

'No, I'm well enough thankee. I've come to check on you two.'

The pair exchanged a puzzled frown. 'Kind of you to visit us, sir. We appreciates it, don't we lobster?' They were clearly pleased but some of the old intimacy of the Auberge du Marin and their escape had evaporated. It might only be a stone frigate and a hospital at that, but it was as if they were on board a ship again where the gulf between quarterdeck and lower deck was vast. His smart new uniform emphasised the point.

Anson realised that, and asked them kindly: 'How are you both mending?'

Fagg ventured: 'Better'n we was 'oppin' an' crawlin' through France, eh, sir?'

'You've been treated well, I trust?'

Hoover nodded. 'Well enough, sir, and now I'm pretty well mended I guess I'm about to get my marchin' orders. I'd kind of like to go back to *Phryne*, but they tell me that's unlikely. More'n likely they'll send me to Chatham to wait on some other ship. '

Anson gestured at the crutches and asked Fagg. 'And how about you? Is the ankle still troubling you?'

'By the time we got 'ere it was 'urtin' agin somethin' cruel.' Fagg grimaced at the memory. 'They said as 'ow it weren't set proper and splinted it up agin. I'm not allowed to put no weight on it for a while. At the minute I'm no good to man or beast. But seems it'll be all right in a while, though I'll proberly always walk wiv a limp, a bit crooked like –

and I can forgit bein' a foretopman. No more friggin' abaht in the rigging, eh, sir?'

Anson looked pained. He could imagine what a blow that must be. But Fagg was philosophical. 'I could serve on as a cook or summat, but not as a proper seaman, so I'll see if they'll give me a discharge – swallow the anchor like. Then mebbe I'll 'op up to Chatham an' get work in the dockyard, in the stores, or the colour loft. Always liked flags, I 'ave.'

'You, a dockyard matey?' Hoover grinned. 'I guess if you were in the stores they'd be wise to nail everything to the floor. And, any road, ain't the colour loft women's work?'

'Awlright then, what if it is? Mebbe I'd be able to get me stiff leg over now an' then!'

'But what about you, sir – are you rejoining *Phryne*?' Hoover asked.

'No, it appears I've already been replaced in the ship, and it seems sea-going appointments are as rare as rocking horse droppings. I've been ordered to rest up for another couple of weeks. But then I'm being given a new appointment – to command a small shore-based force down at Seagate. It's one of those they've set up to counter an invasion, although after Aboukir one doesn't look likely for a while. I'm not entirely sure I wanted to take it, but it'll be better than nothing ...'

'As you say, sir, better'n nothing.'

'That's right.' He deliberated for a moment, then, mind made up, he told them: 'I'm afraid that you two are in it with me – as soon as the surgeons pass you as fit, of course.'

Both gasped in astonishment. 'Us?'

'Yes, you. We made a pretty good fist of escaping from France together and for this appointment at Seagate I'll need a bosun and a master-at-arms – people I can trust.'

Fagg, genuinely amazed, stuttered: 'I'm, well, like what they say, speechless.'

Hoover observed: 'That makes a change.'

'But we ain't got the rank fer them jobs—'

'You have now.' Anson took a letter from his pocket and waved it at them. 'I've got an official document here that says I can do more or less whatever I want. You won't have a Navy Board warrant. That don't apply in the fencibles, but you'll be rated petty officer, and Hoover here's to be promoted to sergeant.'

Both were now truly speechless.

'So, are you up for it?'

There was no need for them to reply. Their broad smiles told him they were.

'Now,' Anson rose, 'I'm off to beard the commander and inform him what's afoot. Then, as soon as you're passed fit to travel, we'll get you over to Seagate and the fun will begin.'

Then, he had an afterthought. 'Corporal – sorry, Sergeant – Hoover, did you say they're about to discharge you as fit?'

'That's right, sir!'

Anson rubbed his chin. 'Good, then I need you for a rather special task. Have you got what you need in the way of uniform and what-not?'

'I've just got to go and get a new uniform and all the trimmings at the barracks. Everything's going to be brand new, sir, on account of them selling our kit in the old *Phryne* because they thought we were dead.'

'New, you say? That's fine. You'd best make sure the uniform the stores wallahs issue you with is showing you with the right rank – sergeant. Then get your dunnage together and I'll square it with the commander that you can come with me now. The paperwork will catch up soon enough.'

Sergeant Hoover had never looked happier, but Fagg could not help showing his disappointment not to be escaping from the hospital along with him.

Anson considered for a moment before telling him: 'Don't worry, the minute you're passed fit enough you'll be given the necessary paperwork and money for you to coach it to Canterbury. When you get there seek out the carrier who calls three times a week and he'll bring you to me at my father's rectory. The carrier will be told to look out for you.'

Fagg queried: 'What abaht uniform or whatnot, sir? All I got is this 'ere horspital stuff and I 'spect they'll want it back.'

'Apparently the Sea Fencibles don't have a particular uniform, but as bosun you'll be expected to look the part, so you'd better get into Deal as soon as you're up to it and get yourself kitted out. A blue jacket with brass buttons, japanned hat – that kind of thing. The hospital purser will advance the money.'

Both were clearly overjoyed with this totally unexpected upturn in their fortunes, and Fagg nodded enthusiastically.

'Now, I'll go and sort things out with the commander. If all goes well we can soon get to grips training a parcel of fishermen, boatmen and smugglers to prevent the French hordes landing on our stretch of coast.'

'Amen to that!' said Fagg, taking a long swig of his ale, while Hoover scuttled off to the barracks to collect his smart new uniform and get his kit together.

18

Back at the rectory, Anson introduced Hoover to the family and settled him into a room in the servants' quarters. For anyone like him, used to sardine-cramped hammocks, his spartan room with single bed, chair and table with washing bowl and water jug was the height of luxury.

Over a glass of pre-dinner sherry, Anson told his expectant father how his appointment at the Admiralty had gone. The rector was taken aback. 'Sea Fencibles? Isn't that rather a come-down from sea service?'

'Somewhat, I suppose.'

'And removed from action and the opportunity for advancement?'

'If the French invade, it's the Sea Fencibles who'll be in the front line – even in front of the front line, attacking the landing craft with our boats.'

'But we hear that after his fleet's drubbing by Nelson at Aboukir even the French First Consul himself is of the opinion that the invasion of England is beyond French capabilities.'

'That may be the case now, but the ultimate aim of the French must be to defeat us in these islands so that we cannot sustain our navy. Without achieving that, they cannot command the sea and dictate what happens outside Europe. The situation can easily change and we must prepare for that day.'

His father's disappointment needed no words. To him, such land-based appointments were for unambitious, comfort-loving has-beens. Hopes of having a rising hero in the family were dashed, at least temporarily.

Mrs Anson appeared not to know or care about the nuances of the naval appointing system and was delighted that her son would be serving ashore rather than afloat. For one thing, it would make him more readily available for match-making.

She was also quite taken with Hoover. 'He's such a clean, smart and well-mannered young man, although almost as thin as you, dear. I've told Maggie to do her best to fatten him up. I trust all your men in the navy are as well spoken and as well groomed?'

Anson thought of Fagg. 'Not quite all, mother. Hoover's smart because he's a marine, not a ragamuffin sailor, and his speech and manners could be the result of his American upbringing rather than his time afloat mixing with coarse, ill-mannered navy people like me ...'

'An American? Good heavens!' exclaimed the rector. 'I hope he's not a rebel!'

Rebel or not, the Anson daughters were also much taken with him, but as Elizabeth remarked to Anne when they were alone: 'He's gentlemanly and a very personable and good-looking man. Such a pity he's not an officer!'

*

Over the next few days, Anson and Hoover spent a good deal of time together drawing up plans for training the fencible unit they had not yet clapped eyes on. They worked out a system of training with the great guns, musketry, half pike and cutlass.

Boat-handling was to come, but they agreed that should be no great problem since many of the men would have been in and out of small craft since boyhood.

'Until such time as we can find an experienced gunner, you and I must lead on gunnery as well as small arms drill. Fagg can take the lead on recruiting and discipline. But, first and foremost, we must find out who we've got and assess their level of training and so on.'

'Just so, sir. And then recruit however many more we need?'

'Indeed.' Anson made a note. 'So I had best draft a notice that we can put about, stick up in the pubs and so forth. I've seen one from another area in a newspaper, so no sense in reinventing the wheel. I'll pretty much copy that, well, the style of it anyway.'

He also told Hoover what little he knew about the disappearance of his predecessor at Seagate.

'We'll need to get to the bottom of that, but it'll be a while before I take up my appointment and I don't relish going in there blind.'

'So mebbe I could kind of spy out the land, sir?'

Anson liked the way the sergeant always seemed to be one thought ahead. It augured well.

'Exactly, I'd like you to do just that. I'll give you a letter quoting Admiralty authority to show in case you have any problems, although I doubt anyone will bother a sergeant of marines going about official business. You could put it around that you're there to inspect the cannon. Put yourself up at one of the pubs and see if you can find out what's happened to this Lieutenant Crispin, what sort of man the bosun is, and so on …'

A sudden thought struck him. 'Damn, I've just remembered the special task I mentioned I had for you – and it isn't this reconnaissance mission …'

'Sir?' Hoover was puzzled.

'No, damn it. I wanted you here in your smart new unform to, er, support me at a glorified bun-fight my mother's laying on next week for the neighbourhood toffs to welcome me home.'

'So, shall I delay going to Seagate?'

Anson shook his head. 'No, no. That's by far the shark nearest the raft. No, Fagg should be discharged from the hospital by then – and you heard me tell him to get some kind of uniform – so he'll have to stand in place of you. It'll be fine, just so long as he buttons his lip.'

They shared a knowing smile.

Before leaving the following morning, Hoover asked: 'By the by, sir, just to settle my mind so to speak, will you tell me what it was you wrote on the barrow with that bit of chalk when we borrowed that boat at St Omer?'

'The *bacôve*?'

'Yeah, by the river with the funny name.'

'The Aa?'

'That's it, sir. It's been puzzling me and Sam.'

Anson thought for a moment. 'Well, we weren't thieves. We paid for the wheelbarrow, remember? And it was important to pay for the boat, so I wrote *Pardonnez moi* – forgive me. *Trouvez votre bateau près de Gravelines*. And I left a guinea wrapped in a piece torn from my shirt.'

Hoover gave an understanding nod. 'Good of you to do that, sir, when you didn't need to – they being Frogs and us being at war with them and all.'

Anson shrugged. 'It was a matter of honour.'

*

Hezekiah reined in outside the Three Tuns, his usual pick-up point for parcels and passengers destined for the villages. For many a year his carrier service had operated from here, regular as clockwork, on

Mondays, Wednesdays and Fridays, taking passengers to or from Canterbury and bringing back goods to order that were unavailable out of town.

He brought back everything from bespoke clothing to pots and pans, crockery, cutlery, spices, books and, importantly, the latest newspapers of which *The Times* and the county's own *Kentish Gazette* were by far the most sought-after.

The passengers were usually country folk bringing their goods to market, others on periodic shopping expeditions, visiting relatives or on occasional business with the men of law, accounting or banking who plied their professions in the cathedral city.

But today was different. Hezikiah had instructions to look out for a naval person and, sure enough, after a brief wait one such appeared from the public bar followed by a young lad carrying a kitbag almost as big as himself.

Tilting his pointy hat back with his whip handle, the carrier appraised the said naval person. You could hardly miss him. The first thing to hit you was the newcomer's tall, black-lacquered hat tilted jauntily to one side with the letters SSF picked out in white paint to the fore. Aft, the beginnings of a pigtail could be discerned by the observant, and Hezikiah was ever sharp-eyed.

Beneath, the naval person wore a blue and white check shirt, blue neckerchief and red waistcoat topped with a dark blue cutaway jacket with a row of highly polished brass buttons down the front. His trousers were red and white-striped and the silver buckles on his shiny black shoes flashed as he walked – or rather hopped. And from a cord round his neck hung his unofficial badge of office, a silver bosun's whistle.

A Malacca cane under one arm and a crutch under the other completed his rigout, giving him more the look of a pirate chief than a navy petty officer, and Hezikiah could not help staring.

'Are you name of Fagg?'

'Who's arsking?'

'Hezikiah Dale, the carrier, at your service. But I was told to look out for a sailor and you look more like a hadmiral t'me …'

'Not quite a hadmiral mate. Leastways, not just yet,' said Fagg. 'Mebbe it's me 'at,' and he pulled it off by the brim, instantly revealing himself to be a foot shorter than he had at first appeared. He tapped it with his cane. 'Waterproof see? On account of how they give it coat arter coat of black varnish.'

'Well, shame it ain't raining then,' observed Hezikiah. 'So 'op aboard and let's get this here voyage on the road.'

Fagg obliged, flicked a coin to the porter lad and settled down to enjoy the journey to Hardres Minnis, instructing the carrier: 'Now, so as us don't get bored nor nuffink, p'haps you can tell me all about Mr Anson and his family so's when I'm hobnobbing with them at the rect'ry I'll know who's who and what's what.'

And Hezikiah, who so often endured the tedium of the trip alone, was more than happy to oblige.

*

Fagg's arrival at the rectory caused something of a stir, and Anson was roused from his post-lunch nap in the summerhouse with the news that there was 'a navy gennelman' asking for him.

This, he thought, must be Fagg – hopefully smart in his new rig. He instructed the servant: 'Kindly show him round.' But he was quite unprepared for the startling apparition that manifested itself a few minutes later in the summerhouse doorway in the shape of Samuel Fagg, boatswain designate of the Seagate Sea Fencibles.

Anson took in the tall japanned hat, the brass-buttoned blue jacket, red waistcoat, striped trousers and glinting shoe buckles with astonishment, gasping 'Good grief!'

The apparition raised his hat. 'Beg pardin, sir?'

Anson stuttered. 'I said good, er, yes very good! I told you to find yourself a uniform and you've most certainly done that. Very, well, very ...' He put his hand over his mouth to smother his grin.

'Smart is the word what I 'ope ye're searchin' for, sir,' said Fagg, glancing down at his flashing buttons.

'Smart indeed, bosun. You look, well, I cannot seem to find the words to express it ...'

Fagg knuckled his forehead. 'Thank you very much, sir. Obliged to ye. Can't help being a bit chuffed wiv it meself.'

Anson could not trust himself to disguise his amused astonishment, so waved Fagg to a chair and told him of Hoover's mission. 'It'll keep him away for some days so you can have his room and stay here until I take up my appointment. It'll give that ankle of yours a bit more time to right itself.'

Then he remembered the coming dinner party, pictured Fagg waiting on him in his magnificent new full fig, and, with some relish, explained the role he wanted his new bosun to play.

19

While Anson was being introduced to the company over sherry, the butler buttonholed Fagg. 'Ever served at table before?'

Minus only his japanned hat from his otherwise gaudy uniform, Fagg said unapologetically: 'Only on board ship when it's me turn to fetch me messmates their dinners.'

The butler had no idea whatsoever what that entailed, but took it to mean waiting experience rather than the unruly scrum it usually was. 'Good, then you'll know to serve from the right and keep your thumb out of the soup. You'll stand behind Master Oliver. I'll tell you when to do what, and if in doubt look to me.'

'Aye aye butler,' Fagg responded, reminding this jumped-up landsman who was who.

The guests, now fully mustered and plied with sherry, moved to the dining room which sparkled with the light of many candles glittering on the silver and glassware and flickering on family portraits – a mixture of undistinguished clergy and a few second-son military men, including the unfortunate Hannibal Anson.

The rector was flanked by Squire Brax's portly wife Elizabeth and Mrs Todd, a neighbouring clergyman's plain but wealthy young widow, only recently out of mourning. At the other end of the long table, Mrs Anson had seated Colonel Redfearn, of the engineers, on her right and Squire Brax on her left.

The other places were taken up by Lady Brax, Colonel Bumstead of the yeomanry, his horsey-looking wife and surprisingly pretty daughter Caroline, a chubby, unaccompanied magistrate called Smythe from Canterbury who was seated between the Anson daughters, and the archdeacon, whosehistorical pinch-faced wife and angular daughter were next to Augustine Anson.

Just as his mother had predicted, Anson was seated between the two eldest Brax girls, Charlotte and Jane. Their younger sister Isobel sat opposite, looking not at all ill at ease next to the colonel of engineers.

In Anson's honour, it was a meal with a nautical flavour.

The soup appeared and, noting that his mother had taken her first sip, he took a mouthful. Spoon poised, Charlotte Brax asked Anson,: 'What's the fish soup like?'

Anson raised an eyebrow. 'Fishy.'

She giggled, drawing a disapproving glance from her mother, but dismissed it with a toss of her head. She was exceptionally pretty, well-covered, verging on the voluptuous, done up to the nines, and spoilt, Anson concluded.

He noted that Jane, slimmer although not half as pretty, was nevertheless attractive in her way, perhaps largely due to the way she deported herself – with poise and apparent charm. Being the centre of attention between the two could be more fun than he had imagined.

Soup dishes disappeared without mishap and on came the next course. Fagg nudged Anson and nodded at the plate he had placed in front of him, hissing loud enough for those nearest to hear and pause in mid-chew: 'I'd take care to clean orf that green stuff with yer knife if I wus ye, sir. It's covered in snail shit.'

This set Charlotte off giggling again, and Jane put her hand to her mouth to stifle a grin. Anson near choked and spluttered: 'It's, er, caviar,' and, sensing all eyes on him, added, 'Yes caviar, how nice!' And turning to his mother with an embarrassed, apologetic shrug he managed to add: 'How clever to acquire some, mother. Haven't seen any since the Baltic,' adding diplomatically, 'Clearly my bosun has never seen caviar there or anywhere else.'

This provoked a nervous laugh from the nearest diners, and one or two surreptitiously cleared their salad leaves of the precious eggs – just in case.

His mother looked relieved at her son's compliment, and protested: 'We can thank Lady Brax for this treat. One of her servants rode over with it this morning.'

Anson prayed he was alone in hearing Fagg's muttered: 'Pick it orf the cabbages, did she?'

Mrs Anson hastened to complete mending the fence by turning to Lady Brax and gushing: 'We are so very grateful. Caviar is such a rare treat. It's such a luxury in these trying times.'

Her ladyship had not registered Fagg's snail shit remark and took the compliment at face value. 'It comes in jars, of course, imported from

Scandinavia packed in ice blocks. My grocer rushes a few jars to the hall as soon as it arrives in port. It keeps for a while in our ice house.'

Squire Brax grumbled. 'An acquired taste if you ask me. Damned salty stuff, but it's just about edible with a good wine.' He turned to the rector. 'War don't trouble your cellar, eh, parson? Use the same firm of suppliers as we at the hall, I'll be bound!'

Various meat dishes followed and Anson struggled gamely on, watched closely by Charlotte and Jane for signs of flagging. Looking round at the way his fellow-diners were tucking in, it was small wonder that most, including Charlotte, were carrying what was known afloat as 'a bit of cargo'.

Her mother was certainly provisioned for a long voyage, as a seaman might say of a paunchy landsman.

Mrs Anson caught her son's eye. 'Is the meal satisfactory, dear?'

'Very much so, mother – a rare treat for someone more used to salt beef, salt pork and dried peas.'

Charlotte Brax insisted on hearing more about life afloat. 'You men are so lucky. You go off to war and have all the fun while we poor girls have to hang around leading boring lives at home waiting for the heroes to return if we are ever to find a husband.'

Anson glanced her way and was immediately conscious of the expanse of pink flesh cleaving dramatically as it disappeared into her gown. 'Er, so, do you aspire to a martial life, Miss Brax?'

She noticed his interest, fixed him with an amused half smile, and replied archly: 'A marital life might suit me better, sir.'

Anson spluttered. 'Some women do go to sea, but it's not an ideal life for ladies.'

Charlotte gave him a knowing look. 'So I've heard Mr Anson, so I've heard.'

He realised he had left a chink in his armour and hurriedly explained. 'What I mean is, that warrant officers like the gunner sometimes have their wives on board – with permission of course. They perform useful tasks, help look after the sick and wounded and so on …'

'How noble! If you had a wife, Mr Anson, would you have her on board?'

He was still contemplating how to answer without digging himself in deeper when Jane Brax came to his rescue.

'I would definitely opt for a martial life, were it possible, Mr Anson.'

He turned to her, mightily relieved at the opportunity to steer the conversation out of dangerous waters. 'Really, Miss Brax?'

Anson's concentration received a sudden jolt. Something brushed against his thigh and for a moment he thought one of his father's gundogs had sneaked into the room and hidden under the table. But then he felt a light stroking. It was a hand, approaching from starboard: Charlotte! While her left hand continued its exploration she reached for her wine glass with her right, countering his look of alarm with an amused pouting smile. Clearly, she was ambidextrous.

Flustered, he looked round hastily to reassure himself that no-one else had noticed and reached down to capture her hand and push it away. It fluttered like a small captive bird in his ship-toughened paw, and as he let it go she gave his fingertips a slow, gentle squeeze.

'Do you agree, Mr Anson?'

Startled, he turned back to Jane. 'Sorry Miss Brax … er, I believe one of the, er, dogs has crept into the room and was nuzzling me under the table.' Charlotte suppressed an explosive snort as Anson added weakly: 'I'm afraid I missed what you said.'

Jane appeared not to have noticed her sister's mischief-making and repeated: 'I asked if you agreed that women should be allowed to form their own yeomanry, acting as nurses, message carriers and so on.'

Anson played for time by reaching for his wine glass and taking a long sip.

'It's absurd and unfair that boys always have the fun and adventure,' Jane insisted. 'We can ride, so why cannot we be volunteers, yeo-women or whatever?'

The youngest Brax sister, Isobel, was following the conversation intently from the other side of the table. 'At least we should be able to dress in regimentals to show support. I've heard of Scottish ladies dressing up in red coats with military cuffs and epaulettes. And some girls are wearing velvet dresses of rifle green—'

Jane interjected, 'And I've read in the *Morning Post* that the women of Neath have petitioned the prime minister to be allowed to form their own home defence regiment. Since our frontline county is most likely to be invaded, do you not agree that the Maids of Kent and Kentish Maids should do the same?'

Before he could think of a suitable response, Charlotte butted in. 'Yes, and of course we should be allowed to fight, too.' She looked him straight in the eye and added, 'I'm sure I could kill a man ... given time.'

Anson coughed nervously, turned to Jane and spluttered: 'There is s-something in what you suggest, Miss Brax. Yes, I think non-combatant roles such as nursing, carrying messages and so on might become acceptable for the, er ... fair sex, eventually.'

From starboard, Charlotte murmured softly: 'Balls ...'

There was an audible titter from Fagg behind his chair as, taken aback, Anson spun to face her, spluttering: 'Er, I'm sorry Miss Brax, I didn't quite catch your drift.'

Charlotte, with a look of total innocence, asked: 'I was querying if you like balls Mr Anson. You know, music and dancing?'

'Ah yes, balls,' he gasped, much relieved. 'I can't say that I'm an expert on ... er balls, Miss Brax. We don't have much call for them at sea, except cannon balls and musket balls of course, ha ha,' he laughed nervously. 'But I daresay they are quite the social thing ashore, there being ladies available as partners and all.'

She smirked: 'Quite so. Then you would accept an invitation should one be held hereabouts?'

'Well, er, in principle I daresay a ball would be a jolly thing to attend.'

She leaned forward, her bosom straining against her gown, and addressed her sister triumphantly. 'There you are Jane, he would love to attend a ball. We must get to work on mother and father immediately. It's an age since we had one at the hall, and now we have the perfect opportunity. The countryside is alive with army officers, volunteers, yeomanry and such.' And, turning to Anson, she asked: 'Will you bring some of your unattached fellow officers?'

'I don't have ... er, that is I will, er ... have to give some thought to that.'

But before he could dig himself into a deeper hole, his mother tapped a glass with a spoon and invited the ladies to withdraw and leave the gentlemen to their port.

As he stood to pull back the sisters' chairs, Anson turned surreptitiously to Fagg, raised his eyebrows and mouthed: 'Phew!'

20

Mindful of Anson's concern about stumbling blindly into Seagate, Hoover had booked himself a room at the British Lion near the gun battery on the Bayle in Folkestone.

He let it be known to the landlord, and therefore no doubt soon to every busybody in town, that he was on a tour of inspection of all great gun batteries in the area. This gave him the excuse to have a long chat to the Bayle battery master gunner and take a careful note of his claims regarding manning and stores deficiencies – all without being once asked for proof of his identity or what his authority was, despite what remained of his New England accent.

'Could've been a spy and he'd be none the wiser,' the sergeant muttered to himself as he made his way to the Seagate battery.

There he found a large gun platform on the high ground away from the seafront, but instead of the expected six 18-pounders there were just two, both showing signs of rusty neglect. Nearby stood a long, tile-roofed building with a board over the door identifying it as the base of the Seagate Sea Fencible Detachment.

He made a great show of measuring and examining the guns, deliberately attracting attention to himself until at last a passing gnome-like figure paused to stare at him for a moment or two and then scuttled into the Sea Fencible building, no doubt to report his presence.

On cue, a surly-looking, scar-faced, thick-set, balding individual emerged, took a long look at the scarlet-jacketed stranger apparently appraising the guns and ambled over. 'Looking to buy one, sodger?' he enquired sarcastically. 'Everythink's got its price.'

Hoover straightened up from peering at a spider's web down one of the barrels and laughed. 'No mate, I wouldn't give you tuppence for one of these. Give me 24s every time.'

'Know a lot abaht guns, do yer? If so, mebbe you can tell me when us'll be getting the rest of what we're entitled to?'

Hoover seized the opening. 'That's exactly why I'm here – just making sure what you've got and what's still needed. Four more 18-pounders, am I right?'

'Blimey, that's it right enough. We've bin waiting for 'em ever since this 'ere detachment was formed.'

'Well mate, your long wait might soon be over – once I've made my report.'

The man was clearly impressed. 'Who are you when you're at 'ome, then?'

'Me? I'm Sergeant Tom Hoover from the marines, checking on the guns down this stretch of coast. How about you?'

The man waved towards the building. 'Sea Fencibles – name of Lillicrap, bosun's mate.'

Hoover nodded. 'Is the bosun at home?'

'No, he's orf on, er, official business up Folkestone way,' Lillicrap lied easily. It was well known around Seagate that Bosun MacIntyre's business at this time of day was with a bottle, and, if he was lucky, a floozy.

'Well, ain't that a pity? I was bent on inviting him for a drink at the Mermaid here while I make notes about the guns you need and all.' Hoover hesitated. 'I guess you'll be too busy to join me instead of him?'

There was no way Lillicrap was going to refuse a free drink, and a short while later they were in the nearby pub, Hoover sipping a weak beer and pretending to take a few notes about the guns while he plied his dupe with tots of rum.

When asked innocently if the detachment had an officer, Lillicrap, warming to his benefactor by the tot, was only too willing to recount the tale of Lieutenant Crispin's downfall, and the more he imbibed the stronger the hints he dropped that the bosun had turned the situation to his advantage.

'He's a right bastard is Black Mac, but 'e's clever wiv it – and I can't complain seeing as how 'e's seein' me orlright. Them there Admirality orficers would 'ave a fit if they knew 'ow he works their own book!'

He slung back his latest tot, gave his new best friend a gap-toothed smile and, overcome with generosity, slurred: 'Let me buy you one this time, Tom. Thanks to Black Mac, I ain't short of a bob or two these days.'

Once the ladies had withdrawn, decanters of port and Madeira appeared and commenced their voyage to larboard around the table. Anson was at first engaged by Colonel Redfearn, who wanted to hear of his adventures in France.

Anson gave him a selective summary, an outline of the raid on St Valery-en-Caux and his wounding, subsequent capture and escape – omitting any mention of the Auberge du Marin and glossing over precisely how he and his fellow fugitives had secured their passage home.

'Commendable, commendable!' the colonel enthused. 'You showed the kind of initiative we sappers prize! Wouldn't care to transfer, would you?'

The colonel's attention was captured by the portly magistrate and Anson looked across the table to see Squire Brax staring at him.

Having already downed several glasses of port on top of the sherry and various wines, the squire was red-faced and well on his way to being comprehensively drunk. 'Well, my boy, now you've had a sniff of my young fillies, do you fancy a canter with one of 'em, eh?'

Taken aback by the squire's directness, Anson stifled a nervous cough and decided not to be led down that dangerous path.

''Fraid I'm not much of a hand at riding, sir. Horses and naval men tend not to mix too often – nor too well.'

The squire registered pretended outrage. 'Can't ride! Never heard of such a thing. Good God man, the son of a hunting parson and you can't ride!'

Anson, keen to steer away from the fillies the squire had in mind, stammered: 'I can ride, of course, but not well and it takes a few weeks ashore to get over being saddle sore. As to hunting, I'd prefer to harass Frogs rather than chase foxes.'

Brax quaffed his port, thought for a moment, and countered: 'Oh, very good! Daresay the Frogs leave a scent in their wake. Strong whiffs of garlic, eh?'

Turning to the rector, he added: 'Never thought of that when you were off a' huntin' did you parson? Chasing a snail-scoffin' Frog would be capital sport, what!' Polite chuckles greeted his remark, but Brax thought it hugely amusing and guffawed.

Then, to Anson's horror, the squire seemed to realise he had been taken off at a tangent and dragged him back to the subject of his daughters. 'Fobbed me off, didn't you, my boy? I was askin' if you fancied one of my gals?'

'All three are quite delightful young ladies, sir. But I wouldn't presume—'

'And pray why not? Not one of those navy wallahs who prefers boys to gals, are you? I've heard all about you navy men.'

Anson was stung. 'Certainly not, sir!'

'So what is it then? Didn't get some of your faculties blown off when you were wounded, did you?'

'I can assure you, sir, that I am completely … er, intact.'

'Good to hear that, but if so, what's wrong with me daughters?'

'As I said, sir, all three are delightful, but—'

Brax mused, 'Isobel is a touch young, I'll grant you – only 14. Jane's 18 and sturdy enough, but a bit on the plain side. Gets it from her mother's family, I s'pose. But Charlotte's old enough, pretty enough and certainly she's ripe enough for the marriage stakes.' He smiled salaciously. 'And she'd come with a tidy dowry.'

It was well known that there were few enough eligible suitors around and he would not be sorry to marry his eldest daughter off before she ran to fat like her mother.

The rector nodded encouragingly, but Anson was highly embarrassed at the turn of the conversation and struggled to extricate himself with honour. 'You have me on a lee shore, sir. You will appreciate that apart from seeing your daughters in church on Sunday, today is the first time I have been with them since they were playing with their dolls and I was not much older.'

And, recalling Charlotte's full bosom straining at her dress and hypnotising him during dinner and her hand stroking his thigh, he added: 'Most certainly I hope to see much more of them before duty calls again, sir.'

Brax grunted, and apparently satisfied, turned to the engineer colonel. 'D'you hunt sir? Not going' to tell me that the army ain't any good at ridin' either, are you, eh?'

The port and Madeira decanters continued their voyage and the conversation reverted to hunting, shooting and fishing – and, predictably, the infernal nuisance that the war with France was becoming with its outrageous tax on income that was about to be introduced, and the inflated prices of everything.

Anson shrank back into his chair and held his peace, relieved to be out of the verbal firing line. Clearly, navigating the society minefield was far trickier than life afloat.

While the rest of the male guests were burbling on about field sports and politics, it was something of a relief for Anson when Colonel Redfearn turned to him again and asked if he yet knew what his next appointment would be – or if he had a preference.

'The Admiralty has informed me that I cannot return to my frigate, sir, nor will they give me any other sea-going appointment. So, against my wishes, I've had to accept a Sea Fencible appointment.'

'I venture this is not a time to concern ourselves with our personal aspirations, Anson. We need good young naval fellows like you to sort out our shoreline defences. After all, as Miss Brax – that is, one of the Miss Braxes – said earlier, this is the frontline county.'

'Indeed sir, but—'

The colonel waved his hand dismissively. 'Never mind all that. You've been over the other side more recently than anyone. Give me your assessment of the mood of the French.'

In truth, Anson had little to offer other than to say that the ordinary people had not seemed overly concerned about the war unless it interfered directly with their lives. There had been a general belief in French invincibility, he recalled, but as to the overall strategic picture, well, the average peasant had little or no idea what was going on outside his patch. Nor did he much care.

The colonel listened intently nevertheless. 'You are a resourceful fellow Anson, and did well to make your way out of an enemy country. Tell me, in your opinion, how easy or otherwise would it be for someone to infiltrate and make their way around the Pas de Calais observing what the Frogs are at?'

'If you had some French and went in disguise, ideally as a Dutchman or some such in the French service, I think it would be relatively easy, sir. Gold talks, of course, as it did for me. I was lucky enough to have taken some of my prize money sewn into my jacket. It proved better than a passport.'

Colonel Redfearn went on to ask Anson's opinion about shore defences, whether he had heard anything of invasion preparations in Normandy and the Pas de Calais ports, and how troop-carrying barges might best be destroyed if they ran the gauntlet successfully to evade the British fleet and attempt a landing on the south coast. Tongue loosened by the wine and port, Anson was happy to air his views with all the assurance of an admiral.

By the time they rose to join the ladies, he had the feeling that he had been almost surreptitiously but thoroughly interrogated by the colonel and perhaps out of bravado had made wandering around France and blowing landing craft out of the water sound all too easy.

He had an uncomfortable feeling that had he been a soldier the colonel could almost have been sizing him up for a return trip across the Channel. But that could not be. Interested though he might be, surely the engineer could play no part in his destiny.

*

Back from his reconnaissance mission, Hoover recounted what he had learned from his session with bosun's mate Lillicrap at the Mermaid tavern. 'He was three sheets in the wind by the time I got around to asking him about Lieutenant Crispin and he was more than happy to talk about it.'

Anson smiled. 'Excellent. I felt sure a bit of digging around would pay off.'

'It did that, sir. It appears the early training had not gone well and Lieutenant Crispin took this bully boy, name of MacIntyre, on as bosun to sort the men out. But, from what Lillicrap told me, he treated the volunteers as if they were raw lubbers in the devil's own man-of-war.'

Hoover's turn of phrase amused Anson. 'Go on …'

'Well, the bosun made up two or three like-minded mates, including Lillicrap – each of them known bad hats and bullies – who took cane or rope's end to the men for the merest trifle. That idiot Lillicrap actually boasted about it to me after half a dozen tots.'

Anson held up a finger. 'You must give me a note of what you've spent. I can't have you being out of pocket.' And, frowning, he queried: 'The men didn't retaliate?'

'They could do nothing for fear of worse official punishment, or of being shopped to the impress. It was kind of a regime of fear and it seems you can't get away with treating volunteers like that ashore.'

Anson agreed. 'But didn't this Crispin do anything about it?'

'Seems he is, or was, a weak man and the bosun despised him and wanted rid of him so that he could operate some kind of swindle. Lillicrap told me that MacIntyre forced it to come to a head when he persuaded Lieutenant Crispin to give the fencibles pike drill down by the harbour when he'd drink taken as usual. He couldn't remember the correct commands and the men were stumbling every which way in confusion, dropping their pikes and muttering. You can imagine it – the gawpers made fun of them and fell about laughing.'

It was easy for Anson to picture the scene. There was nothing half so effective as public ridicule for putting men who were trying to do their best out of sorts.

'Crispin kept giving rambling instructions that only made the situation worse and at that point the bosun, MacIntrye, stepped in and ordered them to fall out for a short rest. They broke up into small groups, talking loudly of going home, and when they were ordered to fall in again it was well nigh impossible to get them to obey – even with the bosun's mates threatening them with the rope's end. When they did eventually get back into some sort of order, Crispin tried to continue with the exercise, but got the orders wrong again.'

'Good grief!'

'The word had gone round and drew a crowd, including some off-duty soldiers, and as you can imagine they found the scene real funny ...'

'Sounds like a complete shambles!'

'That's the impression Lillicap gave me, sir – a complete farce. And the more Lieutenant Crispin tried to remonstrate with the men the more they hooted and hollered, shouting "Wrong, wrong, wrong" and "Home, home, home!" It was only when the officer staggered off that the bosun managed to quieten them down sufficiently to dismiss the parade. Since then MacIntyre – I understand the men call him Black Mac – has taken complete charge, but there's been no more drilling in public, many of the men have melted away and the detachment seems to be totally ineffective.'

'Did you get any hint of what's happened to Lieutenant Crispin?'

Hoover shook his head. 'All I could get out of Lillicrap was that he'd be seen no more this side of the Channel.'

'What do you think he meant by that?'

'Sounded to me as if he might have been deliberately marooned over the other side, but I can't be sure.' He paused. 'There's one other thing, sir. I got the impression from Lillicrap that, with the officer out of the way, MacIntyre has got some kind of swindle going at the detachment.'

'What sort of swindle?'

'He spoke about the bosun coming up with a clever scheme and cutting him in on it. He let slip that it was something to do with some kind of official book, but I couldn't get any more out of him. He was pretty well soused by then.'

Anson rubbed his hands. 'Good work. Sounds as if I need to pay them a surprise visit before they find out they're about to have a change of command.'

21

On the appointed day at the appointed hour, Anson sought out the temporary office Commodore Home Popham was using at Dover and handed over the letter of introduction from Captain Wallis.

A clerk bade him take a seat, knocked on the inner office door and handed in the letter with a muttered explanation. After a few minutes, an officer with iron-grey hair, startling eyebrows, side whiskers and an air of dynamism about him, appeared in the doorway and fixed his visitor with a friendly stare.

Anson rose and the commodore shook his hand. 'Lieutenant Anson? I'm Captain Home Popham, well, temporarily a commodore, the fellow to blame for creating the Sea Fencibles and the reason you are here today. Come in.'

He led the way into the inner sanctum and gestured to Anson. 'Do sit.' He pulled up his own chair and appraised the young lieutenant for some moments before asking, 'Any connection to the Anson?'

Anson's eyes went ceiling-wards and he answered for the umpteenth time: 'Only a very distant kinship, I'm afraid, sir, many times removed.'

Home Popham snorted. 'Distant eh? Still, not a bad name to be saddled with in the navy, what?'

'No, sir, I've heard worse.' Then he realised the commodore might think he was referring to his peculiar name and wished he could un-say what he had just said.

But Home Popham had clearly not taken the remark personally. He murmured 'Quite, quite,' and, elbows on the desk and hands clasped in front of him, the commodore got down to business. 'Perhaps I should explain that as a result of my experience as a naval staff officer with the Army in Flanders four years ago, I came up with a plan for the organisation of a kind of naval militia for flotilla work.'

'What are now called Sea Fencibles?'

'Just so. My plan was adopted and I've been appointed to command the most important section of the force – covering the area from Beachy Head to Deal. Each area under me is commanded by a naval captain, which is why I'm temporarily a commodore, and a lieutenant commands each detachment.'

He held up the letter of introduction and fixed Anson with a steely look. 'I need competent officers to serve under me. Captain Wallis has told me something of your record. Your escape from France tells me you are a man of initiative and courage, and that is why we want you to take over a special detachment, based at Seagate. And you've accepted, I gather?'

Anson nodded. He was flattered but still not entirely convinced about his competence for leading what he saw as essentially a part-time, part-trained parcel of man-of-war dodgers.

'Yes sir, but may I ask how do you suppose these untrained, er, fencibles, will be able to frustrate the French?'

Home Popham banged his fist on the desk. 'By getting in among their invasion barges and sinking them off the coast! The only Frenchies I want to see coming ashore are floating bodies!'

Anson smiled wanly. It was clearly not wise for a junior officer to argue the toss with this man.

Home Popham softened. 'The whole point is that I need officers like you to train them. These detachments comprise mainly south coast boatmen and fishermen, no doubt including many a smuggler, because I've little doubt most south coast boatmen and fishermen are smugglers.'

'And you believe that given training they could successfully counter an invasion, sir?'

'Correct. They are being trained in the use of guns and pikes, and the idea is to use small gunboats and batteries ashore to oppose and frustrate any attempts by the French to land on our coast.'

Home Popham read the scepticism on the lieutenant's face and added sharply: 'Recruiting, training and commanding them is a most proper and worthwhile task, young man. I can assure you the threat of invasion may have diminished somewhat since Nelson whipped the French in Aboukir Bay, but it is still very real.'

'So Captain Wallis was telling me, sir.'

'Quite so, and as the lieutenant at Seagate you'll be covering the stretch of coast from the west of Folkestone to the edge of Romney Marsh – as likely a landing area as you'll find.'

'Leaving aside Deal and Pevensey?'

'Where the Romans and Normans landed?' Home Popham arched his eyebrows. 'I like a man who knows his history. Yes, but this General Bonaparte has read his history too. If I were him I would opt for the beaches between Seagate and Dungeness on the marsh. Let's not forget that the Armada planned to land troops there. And, if the French try something similar, the officer based there will be in the thick of it.'

Anson still had his doubts about a motley crew of Kentish fishermen and smugglers fending off the hammers of the Austrians, Prussians, Spaniards and Italians. But he was beginning to accept that life with the Sea Fencibles could be a worthwhile challenge. 'What craft do we have, sir?'

'At the moment we've a hotchpotch of commandeered boats – whatever we can beg, steal or rent. But we have plans for something much, much better. And this, Anson, is where you figure – in a special role.' The commodore rose, walked to the window, and turned to face him. 'At this stage this is for your ears only, d'you follow?'

'Of course, sir.'

'I am having built here at Dover a new type of row-galley to carry a gun for use by my fencibles. Now, if I can demonstrate the suitability of such a craft in the anti-invasion role, I believe the Admiralty will give orders for many more of the same to be built. Indeed they have already applied to the Treasury at my request to order three smuggling vessels, lately taken by the Custom House cutters, to be delivered over to me for the purpose of being fitted as galleys.'

Anson was surprised. 'Smuggling vessels?'

'Certainly smuggling vessels! You are a man of Kent, are you not? So you must appreciate more than most that your average smuggler is a wily fellow who knows exactly what craft are suitable for his trade. And it follows that on this coast what's suitable for him is bound to be suitable for us. When I get these vessels under my orders I think I shall be able to prevent the French row-boats – and larger privateers – from coming near this coast, either to reconnoitre or annoy our trade.'

'And you want me—?'

'As far as the world and his wife are concerned, your role is no more or less than to lead the detachment that will trial two of these new craft and train up crews to fight them. This means precision handling, rowing to manoeuvre them into position to attack enemy landing craft when they are most vulnerable as they come inshore. It means speedy and accurate gunnery – not easy, I daresay, when bobbing around in not much more than a Portsmouth bumboat with Frogs popping their muskets at you. If the French escape the blockade and get past our screen of ships we have to kill them off as they near the beaches. They must not be allowed to come ashore.'

'But the French have crossed wide rivers to win many battles—'

'Yes, and if they get a foothold ashore it will be a devil of a job getting rid of them. They must be destroyed before they set foot on English soil. We must make the waves run red with French blood!'

He stabbed the air with his index finger. 'But there is more – the special role I have in mind for you.'

Home Popham paused for effect and added: 'The French have many ears in our Channel ports, especially among the smuggling fraternity. Security will be a problem and some misleading ruses and false trails will be necessary.'

Anson listened intently as the commodore added, conspiratorially: 'Not only do I want you to frustrate the French sniffing around this part of the coast, but in due course I want you to obtain intelligence from them – and when necessary to do some sniffing of your own on their side of the water. You are well fitted for tip-toeing round France following your recent escape, are you not?'

This thrilled Anson beyond measure. 'I believe I am, sir.' He could hardly have dreamed up a better scenario for himself: a virtually independent command, trialling new craft, engaging the enemy – albeit in penny packets – and gathering vital information about French invasion intentions.

Short of being made post and given command of a frigate or better, this was about as good as it could get.

Home Popham continued: 'There will be times when we positively want the French to receive certain information and you may be called upon to, let's say, assist in getting it to them. We also have a number of French royalists helping us, and there will be times when we need to insert one or two of them back into France – or fetch them back when their missions are accomplished.'

Anson remembered his own escape from France courtesy of smugglers. 'That should not present a problem, sir.'

'Your stretch of the coast is, of course, of special interest to us. You will be, after all, only some 25 miles from France. I will expect you to furnish me with such intelligence as comes your way. As we know, many of these Kentish Sea Fencibles have smuggling as a sideline – and many are boatmen and fishermen who dabble in what they like to call 'free trading'. With you commanding them, you are in every way perfectly placed for this role, just as Colonel Redfearn told me—'

'Colonel Redfearn?' Anson gave a start at the mention of that name. So even at the rectory dinner party he was being sounded out.

Home Popham smiled at his new protégé's realisation that he had been assessed so carefully, but added: 'Make no mistake, these clandestine tasks must remain totally confidential between you and I. It is of crucial importance that none of your men, not even the divisional captain himself, must know that you are other than a bog-standard Sea Fencible officer training a bunch of base rats in handling the new gunboats and sitting on his backside awaiting the invasion. Is that fully understood?'

'It is indeed, sir.'

'Good, then you will hear from me from time to time, but meanwhile I want you to crack on at sorting out the Seagate detachment.'

Home Popham sent for the gunboat plans and they pored over them, discussing capabilities and tactics. The more Anson heard, the keener he became. And, by the time he left the commodore's office, his senior was clearly convinced that this eager young officer was exactly the right man for the job.

22

While enduring yet another carrier ride back to Hardres Minnis, Anson made up his mind to buy a horse and it was the carter himself, Hezikiah Dale, who suggested he should approach a smallholder called Horn.

'Old Willie Horn knows his 'orses and does a bit of dealing on the side. I hear tell he's just come across a big gelding he's bought from a lady what's just been widdered down on the marsh, Isle of Oxney way, that might suit you.'

'The widow?'

Hezikiah cackled. 'You want 16 hands or more and she's only got the two! Willie Horn's a cantankerous blighter and like as not he'll give you a load of lip afore you get around to looking at the 'orse. But there's few round here as knows their 'orseflesh as good as him. You'll pay top whack but he won't cheat you with a wrong-un.'

The advice was spot on. Next day, Anson found the smallholder leaning over a five-bar gate beside his cottage, puffing at a clay pipe and watching the world go by.

'Good afternoon. Mr Horn?'

Horn looked him up and down, almost insolently.

'You'll be parson's son? I heard you'd be along sometime.'

Anson nodded. The Kentish equivalent of jungle drums had clearly been at work and the uniform was a give-away. 'I hear you've a horse for sale?'

Horn sucked his pipe. 'Mebbe.'

'I'm looking for one of 16 hands or more – and not some flighty creature. I'm a sailor, not a cavalryman.'

'I just might have one o' 16 hands, but it'll cost mind.' He waved his pipe at a large black horse grazing in the meadow alongside his Kent peg-tiled house. 'It'll cost 'cos this 'ere 'oss ain't no nag. It's quality.'

'Good, that's what I'm looking for.'

'An' I s'pose money ain't no object to the likes of you.'

Anson smiled at the barb, taking it as part of Horn's bargaining style. 'I'm not rich. Just a navy man temporarily marooned ashore and on the look-out for a reliable mount.'

Horn sneered. 'That there smart uniform, buy that out of yer sailor's wages, did yer? Or was it paid for private-like, out of the money yer parson daddy gives yer? 'Cos if it were, then that's come from the tithe money forced out of us poor farmers by the blood-suckin' church!'

Anson knew 'minnisers', as the local commoners called themselves, had a reputation for their strong independent streak and plain speaking, but was nevertheless taken aback at the man's vehemence.

Before he could frame any sort of answer, Horn wagged his pipe and growled: 'That comes from the sweat of our brows and keeps poor men's children 'ungry while the likes of yer father lives like a lord, just for preachin' one sermon a week, and that more'n likely copied out o' some book.'

There was truth in that, Anson reflected. His father did indeed appear to copy his weekly diatribes against non-conformism out of a sermon book, and jolly boring they were, too. But Horn's tirade against tithes was something else. It was not an issue Anson had ever thought about before and he felt distinctly uncomfortable. Suddenly, the hundred a year he got from his father seemed somehow tainted. He ventured: 'I'm sure it cannot be quite that simple, Mr Horn.'

'Can be and is that simple,' the small-holder countered. 'Fact is, the parson gets ten per cent of all we sweat to grow, beasts, crops, hay even. A tenth of everything! That's the tithe, and parsons like to tell us it's what the good book calls rendering unto God the things what's God's. But your daddy ain't God. You'd best remind him the Bible also says it's easier for a camel to go through the eye of a needle than for a rich man like him to enter the kingdom of God. So you tell 'im to put that in his pipe and smoke it!'

Anson held up his hands in protest. 'Look, I'm not my father and I know nothing of tithes and church politics. I've just come about your horse.'

But Horn was not finished. 'And where does that tenth of all our labour end up? I'll tell yer – in that blurry great barn next the church. Tithe barn? They should call it the tyrant's barn, 'cos that's what it is. There's folk round here that's lucky to have enough food to put on the table. An'

I'll tell yer, a tenth of not a lot when you're a poor smallholder is a lot. I wouldn't mind so much if it was goin' to fight the war.'

Anson was not sure what to say. He offered: 'But the clergy will pay the new income tax to help pay for the war, so some of your tithe money will help us to fight the French.'

Horn was not to be fobbed off and was accustomed to getting the last word down at the alehouse. 'P'raps we'd be better orf with them revoluntioners over 'ere, anyways. I bet the blurry Frogs don't pay tithes!'

Anson was beginning to get irritated and it showed. 'Look,' he said, 'I came to buy a horse, not to hear a lecture—'

'Fair enough, but I tell ye, 'tis a poor thing to see a man like yon parson father of yourn in what to the likes of us is a palace, eatin' rich food, drinkin' the best wine and such, wearin' fancy clothes – an' all paid for by us. And using his parson's pulpit to pull the wool over the eyes of his iggorant fellow creatures with Bible words they don't unnerstand. That ain't Christian – not in my book it ain't.'

His point well and truly made, there was business to be done. Anson examined the horse carefully, looking for obvious faults, but found none. Horn insisted it was 'honest, genuine – a gennelman.' And, when led into a lean-to beside the barn to be tacked up, it certainly seemed placid and easy to handle, as might be expected of a gelding of maybe seven or eight years.

Quizzed about its provenance, Horn was evasive. It was a good horse that had come from a good home where there was no longer a need for it, and it had come at a high but fair price, he said. Others were interested and it would sell within the week.

Anson scrambled untidily aboard, uncomfortable as ever when exchanging a rolling deck for a lurching horse, and first walked, then trotted the gelding round the meadow. Nothing nasty happened, and as he swung down from the saddle he noted Horn's knowing look – the look of a dealer who knows he is about to shake on a successful deal.

Was it Anson's slight feeling of discomfort over the tithe tirade that made him agree the asking price for horse and tack without argument? Whatever, the seller was satisfied, and he had a horse. He smiled knowingly when Horn told him its name – Ebony. There was a place of that name on the Isle of Oxney, so it had come from the widow there as Hezekiah had said.

As he rode slowly back to the rectory, Anson reflected on Willie Horn's tirade. It did seem unfair that poor men, little more than subsistence farmers, should be forced to give a tenth of what they earned to the church.

What did the church give them in return? And why should men like his father – and his self-seeking brother – grow rich and fat at the expense of men who slaved on the land in all weathers to feed their families? Were churchmen little better than parasites, cuckoos in the nests of the poor? It was a debate he must take up with his father, or Gussie, who it would irritate beyond measure – but not today.

23

The thought of staying at the rectory, with his ears under daily assault from his match-making mother and his father's church politics at every meal, filled Anson with horror. It was not difficult to convince them that, now fully recovered, he needed to be at the centre of his new command and he determined to find suitable lodgings at a Folkestone inn.

Although he had learned to ride as a small boy, long absences at sea were not conducive to familiarity with the saddle. It took Anson some time to re-master the rising trot, so that when he disembarked in Folkestone not only did his thighs ache but there was a soreness in his nether regions that forced him to mince somewhat to avoid further chafing.

Fagg was there to meet him and, ever the eagle-eyed topman, he observed: 'Sore arse, sir?'

Anson grimaced. 'You could put it like that. First days afloat and your sea legs have deserted you, and first days ashore and your horse has turned into an instrument of torture.'

'Nuffink that a drop of lard won't cure overnight, sir,' Fagg advised. 'But 'scuse me if I don't volunteer to rub it in for you. Mebbe one of the rectory maids'll do that, eh?'

Shared experience of their escape had made Anson tolerant of cheeky bandinage from Fagg that, afloat, would most definitely not be permitted coming from lower to quarterdeck.

'Your concern is commendable, but if I need advice on medical matters I will turn to a medical man, not an uppity retired topman.'

It was not a serious rebuke, and, not a tiny bit chastened, Fagg could not resist adding: 'Cor, I wouldn't mind some woman, like that one what looked arter you in France fer instance, rubbing lard on my arse...' But Anson's darted frown told him he had overstepped the mark.

'Sorry, sir,' he added quickly, 'me tongue ran orf wiv me on account of being what they calls deprived, like. Mind you, now we're 'ere, I'll soon put that right ...'

But his voice tailed off to silence under Anson's withering stare.

Anson booked himself into the Rose Inn, in Rendezvous Street. It was that or the nearby King's Arms – both coaching inns and a cut above all the others, but the Rose reputedly had better rooms and stabling. And it was well-known as a venue for mayoral dinners, so the food was likely to be good.

Before showing him the rooms, the landlord enquired diplomatically: 'You indicated a longish stay, sir. Might I enquire 'ow long you envisages?'

'So long as the bed is comfortable, the food good and the stabling's up to scratch, I think you might say it will be for the duration, Mr Griggs.'

The landlord, wisely wary of that well-known sub-species – potential Channel port moonlight flitters – was clearly delighted at the prospect of hosting a long-stay naval officer, and gave Anson the choice of the inn's five guest bedrooms.

Anson favoured a good room with two windows, furthest away from the Free School next door, but two travelling trunks and some clothing on hooks indicated it was already taken.

'I'd like this one when it's free. Meanwhile I'm happy to camp out in any one of the other rooms.'

Without hesitation, Griggs countered: 'Say no more, sir. It shall be yours this very day,' mouthing under his breath, 'as soon as I've shifted this other lot.'

Having settled his accommodation, Anson partook of the inn's ordinary, a wholesome beef dinner that augured well for his messing requirements, and set off to report to the divisional captain and find out about his new command.

He learned little more of the Crispin affair – what Captain Wallis had referred to as the 'little local difficulty' – when he reported to Captain Arthur Veryan St Cleer Hoare, the divisional captain.

Hoare, proud of his albeit distant connection to West Country aristocrats, was a jolly, plump fellow with side-whiskers bordering on the extravagant 'buggers' grips' variety – and was well into the local social scene.

He immediately made it clear that he was happy to let his lieutenants do the work. 'There's one thing ...'

Not one to mince words, the captain chose them with care. 'Have you been made aware of the cock-up at Seagate?'

'Sir?' Anson held his tongue about what he knew in case Hoare could throw some further light on the affair.

The captain toyed with his whiskers and sighed. 'It's not a pretty tale. The lieutenant who formed the detachment you're taking over, one Crispin, is a gentleman but unfortunately given to drinking to excess. He was not popular with his men – not that popularity is necessarily a virtue. At any rate, he appears to have been highly unpopular, and while drilling them in public when drunk provoked what would have been called a mutiny if it had happened among real sailors at sea.'

'So I'll have my work cut out to get them up to scratch?'

'You will indeed, especially as you're to trial the first of the new gunboats. The men will need careful handling. We cannot have a total want of discipline and subordination, but I have to accept that they were appallingly badly-led by Crispin and have been systematically bullied by their bosun, a man called MacIntyre.'

'And he's still here?' Anson asked.

'Yes, and by all accounts he's a devil of a tyrant. No bounds what he's been up to since Crispin cleared off. If necessary, get rid of him and his mates, and start again, ideally with subordinates you know and trust. The impress service would no doubt be happy to take MacIntyre. They're in need of bully boys.'

Anson chose not to reveal that he already had his replacement, two in fact, standing by, and asked: 'May I enquire if you know what has happened to Lieutenant Crispin, sir?'

'That drunken sop was last seen an hour or two after that disastrous pike drill, three sheets in the wind and still knocking it down in one of the pubs. That was over a month ago, since when there's been neither sight nor sound of him. It's hardly surprising that he dare not show his face after what happened.'

'You don't think he'll reappear, sir?'

'I've marked him down as run, and good riddance to him! Disgraceful behaviour for an officer! Wherever he is, I sincerely hope he stays there and drinks himself to death to save us the expense and embarrassment of a court martial.'

The pair spent the next hour discussing the nuts and bolts of Anson's new command – the Seagate Detachment – and arrangements for the acceptance of the gunboats. Captain Hoare made it abundantly clear that the less he was troubled about day-to-day operational matters the better he would like it.

'I've got an important job to do, liaising with the military and civil authorities, and cannot be arsed about getting involved in the nitty-gritty of every fencible detachment.'

'Understood, sir.' Anson was relieved that there would evidently be minimum interference from this quarter.

Like Home Popham, Hoare had clearly warmed to his new subordinate. He added, kindly: 'You know what is expected of you Anson, so do me the favour of getting on with it and only bother me when absolutely necessary. You're a grown-up and you can be confident that I'll back you up as long as you make a good fist of sorting out your detachment and making them efficient, which they'll most certainly have to be if they are to operate these new-fangled gunboats effectively.'

'I will do my utmost, sir.'

'Of course you will, there's a good fellow. However, if you come across any society types who need influencing about the navy and suchlike you might suggest they include me on their invitation lists.'

Anson reflected that the captain clearly had little if no idea of the special role Home Popham envisaged for his new lieutenant, nor did he appear to give a damn what he did with the fencibles – unless it reflected well or otherwise on him, or in any way affected his burgeoning social life.

*

Hoare's early naval career had been pretty much of a doddle, as befitted an almost aristocrat with a silver tongue and a ready pen devoted to ensuring his personal success.

True, he had served his time as a midshipman and junior lieutenant without blemishes, and his perceived connections and influence had smoothed his early years in the service. But it was when the captain of the frigate HMS *Seraphim*, in which he was serving as first lieutenant, was decapitated by a cannon ball during a skirmish with a French fifth rate in the Bay of Biscay, that his chance had come.

Heavily outgunned, and in grave danger of being raked by another broadside, Hoare had taken command, wisely broken off and fled, managing to get off a couple of balls from his stern-chasers as he manoeuvred out of danger. At many a dinner conversation since, these two balls had become a broadside.

However, the incident had been sufficient for him, with his literary flair, to claim that, despite their patent inequality, he had damaged the Frenchman and avenged his unfortunate headless captain.

Promotion to post captain was the desired, and as far as the Admiralty could judge from his somewhat extravagant report, fully justified result.

But to Hoare's chagrin, *Seraphim* went almost immediately into refit and he to a shore post. As divisional captain for a clutch of south coast Sea Fencible detachments, he found himself commanding half a dozen lieutenants, assorted human flotsam and jetsam of the Channel ports, and temporary owner of the scruffy huts that served as their bases.

This was not the glory he sought, but he had soon discovered that he could leave all the work to his lieutenants and devote his own more valuable time to embellishing his social life and keeping his name, and the minor fame he claimed at every opportunity for his skirmish with the French, in the eyes of the county set.

In short, Hoare, the almost aristocratic self-proclaimed hammer of the French, was a poseur and social climber par excellence.

*

Before parting with Anson to attend another a social event, he told him: 'Let's get this clear from the outset – if you want rid of your bosun or to make any other changes, just do it. I expect an officer of your rank and experience to get on with your job and not come bleating to me whenever you have a problem.'

Anson was deadpan. 'Of course, sir, with your permission.'

'Carry on Anson, there's a good fellow.' And, as an afterthought: 'By the by, as I was saying, about the importance of the social scene, your people are local, ain't they?'

Anson nodded. 'More or less, sir. My father's rector at Hardres-with-Farthingham and my brother's a minor canon at Canterbury Cathedral.'

'Really? That's splendid. Perhaps you'll ensure that they put me on any invitation lists that might be going. In my division I need to get in among the county movers and shakers, what?'

Anson replaced his hat. 'Of course, sir. I'm sure there're many who'd like to meet the hero of an engagement with the French.'

Appallingly, Captain Hoare showed no sign of registering the heavy irony.

Whatever, Anson left with a sense of relief. Hoover and Fagg could be brought in without further ado and clearly he would be able to run the detachment exactly as he wanted without any interference from the gallant captain.

As he walked up the old High Street heading for the Rose Inn, Anson wondered what had really happened to his predecessor. Was the pike training kerfuffle enough to make him want to vanish? Would even a drunkard risk his career by disappearing of his own accord? If he cared nothing for his commission, why had he not simply resigned?

Or was there a more sinister reason for his non-appearance, and could he have been marooned in France as Lillicrap had hinted to Hoover?

As he crossed Rendezvous Street and entered the inn, Anson resolved that as soon as he was able to establish himself as the new detachment commander down at Seagate he would seek to discover exactly what had befallen Lieutenant Crispin.

24

Charged with finding their own accommodation, Fagg and Hoover had steered well clear of the Rose. 'That there's orficers only now, so us'll find somewhere a bit more lower deck,' Fagg announced, and the marine was happy to agree.

Life under the same roof as their officer would be like being on parade round the clock. The other main coaching inn, the King's Arms, was also frequented by what passed in these parts as the upper crust, and was a might too expensive.

Somewhere a little more relaxed beckoned. If they checked into one of the Seagate pubs they would be mixing with the fishermen and boatmen who were likely as not members of the detachment, men who would be unhappy to have their new bosun and master-at-arms living in one of their drinking dens.

So Hoover proposed the British Lion in Folkestone, where he had stayed during his reconnaissance visit and where he was again welcomed by the obliging landlord. It was cosy and friendly, the clientele being mainly shopkeepers and the like rather than seafarers who would have viewed any uniformed stranger as a potential threat to their liberty.

So it was that over another tankard of ale they quickly struck a bargain with the landlord, taking two small rooms for an indefinite period.

Once settled, Fagg confided: 'What I need now more'n anyfink is to find meself a woman. I could just go a round or two with some nice cuddly lady, a widder woman with a bit of flesh on her, p'raps. One of them as you can pull on comfortable, like an old sea boot!'

Hoover, brought up far more straight-laced than Fagg had been in the stews of Chatham's Smithfield Banks, frowned his disapproval.

But rather than get into a debate, he announced that he was off to inform Lieutenant Anson where they were now lodging. And with some relief, Fagg clumped up the stairs to his newly acquired room to try out the bed, study the ceiling and give his throbbing ankle a rest.

*

While Anson was in the inn's stables, supervising as Ebony was being tacked up for his ride to Seagate, the landlord called him to the bar where a fellow officer was waiting for him.

The man, well-built with a lived-in face, blond hair queued at the back and wearing a naval officer's uniform that had clearly seen much service, stood as he entered and offered his hand. 'Anson? I'm the most popular man in town – Matthew Coney of the impress!'

Anson smiled at the irony. The lieutenant commanding the local press gang would be about as popular as a fox in your hen-house. He shook the proffered hand and asked: 'Will you take a drink?'

They sat alone in the bar that had miraculously emptied in seconds. Coney raised his hands in mock surrender. 'See what I mean? Wherever I go, all the men suddenly find an urgent reason to be elsewhere.'

The landlord appeared with a jug of wine and two glasses and Anson winked at him. 'Worry not, Mr Griggs, Lieutenant Coney's off watch – and anyway, I expect he'll think you a touch too old to be taken up for sea service!'

The impress officer was used to such banter and took it with good grace. 'Yes, yes, all very amusing. But as you might imagine, the impress service wasn't my choice. It was either this or being cast up on the beach on half pay.'

Anson sympathised. 'You could say the same for me. I would have given my eye teeth for almost any job afloat, but that wasn't to be, so here I am, about to take command of a bunch of harbour rats.'

Coney confessed: 'I'd rather be in your shoes than mine. Pressing men who don't want to serve is no sinecure and it can be devilish unsettling if you allow it to get to you. Wailing wives and children, complaining mayors and magistrates – you've no idea ...'

Anson asked about the fate of his predecessor, but Coney knew no more than he did himself. 'Crispin was not just a hard drinker. It was more like an illness with him. It's hardly surprising that he appears to have come to a bad end.'

'What about his bosun? MacIntyre, isn't it?'

'He's a bit of a bully boy and I could do with more like him in the impress. In fact, he's given us some pretty good tip-offs of late.'

'Would you consider taking him, if I wanted to bring in my own man, that is?'

Coney shrugged. 'In my line of business you need a few hard cases like him, so I'll certainly give it thought. '

'Thank you. I'm just off to Seagate but will be in touch.'

'Then I wish you joy of your new command and hope you'll be happier in your berth than I am in mine!'

They parted swearing mutual support should the need arise.

*

Over the door of the large shed-like building was a chalked sign that read 'S. Fencibles – Seagate Det.'

Anson tied Ebony to a rail outside and pushed at the door. After the sunlight outside, he had to peer into the gloomy interior for some seconds before he could make anything out.

A lone, grizzled man in a striped shirt was seated at a trestle table, engrossed in making entries in a large leather-bound book. He looked up, blinking as he focused on the tall figure silhouetted in the doorway.

'An' vot can I do fer you, cully. Come t'join the fencibles has you?'

Anson guessed, correctly, that this was one of Bosun MacIntyre's bully-boy mates. He barked: 'Stand up when a naval officer enters!'

There was something so authoritative about the gaunt figure that convinced Bosun's Mate Lillicrap this was no joker. Sullen and reluctant, and after a pause bordering on insolence, he rose slowly to his feet.

Anson entered, strode up to the table and looked the man in the eye. 'My name is Anson, the new detachment commander. And you are?'

The man did not respond quickly enough and Anson barked: 'Answer, damn you!'

The man croaked: 'Lillicrap, bosun's mate …'

Anson growled: 'Sir!'

'Lillicrap … sir.'

Anson wrinkled his nose. 'Ah well, a rose by any other name.'

Puzzled, the man asked: 'Rose, what rose?'

'Never mind. Now, Mr Bosun's Mate Lillicrap, where is the bosun?'

'Down at the pub gettin' 'is, er, dinner … sir.'

Anson's eye fell upon the ledger. Lillicrap made to close it, but the officer read much into the move and held out his hand. 'I'll take the book, thank you. The detachment's muster and payroll I presume?'

'But the bosun says not to let anyone 'ave the book, sir, it being conferdential like.'

Anson stared him down. 'As I have told you, I am the new commander of this detachment. Now, give me the book.'

Reluctantly, realising there was no alternative, Lillicrap pushed the heavy ledger towards the officer.

Anson sat down in the only chair and opened the book. The pages were laid out in columns. To the left were the names of detachment members with their civilian occupations, addresses, ages, marital status, number of children and so on, and to the right were what appeared to be records of attendance at training sessions, and pay.

He noted that most of those listed were connected to the sea – boatmen, fishermen and the like. Their ages varied from 17 to a few men in their 50s. Most of the married men had several children.

Some of the names, he noticed, were marked with a small cross.

Anson demanded: 'What do these marks mean?'

Lillicrap shook his head. 'No idea what-so-hever … sir.' He had responded a little too quickly and emphatically to be entirely believable, and again the delayed 'sir' bordered on insolence.

His hasty denial confirmed Anson's gut feeling that the book might reveal some kind of wrong-doing.

Making a mental note to deal with Lillicrap when it best suited him, he snapped the volume shut and rose, putting it under his arm.

'Bosun won't take kindly to the book leavin' here,' Lillicrap blustered. 'He'll be needin' it for dolin' out the trainin' money.'

Fixing the man with a steely stare, Anson spoke menacingly. 'You can tell the bosun that he has a new master. Tell him that I will be going through this ledger with a toothpick. And tell him to wait on me at the pub here, the Mermaid is it not, at noon on Friday when I will be ready to interview him.'

Such was the authority in the officer's voice that Lillicrap could not help himself replying: 'Aye aye, sir!'

*

Next morning Anson rose early and began to study the detachment muster roll in detail, making notes as he went.

What struck him, immediately, was that those men with a cross after their names appeared to be the most regular attenders at training sessions. In fact, according to the book, every one of them had attended every session to date, receiving the shilling they were entitled to each time they turned out.

Attendance by the rest was more haphazard, and a few who had the letter P after their names appeared to have left the unit after only a few weeks.

The entries took up only a few pages, but some instinct told Anson to flick through the rest of the book, and there, sure enough, on the last page was another, shorter list of names. There was a series of weekly dates, and against each name a row of ticks up to date as of the previous Friday. But in several cases the row of ticks had ended a month or two ago, except for a man by the name of Jacob Shallow. The row of ticks against his name had ended two weeks before and the letter P entered after the last tick.

Lacking up-to-date local knowledge, Anson decided to take the Rose Inn's landlord into his confidence. Years of weighing up men told him Griggs was trustworthy, and, like most publicans, a mine of local information. He seemed to know everything and everyone in and around the area and had clearly taken a shine to his new, potentially long-term, paying guest.

After breakfast Anson asked him back to his room and took him through the list of names.

Griggs knew almost all at least by name, except those marked in the ledger with a cross. He knew none of these. 'I'm taken somewhat aback, sir. Thought I knew pretty well everyone round here, or at least had heard of them by name. But I've never heard of these men. Must be newcomers.'

The few marked with a P he did know, as local tradesmen. But they had recently been pressed into the navy and were now serving afloat. Hence the letter P, Anson surmised. But how could that be, if they had a fencible's protection?

He turned to the back of the ledger and showed Griggs the list of names with ticked dates. 'Do these names mean anything to you?'

'Indeed they do! These are tradespeople and the like. Tom Oldfield's a butcher, Joe Hobbs is a cobbler, George Boxer's an undertaker and Sampson Marsh is a fish-monger down at the harbour.'

'What about Jacob Shallow?'

Griggs frowned, trying to make sense of it all. 'Why, he's a greengrocer. Well, he was 'til he got pressed into the navy a couple of weeks back. His wife hasn't heard from him since he was taken, and she's havin' to run the business with only their children and Jacob's old father to help her. They've been trying to get the mayor to complain to the impress officer, but nothing's been done. Pity, the business was already failing and I doubt they'll be able to save it now.'

'Tell me, did Shallow and the rest on this list have any association with the navy or the sea?'

The landlord smiled. 'It'd be difficult round here not to have some sort of connection to the sea. Jacob Shallow was a boatman afore he married into a farmer's family and set himself up as a greengrocer. Oldfield and Hobbs were both fishermen afore they swallowed the anchor.'

He explained: 'Hereabouts when times is hard or you get a long spell of bad weather you need a second string to make a living and anyone like Tom Oldfield, who's good at gutting and boning fish, makes a fair job of butchering, too. Joe Hobbs was always one for mending nets, splicing ropes an' all, so he took to cobbling pretty well.'

'What about Boxer and Marsh?'

The landlord scratched his head. 'Don't know much about Boxer. He has the look of a navy man, but I try to keep out of the way of undertakers, so I don't know for sure. But there's not a lot of doubt about Sampson. Well, at any rate 'tis rumoured he was captain of a gun in a man-of-war. Yes, I reckon all those on this here list could have more'n a drop of seawater in their blood.'

'Is Marsh a deserter?' asked Anson.

The question provoked amusement. 'Dear me no, sir! He's what you might call a God-fearing man, a reg'lar chapel-goer, true as a die.'

'And now he's a fishmonger down at the harbour, you say?'

'That's right. His shop's the smartest and cleanest on The Stade. You can't miss it.'

Thanking him, Anson asked him to keep the matter to himself and the landlord readily agreed.

As Griggs went to close the door, Anson held up his hand. 'One more thing, tell me, do you know what became of Lieutenant Crispin?'

The landlord glanced behind him to make sure no-one was listening. 'You know about the rumpus down at the harbour when your lot was training with pikes?'

'I do, but do you know what happened to the officer afterwards?'

The man gave an evasive look. 'I can't get involved in this, sir. A landlord hears a lot of things, 'specially when there's been drink taken … but we're a bit like priests who never let on what they hear in confession. If word got out that I was tale-telling, I'd pretty soon lose custom, or worse.'

It was clear from his answer that the man did know something about Crispin's disappearance. Anson reassured him: 'Anything you tell me will stay with me, on my honour, never fear.'

Still clearly uneasy, the landlord replied almost inaudibly: 'Some say as he was put ashore in France, drunk, still in his uniform, and not a penny piece in his pockets.'

'By whom, smugglers?'

The man nodded reluctantly.

'Local men?'

He shrugged and whispered: 'Couldn't say, even if I knew.' And before Anson could ask anything else, he quickly closed the door and left, his footsteps setting the floorboards creaking in the passage as he headed for the stairs.

Alone again, Anson pondered his predecessor's likely fate. After the shambolic pike training it would not be surprising if some of the fencibles had decided to rid themselves of the man who had made them a laughing stock.

Or had the bosun seized the opportunity to off-load him? If it were true that Crispin had been marooned across the Channel, the likelihood was that he would have been quickly picked up by the authorities and would by now be kicking his heels in a French prison, or, worse, selling everything he knew about English coastal defences for drink.

Either way, Anson could do nothing about it now.

Instead he stared at the muster payroll. It was pretty clear now. Those names completely unknown to the landlord were almost certainly fictitious, and their 100 per cent recorded attendance was no doubt aimed at falsely obtaining the maximum amount of training pay for the perpetrators of the swindle.

The list at the back of the ledger was of real men and the P after the names of local tradesmen was self-evident. It marked those the landlord knew to have been victims of the press gang, the most recent being Shallow. But protection against the impress went with membership of the Sea Fencibles. So why had these particular men been pressed?

And as for the others listed at the back of the ledger, did the regular sums of money against each name mean that they were being blackmailed to keep themselves clear of the press? Had Jacob Shallow's failing business meant that he could no longer pay for protection, and had the blackmailers arranged for the press gang to take him, maybe as an example to the others on that list?

Anson was now convinced he had uncovered a lucrative fraud – claiming pay for men who did not exist. And he guessed it probably also involved fingering into naval slavery anyone who did not go along with MacIntyre's schemes, or could not or would not cough up protection money.

And could this be the real reason for Lieutenant Crispin's disappearance? A drunkard he may have been, but supposing he had found out about the racket, threatened to expose the perpetrators, and been silenced? If so, Anson could be placing himself in grave danger if he took the matter further.

In order to prove wrong-doing, he needed to find victims willing to provide evidence and to that end he now went systematically through the list of supposed blackmail victims.

Then he sent for Fagg, instructing him to seek out Sampson Marsh down at the harbour, and despatched the inn's pot boy to find George Boxer.

25

Summoned to the Rose, where Anson was sitting waiting for him in a secluded corner of the bar, Boxer was sullen. 'Why've you called me in? Your bully-boy isn't due until Friday.'

Anson gestured to a vacant chair and passed the ledger page with the blackmail list across the table. 'Check the number of ticks for payments you have made. Are they correct?'

The man glanced at them. 'You must know they are.'

'Will you sign a statement confirming how much you have paid, and to whom?'

Boxer was mystified. 'Why would you want that? You know the figures.'

Anson shook his head. 'No. I know you have been blackmailed into paying protection money, but I do not know the amounts. Armed with that information, and a sworn statement from you, and from others on that list, I will be able to bring the blackmailers to justice.'

Boxer's face showed a mixture of hope and disbelief.

'I am what you might call a new broom here, Mister Undertaker, and I intend to clean out this Augean stable. There will be no more blackmail and no more fingering men for the impress. But I need your help, so will you co-operate?'

The undertaker might not have been familiar with the Labours of Hercules, but he caught the officer's drift. He pondered for a while, then nodded. 'I've felt shame at giving in to blackmail, but I had to for the sake of my family and the business. Yes, I'd like to nail the bastards who've been screwing me – and who gave poor Jacob Shallow to the press gang.'

'Good man!' Anson was triumphant, but could see that Boxer, although determined, was still a worried man.

'I promise you that you'll not regret this.'

Boxer shrugged resignedly. 'I won't regret MacIntyre and his bully boys getting their comeuppance. But I'm old enough and ugly enough to know that the impress will hear who's shopped their slave-traffickers and will come for me one of these nights.'

'Then you need a proper protection and I can offer you one.'

'You can … sir?' It was Boxer's first acknowledgement of Anson's commission – and that he was now dealing with a proper officer.

Anson explained: 'I have now taken over the Seagate Sea Fencible detachment. The blackmailers are being removed and the unit will forthwith be run on proper official navy lines. Those who sign up will get a shilling a day for the time they put in, and a cast-iron protection against the press gang. Are you interested?'

Boxer nodded. 'I knew that before, sir, and I would have dearly loved to have the protection but, protection or not, MacIntyre shopped anyone who wouldn't toe his line and I couldn't have done that, so I paid up.'

'Well, you can join now although in truth you'd be more use as a pioneer, digging holes and suchlike. It's what you do, is it not?'

Boxer protested: 'It isn't digging holes, sir. Undertaking is making all the arrangements when someone passes on: dignified funerals, black horses, hearse an' all the trimmings for them as can afford it – more modest interments for those as can't.'

Anson asked: 'Since I've yet to meet anyone who's lived for ever, I take it you're probably not short of a guinea or two?'

'That's right, it's a good business, and I've got a nice house up the town.'

'But to get the proper protection, you're willing now to enlist for the fencibles?'

Boxer pulled back the sleeve of his coat to reveal a tattoo of a fouled anchor.

'Now that you've told me the score, I'll come clean with you. It's this, sir. What with the press always on the go and knowing that I've helped shop MacIntyre it'll only be a matter of time before they stop me, see this here anchor and take me up.'

No landsman would sport an anchor, ranking in popularity as sailors' adornments with ripe-chested mermaids, bleeding hearts, old ships and a variety of wildlife from serpents to – British – lions.

'So you were a man-of-war's man before you took to undertaking?' Anson asked.

'I cannot deny it, sir, but—'

'Run?'

'No, no, not run, sir. I'm no deserter. I never ran. I was a seaman and sometime pusser's assistant in the old *Brunswick* on account of being able to read and write and being good with numbers. But I was wounded at The Glorious First of June.'

'In that scrap with the *Vengeur*? A bloody encounter that was—'

'Aye, sir. Anyway, they paid me off. Thought I'd most probably lose my leg. But over time it's got better so's I only limp on a damp day or when I've walked too far. So I took to undertaking on account of this girl I met. Well, her father had followed the business all his life, and his father afore him. So he took me into the business when I married my Lizzie, and now he's retired I run it. Someone must have told MacIntyre I'd been a navy man and that I'd now got a good business. And that's why he got his claws in me.'

Anson stroked his chin. 'And now that you're not going to be paying him for protection you fear the impress men will still take you for a seaman on the strength of that tattoo?'

'That's right, sir. When there's a hot press they'll take anyone they can get their hands on whether or not he smells of tar and rolls when he walks.'

'And you have had some close shaves?'

'They're always a-hunting through Seagate, Folkestone and Dover and I've come close to being taken several times.' He added meaningfully: 'It's cost me a bit paying off the gangs, too. So to be honest with you, I'm desperate for a protection – desperate enough to pay the blackmail money. And now, if you've got rid of the likes of MacIntyre, I'll be happy to get one with the fencibles.'

Anson nodded. 'Alright Mr Boxer, you've got yourself a protection. But only as long as you, er, undertake your duties as a Sea Fencible with due diligence. I will carry no passengers.'

The undertaker was delighted. 'I surely will. And thank you kindly, sir.'

Hoover came into the bar and Anson beckoned him over. 'Fall out, Mr Boxer, and give the sergeant here your details: full name, age, marital status, abode, number of children, trade. Sergeant, put him down as a seaman undertaker.'

'Aye aye, sir.'

'Then, once you're sworn and have your precious protection, I'll take down your statement myself and you can put your name towards getting MacIntyre the desserts he deserves.'

It was a mutually advantageous bargain. Boxer had his protection, and instead of yet another lubber, part-time smuggler or near simpleton, Anson had a prime man-of-war's man, and a pusser's writer to boot, intelligent, clearly honest; a man who had come through a major sea battle. And a man whose undertaking skills might also come in useful.

*

From his scruffy appearance there was nothing to suggest that Fagg was a newly-promoted petty officer of the Royal Navy.

Seated on a bollard, he had a mug of ale purchased from a nearby pub in one fist and a long clay pipe in the other. From time to time, he sipped one and sucked on the other as he watched the comings and goings of small craft in the harbour. His game leg was stuck out in front of him, testament to his sacrifice for King and country.

Seagulls strutted around him, cackling and brawling over scavenged scraps.

For a while he continued to gaze seaward, showing no interest in the fishmonger's shop behind him. But when the fishmonger emerged during a lull in trade, Fagg half turned and touched his knitted woolly hat in salute.

'Mornin'.'

Sampson Marsh wiped the fish scales from his hands on his apron. 'Mornin' to you, brother. You're a new face round here.'

'That I am brother, jest washed up here on account of the navy ain't got much use for game-legged foretopmen. But you'd know that, 'avin' swallowed the anchor yerself ...'

This clearly puzzled Marsh. 'And what makes you think that, brother?'

'The same fing what makes me fink you've done some years afore the mast, captained a gun, left honourable like – and now 'as t'pay a certain Bosun MacIntyre to forgit that you'd still make a prime seaman worth the impress men draggin' orf to a receivin' ship ... brother.'

Startled now, and apprehensive that unpleasant things were in the offing, the fishermonger looked nervously around as if expecting a press gang to be waiting to pounce. Reassured that the threat was not imminent, he beckoned Fagg into the shop, hung a closed notice on the door and locked it.

'Now brother, p'haps you'll tell me what this is about.'

'Gladly, mate. I've come t'warn you that the next hot press will take you, bribe or no bribe.'

Marsh showed his annoyance. 'MacIntyre knows full well I'm paid up to date. Who in hell are you? How d'you know about me? And who got you to put the squeeze on me? Is it Black Mac?'

'No, no matey. I'm not puttin' the squeeze on anyone and I'm nuffink to do with Black Mac. I've come from the detachment's new orficer to offer you a protection, watertight agin any press, and you won't 'ave to pay a penny piece. Matter of fact, we'll pay you. All you need to do is tell the orficer 'xactly what this MacIntyre bloke's bin up to …'

Half an hour of persuasion, and Fagg emerged clutching a bag of fish along with the fishmonger's word, sealed with a spit-and-handshake, that he would appear next morning at the Rose to sign on the dotted line for a Sea Fencible, and dish the dirt on Black Mac.

For Sampson Marsh, the encounter had clearly come as a great relief. A shilling a day for the odd bit of showing the greenhorns how to fight the great guns was a bargain compared to paying out bribes and risking being taken by the impress anyway.

And Fagg was cock-a-hoop, bursting to report his success in finding someone else willing to testify against MacIntyre and at the same time recruiting a trained man-of-war's gun captain. Lieutenant Anson would be delighted.

*

Next morning, after spending two hours with the lieutenant, Sampson Marsh happily signed the statement the officer took down, spilling the beans on the rackets MacIntyre and his bully boys had been running. Then he signed on as a Sea Fencible, drank off the free tankard of ale Fagg brought him, and pocketed his first shilling, confessing ruefully: 'That's a first. Usually it cost me every time I had a brush with your lot …'

Next to appear in answer to the officer's summons, were the butcher Oldfield and Hobbs the cobbler. Both had similar stories, were visibly relieved to hear that MacIntyre was no longer a threat – and were happy to sign on as fencibles.

After they had left, Anson took out his watch. Bosun MacIntyre had much to answer for – and there was just time to get to the Mermaid for noon.

*

When he entered the bar and looked around at the handful of drinkers, his eyes were immediately drawn to a thickset man with the look of an old sailor, short but with powerful shoulders, tattooed neck, shaven head, and a nose that looked as if it had been broken several times. It was noticeable that the other drinkers were keeping their distance.

'MacIntyre?'

The man remained leaning on the bar, tankard clutched in his big misshapen right hand. He took a deliberate sip of his drink before half turning and staring at the newcomer. 'Who wants him?'

Anson reddened. The man had been summoned and must know by whom. If there had been any room for doubt, the uniform said it all. No, this was studied insolence.

'I think you know exactly who I am, Mr Bosun MacIntyre.'

The Glaswegian took another swig of his drink and wiped his mouth with the back of his hand, revealing teeth like ancient lichen-covered tombstones, leaning every which way.

He looked the officer up and down with a malign leer, starting slightly when he saw the ledger under his arm. 'So, you're Anson, are ye?'

'Lieutenant Anson. That I am, and now you may put down your drink and walk over to the detachment where we can speak privately.'

MacIntyre looked round at the other drinkers who were pretending not to be listening. They had learned from experience not to get on the wrong side of this hard nut who had been known to deck a man just for looking at him in the wrong way.

'Why should I care if these fuckin' southern worms hear what I say t'ye? Anyways, I've paid for this wet and I'll drink it doon afore I go.'

Ignoring the man's insolent tone, Anson turned on his heel and walked out of the bar into the street. MacIntyre knocked back the dregs of his drink and banged the tankard down on the bar, startling the other drinkers. He gave them a last contemptuous stare and slowly followed the officer outside.

They made an incongruous pair: the tall, slim, smart young officer and the short, bull-necked bruiser lurching alongside him with an alcohol-fuelled rolling gait.

Saying nothing, Anson strode off.

'Where're yous going?'

'As I said, to the detachment. I have questions to ask you.'

MacIntyre snarled: 'Ask away, it's all shipshape and I'm the one who's held it together since that other officer clown pissed off.'

But Anson held his peace until they reached the detachment hut.

Inside, he sat down in the one chair at the small table, leaving the Scotsman standing, and placed the ledger in front of him. 'Now, Mr Bosun MacIntyre, let me give you the facts of life. You are history as far as the Seagate detachment is concerned. I have my own men. I want you out.'

MacIntyre responded with a belligerent stare, but Anson faced him down. 'I am not Lieutenant Crispin and I am not a southern worm, but your superior officer with the full power of naval discipline behind me, and I am sir to you, whether or not we are in public. Understand?'

The petty officer clasped and unclasped his fists and stared sullenly back. 'Didna' call ye a southern worm—'

'You can call me what you like so long as there's a sir at the beginning or end of it. Now, answer me this: how many phantom fencibles have you been drawing money for and how many men have you blackmailed into paying you not to shop them to the impress?'

MacIntyre looked down at the ledger shiftily, but said nothing.

'I'll say this for you. You've kept a good record – good enough to show your court martial exactly what you've been up to these past months. You've made a pretty penny and no doubt you've made some of these men's lives a misery.'

'It wasna' me ...' the Bosun blustered, but Anson shook his head. 'You're about to try and blame it on Crispin aren't you? Well, that won't wash. I have witnesses who will finger you. You are a crook and a bully and you are hereby drafted out of here. If you're lucky the impress service will take you on. They need hard nuts like you. But if you give me or any of my men any further trouble, it's a court martial.'

He tapped the ledger. 'Just remember, there's evidence aplenty here and I'll be holding on to it – just in case!'

With a sudden kick that belied his stocky build, MacIntyre knocked the table away and made a grab for the ledger. Anson, although expecting something of the sort, was genuinely taken by surprise at the speed of the man's move, stumbled as he tried to rise, and was sent sprawling by a wild punch from the bosun that caught him on the shoulder.

Before he could rise, MacIntyre had fled the building clutching the precious ledger under his arm.

26

Rising slowly, Anson massaged his shoulder. There was no doubt that the man packed a powerful punch – and now he had the ledger.

But the new detachment commander had read his man well. By grabbing the muster book the bosun had confirmed his guilt, but it would do him no good whatsoever. When he came to dispose of the evidence he would discover to his alarm that it now contained only the remaining blank pages.

Back in his room, Anson had used his cut-throat razor to remove all the sheets containing information about the detachment, including the incriminating lists revealing the extent of the blackmail and fictitious names scams. Those pages were now secreted in his room at the Rose Inn.

Maybe the former bosun would come in search of them. If he did, Anson would be ready for him, but for now he needed to meet up with Lieutenant Coney again to confirm MacIntyre's transfer to the impress service.

A court martial for fraud and blackmail, let alone striking a superior officer, would have been in order, but first and foremost in Anson's thinking was the need to avoid embarrassment to the service and further disruption to the rebuilding and training of the Seagate detachment.

*

He found Coney at the impress rendezvous, dealing with the inevitable pile of paperwork that seems to dog naval officers serving ashore, and fending off a tearful group of female supplicants pleading for the release of their recently pressed menfolk.

Relieved at the opportunity Anson's arrival gave him to escape his duties for a while, he motioned his visitor to the privacy of an adjoining room and asked: 'What can I do for you?'

Anson rubbed his bruised shoulder. 'I have had, shall we say, a brush with MacIntyre. I found evidence that he had been extorting money from some of the men, threatening them with being taken up for sea service, and claiming for men I don't believe exist.'

'So he has a good imagination?'

'You could say that,' Anson said ruefully.

'So you will start your new command with a court martial?'

Anson shook his head. 'Certainly there is a case to answer. I already have statements from reliable witnesses and I believe I could find plenty more willing to finger him, but it would be time-consuming, disruptive and bad for the navy's reputation. My mission is to re-form the detachment and train the men to meet the invasion threat, not drown myself in court martial paperwork.'

That appeared to strike a chord with the paper-plagued impress officer. 'So?'

'So, I just want to be rid of him, forthwith!'

Coney sighed. 'Well, I've thought it over, as you asked, and from what I've seen and heard of the man I cannot say I warm to him. But if it helps we'll take him. My lot are hardly angels, so he'll be among fellow ruffians.'

Relieved, Anson warned: 'He'll need to be watched in case he gets up to more mischief.'

'Where is he now?'

'Probably in one of the pubs drowning his sorrows at the sudden drop in his income.'

'Right, I'll put feelers out and summon him to report to me.'

'And you'll be sure to get a grip of him?'

'Never fear. I'll let him know in no uncertain terms that if he puts so much as a toe, let alone a foot, wrong we'll bring up the evidence for a court martial.'

Anson smiled. 'That's very good of you. I will be greatly in your debt, but I have one further favour to ask of you. I'm anxious to discover the fate of a man called Shallow. He was blackmailed by MacIntyre and when he couldn't pay up he was betrayed and taken by the impress in Hythe not long since. If it's not too late, I'd like him back.'

By law only professional seamen could be pressed, and Anson stressed: 'Shallow has done a bit of harbour boatwork in the past but he's no seaman – he's a greengrocer.'

'Taken up recent, you say?' Coney queried. 'If that's so, he'll doubtless still be in a receiving ship – at Chatham more than likely. I'll look into it and see what I can do.'

'In return, you can have MacIntyre's mate Lillicrap and a couple more of his bully boys with tar on their hands if you wish. I believe they were in on his rackets. We'll be well rid of them in the fencibles but they'll make very satisfactory man-of-war's men.'

The impress officer well knew that to suggest a man had tarred hands indicated he was a professional seaman – and therefore prime press fodder. 'Done! A press gang hard nut and several right seamen for one greengrocer is a pretty fair exchange.' Coney held out his hand and Anson shook it warmly.

*

Before the week was out, ex-bosun MacIntyre was with the press gang that cornered Lillicrap and two more of his former mates in a raid on a Seagate drinking den and hauled them off, protesting vociferously, to the hold of a pressing tender with an iron grating and armed marines ensuring that they stayed put. For them, a long spell of virtual sea slavery had begun.

Two days later, they were transferred on board an old man-of-war employed as a receiving ship in Chatham to await allocation to undermanned vessels of the Royal Navy.

While they were being processed, the bewildered greengrocer Jacob Shallow was told he was being discharged, handed a shilling to help him on his way, and told he was free to go home.

*

Fagg and Hoover lost no time in making the shabby detachment building shipshape.

In his element as master procurer, Fagg set about obtaining everything needed to get the near-bare building up and running as a training base. As a marine, Hoover's eye for smartness was exercised. Rubbish disappeared and such equipment as he found there was tidied.

Word soon got around that the Seagate Special Boat Detachment of the Sea Fencibles was under new command: new officer, new bosun, and new master-at-arms, and that all existing members were to report at six o'clock the following Friday evening whereupon they would receive a day's pay apiece.

It was a clever ploy. The fencibles would quickly work out that they could do their normal day's work and still receive a shilling for just an evening in the service of King George.

With detachment numbers severely depleted thanks to Black Mac's machinations, Anson set about composing a handbill:

'SEA FENCIBLES
NOTICE IS HEREBY GIVEN
That all persons residing on the Coast between Folkestone and Dymchurch, or in adjacent parishes, who are not already engaged in any Volunteer Corps, and are ambitious of stepping forward at the alarming crisis, in defence of their King and Country, and for the protection of their Families and Property, against the formidable threats of an infatuated and implacable enemy, have now a glorious opportunity of manifesting their loyalty by enrolling in the Seagate Special Boat Detachment of SEA FENCIBLES, raised in the above district, for which purpose Lieutenant Anson will attend on WEDNESDAY, at the Mermaid in Seagate, in the forenoon and there explain to such as may be inclined to enrol themselves, the nature and extent of the service.

God Save the King and State.'

Within a few days the printed version was to be seen posted around the town, and Fagg delivered copies for publication in the local newsheet.

*

Next Wednesday, the first of what was to prove a steady trickle of would-be new recruits sought Anson out.

The call to arms in his poster had clearly begun to lure fish. Those who could read were no doubt spreading the word. And a regime that did not include MacIntyre but did include a shilling for a day's training, and the promise of a protection against the press gang, had great attraction, as Anson learned from his first caller.

He sat at a table in a corner of the Mermaid bar, apparently engrossed in paperwork, a pile of coins at his elbow, and pretended not to notice the first man who came looking for him.

The man, shabbily dressed and wispy-bearded, but thick set and sturdy, looked around furtively before sidling up to the table. Anson's pen continued scratching, and after being ignored for some minutes the newcomer cleared his throat noisily and ventured: ''Scuse me. Are you …?'

Anson paused mid-scribble and looked up, noting the man's single gold earring, a sure give-away of someone whose work took him afloat. 'The new Sea Fencible officer? Indeed I am. And what can I do for you?'

The man snatched off his hat revealing an almost completely bald pate which he proceeded to knuckle in salute. He mumbled: 'I've come 'bout the notice what's bin put up round about. Sea Fencibles and whatnot ...' And, clearly wishing to be respectful, he added 'your worship'.

'Sir is quite sufficient for an officer of His Majesty's navy. You are what ... a fisherman, boatman?' Anson avoided the temptation to add smuggler, which he knew most of the local harbour rats were when the opportunity arose.

'Yes, sir, sorry, sir. A bit of both, sir.'

'So you've come to find out more about joining the fencibles?'

'Yes, yer worship, I mean sir.'

Anson looked him in the eye. 'Why now? Why not sooner? The detachment has been here some time.'

''Twas your notice, sir.'

'Come, man. There was a notice calling for recruits before. Why didn't you come forward then?'

The man looked shifty, wringing his hat in his hands, and Anson coaxed him. 'Come on, no one's listening except me. Let's have the truth now.'

Looking round to make sure no one could overhear, he muttered: 'It was Black Mac, sir.'

'Do I take that to be Bosun MacIntyre?'

'That's the truth, sir.'

Anson leaned back in his chair, balancing on its back legs. 'And now you know Bosun MacIntyre has been drafted out of the fencibles?'

'I do, yer worship.' Anson raised an eyebrow. 'I mean I do, sir. I know 'e's gorn, from the fencibles like.'

'Very well, let me get this straight. You didn't want to join the fencibles because of MacIntyre?' A nod. 'And now you want to join because of MacIntyre?'

Another nod. 'On account of 'im being gorn, like. Y'see, sir, he's got a bit of a repitation like.'

'So I've heard. Well, join now and you'll have a protection. But you'll have to work for it, and for your shilling a day.'

'Not afraid of 'ard graft, sir.' His gnarled hands and powerful shoulders confirmed that.

'Good to hear, Mister what's-your-name?'

'Minter, sir, Jeremiah Minter, but they always calls me Jemmy.'

'Right Jeremiah, alias Jemmy, Minter. Pull up a stool. The landlord'll draw a mug of ale for you, courtesy of the navy, and you can give me some particulars. I'll jot 'em down in this ledger and get you to sign your name or make your mark. Then you'll be a fencible.'

Minter looked anxious. 'And will I get me protection chitty straight off, sir?'

Anson waved his hand dismissively. 'Yes, yes – and your first shilling just for turning up to volunteer.'

Minter nervously grasped the tankard that the landlord, with a knowing wink at Anson, had placed in front of him and took a tentative sip of ale. 'Thankee sir, thankee very much.'

'And, Master Minter, you can do something for me?'

'I can, sir?'

'Yes, you can tell all your boatmen mates that Bosun MacIntyre really has gone, and if they'd rather be Sea Fencibles than be pressed for men-of-war they'd best get along quickly and sign on with me.'

The formalities completed, Minter left with a beaming gap-toothed grin, clutching his precious protection and first day's pay.

Anson caught the landlord's eye. 'Best start lining up the tankards, Mr Griggs. I've a shrewd suspicion we'll soon have a queue of recruits.'

27

Anson spent a night at home and breakfasted with his parents, his father scanning the *Kentish Gazette* between mouthfuls.

The Reverend Anson snorted and gesticulated at an advertisement on the front page.

'What is it dear?' His wife was well used to the rector's little outbursts whenever he spotted some annoying item in the news sheets.

'That Baptist quack is peddling his fake wares again. Bare-faced effrontery ... should be a law against it.'

'Who? And what's he peddling, father?'

'Just listen to this!' The rector jabbed the paper with his finger and read:

'Hardres Minnis. Phin. Shrubb desires to acquaint the Public, that he innoculates in the new and most approved Method (with all desirable Success) on the most reasonable Terms.'

'Against the smallpox? Why shouldn't he father? It's being put forward as a good preventative is it not?'

The rector huffed. 'Certainly, when in proper hands. But this fellow's a dissident, a Baptist! And listen to this, the newspaper informs us that his specific powders, for the cure of all sorts of agues, are sold by him at 2s 6d per dozen. That's more than a day's wage for most poor labourers. ...And he has the cheek to use God's name to sell his quack cures. He's appended this ill-written verse to his advertisement!'

Almost apoplectic, Reverend Anson quoted:

'See Britons now what Mercies God hath sent,
An Epidemic Evil to prevent,
Trust in the Lord therefore, and use the Mean,
Which safely will you from this Evil screen.'

He flung the paper down. 'Why, it's bordering on blasphemy, and what's worse, it doesn't scan!'

Anson was amused at his father's vehemence. Any mention of non-conformists had always produced a strong reaction at the rectory. And the Baptists, partly because of what the rector considered as their puritanical streak, and the fact that most had settled in an extra-parochial enclave to the west of the common to avoid having to pay tithes to the established church, were absolute anathema to him.

But of course, in a household maintained in some style by the church's own taxation system, it would be impolitic to raise that controversial subject just now.

If non-conformists of all persuasions – Methodists, Moravians, Muggletonians and whomsoever else – were normally taboo at the rectory, the local Baptists were doubly so.

The rector claimed they slunk about dressed in puritanical black preaching against just about everything including horse racing, card-playing, dancing, cockfighting – cricket, even – and ensnaring gullible yokels from his own flock. In fact, they abhorred most of the pastimes a sporting gentleman parson like him enjoyed.

Yet in his narrow view, despite their holier-than-thou demeanour and certainty about the rightness of adult baptism, they, too, had their own schisms – the General Baptists believing in unlimited atonement versus the Particular variety favouring redemption for the chosen elect.

Not least, it had grieved the rector greatly to have to admit in his official returns for church hierarchy visitations to parishes in the Canterbury Diocese that there were any non-conformists locally.

In fact, in answer to the questions on the printed form about the presence of chapels and dissenters in his parish, he had consistently written 'none' and 'six or seven' respectively, justifying – to himself at least – his misleading response by the fact that the nearest General Baptist enclave and meeting house was just outside his boundary, in extra-parochial no-man's-land between his parish and the two neighbouring livings.

'This Phineas Shrubb, was he not once a surgeon's mate in the navy?' queried Anson.

The rector nodded. 'So I understand, and you can be certain the navy's well rid of a mean-minded, dissenting, pinch-penny quack like him. Well rid!'

Anson chose not to comment, but determined to call upon the former surgeon's mate.

*

Somewhat gingerly mounted on Ebony, he rode over the downs that very afternoon to the quaintly-named hamlet of Wealden Bottom, tucked away in a narrow fold that perhaps once had been a river valley. From memories of taking part in the annual beating the bounds of his father's parish as a small boy, he recalled that it was indeed outside the grip of the Anglican church.

A scattered handful of smallholdings flanked the rough track, and a peg-legged man sitting breaking flints with a club hammer to fill potholes, pointed the way to Shrubb's flint and pink-bricked and tiled cottage with a cheery: 'Arter a cure, are ye, brother?'

Anson touched his hat and rode on, lowering himself stiffly from the saddle at the apothecary's gate.

A young woman emerged from the cottage and watched, hands on hips, as he tied his horse to a gatepost.

'If you are seeking my father I'm afraid he is out gathering, sir.'

'Lost souls?' Anson asked playfully.

She smiled. 'Always that, sir, but it's plants for his cures that he's seeking today.' Despite her severe dress and black bonnet, her smile revealed that she was no pinch-faced, dried-up old maid, but a handsome woman. Anson calculated she must be in her mid-20s.

'Miss Shrubb?'

'That is me, sir.' And noting his uniform she added: 'You are in the navy, I see.'

'As was your father?'

'He was, sir – a surgeon's mate during the American war.'

'That's why I'm here. The navy has need of his skills again.'

'I am very much afraid he is too old for the navy now, sir. He has kept to his cures these many years since my mother died. His life's work now is saving souls as a preacher and treating ailments of the body as an apothecary. I was born soon after he returned from the wars and I have never known him to go afloat in all that time ...' She hesitated as the thought occurred to her: 'Are you with the impress, sir? I hope that it has not come to taking old men ...'

196

He smilingly shook his head. 'No, no. My name is Anson, Lieutenant Anson. I am taking command of a detachment of Sea Fencibles on the coast and need a good surgeon's mate to check that they are sound of wind and limb.' And he added: 'For a price, of course.'

'Why not a doctor?'

'Because only a navy man will know if a sailor's fit to serve – and all the tricks he can pull to escape duty.'

She smiled. 'He will hear you out, sir, I'm sure, but I cannot promise more. Will you come in and I'll fetch you some beer while you are waiting?'

Following her into the cottage, he countered: 'I thought those of your religion forswore the demon drink?'

'We do, sir, just as we recommend to our members to abstain from worthless games like cricket and all forms of gambling, dancing and other such disgraces to the Christian name. But small beer is an exception. You would have to drink a great deal of it to become even mildly intoxicated and father says it's safer to drink than the water – something to do with the brewing process, I believe.'

'He should know,' said Anson. 'For myself, whenever possible I have long drunk only alcohol or boiled water. I've heard boiling it kills the creatures we can see swimming in it when we draw it from the barrels on board ship. And, by the by, I've not played cricket these ten years or more. It's a little tricky at sea ...'

She smiled at the thought, and he sipped at the beer she brought him, pleasantly surprised by the taste. Noting his approving look, she added: 'Father has a small hop garden and he is meticulous about his brew.'

'I've heard of his advertisements.'

'For cures?'

Anson nodded. 'And do they work?'

She smiled gently. 'With the Lord's help.'

'But if you take the Lord out of the equation?'

'The Lord is everywhere, Mr Anson, wouldn't your own father agree?'

He blinked. 'You have flushed me out as the parson's son, Miss Shrubb. My problem is that everyone hereabouts tars me with my father's brush. He's the man of God, not me.'

'And you are more of a man-of-war?'

He grinned at the teasing. 'Well said, Miss Shrubb. But leaving God out of it, do these cures work or no?'

'Let's say that they help, sir. Certainly boiled nettles and a root tea of bracken fern relieve diarrhoea, and sphagnum moss makes a fine bandage.'

She glanced towards the bottle-laden shelves that lined the wall. 'As you can see, there are many others – for wounds, sores, rashes, coughs and colds, headaches and stomach problems.'

'Cures for all ills then?'

'The ills are natural, so it seems natural to use the healing qualities of plants, does it not?'

Anson teased her further. 'So, conveniently your father is able to pluck these curing plants from the hedgerows and sell them on, for half a crown a time I understand?'

She flushed. 'They are God's bounty sure enough, and yes, anyone can gather them. But only a few have the knowledge to transform them into cures.'

Anson smiled. She was unlike any female he had ever met – intelligent, articulate, confident, yet gentle and vulnerable too. And attractive, in a wholesome way, despite her plain dress and bonnet. A God-botherer obviously, but somehow alluring.

'I'm teasing you, Miss Shrubb. Our naval surgeons and their mates, the better ones at least, know something of the curative properties of plants, of fruit against the scurvy and so on ...'

'It is the knowledge that counts, sir, passed down since biblical times. Like fungi, handling and consuming plants or extracts from them can be risky. Only those with certain knowledge can do this in safety. Even some who rated themselves experts have died through misidentifying and consuming poisonous species.'

'And you, too, are an expert?'

She blushed. 'I am learning, sir, ever learning. My father is the expert.'

'May I?' He indicated the bottle-filled shelves.

Nodding, she pointed out some of the labels. 'There's essence of catnip, good for alleviating headaches, and you chew the leaves to cleanse the teeth. This one's wild mint. You make a tea of it to induce sleep, and boiling these acorns makes a wash that soothes skin irritation and stops bleeding.'

'Sarah?' A call from outside heralded her father's return. Silhouetted in the doorway, Phineas Shrubb, former surgeon's mate, saver of souls and curer of the ills of the body, was a kindly-looking man, but put Anson in mind of a throw-back puritan, severely dressed as he was from head to foot in black except for the collar of a white shirt showing at his neck. He was carrying a basket of plants that he set down beside the door.

Sarah told him: 'This is Mister Anson, father, come to talk with you.'

Shrubb removed his black tricorn hat revealing a mane of iron-grey hair and luxuriant white eyebrows that gave him an oddly beetle-like look. 'Anson?' he said. 'So you must be the rector's sailor son?'

'Correct.'

'Welcome to Mount Zion.'

'Zion?'

The preacher wrinkled his nose. 'It's a small biblical conceit of mine. To us, what you would call non-conformists, naming our meeting houses and homes after sites in the holy land is a way of demonstrating our simple faith. Have you come to seek a tithe, perhaps?' the old man asked mischievously.

Anson was beginning to get the picture that the tithe system was not exactly popular.

Shrubb added: 'You may not be aware that this barbarous enclave is outside your father's, shall we say, control?'

'Please do not label me, Mr Shrubb. I am a naval officer, not an Anglican clergyman like my father. I am the navy's man, not his.'

Shrubb shrugged in surrender. 'You are a plain speaker, sir, as I hope I am. You may not know, I was once in the navy myself.'

'That, Mr Shrubb, is precisely why I'm here. I am on the navy's business, not my father's, and I am here to talk to the apothecary – the surgeon's mate – not the preacher.'

'Nor the glover,' Shrubb teased. 'I also make gloves for the winter time, you know?' He smiled. 'And what might that navy business be? I swallowed the anchor long since, sir.'

'I have come to enlist your aid, Mister Shrubb. I am just taking command of a detachment of Sea Fencibles at Seagate and I need a medical man to look over my recruits.'

Shrubb raised a bushy eyebrow. 'There are medical men aplenty in Seagate, Folkestone and Hythe, are there not?'

'I don't want one of those fashionable doctors who tell their patients what they want to hear and charge them for it in guineas. I want a naval man who's used to seamen's ways and ailments, someone who knows if they're fit to serve and when they're swinging the lead. And I have a notion that you fit the bill, Mr Shrubb.'

The preacher sat, appraising Anson, his gaze falling on the powder burns and the clearly recent v-shaped scar, while Sarah brought him a mug and poured him a drink.

'I heard about your escape from France, and what you ask is flattering to an old man, but there is a hindrance.'

'Age makes no matter to me. I can see you are as fit as men half your age.'

'It is more than that. You are the son of the rector and I am a Baptist preacher. You've been long at sea and doubtless not twigged why I mentioned that this little hamlet is extra-parochial – just outside the parish.'

Anson nodded: 'I know that. You are not part of my father's flock.'

'He might call us lost sheep. Here we are in no-man's-land and that's why we non-conformists – what your father calls dissenters or worse – choose to live here. We're not on the tithe map so we pay no taxes to your church.'

Anson bridled. 'It is not my church and my father doesn't command the Sea Fencibles. I do.'

'That may be, but he'll not look kindly on you using a dissenter to cure your men's ills.'

'Ills no, souls may be. But it's fitness you'd be assessing, and it'll be illnesses and in due time maybe wounds you'd be healing, not souls.'

Sarah, who had been following the discussion with close interest, asked: 'Do you not have faith, sir?'

Anson nodded. 'At sea, when you look up at the heavens, you can but believe in a supreme power. But I cannot abide the politics of the church. I leave that to my father and my brother.'

A knowing look passed between father and daughter. It would be difficult to live only a few miles from the rectory without being aware of the doings of Anson's father and his much disliked older son.

'You realise that as Baptists we do not accept state religion? We live by Hebrews Chapter Six, and would never do anything that might compromise our beliefs.'

From his rectory upbringing, Anson knew this referred to the biblical doctrine of general redemption and the pursuit of perfection, of baptisms, laying on of hands, resurrection of the dead, eternal judgment ...

He countered: 'As a naval officer I abide by the navy's Bible – the 37 Articles of War. There is no hindrance. Didn't Jesus say something about rendering unto Caesar the things which are Caesar's?'

'And unto God the things that are God's. The book of Matthew.' Shrubb smiled, enjoying the repartee, and sipped his beer, contemplating Anson's invitation.

Anson sensed he was close to agreeing and pressed on. 'The men we have so far are a mixture. Some are strong, right seamen – no doubt smugglers in the main – only too glad of a protection from the impress. Others are poorly nourished, sickly, and the older men have few teeth between them. I should like you to at least look 'em over and refit them as needs it. You'll be paid, of course.'

The preacher shook his head. 'This is not about pay. I will come and take a look at your men and tell you what's what and who to keep and who to reject. But that is all, and I will take not a penny piece for it. As an old navy man I will do this for the service.'

Anson gripped his hand, delighted that he had achieved all he could for now, and determined that Shrubb should become a permanent member of the detachment.

As he left he caught Sarah's eyes on him, and they exchanged the ghost of a smile.

28

A commotion greeted Anson on return to the fencible building that his new bosun had dubbed the 'stone frigate' as many a land-locked naval establishment was named despite the fact that it was built entirely of wood topped by Kent peg tiles.

Fagg, hands aloft, was fending off a short, stocky, crippled young man who was supporting himself on one wooden crutch and gesticulating with the other.

'Bugger orf, we can't take yer!'

Anson asked: 'What's the problem?'

'This bloke wants to join, sir, but we can't take 'im, can we, 'im bein' a cripple an' that?'

Anson turned to the crutch-waver, who had temporarily fallen silent, perhaps sensing different tactics would be required in the face of higher authority. 'Who are you?'

'Marsh, sir. Tom Marsh.'

'Any kin of Sampson Marsh?'

'Sampson's me uncle.'

'And you want to join us?'

'Yes, sir – an' peg-leg here won't let me, but if he's allowed to be in it why can't I? It's not as if I'm going' for a sodjer. Sea Fencibles don't march, do they?'

Anson smiled at the man's incontrovertible logic. 'No, not a lot. Mostly we'll be firing the great guns – and rowing ourselves about killing Frenchmen.' He appraised the young cripple's powerful over-developed shoulders, the result of maybe 20 years of manipulating his crutches. 'Can you row, Tom Marsh?'

'Yes, I surely can, sir. Put me in a boat with an oar or a pair of 'em an' I could row you across to Boologny single-'anded. And I can drive a pony and trap. Mebbe I can't march, but I can 'op along on these ...' he waved a crutch aloft '... good and quick as any of them you've got so far.'

'And why are you so keen to join? Do you need the shillings?' For some, he knew, the guaranteed shilling for a day's training was a strong lure.

'I ain't 'ard up,' Marsh protested. 'I've got me work as a snob, mending boots and such, and I've got me own pony and trap to get around and do a bit o' this and that to turn a penny or two. No, it ain't for the money. I want to do me bit for old England.'

Anson considered for a moment. The man could row, work horses – and his cobbling skills could prove useful. Above all, he didn't have need of a protection; even the most desperate impress officer would jib at taking a cripple. So, crippled or not, his keenness to serve made him a worthwhile acquisition.

'Very well, Tom Marsh. You shall do your bit for King and country. Get him to make his mark, bosun. He is to be one of us.'

Marsh could clearly not believe his ears. 'Oh thankee, sir, thankee. I promise you shan't regret it.'

'Somehow I'm sure I shan't, Tom Marsh. As you have your own pony and trap I will hire it when needed, for the going rate, and you can ferry me about on the King's business as well as being my personal oarsman and runner.' He shrugged. 'Well, let's say message-carrier. On a month's trial to see how it goes.'

Marsh's face was a picture of joy at his new status, but behind him Fagg grimaced. 'Some runner,' he muttered just below hearing level. 'Hopper, more like!'

*

Bosun Fagg was again taken aback when Anson announced before the men paraded for their first day's training under the new regime: 'There will be no starting – and certainly no flogging.'

'Starting' was the naval euphemism for chivvying up slow-off-the mark sailors, or beating them when they transgressed, with a rope's end.

Anson saw the doubt in the bosun's eyes, so he quickly added: 'I prefer encouraging our sailors to do their duty from cheerfulness and inclination rather than from abuse.'

'So 'ow are we goin' t'keep this bunch of vagabonds and lubbers from skiving an' slopin' orf?'

'Simple. If they slope orf, er, off, or give us any trouble whatsoever we tear up their protection and we pass their names to the impress service. They'll do the necessary.'

The mere mention of the press made Fagg shudder, safe though he was from it on various counts, not least due to his current legitimate employment with the fencibles – surely protection enough.

To every seafarer and any man of likely age living anywhere near the coast the impress conjured up a fearsome image. The press gangs, made up of rough, tough, man-of-war's men, were licensed to target, beat and virtually kidnap any man bred to the sea – 'seamen, seafaring men and persons whose occupations and callings are to work in vessels and boats upon rivers as shall be necessary to man His Majesty's Ships'. But no landsman in the coastal towns could count himself entirely safe, either.

In return for their services, the press gangs – these fishers of men – enjoyed coveted privileges: wenching, boozing and messing ashore, with plenty of licensed assault and battery, and opportunities for extorting money in exchange for better-breeched citizens' freedom – and occasionally even for sexual favours from the womenfolk of the riffraff.

Small wonder it attracted the worst, hard-drinking, womanising bullies.

Once in the bowels of a receiving ship even a bishop would have a problem disentangling himself from the navy's embraces. Possession, as far as a service desperate for hands was concerned, was all of nine points of the law.

*

'So let's get this clear, shall us? The new orficer, Mister Anson 'ere, sez there's t'be no floggin' and no startin' – right?'

There was a murmur of approval from the raggle-taggle crew of the Seagate Sea Fencibles.

'Nah, you lot are so special we ain't goin' to touch you if yer fouls up, fergets to report an' suchlike. What we're goin' t'do instead, is tear up yer sustificates. An' no sustificate sayin' you're a Sea Fencible means yer won't have no protection.' Fagg pointed at a grizzled veteran in the front rank. 'You, what's-your-name, what does no sustificate mean?'

The veteran spluttered, 'The press, bosun?'

Fagg paused theatrically. 'That's right, sailor. The press gang'll come for yer, an' I'll tell you why. The nice gentlemen from His Matey's impress service'll come and fetch you to go orf to sea in one of 'is fine men-of-war 'cos we'll tell 'em 'oo you are and where to find you. Point taken?'

The fencibles were, indeed, visibly impressed. A mumbled chorus of 'Yus bosun' confirmed that the point had struck home.

Anson had seen some ragamuffin crews before, especially at the start of a ship's commission when a good half of the men were landsmen hauled in by the press gangs. But this scarecrow bunch took some beating.

There were a score of them, their weathered faces, calloused hands and rolling gait marked most of them as fishermen and small boat seamen of all types – no doubt most of them smugglers, occasional or otherwise.

They were all shapes and sizes, all ages from boys who looked as if they had only lately escaped their mothers' apron strings to prematurely elderly men with little hair and few teeth between them, and dressed in everything from ragged work clothes to the undertaker's smart funereal garb.

Taking station behind Anson, former surgeon's mate Phineas Shrubb whispered to him: 'As directed, I have examined all the would-be recruits and these are the ones who passed muster.'

The lieutenant winced. 'If these are the best, what was wrong with those who failed?'

'Oh, rickets, consumption, ruptures, lunacy – that sort of thing ...'

'Good grief!'

'But you have accepted a cripple I should have been sure to fail?'

'Tom Marsh? His spirit makes up for what he lacks in the foot department.'

Anson waited, standing rigid and silent in his smart new uniform, while Fagg, aided by Hoover at the back in the role of an ankle-biting sheepdog, verbally whipped the rabble into two muttering lines.

'Silence fore and aft!' Fagg roared, so fiercely that he won their immediate attention. 'These here's the rules. When I says form two lines, you forms two lines. And when I says silence, what do I mean?'

'No talking?' ventured one of the cheekier volunteers from the back row.

Fagg was beside the unfortunate in a split second screaming 'Silence!' into his ear and making all those around him flinch violently. 'What's your name sailor?'

The man hesitated, too nervous to speak until Fagg shouted 'Answer!'

No longer cheeky, he managed to stutter: 'F-Ford, master.'

'I'm not your master. I'm the bosun of this here land-locked looney-bin. I worked long an' 'ard to get this.' He brandished his highly-polished Malacca cane. 'That's why I likes to be called bosun. What should you call me?'

'B-bosun.'

'That's right, master effing Ford. Now we've got that straight and you're all stood more or less in two wavy lines, the master-at-arms here'll call you to attention.'

Hoover marched smartly to the front and stamped to attention, ramrod straight.

'Allow me to introduce myself. I'm Sergeant Hoover of His Majesty's Marines and you are a shambolic bunch of scallywags who'll soon be smart Sea Fencibles or wish you'd died in the attempt.'

He marched along the front rank, glaring fiercely into startled faces, came to a halt with stamping feet and shouted, 'Atten ... shun!'

The two lines shuffled to various interpretations of attention and Anson stepped forward, acknowledging Hoover's exaggeratedly smart salute with a sloping-handed touch of his bicorn hat.

His eyes swept down the ragged lines. First impressions might have been on the gloomy side of positive, because he could now see that there were a fair few useful-looking sun- and wind-burned salts among them. They included the blackmail victim Jacob Shallow, still smiling at his miraculous escape from the impress, the butcher Tom Oldfield and the cobbler Joe Hobbs.

'I am Lieutenant Anson of the Royal Navy, and I have been appointed by the Lords Commissioners of the Admiralty to command this detachment of Sea Fencibles.'

He paused for effect, then added: 'Whatever happened here before today is history. This detachment will henceforth be run in proper navy fashion. I am pleased that some of the old hands are staying on – and I welcome the newcomers.'

His eyes again swept the lines.

'You have volunteered to become Sea Fencibles and I commend your loyalty and obvious zeal to train with musket, pike and great guns to frustrate any attempt by our enemies the French to land on these shores.'

'Amen,' said Fagg.

Anson darted a wintry glance at him before continuing: 'But I would be taken for a fool if I believed all of your motives were so high. There are prime seamen among you, fit for any man-of-war. The Royal Navy needs good seamen and the press will soon be out looking for loyal, keen men like you to serve afloat from the Channel blockade to the West Indies ...'

At the mention of the press gang a visible shudder swept the ranks.

'But of course, as Sea Fencibles you have a written protection against being pressed. If you bump into those gentlemen on a recruiting sweep and show them your piece of paper they'll thank you and tell you to go about your business – all matey. You have that protection. But, as Bosun Fagg has told you, you will keep it only as long as you parade when you're told, train hard, obey orders and become effective Sea Fencibles for the defence of this coast. Is that clear?'

Their mumbled assent was drowned by Sergeant Hoover's barked: 'Answer the naval officer, 'aye aye, sir!''

They aye ayed, and now that everyone knew where they stood, Anson outlined his training programme, when and where they were to report, and how they would be paid.

In the coming days more volunteers joined, attracted by the promised protection from the dreaded press gangs, and bringing the detachment more or less up to strength.

The newcomers' mates and neighbours already enrolled told them it was not so bad for a shilling a day. MacIntyre and his cronies had been seen off. The new, game-legged bosun and the sergeant of marines were black bastards, but their bite was not as bad as their bark. As for the officer, he'd clearly seen a bit of action, but he treated them fair and he seemed straight as a die.

29

Training was soon under way, with the master-at-arms introducing the men to musket and pike handling, and Fagg – ably assisted by Sampson Marsh, the gun captain turned fishmonger – demonstrating gunnery drills.

But the most significant event was Anson's visit to the Dover boatyard with a party of fencibles to take charge of two of the new gunboats ordered by Commodore Home Popham.

Clinker-built row galleys, each had a slide for'ard extending back to the third thwart for mounting a 12-pounder carronade and, aft, were pairs of throle-pins to accommodate eight oars a side.

Anson looked them over with approval. They were well built and he was particularly impressed with the slide, pivoted at the fore end so that it could be elevated or depressed, and on rollers at the after end for training the gun to starboard or larboard. There was only one problem. The carronades themselves were missing.

'There's none to spare in Dover,' he was told. 'You'll be getting them from Chatham Dockyard.'

'And when will that be?'

The chief shipwright scratched his head. 'Your guess is as good as mine, sir, but knowing the pace those dockyard mateys work at I shouldn't expect anything to happen in a hurry. They haven't got, let's say, the financial incentive that we commercial yard men have.'

Unimpressed, Anson twitched his nose. 'Hmm, we'll see about that.'

He had chosen Hobbs and Oldfield as coxswains, and they steered, somewhat cack-handed to begin with, out of the boatyard. On their way to Seagate, he set them to getting the crews, each made up of eight oarsmen who were more used to rowing solo, trained up to stroke together and at speed. Working the carronades would have to come later when they could be prised out of the dockyard.

*

Called to the Seagate slipway by an excited off-duty fencible to see the arrival of the boats, Fagg was deeply unimpressed. 'You couldn't make it up! Gunboats wivout guns is just boats. If the Frogs invade we'll 'ave to throw pebbles at 'em!'

Anson reassured him: 'No doubt we'll get them long before any Frenchman ventures over here.'

'Sometime never, if them dockyard mateys 'ave anyfink to do wiv it. Don't fergit I'm from Chatham, sir, so I know 'ow slow they can go. And, let alone the boats, we're still short of four guns for the battery ...'

The officer sensed that Fagg's warning of dockyard delays was the truth of it. 'Quite right, bosun. We must equip ourselves with our entitlement if we're to be effective, so we'll send Boxer to the dockyard. If anyone can sort them out, it's him.'

*

When the undertaker returned two days later he reported that the Ordnance Wharf's quaintly-titled 'clerk of the cheque; had confirmed that the detachment was indeed entitled to four more great guns for its battery and a carronade for each of the gunboats. 'I tried my best, sir, but—'

'Don't tell me, I can guess,' said Anson. 'We rate behind every ship in the service, rated or unrated.'

Boxer smiled ruefully. 'That's the long and short of it, sir. The dockyard mateys said we'd just have to wait our turn.'

'That could be a very long wait and the French could be here before our turn comes around, so we'll just have to jump the queue.'

*

News that Black Mac had left the detachment for the impress service had at first been greeted enthusiastically, but as they began to get used to the idea there was some unease among the fencibles.

Sampson Marsh and George Boxer sought out Sam Fagg and explained the men's fears. 'He's out of the fencibles sure enough and that's a relief to all, but now he's with the press gang he could still cause a lot of problems. What if he targets our boys, pink chit or no pink chit?'

Fagg agreed. 'He's got to disappear. Lieutenant Anson can't make that happen, but we can.'

They met that evening in the privacy of Jacob Shallow's store to devise a fitting fate for MacIntyre. Marsh and Boxer had persuaded Fagg that no one deserved a crack at his former blackmailer more than the greengrocer.

And they agreed that the Scotsman's well-known appetite for strong liquor and easy women was to provide the opportunity to get rid of him, the sooner the better.

****

As the former bosun set off from his lodgings for his night's carousing, he failed to notice that he was being followed. Shallow knew the town inside out and shadowed him to the True Briton down on Harbour Street.

With the quarry safely inside and no doubt quaffing his first tot of the evening, Shallow made his way back up the old winding High Street and headed for the British Lion.

There, Boxer, Sampson Marsh and Fagg had gathered to await the summons. They had cudgels hidden under their clothing and sipping ale with them was Fagg's new lady friend, Annie.

They looked up as Shallow entered and Sampson asked: 'What's afoot?'

'He's drinkin' in the True Briton.'

'Alone?'

'He were when I seen him not ten minutes since. The locals give him a wide berth, what with him being in with the impress an' all.'

Sampson rose. 'Right mates, time to set a trap for a rat.'

They finished their ale and set off for the Stade. On the way Sampson asked Annie. 'You sure this MacIntyre don't know you?'

Annie grinned. 'Don't drink in the Lion, does he? An' I never have nuffink to do with them press gang scum. I know I ain't no nun, but that'd give a girl a bad name, that would.'

'But you'll do this, will you?'

'I heard what he did to your mate here, an' I'll do what it takes to get him his comeuppance.'

'Good girl. All we want is for you to get him outside and down the alley.'

Annie sniffed. 'Make sure you take him quick. I don't want his filthy hands all over me.'

Sampson patted her on the back. 'It'll be quick, never fear.'

And Fagg promised her: 'Don't fret. We'll 'ave 'im down afore 'e can touch you, love.'

They had reached the bottom of the High Street and Sampson motioned to Annie to walk on alone.

He and the others split up and made for the alley beside the True Briton.

When she reached the pub, Annie faltered for a moment and then pushed open the door and walked boldly in, looking around the smoke-filled taproom until she spotted her target, sitting alone on a bar stool, elbows on the counter and a tot in his right fist. It was time to spring the trap.

*

News of the MacIntyre's move to the impress had long since reached the True Briton and by common consent the local tipplers had left an obvious *cordon sanitaire* around him.

In a coastal town, it was not wise to be seen drinking in close company with such a man lest the word got around and you were rumoured to be fingering your neighbours for the press gang for a few Judas pints of ale. In such cases guilt was assumed and the vengeance of those who daily walked in fear of being pressed could be swift and vicious.

A fisherman spotted passing the time of day with MacIntyre a year since had been given such a kicking by his former mates that he had upped sticks overnight and fled to Yarmouth, where he now lived under an alias – in constant fear of meeting up with a Folkestone boat and being forced to run again.

Annie knew nothing of cordons – sanitaire or otherwise – and felt safe in the knowledge that she would be seen as heroine rather than tell-tale after what was about to happen to the detested bully.

For a moment, she stood in the doorway until her vision adjusted to the smoke-filled, candle-lit bar-room.

Then she set a course for the stool next to MacIntyre, hitched up her skirts to reveal several inches of ankle, and plonked herself down. She pulled her already low-cut blouse down a little further and called to the landlord for a shot of gin.

MacIntyre, used to being given a wide berth, looked up, somewhat surprised, and immediately took the bait. 'Have'na seen you here afore, sweetheart.'

'Never bin in this den afore, have I?'

'If ye had I'm certain sure I'd recognise a pretty wee thing like yous …'

Annie shrugged the compliment off and took a swig of her gin. 'Just up from Rye visiting me sick aunt, ain't I?'

The locals gawped at the encounter. Some were already marking her card for getting familiar with the hated MacIntyre. He, however, had brightened considerably – his interest fully aroused by this dolly showing enough of her chest to make it clear she was open to overtures.

'Another tot, sweetheart?'

'Me muvver told me never to drink with strange men,' she countered.

The Scotsman responded with his gravestone-toothed grin. 'In that case I'll interjuce mesel'. MacIntyre's the name. Billy MacIntyre – at your service. Landlord, look lively an' gie us two mair tots over here!'

Annie forced a smile. 'Navy man is it?'

MacIntyre was happy to admit to that.

'So what're y'doin' ashore, Billy MacIntyre?'

He hesitated. She must be one of the few people in town who didn't know him as the former bully boy of the fencibles and now of the much-feared press gang.

'Recruitin' – that's what I'm on.'

She tossed back her tot. Looking to recruit me, are yer?'

MacIntyre grinned lasciviously and reached out to squeeze her knee. 'Mebbe I will. I like a willin' recruit.'

*

Outside, the ambush team lurked in the shadows.

Marsh nudged Shallow. 'You're sure the boys are ready with the boat?'

'Told yer they were. I checked, didn't I?'

The undertaker asked: 'How long afore they have to sail?'

It was a good question. Unless they caught the tide they would have to hide their man ashore until the following night.

Fagg guessed: 'Reckon we've got about an hour, no longer.'

'What's keeping that girl?' Sampson muttered.

As if on cue, the door of the True Briton swung open and MacIntyre emerged in a shaft of smoky light, Annie on his arm. She faked a stumble down the single step and the Scotsman pulled her to him. 'Steady there, sweetheart. Ye're a bit too keen. Wait 'til we're in the alley afore ye get down on yer back!'

They negotiated the corner into the alley and MacIntyre grunted in surprise as unseen hands dragged the girl away from him. Startled, he reached for the knife in his belt but before he could pull it free he took a sickening blow to the head from an apparition that had loomed up behind him.

From his right side, another assailant cudgelled him across his forearm, sending the knife clattering on the cobbles. He staggered and fell forwards, blood already running down his neck from the blow he had taken below his right ear.

As he lapsed into unconsciousness, he took a kick to his ribs from one of his attackers who was immediately dragged back by one of the others.

'Leave him, Jacob, leave him! You want the swine to suffer, don't you? And he'll not suffer if you kill him now – but likely you'll swing for it if he snuffs it here.'

Annie's eyes had adjusted to the gloom and she could see it was Sampson Marsh who had pinioned Shallow from behind and was pulling him off the stunned bosun.

Shallow struggled for a moment but then went limp. 'You're right Sampson, I know you are. I'd like to 'ave killed the bastard for what 'e done to me and me family. But I know you're right.'

Marsh let him go and Fagg put an arm round his shoulder. 'Sampson's right, Jake. With what we've got in mind for this piece of Scotch shite 'e's gonna suffer orlright. Come quickly now. Let's get 'im down to the Stade afore the boat's high and dry.'

Boxer was the acknowledged expert at moving bodies, dead or alive. As soon as the Scotsman had hit the deck, the undertaker had disappeared round the back of the pub and emerged pushing a barrow he had noted earlier and borrowed for the job in hand.

The undertaker took the feet, Marsh and Shallow an arm each, and they hoisted MacIntyre into the barrow.

With his head lolling back between the handles, an arm dangling each side and legs hanging akimbo for'ard, they wheeled him off towards the Stade.

Anyone seeing the strange little procession could assume this was a drunken sailor being wheeled back on board by his mates, with his worried woman walking alongside.

Annie was muttering right enough, but not out of concern for MacIntyre. 'Don't know how I let you lot talk me into acting up to him, 'orrible beggar. Still feel him groping me – wiv all them people staring, too. Now they'll all fink I'm 'is tart—'

Sampson Marsh reassured her. 'This is my neck of the woods. Once word gets round about how MacIntyre got his comeuppance and disappeared, folk'll put two and two together and you'll be a heroine for luring him out.' Unconvinced, Annie muttered on until they reached the Stade.

Among the fishing boats lying there was one showing a green light. 'There she is,' whispered Shallow. 'The boys have had to take her out a bit.'

'Aye, so we'll need to row him out,' Marsh confirmed. Their timing had been governed by MacIntyre's movements, and for whatever reason he had entered the True Briton much later than usual.

But this eventuality had been foreseen as a possibility. At the bottom of the steps leading down from the Stade, a small dinghy tethered to an iron ring set into the stone was bobbing with the swell. Nevertheless, there was barely enough depth to row out to the fishing boat.

'Hurry!' urged Marsh. 'We'll just about float with him and me in the boat. I'll have to row him by myself.' To cause a commotion by getting trapped in the mud would be unwise, as military patrols were a well-known hazard in these parts.

Shallow and the undertaker grabbed the unconscious man fore and aft, lifted him from the barrow and carried him to the top of the stone steps.

It was at that moment, as if on cue, that the sound of hobnails striking cobbles made them freeze. 'Patrol!' hissed Marsh. 'Let me do the talking.' Instinctively, Annie slipped away, her duty done, and Fagg followed her. He had no wish to answer awkward questions.

A corporal, carrying a lantern and accompanied by two privates of the Cinque Ports Volunteers, appeared out of the gloom. 'Hello! What we got 'ere then?' the corporal enquired with the touch of sarcasm expected of a man of his rank. 'A robbery is it, or … heh heh, mebbe a burial at sea?'

The two privates simpered, and Marsh signed to his companions to lower their burden.

'Evening corporal,' said Marsh. 'No, no – nothing so exciting. This poor sailor-lad has imbibed of spirituous liquor a little unwisely. We're, er, escorting him back to his boat.'

The corporal, a shopkeeper in Hythe when not in uniform, and a staunch chapel man, knew his Bible. 'Be not drunk with wine, wherein is excess; but be filled with the Spirit, eh?'

The quotation provoked more chuckles from the privates – and from Marsh. 'Very apt brother, very apt. Ephesians, is it not?'

The corporal smiled, recognising a fellow chapel man. 'Heh, heh. Spot on, brother. Chapter five, verse 18 if memory serves me true. Now, d'you need a hand to get this sinner down them slippery steps?'

Shallow could not resist poking his oar in. 'This here cully's bin on the slippery slope for ages orlright!'

Marsh shushed him. 'Now, now Jacob. There, but for the grace of God …' and smiling at the corporal he added: 'It'd be a kindness. He's already bashed his head a-tripping down the step outside the pub door. If he takes another tumble down these here steps it could be the death of him.'

The corporal examined MacIntyre by the light of the lantern. 'Hmm, he's taken a nasty blow to his head alright. Almost as if someone's coshed him, eh?'

Marsh knelt beside the unconscious Scotsman. 'He'll live, and once we've got him in his cot he can sleep it off.'

'And mebbe foreswear the demon drink when 'e wakes with a thumping headache,' Shallow volunteered.

The corporal was still somewhat suspicious. 'Are you shipmates of his?'

'No brother,' Marsh answered quietly. 'We're Sea Fencibles just come off duty. We saw him fall and came to his aid like. We're what you could call Good Samaritans. Couldn't just pass by on the other side, could we?'

The corporal smiled at the reference. 'Heh, heh. Fair enough. Better get him out to his boat afore the tide goes right out, otherwise you'll be draggin' him across the mud.' Turning to his men he barked: 'Look lively, lads, and give these 'ere good Samaritans a hand! But careful mind – those steps'll be treacherous and I don't want to lose half me patrol. Wouldn't help me make sergeant, that wouldn't.'

Marsh went down first, taking care not to slip on the slimy steps that were covered at each high tide. The undertaker and Shallow took a leg each and the two soldiers grounded their muskets and linked arms to support MacIntyre's head and shoulders. Gingerly they began their descent.

At the bottom of the steps, Marsh felt for the rope holding the dinghy and pulled it close so that he could step in without it capsizing.

The others negotiated the steps slowly with muttered instructions to one another. At the bottom, Marsh held the dinghy steady by its mooring rope while they swung the unconscious man aboard.

Laying the Scotsman in the thwarts, Marsh unshipped the oars, touched his hat to the corporal, and signed Shallow to let go.

As soon as the rope was untied and thrown into the dinghy, Marsh dipped his oars and rowed skilfully towards the boat showing the green light.

The two soldiers mounted the steps to muttered thanks and picked up their muskets. With a wave, the corporal led them off to continue their patrol, while Boxer and Shallow headed for the British Lion to celebrate a successful operation.

It had begun to rain, and the small pool of blood at the top of the steps gradually drained away until no sign remained of the drama that had been played out there.

30

It was three days before Sampson Marsh returned.

He sent word to Fagg, Boxer and Shallow to meet him in the churchyard, where they could not be overheard, and reported that the cargo had been landed successfully at Hastings.

MacIntyre, he told them, had recovered some of his wits by the time he was taken ashore, but not sufficient to be able to talk his way out of being pressed.

The impress men had found him, just as they had been informed, in a back street pub with a tot in his fist. There was a mess of blood-matted hair behind his right ear, a bewildered look about him – and he had no convincing story as to why he should not be taken to serve His Majesty in a man-of-war. His horny hands, tattooed arms and pigtail so clearly indicated a man who had followed the sea, and was therefore ripe for the taking.

Even if his befogged brain had recalled what had happened and if he had protested that he was a proper navy petty officer serving with a press gang in the next county, who had been clubbed, kidnapped and cast ashore here, it would have cut no ice.

Worse, if he had claimed he was already serving elsewhere, he could easily be branded as a deserter. And branded was the word: the minimum punishment was a flogging and having the letter D hot-ironed into his forehead.

No, even in his still-befuddled state, MacIntyre had known it was wisest to hold his peace, go quietly – volunteer under a false name even, with the perks that offered over being pressed – and take the first opportunity to disappear, and avenge himself in due time.

As he was led away, he had glimpsed a half-familiar face among the watching crowd. He stared at Marsh and as he passed him growled: 'Ye've got somethin' t'do with this y'bastard. I've marked yer card!'

But Sampson had blanked him. And the press gang led their latest catch outside.

*

When the word got around Folkestone that the hated MacIntyre had received his long-due comeuppance, and that she was the one who lured him to it, Annie was indeed regarded as something of a heroine.

How the Scotsman had been spirited away, no one knew other than those closely involved. And they were keeping quiet.

Rumours abounded as to what had happened to him. Some said he had been marooned ashore in France; others that he had fallen from the Stade while drunk and been washed out to sea. Some were convinced that he had had his throat cut and been buried on top of another body in a recent grave.

From his fish shop on the Stade, Sampson Marsh quietly started hinting that MacIntyre had spoken of being sick to death of Sassenachs and wanting to go home to Scotland. Within a few days, that was the version that reached the ears of authority.

As for the officer commanding the impress service, the easiest option was to settle for that explanation for the Scotsman's sudden disappearance. And it was with little regret that Lieutenant Coney entered R, for Run, against MacIntyre's name in the nominal roll.

*

Anson rode off cross-country towards Barham Downs and then headed north on Watling Street, the old Roman road that ran from Dover to London.

He overnighted at Ospringe and set off again at dawn, arriving stiff and chafed at Chatham Dockyard around noon.

A naval officer was naturally a familiar sight in a dockyard with several warships alongside for repairs or replenishment, and Anson attracted no attention as he spent the rest of the day on intelligence-gathering.

In the main dockyard, he was able to wander at will, admiring the newly-launched second rate Temeraire, now fitting out, and a new fifth rate under construction.

He noted the great mixture of tradesmen: shipwrights, caulkers, smiths, carpenters, plumbers, riggers, sawyers, sail-makers and labourers going about their business.

The new rope-house was of special interest to him. It was more than 1100ft long to accommodate the longest ropes made, and three storeys high, divided into 100 bays.

Noting his obvious interest as an end-user of this vital product, a friendly foreman pointed out the two separate sections, the spinning floor where hemp was spun into yarn ready for tarring before being transferred to the laying floor, to be spun into rope – a bewildering myriad of thicknesses for as many uses at sea.

But, however riveting Anson found all this, it was to the Gun Wharf that he paid particular attention.

31

They travelled with two large wagons, each drawn by four carthorses hired by Boxer on Anson's instructions, and sturdy enough to carry a couple of 40-hundredweight objects.

On arrival at the Ordnance Wharf that lay at the Chatham end of the dockyard, between St Mary's Church and the river, a waved document was enough to allow them entry.

A naval officer on one wagon and a sergeant of marines on the other were proof enough of official business for the porters who stood duty during the day. They were more interested in searching men leaving the yard to combat pilfering than in holding up apparently perfectly legitimate arrivals.

The wagons drew to a halt beside storehouses containing great quantities of cannon of all calibres, plus carronades and mortars stored in regular tiers. Hundreds of gun carriages were laid up under cover and thousands of cannon balls were piled up in large pyramids. Nearby were cranes used for lifting the guns on board ship.

Other storehouses and an armoury contained vast numbers of muskets, pistols, cutlasses, pikes and pole-axes. It was a treasure trove of weaponry.

Anson strode off towards the offices, pausing briefly to look over his shoulder to check with Hoover: 'You've got the necessary, and you know what to do?'

'Sure do.'

A lurking storekeeper looking as miserable as if he had the troubles of the world on his shoulders was told by the marine: 'The officer's just off to sort the paperwork. We've got to load four 18-pounders and two carronades.'

The man sniffed. 'That's as may be, but there's plenty more ahead of you lot.'

'Right mate, but I bet they ain't all gonna give you one of these.' And Hoover produced a golden half guinea from his pocket and spun it nonchalantly in the air with one hand, catching it in the other.

The storeman perked up immediately. That coin represented a lot more than a week's pay.

Hoover ventured: 'Why don't you drum up a crane crew to get our cannon loaded, so's when the officer gets back it'll all be shipshape and these here wagons will be ready to roll.'

The man looked interested but doubtful, so Hoover pressed on. 'He's a generous man, this officer, and I reckon if we're all loaded up they'll be another half guinea to join this one. So what's it to be? Do we join the queue and you get nothing, or do we jump it and you get to treat yourself and your missus to a few comforts?'

Convinced, the storekeeper looked around to make sure no one was watching and reached out his hand for the coin. Hoover handed it over, but as soon as the man had pocketed it he threw in: 'You'll need to treat the labourers, too. They know what's next to be loaded and they ain't going to get off their arses for sod-all. We gets paid a pittance in this here yard – not enough to make us want to jump to it every time some smart-arse in uniform comes demanding guns.'

Like any marine or navy man, Hoover knew of the poor rates of pay dockyard men had traditionally received – the downside of a pretty safe job for life. There had been trouble in years past, when not only were the men badly paid, but sometimes received nothing at all for months at a time when their masters failed to pay them.

So it was not surprising that they had earned a reputation for idleness and susceptibility to bribery and theft. It was different now that the war had imposed greater demands on the dockyard, a vastly increased workload that brought with it greater prosperity – and the promise of pensions – for the workers. But the old attitudes still prevailed, and Hoover was under instructions to do what it took to promote his demand to the head of the queue.

He clapped the man on the back. 'Right you are, mate. You can tell your boys there'll be a half crown in it for each of 'em when the wagons are loaded.'

The man nodded. 'You're on, but give 'em it surreptitious like. We don't want no come-back – and your officer's paperwork better be straight afore you leave, else the clerk of the cheque'll be arter all on us.'

That official would have to be squared by Lieutenant Anson, Hoover decided. Greasing the palm of a storekeeper was one thing, but dealing with the senior men in charge of issuing ordnance was something else altogether.

Meanwhile there were half pikes, muskets, pistols, ball ammunition and powder to be drawn and the cannon to be secured aboard the wagons, and he called to Boxer and Marsh to bring them up to the pile of 18-pounders.

****

Anson's earlier visit had provided him with invaluable intelligence, and when he called upon the Ordnance Board office he was ushered after a brief wait into the presence of a senior officer who greeted him warmly.

Signing Anson's paperwork, the officer confessed: 'This smacks of queue-jumping, my boy, and it may not be strictly legal. But, after what you did during the Nore Mutiny and the fact that you are now in the front line agin the French, I'd be willing to be court-martialled for helping you over this.'

'Thank you, sir. I am greatly in your debt.'

'Think nothing of it. All I ask is that you don't go around gossiping about my part in this. If certain man-of-war captains hear that a Sea Fencible has jumped the queue there'll be hell to pay!'

'My lips are sealed, sir.'

The officer chuckled at a sudden thought. 'In any event, by the time the paperwork comes home to roost, the war will probably be long over and we'll either be speaking French or laying up our victorious fleet and melting down the cannon to make doorstops or turning them into street bollards! Meanwhile, sailing a desk is thirsty work. Will you join me in a glass?'

Mission completed, Anson was happy to oblige.

*

Leaving Hoover in charge of loading the wagons, Fagg stomped off to the poorest area of Chatham: Smithfield Banks.

This bleak, overcrowded stew of crumbling tenements, only a musket shot from the yard, was distinguished by the grandiose names of its chief thoroughfares – King Street and Queen Street – but it was a safe bet that royalty had never trod, nor was ever likely to tread, these mean streets.

Rather, they were frequented by the very dregs of society – hopeless alcoholics, beggars, cutpurses and raddled sixpenny whores who had reached the very end of the prostitution line.

These were filthy, smelly, grim and depressing streets, but for Fagg they were home.

A snaggle-toothed crone offered from a doorway: 'Oi, sailor boy – want a good time, dearie?'

Sam Fagg was a changed man, woman-wise, since he had got himself hitched up with Annie back at Seagate, and in any case this tart was well past her shag-by date even for him. 'Not just now, sweetheart. I'm orf t'meet me Ma.'

'Can y'spare a couple o' coppers anyhow? I need milk fer me babby?'

Fagg shrugged and threw her some coins. There would be no baby, and no doubt the money would go on a pint of gin – and temporary oblivion. But so be it.

She bobbed and grinned happily. 'Ye're a real gent, cap'n, that's what y'are.'

Fagg stomped on happily. Instant promotion for a few pennies was not half bad.

This was the jungle of sordid streets where he had played as a child, where he had learned to fight, beg, steal – and to survive. And it was in the dark back alleys that he had learned pleasures of the flesh with willing older girls desperate to be wanted even for a few minutes in their otherwise loveless lives.

At the junction with Cross Street he came to a house he could never forget. This was where he had been dragged up, in a couple of scruffy rooms up a flight of rickety stairs.

He hesitated, fobbing off another cruising whore, before stumping up the stairway that reeked of stale cooking, urine and worse. At the very top was the familiar brown door. This had been home until at 12 he had run off to escape his drunken, bullying stepfather and volunteered himself as a powder monkey in a man-of-war.

A rap at the door provoked a stirring inside and a female voice asked: 'Who's there?'

'It's me, Sam.'

'Who?'

'Is that you Ma? It's me, Sammy.' It was what she had called him as a boy.

The door creaked open a crack and a dishevelled elderly woman peered out, repeating: 'Who?'

It was not his mother.

'Where's old Ma Fagg?'

'Depends 'oo wants ter know.'

'She's me muvver and I ain't seen 'er fer a year or two … 'ow long you bin 'ere?'

The woman sniffed. 'Must've bin more like three year. She's bin dead long since and I bin 'ere comin' up three year.'

Fagg nodded. It was not unexpected, but he could not in all honesty feel grief. She had been racked by a constant cough and was thin as a rake when he last saw her. Old, and now dead, long before her time.

*

The arrival in Seagate of the horse-drawn wagons carrying the guns created something of a stir, which Anson encouraged by calling for the tarpaulins covering them to be removed.

Idlers watched with interest as they passed and one wag called out: 'What you got there mates, some popguns at last?'

Anson raised his hat and called back: 'Thankee, sir. They're real enough. Climb up and take a look if you like. These'll keep the Frogs at bay!'

On-lookers laughed. Being first stop on the invasion route made people edgy and the more guns they could see around them the more secure they felt. At present the main defence for Folkestone was the long-established Bayle Battery up on the heights above the town and normally manned by volunteer gunners, and the East Wear Bay Battery, constructed the year before.

And now the new big guns would join the two, commanding the approach to Seagate from the west. They would ease the minds of worried locals and would discourage enemy ships or landing craft from coming too close.

Hoover followed the officer's lead and prised open one of the wooden crates with his bayonet, took out one of the heavily-greased sea service muskets and held it aloft. 'There's plenty of these beauties, too!'

There was no doubting that the watchers were suitably impressed, and Anson knew the arrival of the guns would be the talk of every inn and alehouse by nightfall. And no doubt the news would have crossed the Channel within a day or two.

He had already sent messengers to round up every one of his fencibles who could be spared from his workplace, promising them a training day shilling just for an hour or two's work unloading the wagons.

In truth he needed but a few, but being part of this significant moment would give morale a huge fillip and boost their standing among their fellow townsmen.

*

The unloading complete, Anson climbed, hat in hand, on one of the 18-pounders and Fagg called: 'Silence fore and aft!' as if they were afloat.

Pausing until the excited chattering stopped, Anson stuck his hat back on, cleared his throat and exhorted them. 'Now we've got our very own battery here at Seagate, men – fresh from the foundry and brand spanking new. You'll train on these until you can knock any Frenchman out of the water – if they should dare show their faces round here!'

There was a growled cheer, but one bold soul called out: 'Will it just be dumb show trainin' like before sir?'

Anson nodded his understanding. 'Fair point. Wheeler, isn't it?'

'Aye, sir.'

'They'll have to be some more dry training, but you have my word, as soon as Mister Marsh reports to me that you all know your stuff, I'll authorise live firing from the cliffs.'

The fencibles voiced their approval and on the spur of the moment Anson threw in: 'And we'll have a competition – with, er ...' he hesitated, trying to think up a suitable prize, '... yes, a barrel of ale and a guinea for the gun crew that's first to blow a floating target to kingdom come!'

This was greeted with great enthusiasm, and Hoover, standing close to the gun and conscious that he would be leading the training with the muskets, called up to Anson in a stage whisper: 'Could we do the same for musketry, sir?'

'An excellent idea, Sergeant Hoover. D'you hear that men? The master-at-arms proposes a contest for musketry too, and I will put up a ... er ... suitable prize for the best marksman.'

Hoover held up the musket he had pulled from the crate and already marked as his own, and the men cheered.

They were even more cheerful when Boxer called the roll, handed each one a shiny coin and got them to make their mark on the pay sheet. It was the easiest and quickest shilling any of them had ever earned. The ale would be flowing this night.

From the depths of seething discontent when Lieutenant Crispin had made such fools of them in front of a jeering crowd, to their relief at MacIntyre's comeuppance, the arrival of the new gunboats, and now this, it was small wonder that morale was sky high.

And, leaping down from the gun, Anson felt sure at last that he had the makings of a company who would do their duty – and, given time and training, would do it well.

*

The Kentish smuggler's news was greeted with interest by his French military paymaster in Boulogne.

'So the gun batteries around Folkestone and Seagate are now complete – up to strength?'

Apart from the occasional dropped aitch and his rather too precise form of speech, the Frenchman's command of English was impressive.

The smuggler confirmed: 'I've seen the new guns meself. I joined the fencibles to stop gettin' pressed for the navy, remember?'

'Ah yes, the Sea Fencibles. The last line of defence, are they not?' The French officer adjusted his spectacles and queried. 'But what about the gunboats? Do they now 'ave guns too?'

'That's right. What they calls carronades.'

'*Extraordinaire*! So, even the English are not foolish enough to continue to operate gunboats without guns at such a location!'

The paymaster shrugged, moved the pile of the latest English newspapers to the side of his desk and consulted a small red-backed ledger. Then, taking some coins from a cashbox in a top drawer, he handed them to the Englishman. 'We need to know more of these guns – the calibre, where they keep the powder and shot, exact dispositions and so on ...'

The smuggler glanced at the gold before placing it carefully in an inside pocket of his coat. 'I'll see what I can find out, monsewer.'

'Do that, *mon ami*. But, most importantly, I also require a copy of the latest edition of Steel's *Original and Correct List of the Royal Navy*. I find it extremely useful but the copy I 'ave is a little out of date.'

There was no doubt that the list, published monthly, would be of great interest to an intelligence officer, its pages listing every ship in commission, their officers and stations, signal station officers, impress officers – even their pay rates – and sailing dates of all packet brigs.

'It is a wonderfully useful publication, how do you say ... a fountain of all knowledge of the British Navy. With such openness, who needs spies? I fear that we in France do not reciprocate. We prefer a certain, shall I say, mystery?'

The smuggler asked: 'So 'ow will I get a copy of this 'ere list?'

'It will be delivered to you via one of our many sympathisers in London. You will bring it to me ... together with news of the state of the gun batteries. Mr Steel's list costs a mere sixpence at his Union Row warehouse in London, but to me it is almost beyond price – and there will be more gold for you when you deliver it.'

32

Ten days later, over breakfast at the Hardres Minnis rectory, the Reverend Anson called his wife's attention to an item in the *Kentish Gazette*.

'This, my dear, must be our son's doing d'you suppose?' He cleared his throat and read aloud:

'The Sea Fencibles of Folkestone and Seagate consist of upwards of 80 men, and 30 of them, who have been formed into a new detachment, were on Saturday last mustered at one of the batteries there, and trained for nearly two hours in the use of the cannon. Of the strength of those robust sons of the ocean, we had sufficient demonstration, nor do we doubt but their courage will prove as conspicuous, should our boasting foe entertain a serious thought of visiting this part of our sea-girt island. We observed, with much pleasure, several of the respectable inhabitants of the town assisting in this exercise.'

Mrs Anson clucked appreciatively. 'That's nice, dear. How charming of them to call our Oliver a robust son of the ocean. He will be pleased.'

*

It was a training day and the Seagate men had been summoned to Folkestone from their normal work to earn their King's shillings learning the arts required of a Sea Fencible.

Down in the harbour, a dozen of them had assembled beside the detachment's two new gunboats and were preparing to row one of them out where they could practise firing the carronade, albeit without shot.

The carronades had been mounted on their slides and at least the men would be able to work out how to use their turn-screws to elevate them and the rollers to point them to starboard or larboard.

When they did come into action their low-charge, low-velocity balls could plough into an enemy hull and send deadly splinters flying inboard like daggers among its crew. They were faster to load, powerful, yet far lighter than a long gun, and the slides would absorb much of the recoil.

Anson listened as Fagg warned the crews about slovenly boat-handling. 'Wiv the world and 'is wife starin' at us, we don't want t'look like a bunch of lubbers, do we? If you lot of 'arbour rats can't row proper then I dunno who can. So you'll row smart as the crew of a hadmiral's barge. Got that?'

A few chorused weakly: 'Aye aye, bosun.'

'You'd better put more life in yer rowing than ye do with yer aye aye bosuns. I said, got that?'

They responded with a louder 'Aye aye, bosun!' drawing curious glances from the town's idlers hovering on the sidelines to watch what promised to be free entertainment.

'That's better. Now, you've all rowed afore, ain't ye?'

There was a murmur of assent except from Apps, a sawyer by profession. His response, bordering on cheeky, brought a titter from the rest. 'I ain't never rowed, bosun. Not much call for it in the timber trade—'

Fagg gave him the evil eye. 'Orlright, orlright, so you ain't rowed, but you must 'ave some powerful strong muscles from all that there sawin', so jest sit behind someone as can row and do 'xactly what 'e does. Same goes fer anyone else who's a bit rusty on the oars, like. Understood?'

'Aye aye, bosun!'

Satisfied that things were well under way, Anson left the coxswains in charge of the boat crews and he and Fagg walked up the old High Street to the Bayle battery, which commanded the western approaches to the harbour.

There he found the exasperated Sampson Marsh putting two gun crews through their paces. The regular gunners had been stood down for the day and the Seagate men were there to familiarise themselves with the Folkestone battery in case there was ever a need to help out there.

They had been at it for little more than an hour, yet already their attention was wandering. It was dry training – always a problem because the fencibles could not be made to take it seriously without a loud bang at the end of each evolution.

With the officer present, Sampson Marsh adopted a sharper, gun-deck tone. 'How many times 'ave I got to tell you? Sponge out, load cartridge, ram home, wads in, ram home, load with shot, ram, powder, run out, point your gun, stand clear, slow match, fire! Not dilly-dally, shilly-shally, fidget and faff about, you dozy donkeys!'

The crews exchanged grins. What did they care about good-natured chivvying from Sampson when they were already well on their way to earning their King's shilling for the day's duty?

The number two gun captain, a burly boatman happy not to be spending the day scraping uncertain pennies rowing errands around the harbour, risked stating the blindingly obvious. 'It's 'ard to play-act Sampson. Us'd larn much quicker if us could fire these 'ere guns for real.'

Fagg could not resist poking his oar in. 'You'll be doing' it for real soon enough. But 'til then it's Sampson Marsh's job to make sure you knows the drill so's when you does it for real you won't blow yourselves up, miss the enemy and waste the King's powder and shot, not to mention the shillin' a day he pays you out o' the goodness of his 'eart.'

Marsh waved them back to the business in hand and called: 'Let's try it again, number one gun against number two. Check slow match, sponge, load cartridge, ram, load ball, load wad, ram, run out, point, ready ... and fire! Go!'

The crews lumbered into dumb show action yet again, and Fagg could not resist interfering once more, muttering ''Scuse me Sampson' and roaring: 'Get moving' number one gun. Ye're practisin' fer a battle, not a friggin' funeral! Number two, sponge aht, sponge aht – put yer back into it Walker. Ye're pussy-footin' abaht like a fairy with a wand ticklin' a tart's bottom. If yer don't swab prop'ly ye'll likely blow yer bleedin' arm orf wiv the next charge the minute yer shoves it in!'

'Aye aye, bosun.' Walker went through the motion of swabbing out again.

'Wet it fust, ye daft ha'p'orth!' And as Walker knocked over the leather bucket with the sheep-wool swab in his haste to comply, Fagg's frustration was complete. 'Gawd 'elp us when them Frenchies come!'

Anson smiled inwardly. Fagg was a natural at jollying men into action with good-natured expletives and insults passed down from generation to generation of petty officers. And Sampson Marsh was clearly a great acquisition, respected by all as a real man-of-war veteran who had captained great guns in action. If he couldn't teach them the rudiments of gunnery, no one could.

'Well done, and please carry on Mister Marsh. They're coming along fine.'

Sampson raised his hat an inch in salute. 'Aye aye, sir. Thank you.' And the trainee gunners grinned at one another, basking in the unexpected praise and determined to do even better.

Leaving them to it, Anson beckoned to Fagg to walk with him to the heights that commanded a view of the old town and harbour – and the French coast itself on a clear day. Not today though. A sea mist had rolled in so that visibility was down to a couple of hundred yards at most.

Fagg was not as impressed as the officer by what he had seen of the gunnery practise and was expecting similar chaos with the small arms drills. 'Supposed t'be what they calls proficient with the musket, pike and cutlass, but I doubt if any of 'em will know the arse end of one from the other.'

Anson smiled. 'They're raw, but Hoover and I will lick 'em into shape, never fear. You'd best get back to the boats and make sure Oldfield and Hobbs have got everything under control.'

Fagg tapped his japanned hat with his cane and limped off back towards the harbour, leaving Anson to help Sergeant Hoover instil the mysteries of musket and cutlass drill in his group of fencibles.

Just as it was with the great guns, it was hard to get the score of men detailed off to learn how to handle the complexities of the sea service musket to get it right without actually firing their weapons.

Live firing close to the town would not be possible without alarming, and perhaps massacring, the inhabitants.

Hoover had arranged for live firing on the shingle of nearby Hythe ranges, where cannon and musket balls could fly sea-wards and the locals were used to constant big bangs and the crackle of small arms fire.

But first, the fencibles must be able to handle the weapons safely and absorb the firing drills until they became second nature – instinctive.

Anson split the group, and while Hoover continued with musket and pike drill with a dozen of them, he demonstrated cutlass techniques to the rest.

There was no standard drill. But Anson wanted them to practise using the strokes and cuts he had shown them earlier, worked out from experience and experiment and illustrated on a chart propped up on an easel.

Officers used to swordsmanship tended to urge their men to strike with the point, not the edge of the blade. But Anson was well aware of the reality that the cutlass was no fancy weapon for fencing masters to prance around with, but a crude maiming and killing tool.

From his experience of observing its use in the heat of battle, he knew the important thing in action was not to go off guard by lifting your arm to make a cutlass blow. The key was to rush, cutlass straight out, watching for the chance to make a thrust, the slightest penetration spelling death for the opponent.

So it was his preferred cutting weapon. He regarded his standard naval officer's sword as more of an ornament and symbol of office, and far less effective than a cutlass on an enemy quarterdeck.

'Guard your left like this,' Anson grunted as he demonstrated. 'Now, thrust and parry. Keep well apart and copy me ...'

He wanted no accidental wounds resulting from over-enthusiasm flaring into real combat in the heat of the moment. A newspaper report he had read of an affray between two bodies of Essex Fencibles, whose passions had run away with them while training on a beach with pikes, was fresh in his mind.

As he resumed an attacking stance the session was interrupted by a loud crack – unmistakeably a cannon being fired out at sea off to the west towards Seagate.

33

Anson shouldered his cutlass and stared, left hand shielding his eyes. It was misty, but no telescope was necessary. A puff of smoke was still rising from a two-masted, square-rigged vessel, fitted with an apparently new suit of sails, that had evidently put a shot across the bows of a small coaster, now at its mercy.

Training had come to a sudden halt as, to a man, the fencibles craned to watch the drama being played out below.

Anson weighed up the situation instantly. The two-masted vessel was a bark, unmistakeably French-built and a privateer, taking advantage of the mist to mount a sneak raid out of one of the minor Pas de Calais or Normandy harbours and intent on grabbing small coastal craft from under the noses of the English while the Royal Navy was busy blockading major French ports.

Immediate action was necessary if they were to prevent the coaster being boarded. Anson called Hoover to send a runner to Sampson Marsh with a message telling him to bring the battery guns into action against the privateer as soon as he could fetch powder and shot from the store.

As the messenger ran off, Anson shouted after him: 'Tell Marsh we're going to row out and attack the Frenchman. He's only to fire if he can get a clear shot at him!'

He glanced seaward and could clearly see a boat being lowered from the privateer and men scrambling down into it.

Yelling at Hoover to follow him, he doubled away, followed by a score of the fencibles clutching the weapons they had been practising with – and praying that if they did get a chance to attack the Frogs his men would remember enough of their training to make a good fist of it.

By the time he and his best runners reached the harbour, the privateer's boat was alongside the coaster and grappling hooks were being thrown aboard.

Fagg had already joined the first gunboat to supervise rowing practise and a shout from shore warned him what was happening. He quickly registered what needed to be done and brought the boat round, yelling to the oarsmen to head for the coaster.

As more of his men arrived at the harbour, breathing heavily from their run, Anson urged them into the second gunboat. Tom Marsh appeared with his pony and three more fencibles clinging to the trap. The cripple jumped down, grabbed his crutches and hopped and pushed his way on board the second boat shouting: 'Make way for a proper rower!' And within minutes they were on their way, joining the wake of Fagg's gunboat.

*

Out at sea, the coaster's skipper stood on deck watching helplessly. He had been creeping westward down the coast with his mixed cargo when the privateer first appeared out of the mist.

The shot across his bows had forced him to strike immediately. He was unarmed, facing a heavily-armed enemy, and a glance at the crowd on its deck told him that his seven-man crew was outnumbered by maybe ten to one. His greatest concern was to protect his wife, hiding terrified in their little cabin below, and he looked anxiously to see if he could identify an officer in the prize crew so that he could throw himself on his mercy.

Under the protection of the privateer's guns, the French rowers and the half dozen armed men crouching between them were shouting to one another excitedly as they neared the coaster. They would have a free hand to plunder it before ejecting the crew and sailing the prize for the French coast.

The grappling hooks found a grip, and as the first of the Frenchmen hauled themselves on board, the coaster's skipper held up his hands in surrender, shouting to his crew to do the same.

They stood together, arms aloft, and were shoved against the mainmast by men armed with muskets and cutlasses. More of the enemy clambered aboard and began raising the sails, while two disappeared below to search for anyone hiding – and for loot.

The coaster's master watched them with growing alarm. He shouted near hysterically at the boarders: 'My wife, my wife – don't let them harm my wife!' But in the feverish activity to get the coaster under way, no notice was taken of him, and then a scream was heard above the din. They had found her.

*

The first gunboat, under Fagg's command, was already closing the distance to the coaster and the second followed 50 yards behind with Anson urging his oarsmen to row like fury.

Up at the battery, Sampson Marsh had taken an axe to the locked store door and was frantically urging his men to pull out powder and shot.

In the second gunboat, Anson could see that Fagg was sensibly approaching the coaster from the side that faced away from the privateer, so shielding his boat from the French guns.

Sails were being run up in the coaster and the French prize crew's excited shouts could now be clearly heard by the crews of the approaching gunboats.

Anson weighed up the situation. This was meant to be a dry training day and there was no powder or shot for the carronades or the muskets that a few of the men were carrying.

All the boat crews had were a few half pikes and cutlasses between them. If they tried to board the coaster with only one grappling hook and not enough weaponry they would likely be shot and hacked to pieces before even one of them could set foot on the captured deck.

Crucially too, how long would it be before the prize crew fired small arms at them – and before the privateer manoeuvred into a position from which its crew could bring cannon to bear on the gunboats and blow them right out of the water?

As a pessimistic farmer might say, Anson could never have brought his pigs to a worse market.

Clearly, his only hope was that Marsh could obtain powder and shot and fire on the privateer in the next few minutes. But, he agonised, this was extremely unlikely, bearing in mind that the ramshackle teams of trainee gunners might easily miss their targets altogether – or hit the gunboats rather than the Frenchmen.

*

On board the privateer, the French captain stood, hands on hips, monitoring the situation with some satisfaction. Another fat prize represented worthwhile pickings and, with the approaching gunboats hidden from his view by the coaster, there appeared to be no sign of retaliation from the English.

Through the developing mist, he could still see his prize crew hoisting the coaster's sails ready to get under way and head for the French coast while he continued his hunting cruise. Conditions could not be better for a predator, and he had enough extra crewmen for a couple more reasonably-sized prizes.

*

Contrasted with the calm aboard the privateer, there was feverish activity at the Bayle battery. But above the excited shouts of his gunners, Marsh's voice could be heard, loud and clear. 'Number one and number two guns! No need to swab. Take your time and get it right: charge in, ram home, wads in, ram home, ball, ram, spike the cartridge, run out … wait!'

Loading completed, he ran to the first gun, directing the crew to point it at the privateer's sails and rigging.

It took more agonising seconds before he was satisfied and hollered: 'It's for real this time boys! Number one gun, stand clear, slow match … fire!'

The gun erupted and lurched back as the shot swished away only to land harmlessly in the sea 20 yards or so short of the privateer, sending a plume of spray into the air.

Taken by surprise at this unexpected development, the French captain looked up towards the battery, but the thickening mist obscured his view. A quick risk assessment reassured him. Judging from their first attempt, these were inexperienced gunners who had probably never fired in anger before, and the drifting mist would give him and the prize crew time enough to make good their escape.

Up at the battery, Marsh had also marked the fall of shot and turned to the second gun crew. 'Quickly now, elevate and point further to larboard!' And, seeing the inexperienced gun captain dither, he shouted: 'Left, you clown, left!'

They struggled the gun into position and Marsh fussed around it, adjusting the aim at the mist-shrouded, ghost-like privateer – only just remembering to shout over his shoulder at the first gun-crew: 'Swab, swab!'

His shout galvanised the stunned gunners back into action to begin the reloading sequence that had been drilled into them.

Satisfied at last that the second gun was pointing as true as he could get it, he shielded his ears with his hands and shouted: 'Number two gun. Stand clear, slow match … fire!'

As the first gunboat neared the captured coaster, Fagg saw to his horror that some of the Frenchmen armed with muskets were using their bayonets to prod the crew to the side, forcing them to drop into the water or be run through.

Following behind and gaining slowly on his first gunboat, Anson could also see what was happening and cursed. Now they would have drowning seamen to rescue as well as trying to board the coaster.

The rest of the prize crew on the coaster's deck had now made ready to sail, but the roar of the number two gun from the Bayle battery followed by the whoosh of the ball changed everything in an instant.

Simultaneous cries of alarm from the prize crew and those back on board the privateer, and of delight from the gunners and watchers ashore, greeted an extraordinary sight. The shot had missed the French cutter's mainmast, aft, by only a few feet but had torn a gaping hole in the main topsail.

For the Frenchmen, triumph was on the point of turning into disaster. It was blindingly obvious that, mist or no mist, the shore battery had got the range and if the privateer did not make good its escape forthwith it could be disabled or worse within a few minutes.

And now that the English crew had been pitched overboard there was nothing to stop the shore battery targeting the coaster, too.

The French captain shouted his orders and as all hands struggled to get the privateer under way, a red maroon climbed skywards recalling the prize crew.

From up on the heights the number one gun barked again, but again missed the privateer, although this time by only a few yards.

The maroon had been unnecessary. Expecting to come under fire from the shore battery at any moment themselves, and seeing the gunboats nearing them, clearly intent on boarding, the prize crew were panicking and rushing to abandon the coaster, frantically leaping down into their longboat moored alongside, nearest the privateer.

At the same time, Fagg's gunboat reached the larboard side of the coaster and Anson, now less than 20 yards behind, could see that the priority was to rescue the frantic crewmen desperately clinging to one another in the water rather than board the abandoned vessel. He cupped his hands to his mouth and shouted to Fagg: 'Get those men! I'll board the coaster.'

Fagg waved acknowledgment and signalled his crew to pull alongside the men in the water.

Gun number two fired from the battery, but the mist was drifting in and this time the fall of shot could not be observed.

With the fleeing prize crew now halfway to the privateer on his blind side, Anson's gunboat bumped alongside the coaster. Hobbs, his coxswain, desperately swung the grapnel to secure it for boarding.

Still in the water, the coaster's master was shouting near hysterically: 'My wife! Save my wife!'

Two of the coaster's crew were already safe aboard Fagg's gunboat, soaked and retching. Hands were reaching out to the rest. But Anson could see no woman among them, unless the master's wife was exceptionally ugly and bearded. She must still be on board – below deck.

The increasing swell was forcing the only loosely-secured gunboat to bang against the side of the coaster and then yaw away. Anson looked for the cutlass he had brought on board, but could not see it among the jumble of oars and men. He forced his way to the prow and when the boat next slammed into the coaster's side he leapt for the deck, sprawling heavily as he landed.

For a moment he was totally vulnerable, but as he drew his sword he realised the deck was deserted and the coaster was his. Away to starboard he could see the prize crew's longboat had reached the safety of the privateer and the Frenchmen were swarming back on board.

A crackle of small arms fire came from the privateer, but the balls sang well wide and ceased when the bark of another cannon up at the Bayle battery reminded the Frenchmen it was time to make good their escape.

As he stood alone, sword in hand and hatless on the coaster's rolling deck wondering what he should do next, Anson heard a scream from below. The master's wife!

He ran to the small covered wheelhouse, which was deserted and showed signs of attempted looting, with the drawer on the chart table hanging half-open and papers strewn around.

A low moaning 'No, no, no ...' was coming from the open hatch that led below. Quietly and carefully he descended with his back to the laddered steps, sword in hand, his eyes becoming accustomed to the half light.

Aft was the cargo hold, with crewmen's hammocks slung above the sacks and boxes. For'ard was an open door to the only cabin. From it came the diffused light of a candle lantern, and the moaning: 'No, no, please no ...'

He ducked into the low doorway and was confronted with a scene that sparked a wave of anger. A woman, no doubt the master's wife, was sprawled on the bunk bed. Her dress had been pulled up to her waist and ripped open to expose her breasts, and she was struggling helplessly, her arms pinioned from behind by a heavily-bearded Frenchman.

Another man, bald-pated but with long greasy side hair, knelt before her, his britches round his ankles and pulling at her legs, snarling: '*Ouvrez salope, ouvrez!*'

Ignoring the long-bladed knife he held at her throat, his victim was moaning and jerking her head from side to side to avoid his mouth as he tried to force her legs apart. Beside her on the bunk lay a boarding axe dropped by one of her attackers in his hurry to get to grips with the woman.

The Frenchmen had clearly gone below looking for loot, found something more to their taste, and become so engrossed in their lust that they were oblivious to the fact that the rest of the prize crew had abandoned the coaster – and that it was being retaken.

Incensed at what was happening to the woman, Anson leapt forward and whacked the flat of his sword across the would-be rapist's buttocks, raising a livid wheal. With an agonised howl, the man withdrew from her and turned, shirt undone, britches still round his ankles and knife in hand, to face whoever had interrupted his sport.

Enraged, he sprang at the naval officer and grappled with him, grabbing Anson's sword arm with his free hand and stabbing with the other. In the confined space the knife was the more effective weapon and Anson felt a sharp pain in his right arm as the Frenchman pierced his sleeve.

Staggering back into the doorway, he fell to his knees, desperately scrabbling for his sword which had fallen on the deck. The Frenchman's spittle-covered beard parted in a grin of savage triumph, revealing blackened teeth and exuding laboured pants of breath foul enough to stupefy a rat. Small wonder the woman had been so desperately trying to avoid his mouth.

Anson fixed the man with a cold stare, willing him not to notice that his searching fingers had found the sword. Knowing he was literally staring death in the face unless he could raise the weapon, he made a supreme effort of willpower, closing his fist around the hilt and angling the blade upwards as the Frenchman rushed him. Impeded by the britches round his ankles, the would-be rapist tripped and fell forward grunting as he impaled his bare chest on the sword.

The man fell sideways, clutching at the blade buried in his chest. But before the now disarmed Anson could rise, the second attacker let go of the woman, flung her aside and pulled his own knife.

Still on his knees holding his wounded arm, Anson was at the mercy of his new adversary, again staring death in the face. Somewhat optimistically in the circumstances, he shouted at the man in French to surrender. '*Rendez-vous, mes amis sont ici!*'

But this was greeted with a contemptuous snort and the Frenchman closed with him, flicking his knife forward to nick Anson's cheek before seeking a vulnerable point to stab.

Anson tried weaving aside, but there was no escape from the long wicked blade and his attacker sneered at him, confident that the Englishman was dead meat. But the slight pause before he delivered the killer blow was the man's downfall.

There was a sudden movement behind him and, instead of the expected stabbing blow, Anson heard a crunch of bone and the Frenchman's head bounced to one side, blood and brains splattering his body. The knife clattered to the deck from his nerveless fingers and a figure rose behind the dead man as his body slumped slowly sideways. It was the master's wife, boarding axe held two-handed and rising to strike another blow.

Anson lifted his left arm and shook his head. She stared back at him, clearly traumatised by the course of events in the short time since the privateer's prize crew had taken the coaster.

She looked down at the man with his head stoved in and hefted the axe, but Anson told her, softly but firmly: 'There's no need, dear lady. He's already well and truly dead. They're both dead, or very soon will be.'

She stared back at Anson for a minute, and then nodded and dropped the axe, raising her bloodied hands to her face and sobbing – oblivious to her near-naked state.

34

Anson got awkwardly to his feet, raised his wounded arm to stop the blood running away, and tried to reassure her. 'You're safe now. These swine are dead – and you have just saved my life.'

She dropped her hands and looked at him earnestly. 'No, no, it's you who've saved me from these beasts ... and you're wounded.'

He shrugged: 'It's nothing – just a deep scratch, I think. And your husband and his crew are safe. The rest of the Frogs have gone and my men are taking charge of the vessel.'

'Thank God!'

Pointing to the bald would-be rapist he asked, almost shyly: 'Tell me, did he, er ...?'

Puzzled for a moment, she looked down suddenly aware of her near nakedness and pulled her tattered dress round her. The penny dropped. 'Oh, I see – finish? No, he didn't, thanks only to you.'

She hesitated, then added shyly: 'The truth of it is, he didn't have the chance to begin. My mother always told me to keep my knees tight together whenever I met a strange man ...'

'Very sound advice!' Anson gave her a broad smile, and she grinned with relief. She was, he guessed, in her 30s, plain but, as he had seen, with a handsome figure, a keen intelligence and a lot of pluck.

'Another few minutes and I couldn't have held out. Thanks to you I can look my husband in the eye. If they'd finished, I would have been so ashamed ...'

He shook his head. 'Don't even think it, my dear. You can be proud of fighting off these two.'

There was a clatter of someone coming down the ladder and Hoover appeared in the doorway behind him.

The marine took in the scene – his own officer wounded, a woman who to judge from her ripped dress had clearly been assaulted, and two dead Frenchmen – or rather one dead with head bashed in and the other with Anson's sword still embedded in his chest frothily rasping out his last breaths.

'Well done, sir! Are you badly hurt?'

'I'll live. Find something to cover this brave lady. I don't want her husband or our boys to see her exposed like this.'

'Did they—?'

'They did not, but it wasn't for want of trying.'

Hoover nodded and asked the woman if she had other clothes on board. She indicated a wooden chest under the bulkhead and he fished out another dress, almost identical to the one she had been wearing. 'Will this do?'

She took it, turned her back and pulled the remains of her old dress over her head. Hoover turned away and began helping Anson out of his jacket, tenderly pulling his wounded arm from the bloodied sleeve.

More steps clattered on the ladder and Hoover called out: 'Get back on deck and fetch the undertaker. No one else is to come below 'cept him, understood?'

There was a muffled 'Aye, aye' from above and Hoover turned back to Anson's wounded arm.

The woman had pulled on her clean dress and knelt beside them with some of the material from her ripped one. Hoover gently rolled back Anson's shirt sleeve and held the arm up as the woman bound the stab wound. She fashioned a rough sling out of another piece of her old dress and supported his arm with it.

Hoover was impressed. 'You've done this sort o' thing before, ma'am?'

She smiled. 'You have to turn your hand to many a thing when your husband's master of a vessel like this. I get to do all the cooking, sewing, washing and doctoring – and take my watch too, when any of the hands are sick.'

The ladder rattled again and Boxer, the undertaker, appeared in the doorway.

His eyes swept the scene of carnage. 'Jesus wept! What's been happening down here?'

Anson held a piece of the torn dress to his face to stem the blood from the Frenchman's knife cut. 'These two Frogs made the mistake of attacking this good lady and were so busy about it that they didn't realise the rest had bolted. Wherever they are now I trust they've learned the error of their ways.'

The rasps from the skewered man had ceased, and he lay silent at last. Hoover gripped the sword hilt, put his boot against the corpse's chest and pulled. The blade emerged slowly, badly bent from when the Frenchman had collapsed sideways.

The undertaker was impressed. 'Some thrust, that must have been!' He knelt beside the second corpse and examined the Frenchman's squashed head with a practised eye. 'And some blow that, too – smashed like an egg!'

Hoover commented unsympathetically: 'If they didn't like the rules they shouldn't have joined. Pity we can't give this pair back to their privateer mates as an example of what happens to Frogs who muck us about, but they've all skedaddled in a bit of a hurry.'

A voice called down the hatchway. 'Mr Anson, sir, the master of this 'ere tub's desperate t'know what's 'appened to 'is missus.'

Anson signalled Hoover to help him to his feet and shouted back. 'Tell him she's fine and we're coming on deck.' He turned to the undertaker. 'Here you go, this sort of thing's right up your street, ain't it? Be a good man and sort these Frogs out and get 'em buried. There won't be any family mourners.'

The undertaker knuckled his forehead. 'Aye aye, sir.'

Hoover helped Anson up the ladder, followed by the master's wife clutching his bent sword.

They emerged into daylight to a ragged cheer from the fencibles on deck and those bobbing about in the gunboats now secured alongside.

The coaster's master, still dripping from the ducking he and his crewmen had suffered at the hands of the prize crew, thanked Anson profusely and announced himself as William Gray, of the *Kentish Trader*.

He embraced his wife, asking repeatedly if she had been harmed. To spare her blushes, Anson told him, loud enough for all to hear: 'She's a brave lady and fought off a couple of Frogs 'til I caught them with their britches down. They learned the hard way not to tangle with an Englishwoman!'

Amid a chorus of congratulations, a voice was heard from below: 'On deck there, prepare to haul away!' and a rope came snaking up through the hatch.

The undertaker called again: 'It'll need a few of you. Here's the first of the Frenchies coming up …'

Half a dozen of the men took hold of the rope and pulled the first of the bodies up to the top of the ladder, banging against the rungs as it came. The dead man's britches were still round his ankles and the red welt across his buttocks provoked ribald chatter from the fencibles until Hoover silenced them with a barked: 'Lady present, watch your language!'

Nevertheless, they put two and two together to make five when Mrs Gray handed Anson his bent sword. The story of how their officer whipped a Frenchman across his arse so hard that his sword bent would be doing the rounds of a dozen alehouses that night.

The second body was hauled up and the undertaker emerged from below carrying the dead men's weapons. He supervised the wrapping of the corpses in bits of an old sailcloth, bound them with rope, and had them lowered one to each gunboat.

Anson, feeling a little weak from his exertions and loss of blood, advised the master to follow the gunboats back to the harbour until he was sure the privateer had cleared the coast, endured a parting embrace from Mrs Gray, and allowed Hoover to help him over the side.

*

At sea, command had to be exercised somewhat ruthlessly without debate – and rightly so. 'The navy,' as Captain Phillips of HMS *Phryne* had been fond of pointing out on every suitable occasion, 'is not a democracy.'

With Anson, ashore, and with his two trusted subordinates, it was different. He had chosen to let them into his thinking whenever possible; and it was necessary now.

Once the boats were secured, the weapons put back under lock and key, and his face and arm had been patched up by surgeon's mate Phineas Shrubb, Anson took Fagg and Hoover aside. They were joined by Sampson Marsh, still glowing from his success at the Bayle Battery.

'God alone knows how, but you performed a miracle today, Mr Marsh. If you hadn't punctured the Frenchman's sail at the very moment you did, all would have been lost.'

Sampson Marsh touched his hat in salute. 'It were pure luck, sir. Well, a bit of judgement and a lot o' luck. The real miracle was breaking into the powder store. If that lock hadn't given way straight off we wouldn't have been able to fire at all!'

'Locked? Good grief! Surely Hastings had left it open or entrusted you with the key?' William Hastings was the town's chief gunner who had held the post for many years and lived in a house within the battery that was served by its own well and separate powder store.

'No sir. He'd let his men stand down while we were doing our day's training and he was nowhere to be found when the Frenchman appeared. Gone off to visit a relative, some said.'

Anson was truly horrified, but he couldn't fault Hastings – nor Sampson Marsh, who could not be blamed for failing to ask for the key. No, he had acted with exemplary zeal as the situation unfolded and deserved praise.

Instead Anson cursed himself for not thinking to demand the powder store key while his fencibles were manning the battery, and for failing to arm the boats' carronades. These were, in his mind, amateurish mistakes. Unless Marsh had broken the armoury lock, his gun teams could not have fired on the privateer. The coaster would certainly have been lost, and the lives of the gunboat crews could have been forfeit.

As it was, without powder or shot for the boats' guns – and the muskets – his men had been rendered virtually helpless. It was solely Marsh's initiative and a lucky shot carrying away part of the privateer's canvas that had saved the day.

He looked at Marsh, Fagg and Hoover in turn. 'My thanks to you three for what you did today.'

Fagg knuckled his forehead. 'Weren't nuffink, sir. It's Sampson 'ere what deserves thanks.'

Hoover nodded. 'I just wish we'd been kind of more ready – the men, ammunition and all.'

Anson agreed. 'The men may not be properly trained as yet. Not trained well enough in their duties or how to handle their arms, but they've shown willing enough and our boat handling was not too bad.'

'Amen to that, sir.'

'Our arms drill? Well, that still leaves much to be desired, although your gunners deserve a drink Mister Marsh. Oh, and by the way, I meant to tell you before that you are now a petty officer and responsible for our gunnery.'

Marsh smiled happily and touched his hat again in salute. Anson instinctively knew he was a good choice. Nothing succeeds like success and, after that sail-splitting shot, the men would be convinced that their Sampson could do no wrong and he would have no problem keeping control.

Anson's head was beginning to swim, and he swayed and put his unwounded hand to his temple. Shrubb, who had been lurking nearby, noticed and stepped forward to support him. 'You must rest, sir. You have lost blood.'

Sampson Marsh called to the group of fencibles waiting to be dismissed. 'Tell young Tom to fetch the pony and trap.'

'Yes, you must rest', Shrubb insisted.

The officer, supported now by both Shrubb and Hoover, said weakly: 'Very well, very well. But mark this, our boys will be the toast of the town tonight – and rightly so. Instead of being laughed at, they'll be treated like heroes. But we know that I was so busy pushing our dry training that I had no proper plan to cope with the enemy suddenly appearing on our doorstep. We just went at 'em when it was already almost too late and we were lucky not to have got a bloody nose. To have no ready access to powder and ammunition, well, I should court-martial myself. Atrocious!'

'Atrocious it was, sir.'

The bosun's ready agreement to his over-critical conclusion gave Anson a moment's irritation. In truth, it had been far from a debacle. The fencibles had shown spirit and keenness to get to grips with the enemy. They had shown the French that they could not scoop up coastal craft on this stretch without opposition; and, by demonstrating their willingness to spill their own blood, the fencibles would no longer be a laughing stock.

Tonight, the local pubs would indeed be awash with tall stories as the fencibles went over and over the day's action until it assumed the proportions of Aboukir Bay.

Tomorrow, training must be stepped up, intelligence sought and plans made.

He told Fagg: 'Get as many of the men together as you can tomorrow forenoon. I have things to do and you two are to crack on with training –

all hands with the great guns, muskets, pikes and cutlasses. And keep 'em at it.'

'Beg pardin, sir, but we're gettin' through a lot of the King's shillings.'

'His Majesty and those of us who'll be paying this new-fangled tax on income can afford it. If that Frenchman comes again we must be ready for him.'

Fagg knuckled his forehead. 'Aye aye, sir. Press on with trainin' it is.'

Tom Marsh appeared with the pony and trap and Anson was helped aboard.

Turning to Sampson Marsh, he smiled and said: 'By the way—'

'Sir?'

'Let's get a copy made of that damned powder store key!'

35

Over the next few days, Anson was confined to his room at the Rose, his only visitors Shrubb, who checked and dressed his wounds, and Hoover to take dictation in his elegant copperplate hand.

The officer had set himself the task of putting wheels in motion to gather intelligence concerning the privateer.

He dictated, for the divisional captain's signature, a letter to the officers commanding Sea Fencible divisions and detachments from Chichester in West Sussex through to the North Foreland on the Isle of Thanet:

'As Officer Commanding His Ma'ty's Sea Fencible Division at Folkestone I have the honour to request any intelligence you may have of a French privateer, a brig of some dozen guns believed to have been interfering with coastal traffic off Kent and Sussex these several months. The said privateer most recently attacked a trading vessel off Folkestone last week and was brought to action by a shore battery and this Detachment's gunboats but escaped with minor damage. The privateer has what appears to be a new suit of white sails, except that its mainsail is now likely to carry a large oval patch of a different shade. It is believed the enemy vessel carries a complement upwards of some 60 or 70. You are hereby requested to report any intelligence regarding recent and current appearances of the said privateer to Lieutenant Anson of the Seagate Sea Fencible Detachment with the utmost despatch.

Arthur Veryan St Cleer Hoare

Captain, Royal Navy.'

Within days of despatch of the letter, sightings were reported of what could well have been the mystery privateer snatching small coasters off Lydd a week since and off Hastings a day later. Although that fitted the date of the Folkestone raid perfectly, it added little to the sum total of knowledge. And after that there was silence, perhaps, Anson concluded, because the Frenchman had returned to Normandy with prizes and would not be back for weeks or even months.

*

Patched up and feeling fighting fit again, Anson returned to duty in time to welcome a surprise visitor to the Seagate detachment. It was the gallant divisional captain himself, Captain Arthur Veryan St Cleer Hoare, as he was fond of introducing himself even to those he had met before.

Nominally in command of the Sea Fencible division, it was well known that in reality he was merely a figurehead who nevertheless enjoyed the kudos and position in society the appointment gave him.

'The big-wigs have decided to include some jolly Jack Tars in the royal review of the Kentish Volunteers,' he announced, and Anson sensed what was to come.

It would have been next to impossible not to have heard of the review. Thousands of volunteers – yeomanry, infantry, artillery and all – were due to parade at the Lord Lieutenant's residence at Mote Park, Maidstone, for the King himself to review.

Captain Hoare confided: 'Our fellows' little action against the privateer has appeared in the news sheets, y'know. Attracted a fair bit of attention – and so you're going to go.'

Anson sighed inwardly. So he was expected to drop everything to provide a mere token presence.

His protestations that training would be severely interrupted, that his men had no uniforms, and that it would cost many King's shillings to pay them for what would inevitably be a prolonged outing – all fell on deaf ears.

'Nonsense, Anson. Be proud, walk tall! Here's a splendid chance for the navy to score points off some of the bumpkin soldiery. They've not seen action. We have. I'll even go myself.'

Anson's eyebrows twitched. Hoare had been ashore and nowhere near the action.

No doubt the chance to mingle with royalty was too much for a man like him to resist, and Anson muttered 'Thought you would' under his breath. But, noting the captain's questioning look, he added loudly: 'Jolly good, sir – I say jolly good!'

A sudden worrying point struck Captain Hoare. 'Uniform! You mentioned uniform?'

'I'll wear my best of course, sir.'

'No, no, no. The men must have uniform. We cannot have them in sailcloth and rags like a bunch of mendicant beggars.'

Anson shrugged. 'However, I'm afraid that's all most of them have got by way of clothing, sir. A few will have Sunday best, but—'

The captain was growing agitated. 'Think man, think! All the soldiery will be done up to the nines – red jackets, tricorns and all. The yeomanry will be dolled up like dogs' dinners – all gold and silver braid and whatnot.'

'And you think my, I mean our, men will appear rather scruffy by comparison—?'

Hoare was by now almost apoplectic. 'My Godfathers! This is serious! They must be in some kind of uniform and scrubbed up looking at least half decent. Trust the Admiralty to think of setting up the Sea Fencibles without providing uniforms to distinguish them from all the other harbour rats. It's disgraceful!'

'I suppose, sir, that their Lordships reckon what's good enough for proper men-of-war's men is good enough for the fencibles.'

'But dammit, men-of-war's men aren't let off their ships to wander around the countryside. Our men will be seen – and by the King himself to boot. We must provide them with uniform.'

Anson had come to know that when Hoare said 'we' he meant 'you'. 'Are you sure there's money available for that, sir? I'm constantly being reminded that we're spending too many of the King's shillings on the men's pay as it is.'

Exasperated, Hoare neither knew nor cared. 'Just get yourself to Chatham and buy up what's needed. We'll sort out how you get the money back in slower time.'

Anson was dubious. He well knew what slower time meant, and getting money out of the service after you had dipped your hand into your own pocket on its behalf was one of life's trickier problems. However, the captain had a point: the men were going to have to be decently turned out – and Anson still had a fair amount of his Mediterranean prize money.

As Hoare left, an afterthought struck him and he spun around and delivered a final broadside. 'Don't fail to read your men the Articles of War, Riot Act and whatnot to be on their very best behaviour.'

'Of course, sir.'

The captain wagged his finger. 'Assume that they'll get at some drink. These sort of fellows always do sniff the stuff out and knock it back like mother's milk. It'll be the devil's own job to keep them relatively sober. A few tots and they'll be showing off like jolly Jack Tar to the women and pretending to be naval heroes. But in reality they're a parcel of harbour rats. Never forget that and keep a tight grip on 'em.'

Again Anson answered with false enthusiasm: 'Of course, sir!'

*

The task of measuring the men fell to Boxer whose undertaking skills made him best qualified for the role.

Lists were drawn up, and Anson and the undertaker set off for Chatham, where the naval tailors would no doubt be able to supply suitable clothing, as they were increasingly becoming used to providing such items for the ships' companies of fashion-conscious captains, or at least their launch crews.

They made their way into the scruffy, ill-built town and entered the long narrow high street. It was bustling, as befitted a town of some 10,000 souls. And this was not counting the thousands of marines and soldiers in the barracks, and the sailors whose ships were alongside or who were lodged in hulks living in conditions little better than the many French prisoners confined in other rat-infested, rotting, superannuated warships down the Medway.

At the north end of the high street was the large victualling yard with its cooperage, pickling house, bakery and a multitude of stores sufficient to provide the navy's wooden walls with the necessaries for extended periods at sea.

As they made their way down the busy street, Anson noted that apart from the victualling yard the only other handsome buildings were the two breweries, and, from the large number of alehouses and intoxicated people around, it appeared that much of their brew ended up down local throats.

Even in broad daylight, prostitutes were attempting to ply their trade, many no doubt poor country girls lured by the rich pickings to be made from sailors returning from months if not years afloat, pockets full of back pay and lust in their loins.

It was a street that could have few rivals in catering for those who go down to the sea in ships, Anson mused. Within a few yards you could readily obtain a plug of tobacco, a shave, a tattoo or a dose of the pox.

They passed marine stores, bakers, butchers, fishmongers, tobacconists and several tailors before reaching the one who had serviced Anson satisfactorily in the past.

Inside, over a complimentary glass of rum, dark blue jackets, broad red-striped trousers, sea boots and straw hats were ordered at what Anson considered horrendous expense – even after Boxer had used his business acumen to drive down the price as far as possible against the wily tailor, who blamed wartime shortages for his high prices.

Nevertheless, he sensed this could be the first of similar orders for other Sea Fencible detachments all around the Kent coast, and the highest quality of workmanship with prompt delivery was promised.

On the way back, Boxer stated his opinion that it was going to be next to impossible to clean up the fencibles and get them to wear the new outfits in anything like a soldierly or seamanlike manner.

Anson could but agree.

36

Mounted on Ebony, Anson rode ahead, followed by the wagons carrying the tents and rations.

As the miles fell away, first one and then more of the marching fencibles hobbled back to plead with Fagg, who was sitting next to the second driver: 'Can I 'ave a ride, bosun? Me feet's killin' me...'

A nod from Fagg allowed the temporary cripple respite on one of the wagons. But to one he thought was swinging the lead he barked: 'Eff orf an' walk with the rest, yer idle bugger!'

Midway between the small market town of Ashford and their destination, the procession came upon a wayside inn. There were stables and nearby was a large barn. Anson reckoned it as good as they would get for the inevitable overnight stop.

He called to Tom Marsh, who was driving the first cart, and raised his arm to call a halt. The remaining few marching men fell out, collapsing theatrically on the green that fronted the inn. The carts, by now festooned with the sick and lame, pulled off the road and the drivers went in search of water for their charges.

Anson noted this with satisfaction. In this respect alone he subscribed to cavalry rules: first one's horses, then one's men – then oneself.

Fagg limped into the inn and emerged with the landlord – a scruffy, disagreeable-looking man. Anson gave him a stare. 'Good day, landlord. Kindly provide mugs of ale for my men – no strong drink mind – and pray tell me what you can offer in the way of food.'

The inn-keeper pursed his lips and looked doubtful, but when Anson reassured him that he must keep a tally and would be paid in full he managed a crooked smile.

'We got some pies in the larder and I daresay we can rustle up some boiled 'taters, eggs an' bacon,' he ventured. 'The 'taters'll take a while, mind. Will any o' that do?'

'All of the above will do nicely, and you can give me a price for the use of your barn overnight.'

Quick as a flash the landlord responded: 'It'll be a shillin' a man, sir.'

'I'll pay sixpence a man for the food, and the use of all your, er, facilities. That's my final offer. If you don't like it, we'll press on to the next hostelry.'

The man was not going to let this unexpected pay-day slip away and readily agreed. 'Sixpence a man it is, your worship.'

Turning to Fagg, Anson ordered: 'Dole out some midshipman's nuts and water while we're waiting. The boys must be famished.' Fagg grinned at the naval slang for small ship's biscuit and acknowledged the instruction with a touch of his cane to his japanned hat.

Anson followed the landlord into the inn and watched as the man set his wife and a crone who could be her mother to work on boiling potatoes and frying eggs and bacon while he cut triangles from four large pies.

The bar-room was scruffy and smelly, which did not augur well for the food, but they were committed now. Resigned to sticking with the bargain he had struck, he was settling down to study the review orders when he heard a commotion outside.

Through the small latticed window he could see horses ridden by helmeted, blue-coated figures milling about among his men. 'Cavalry! Where the devil did they spring from?'

He hurried outside to find a scene of mayhem, like a hunt meet in a lunatic asylum. The fencibles were retreating before the horsemen to the wagons and a yeomanry officer, distinguishable from his troopers by the extravagance of his uniform, was waving his sabre threateningly and shouting at Fagg. 'Bad luck, Jack Tar! Get your wretched bilge rats away from here. This is where we are going to hole up for the night – and we are about the King's business!'

Fagg stood firm, hands on hips. 'So, sir, are we – and we wus here first!'

Enraged, the officer slashed the air a foot from Fagg's face, shouting: 'Get out now, or we'll run you out!' The other horsemen had reined their mounts in, watching developments. Some exchanged jeering comments, but most looked uneasy and were hanging back.

Anson walked forward deliberately and placed himself beside Fagg.

The red-faced officer demanded: 'And who, sir, are you?'

'I am Lieutenant Anson of the Royal Navy. These are my men, and be pleased to address me if you have anything to say.'

The officer circled his frisky horse and faced Anson. 'I am taking over this inn for the night for my troop. We are on His Majesty's business heading for the royal review and you must take your pirate crew or whatever they are elsewhere, sharp, d'you understand?'

From the corner of his eye, Anson could see Hoover beside one of the wagons, fiddling with his musket. Some of the fencibles were retrieving their half pikes.

Straightening his fore and aft hat, Anson stared at the yeomanry officer. 'It is as my bosun has informed you. We are also on our way to the review and we have already taken this inn for the night. Now, sir, if you will return your weapon to its scabbard and leave us to enjoy our evening meal I shall be greatly obliged.'

Turning away to signify he considered the exchange to be over, Anson felt a blow on his shoulder. The mounted officer had struck him with the flat of his sabre. He spun around, amazed at the man's foolhardy action, but before he could react a musket shot sounded close by, sending the spooked horse skittering backwards and unseating its rider, who fell heavily, losing his helmet in the process – to the ironic cheers of the fencibles.

Hoover stepped forward, smoking musket in hand with bayonet fixed. 'Oh my, oh my! Mighty sorry about that.' And, looking down at the winded officer, he shrugged: 'That must have been what they call a flash in the pan – an accidental discharge. First time that's happened to me since I joined. Usually I only fire on purpose. And I suppose that when you tapped my officer on the shoulder with the flat of your blade, well, that was pretty much accidental, too?'

There was muttering among the foremost troopers, but those who had hung back throughout appeared to be embarrassed at the rumpus. Those who had been harassing the fencibles were clearly uncertain what to do, and it was left to a sergeant to dismount and help his officer, still gasping for air, to his feet. Hoover stooped to pick up the plumed helmet and handed it back.

Another trooper leaned from his saddle to grab the spooked horse and held it as the yeomanry sergeant assisted the officer to re-mount, clearly still dazed, puffing and blowing and rubbing his left arm that had taken the brunt of his fall.

The sergeant remounted, shouted to the troop to form up on the road, and encouraged the captain's horse away from the inn with a smack on the rump. Now that many of the fencibles had armed themselves, discretion was the better part of valour and the sergeant clearly judged a strategic withdrawal advisable.

His officer, helmet askew and still shocked by his fall, was hard put to stay in the saddle. But, as he kicked his horse on, he turned and growled savagely at Anson: 'Be aware – you haven't heard the last of this!'

As the yeomanry troop formed up and trotted off up the road, Anson gave Hoover an enquiring look and spoke quietly so that the others could not hear. 'I saw you loading your musket. That was no accidental discharge.'

Hoover grinned. 'Reckoned a bit of a diversion was needed right then, sir. There was no ball – only powder and a wad. But it made a mighty fine bang!'

Anson nodded. 'Give yourself a verbal warning – and then you and Fagg can see that the innkeeper gets some help in the galley. Some of our boys must know how to cook, and I'm starving.'

*

Next morning the detachment came to the Mote, a mile to the south-east of Maidstone, and the seat of the Right Honourable Charles Marsham, Earl of Romney, the Lord Lieutenant and His Majesty King George's representative in and for the County of Kent.

The old mansion was a venerable rambling building in the lower part of the park, surrounded by trees and by all accounts awaiting its fate – to be demolished stone by stone. Its successor, a far more splendid structure, had already been erected according to the Earl's aspirations with spacious, magnificently-fitted apartments, on a knoll commanding fine views for miles around.

The park itself was of extensive acreage with much fine timber, notably oak, and many of the trees were aged, giant specimens. A broad sheet of water had been created artificially in front of the new mansion and the lake could be crossed via a handsome bridge.

It was already busy, animated by several thousand gaily-uniformed volunteers and a great many horse-drawn vehicles. Anson went in search of the unfortunate officer and his staff charged with organising the review and found them sitting at tables near the old mansion, busily marking up seating plans and dealing with volleys of questions and requests from newly-arrived units.

A harassed, elderly major noted the arrival of the Sea Fencibles and told Anson, 'You are the only navy men, although there are supposed to be some River Fencibles, but God knows where they may be.'

He handed over written instructions about overnight camping and where they were to be seated for the feasting.

Anson saluted and turned on his heel, but as he strode off the major, no doubt remembering the reputation of sons of the sea, called after him: 'I trust your men have no strong liquor about them. We want no intemperance in sight of His Majesty!'

Once satisfied that his men were safely ensconced in the parkland, rigging the tents and canvas shelters attached to the wagons under the direction of Fagg and Hoover, Anson rode, stiffly, into Maidstone.

He was not familiar with the area and knew little of it except that it lay across the River Medway. As a schoolboy he had learned that Wat Tyler had led the Kentish rebels from here, and it had been the scene of a bloody Civil War battle.

It was, he thought, much as Samuel Pepys had described it – 'as pretty a town as he had ever seen,' and by all accounts now supplying London with more commodities than any market town in England.

Riding towards the river, Anson came upon a small crowd gathered under a huge wooden structure, watching carpenters hammering and sawing with obvious urgency.

He dismounted and walked Ebony forward to watch the artisans putting the finishing touches to what he could now see was a massive triumphal arch, under which he had heard the King himself would pass on his way to review the Kent volunteers.

Atop was a crown which on the morrow would be surmounted by the Royal Standard. To the left and right were a lion and unicorn, flanking a representation of a domed building, a ship of war and Britannia. Hanging beneath, where the King would ride in triumph, was a large oval medallion bearing His Majesty's idealised portrait, Roman emperor-style.

A handful of blue-jacketed Cinque Ports Volunteers were keeping at bay the locals who had come to gape and wonder at the great edifice that had grown from wooden frame to pseudo-classic proportions, dramatically changing the appearance of their familiar street within days.

The citizen soldiers were clearly enjoying their role as temporary guardians of His Majesty's ceremonial arch. Men who were mere ploughmen, labourers, potboys and the like in real life, they stood taller, if gawky, with their muskets and unfamiliar uniforms.

Certainly the girls of the town showed more interest in them as soldiers than they had ever been shown in their normal roles as country bumpkins or backstreet lads.

Their good-natured sergeant – a big man with extravagant mutton-chop whiskers and an ample belly, attributable to his normal calling as a butcher – waved his pike at some urchins who had strayed too close and whose furtive air made it obvious that they were souvenir hunting.

'Get back there, you young perishers! If 'is Majesty rides through 'ere tomorrer and finds anyfink missing orf 'is ceremonial harch he'll 'ave my guts fer garters. The fust one of yer that nicks anyfink gets this 'ere pike acrost his backside. And the second will get a good view of the royal party passing under it 'cos 'e'll he hangin' from the top by 'is ankles.'

Clearly impressed, the urchins hung back, and the sergeant acknowledged Anson with a hand to his tricorn.

'Arternoon, sir!' And to the urchins: 'Now you'd better behave yerselves – the navy's 'ere and this hadmiral's proberly lookin' fer powder monkeys to flog!'

'Having trouble with the natives, sergeant?' queried Anson, disregarding his sudden promotion.

'They'd pinch the whole perishin' harch if we didn't keep a close watch on 'em, sir.'

Anson nodded. 'A royal visit's a big thing for Maidstone, no doubt.'

'True enough, sir. And the parade an' tomorrer's review'll be the biggest thing these 'ere whippersnappers will ever see, like as not.'

The urchins, sensing that they were not about to be beaten or strung up by their ankles by the army, nor pressed into the navy, turned their attention to Anson.

'Are you really a hadmiral?' asked the boldest.

'Merely a lieutenant.'

'Can you read?' asked another ragamuffin.

'More or less,' Anson admitted.

'Well, can you read us what it says up there? Only these pretend sodjers says they won't tell us, but they can't 'cos they can't read neither.'

Anson looked up at the arch. It truly was an impressive, if somewhat tacky, edifice. The urchins waited expectantly.

He cleared his throat with a low cough. 'Up there it says: Kent Volunteers – Loyal – Brave—'

'These 'ere pretend sodgers ain't brave. They ain't done nuffink,' protested the bold urchin.

'Not yet, but they will if the French come,' Anson assured him.

Before the ankle-biters could grill him further, hoof-beats clattered on cobbles, drawing the attention of the urchins and the growing crowd of by-standers to a troop of West Kent Yeomanry trotting down to make sure the royal party would have no problem negotiating the arch. Anson remounted Ebony and slipped away back to Mote Park.

*

The park was seething with activity like a disturbed ant hill, with men, horses, carts and artillery pieces higgledy-piggledy all over, and sergeants and corporals struggling to sort out the apparent chaos with raised voices and curses – order, counter-order, disorder.

The officers charged with organising the review briefed those from newly-arrived units, fussed over the morrow's parade order and grappled with the complex logistics required to position and cater for almost 6000 people from the highest in the land to the lowliest volunteer, and hundreds of horses.

Troops of the West Kent Yeomanry, from Sevenoaks, Tonbridge and Tunbridge Wells in the west, to Chislehurst, Greenwich and Woolwich in the north of the county and the Isle of Sheppey in the north-east, resplendent in their richly-decorated uniforms, were exercising their horses, admired by the county set, now disgorged from their carriages and enjoying the spectacle.

The West Kents, under Lord Camden, were to take precedence in the review, but this did not dampen the ardour of their East Kent counterparts, who hailed from as far afield as the Isle of Thanet, Romney Marsh and the string of rural villages between the two extremes.

Companies of volunteer foot from all parts of the county paraded, were counted and re-counted, inspected, re-inspected, exhorted by their officers and tongue-lashed by their sergeants.

For the purpose of the manoeuvres, Major-General Pigott was to command the first line of Kent Volunteer Infantry, and no less a personage than His Royal Highness Major-General Prince William Frederick had been placed in at least nominal command of the second line.

Gunners from Thameside and from Thanet fussed around their artillery pieces and received their instructions over and over from Major Kite, who had brought no less than 100 of his volunteers from Gravesend, qualifying him – if for no other reason – to be commander of the combined Artillery Corps.

With men from Ramsgate, Margate and Broadstairs brought under his command for the review, it was vital that he and his subordinate officers got their act together, for they could afford no mistakes when the 21-gun salute was fired at the end of the proceedings.

A misfire would speak louder than any broadside. With the eyes and ears of the King himself, more than 5000 volunteers, and thousands of spectators concentrated on them at the crucial moment, ridicule for the gunners was but a hairsbreadth from a perfectly-timed salute.

It was small wonder that Kite's men were compulsively cleaning their already highly-polished guns, checking and re-checking the blank charges and advising one another on how to avoid a cock-up.

To Anson, the artillerymen on the whole appeared to be mainly well-built, well turned-out fellows who would not have disgraced a man-of-war gun deck.

He noted that the yeomanry were sparky, proud, and of all the volunteers by far the best-accoutred. But there was no telling how effective they might be on active service.

The standard of their splendid uniforms and the quality of their mounts was no doubt attributable at least in part to the rich young land-owners' sons who commanded them – like the dolt he had clashed with on the way to the review.

The great majority of the volunteer infantrymen looked keen and fit, but among them he spotted more than a few who were only once removed from simpletons and whose ill-fitting uniforms gave them the appearance of beggars in stolen clothes that dogs would bark at if they came to town. For their officers' and sergeants' sakes, he hoped these individuals would escape inspection.

Looking to his own men, Anson thanked God that the social-climbing Captain Hoare had insisted on him providing them with uniforms of a sort. In their normal, shabby, work-a-day civilian clothes they would indeed have looked like a bunch of pirates that had just been pulled through a number of hedges backwards.

As it was, thanks to the expenditure of his personal prize money, they looked half decent in their dark blue jackets, broad red-and-white-striped trousers, sea boots and straw hats. And, all credit to the exacting measurements of the undertaker, the majority of the jackets appeared to fit, at least where they touched.

Fagg and Hoover had managed to get the fencibles cleaned up, too, by forcing them under the pump in the wayside inn yard before they left early that morning. Washed and more or less clean-shaven for once, most now looked unnaturally whey-faced, and one, known to everyone as Darkie Smith, whom most had imagined to have the touch of a tar-brush in his ancestry, turned out to be pink after all. He had just not been seen with a clean face since new-born.

A lavishly uniformed foppish amateur officer minced past, apparently deliberately seeking a salute. Fagg obliged by lifting his hat a good six inches, but Hoover, the previous night's clash still fresh in his mind, turned away, barely hiding his contempt.

Fagg replaced his hat with a flourish. 'What's up lobster? Don't marines salute orficers?'

'Don't mind saluting proper officers, but these ...' He searched in vain for the right word. 'Back home we didn't hold with all this bowing and scrapin' and forelock-touchin' to peacocks like him.'

'Well, you ain't over in Amerikey now. And just 'cos we bows and scrapes over 'ere don't mean we respecks no one,' Fagg observed enigmatically.

37

The large marquees, including the grand royal pavilion, were being readied to receive the King and Queen, the Princesses Augusta and Elizabeth, and the Dukes of York, Cumberland and Gloucester.

Also expected were the exiled Dutch Stadtholder William V, the Lord Chancellor, and all the great officers of state, including Messrs Pitt, Dundas and Windham, along with many of the principal nobility and gentry of the kingdom.

The Lord Lieutenant, as the monarch's representative in the county, was making a tour of inspection with his entourage of deputies and commanding officers of the various corps represented.

Since the time of the Armada, successive Lord Lieutenants from William Brooke, the Tenth Baron Cobham onwards, had been responsible for organising the defence of the county.

Through him and his successors, the monarch exercised indirect rule in this as in all other counties, and, importantly, they controlled the militias, local defence forces of special importance in a nation which came late to acquiring a significant standing army.

Lord Romney also acted as the county's chief magistrate, responsible for the appointment and discipline of the justices of the peace, a role that, like his military power, gave him immense political influence and prestige.

Anson was engrossed in creating order among his fencibles as Lord Romney rode past, and was startled to be addressed by the great man himself.

'You, sir!'

He spun. 'Me, my lord?'

'Yes you, sir. Navy man, ain't you?'

'I am, my lord.' He lifted his hat. 'Lieutenant Anson, here with a party of Sea Fencibles.'

Romney beamed. 'Ain't you the fellows who saw off the French down at Folkestone?'

'In a manner of speaking, my lord. We did have an encounter with a French privateer.'

The Lord Lieutenant guffawed. 'Encounter is it? Gave 'em a drubbing, I heard. Excellent, excellent! We had summoned the River Fencibles from Greenwich, but sadly they have not appeared. Why, I know not. Gettin' all these yeomanry fellows and footsloggers is one thing, but the navy's a bonus that will please His Majesty – especially the jolly Jack Tars who've given the Frogs a kicking and sent 'em packing.'

Anson smiled and tilted his head dismissively. 'Hardly the proper navy, my lord, 'though I do have the honour to be a naval officer, formerly of HMS *Phryne*, now posted ashore to command this detachment of Sea Fencibles under Captain Hoare. But my men here, well, they are part-timers of course, a mixture of boatmen, fishermen and the like—'

The Lord Lieutenant protested. 'No need to excuse them, young man. I've no doubt there are smugglers and harbour rats among them, but the important thing is that they are volunteers, steppin' forward to aid our nation at a time of peril, eh? And as such, your fellows have earned their place at my tables tomorrow.'

The Seagate men within hearing distance shuffled with pleased embarrassment. Being called smugglers and harbour rats was no insult to them, and they were happy at the acknowledgement of their volunteer spirit. Clearly, the Lord Lieutenant was unaware of the protection system that saved them from really putting their lives on the line for King and country in men-of-war.

Nevertheless, Anson was grateful for the compliment. 'You do us proud, my lord. And to bring us here in the presence of His Majesty is an honour we will ever remember with gratitude.'

The Lord Lieutenant turned to his aide. 'Ralls, make a note to bring this young man to the royal pavilion after the feast. I've a mind to present him to His Majesty.'

*

With the men settled, Fagg strolled off, with only a slight limp now, intent on finding out what was on the menu. Behind the mansion he came upon a harassed-looking individual in a cook's rig, out for a crafty smoke.

'Looks like you've bin busy, mate,' observed Fagg.

The cook removed the clay pipe he was puffing on, let out a stream of smoke, and jabbed his thumb at the basements where the kitchens lay.

'Never knowed anyfink like it and that's the truth. There's an army of cooks and skivvies in there, brought from all over. Never in me life—'

'Hard graft, I 'spect, mate?'

'You never said a truer word, brother. You wouldn't believe the amount of stuff we're preparin' – 60 lambs, 700 fowls, 300 hams, 300 tongues, gawd knows how many dishes of boiled beef, roast beef and veal, hundreds of pies ... you name it, we're cookin' it. I hate to think how much old man Romney has shelled out.'

Fagg, more of a drinking than an eating man, enquired: 'And some drink too, mate?'

The cook laughed. 'There's not only more butts of beer and pipes of port up here ready to draw on than you could shake a stick at, but he's had a pump fixed up over there that links to the cellar so's more can be pumped up if you lot drink the barrels up here dry.'

'We'll do our best, mate!' Fagg assured him and made his way back to the wagons. Best see that the men had not yet cottoned on to the ready availability of booze.

He found Anson, who was also acutely aware of the major's warning against drunkenness, but nevertheless ordered: 'Issue a tot of rum, but careful measures mind, and take care the men don't abuse this privilege. I will not tolerate men sneaking off to alehouses or buying drink from pedlars. Any man seen rotten drunk will lose his protection.'

*

At dawn next day, Hoover and Fagg rousted the men out of the canvas-covered wagons and tents and chivvied them into titivating themselves before breakfasting on bread, cheese and water brought with them.

The bosun forestalled any muttering about the spartan fare by assuring them: 'If 'alf what some cook told me yesterday is true, we'll be feastin' orf the fat of the land soon enough. Lamb, beef, chicken, venison ... Gawd, you won't know you're born!'

Before long, parties of gentry and would-be gentry were wandering about taking in the colourful scene and hoping to be noticed later by those of royal blood. Gentlemen were smartly attired as current fashion demanded, mostly in round hats with flat-topped crowns and uncocked brims, tailed frock coats over single-breasted waistcoats, nankeen breeches and short top boots. Many were carrying sticks, some no doubt concealing swords.

The ladies were in their finery, wearing long flowing dresses, bonnets or more elaborate feather-topped hats, and many carried parasols against the afternoon sun.

The adults' equally dressed-up children were little mirror images.

Red-jacketed sentries wearing tricorn hats and crossbelts, their muskets with bayonets fixed, were good-naturedly keeping the lesser mortals at a respectable distance, while the upper crust sauntered around by the house and the cluster of large tents, as much on parade as the volunteers themselves, and pretending to be oblivious to the stares of the perimeter crowds.

On the hilly area looking down on the park, Anson came upon an artist at work behind a large easel, busily sketching the scene laid out before him. As he stopped to take a look, the artist noticed him and asked: 'A darker shade of jacket than the artillerymen or the yeomanry, so I conclude you must be a navy man?'

'Quite correct! Lieutenant Anson at your service.'

The artist put his pencil behind his ear and held out his hand. 'William Alexander. I venture my profession speaks for itself.'

'The official artist for the review?'

'Just so, sir. But may I ask what you are doing here such a long way from the sea?'

'Indeed, sir. I am here with my detachment of Sea Fencibles. We have travelled up from Seagate for the review.'

Alexander nodded. 'Worth every step to be part of such a colourful and historic event, don't you think? I am recording it at the behest of various patrons with a view to publishing a print worthy of framing for drawing room walls around the county, and maybe for the King himself.'

'How will it be reproduced?'

'The plan is for an engraving in aquatint to be made from my finished drawing. In colour, with all the uniforms and so forth, it should make a pretty picture.'

'You have quite a task recording such a busy and extensive scene, sir, but I much admire what you have done so far.'

The artist acknowledged the compliment with an appreciative nod. 'It is indeed a major task, but not all has to be achieved at one fell swoop. I have been working on the background – the old and new mansions, tented pavilions, trees and so forth – for some days now, so today it's a question of putting the soldiery and spectators into the picture. I'll continue to work on the fine detail from my rough sketches for many a day to come before I am satisfied I have done justice to the scene – and the occasion. Are you an artist yourself?'

'Sketching is encouraged in us as midshipmen, so as to be able to do a likeness of an enemy coast or suchlike, and I keep it up as an agreeable pastime at sea. But I fear my skills do not begin to compare with yours, sir.'

Alexander tutted. 'You should keep it up, sir. We all improve with practice.'

Anson pointed to where his fencibles were gathering. 'Pray sir, have you noted the White Ensign above those far tables?'

The artist put a small telescope to his eye. 'I confess I had not noted it earlier, but I see it now.'

'If you'll kindly ensure it is showing in your finished picture, I will most certainly buy a print – a number of prints!'

Alexander smiled. 'Then there is no doubt that I will include it, rest assured. We impoverished artists need all the patronage we can get!'

*

Hoover was with the wagons checking weapons when a lone blue-jacketed horseman approached and dismounted beside him.

He tapped his helmet in salute and Hoover recognised him as the sergeant from the yeomanry troop involved in the fracas at the wayside inn.

'Sarn't Noad, Sam Noad. Remember me?'

'How could I forget? Between us you and I just about stopped a civil war outside that pub. You didn't miss much, by the by – ale was like cats' piss, the food was crap and the barn was full of wildlife!'

Noad laughed. 'We did no better five miles up the road. It took that long for Cap'n Chitterling to calm down enough to stop—'

'So why's he sent you? I guess he wants me flogged for that, er, accidental discharge?'

'I'm sure he does, but he didn't send me. I'm here off me own bat – just to say I reckon I would've done the same as you.'

Hoover was pleased. 'That's mighty thoughtful of you. I appreciate it.'

'Just wanted you to know, sarn't to sarn't, that we ain't all like the captain in the yeomanry. He's got his cronies o' course, but most of the lads are decent enough farmers' sons. Trouble is, they're tenants of the Chitterlings, who own Gawd knows how much land round our parts.'

'You, too?'

'No mate, I was in the reg'lar dragoons. Real soldiers with proper officers, not like the yeomanry clodhoppers. If yer daddy has enough land you can get put in charge like Chitterling is. He's always on about honour, bravery and suchlike, but he's never fought a foreign foe. Poor poachers, foxes, gamebirds and the like are much more to his taste. They gen'rally don't fight back. He's just a spoilt brat with more money and power than sense.'

'So why did you join his troop?'

'I'd just come out o' the reg'lars, got a new wife and wanted to settle down. He needed someone to train his bumpkins and hold things together, so I gets paid as the full-time troop sarn't with all found. He'd be lost without me and he knows it, so he treats me a bit wary-like. Can't be bad, can it? I'm home most nights.'

'Sounds like me, as master-at-arms of these sailor boys. Darn sight better'n sailing the seven seas in the marines!'

The marine's accent puzzled Noad, and he asked: 'You from Amerikey?'

Hoover nodded.

'D'you know a Jack Dawson?'

'Who might he be?'

'Me cousin, well, second cousin.'

'So?'

'P'raps you see'd him there?'

Hoover stifled a smile. 'No mate, 'fraid it's a pretty big country and there's a might few over there as I ain't come across yet myself.'

Noad nodded, apparently satisfied. 'I forgot, 'course it's a big place. I ain't been there, but they do say as how Amerikey's even bigger'n Yorkshire.'

'I guess so,' Hoover agreed.

'No hard feelings about that scrimmage?' Noad held out his hand and the marine grasped it.

'None at all. If I can do anything for you, just let me know. Seagate Detachment, Sea Fencibles, that's where you'll find me.'

Noad swung himself up in the saddle. 'Likewise, Pett Valley Troop, East Kent Yeomanry. Better not be seen talking to you. If the cap'n sees me he'll likely have a fit!' He grinned, touched his helmet in salute, whirled his horse and trotted off.

38

Having left London at five o'clock in the morning, the royal family breakfasted with Lord Camden at his seat at Wilderness, near Sevenoaks, and continued on to Maidstone.

By mid-morning, large crowds had thronged in from all around to see the King review so many volunteers in what was an event of national importance, designed to heighten morale at a time of threat.

Such was the county's pride and enthusiasm, that all roads were almost impassable, but the military ensured that the way was clear for the King and his entourage to enter the town, and to the cheers of the waiting crowds, the procession passed under the triumphal arch, now with the Royal Standard fluttering above, where Anson had encountered the inquisitive urchins the night before.

Lining the route, were red-jacketed volunteers with bayonets fixed and sprigs of oak in their hats – a Kentish custom dating back to the time of the Norman conquest. Every Man of Kent and Kentish Man – the difference being which part of the county you were born in – knew the origin of it, that rather than fight a Kentish army with oak boughs on their shoulders and swords in their hands, the Normans allowed them to retain their ancient rights and liberties. 'That's why,' questioners were always told, 'we call William the Norman rather than the Conquerer, and why our county motto is Invicta – Unconquered.'

Anson was patrolling his detachment's tables looking out for signs of drunkenness and misbehaviour when to his astonishment he heard his name being called in a throaty female voice.

It had to be Charlotte Brax, she of the heaving bosom, wandering hand and suggestive turn of phrase.

Sure enough, there she was approaching like a first rate under full press of sail with her younger sisters flanking her like attendant frigates.

'Good afternoon, Miss, er, the Misses Brax,' he greeted them with more confidence than he felt.

Charlotte, wearing a high-waisted, low-necked dress that displayed her ripe figure to perfection, held out her hand to be kissed. He did so as gallantly as he could muster before the eyes of his men, many of whom ceased their chatter to stare at the newcomers with varying degrees of lust.

'Your servant, ladies. But pray, what brings you here?'

Jane Brax stepped forward and offered her hand. 'We're here to see the royal family – and the volunteers, of course. Father and mother had an invitation from the Lord Lieutenant to the dinner, and brother George is here somewhere with his troop—'

Charlotte interrupted: 'Nonsense Jane, admit to Mr Anson that we're really here to recruit for our ball. We're sizing up the officers! Just about every eligible bachelor in the county holds a commission in the yeomanry or the volunteers, so here's a perfect chance to check that they're sound of wind and limb – and invite the cream of 'em to our ball.'

'I'm greatly relieved that you aren't going to include naval officers in your vetting, Miss Brax—'

She waved her hand at him. 'You've already been vetted and found to be suitable ball fodder, sir – and please call me Charlotte and not Miss Brax. Every time you call one of us Miss Brax, all three of us leap to attention, don't we little sisters?'

Jane and Isobel shrugged, no doubt used to being browbeaten by her.

Anson addressed Jane: 'And having seen so many volunteers, do you still aspire to be in uniform Miss, er, Jane?'

'Certainly, Mr Anson. The next time you see me I will be in uniform!'

'Really?'

Charlotte interjected: 'She's referring to our ball. We are planning some interesting patriotic outfits to compete with all you peacock males in uniform.'

Jane protested: 'Mr Anson is hardly a peacock in his naval uniform.'

And little Isobel offered: 'More of a magpie with all that navy blue and white. But you are a very smart magpie – and your men look very smart, too, Mr Anson.'

She smiled sweetly when he answered: 'You are too kind, er, Isobel. I confess to you that without their new hats and jackets they would look very much like a bunch of pirates!'

There was movement over in the area around the royal pavilion and Charlotte hurried her sisters away, turning to Anson as she went and saying archly: 'We will see you at the ball. I'll make sure you get a stiffy.'

The remark produced stifled guffaws from the nearest tables, and Anson reddened, remembering how she had stroked his thigh at the rectory dinner party. In the navy a 'stiffy' was a stiff invitation card. Surely that was what she meant – or did she?

Anson returned to the allotted tables to find a drunken Sea Fencible, sheep-dogged by Hoover and Fagg, making obscene gestures and shouting challenges to the nearby soldiery.

A couple of redcoats, egged on by their comrades, were all for picking up the gauntlet. But before they could respond, the bosun tripped the drunkard and sat on him.

'Who in hell is that and how did he get in that state so early?' Anson demanded. Fagg yanked his prisoner's head back by the hair. 'It's Longstaff, sir.'

'Longstaff? The man's a liability. Never yet seen him totally sober.'

Hoover offered: 'He's what we in the marines call a topper-upper.'

Anson snorted. 'But where in God's name does he get it?'

'Them as needs it gen'rally finds it,' Fagg observed sagely.

'Well, just keep him out of sight. Tie his hands and stick him under the tarpaulin in the wagon, else he'll shame us all.'

'Aye aye, sir.'

'And bosun, you'd better gag him. The last thing I want is a chorus of sea shanties when he gets to the singing stage.'

Fagg and Hoover pulled the now giggling man to his feet. 'She shanties is it, your worship?' he slurred. 'She shanties ye want and she shanties ye'll have ...' But before he could embark on the first, he was dragged protesting and giggling to one of the wagons, where Fagg expertly trussed him up and gagged him.

Longstaff thrashed about as the tarpaulin was pulled over him, but soon lapsed into a drunken stupor as the first of Major Kite's guns began barking out the royal salute.

His Majesty had entered the park on his charger, attended by the Prince of Wales and the Dukes of Cumberland and Gloucester. The Queen's carriage made straight for the royal pavilion where she and the Princesses alighted and, to honour the Kentish custom, fastened oak sprigs to their dresses.

The King and his entourage, now joined by the generals and members of the nobility, passed the long ranks of volunteers drawn up in two lines and then the troops of cavalry drawn up at the rear.

The ride past completed, the King retired to the royal pavilion and a lone signal cannon ordered the lines to form into their companies for the review proper to begin. There followed a series of manoeuvres, each signalled by a further cannon shot that set the volunteers marching, counter-marching, firing their muskets in sham fight and presenting arms for general salutes.

It was a brave sight. Finally the King passed along the front line once more and the troops marched past His Majesty with bands playing. Sensibly, the Sea Fencibles, more used to rowing than marching, stood fast in the rear watching the colourful scene with interest. But they joined lustily in the three cheers for the King and stood fast for the final general salute.

The review over, the volunteers sat down at the 90 or so long tables in front of the mansion and a sustained attack on the victuals, wine and beer commenced. What the cook had told Fagg proved no exaggeration. It was a truly sumptuous feast and the wine and beer sent spirits soaring sky high.

Once the volunteers were sated, a wagon-load of food was sent to Maidstone to be distributed among the poor, sufficient for 600 families.

Anson was checking that his men were behaving when he heard the jingle of spurs and sensed a presence at his elbow. It was the yeomanry officer from the skirmish at the inn.

Dismounted, his high plumed helmet made him appear taller than he was, and Anson again noted his florid cheeks and the beginnings of a paunch, only partly hidden by his tightly-buttoned brocaded jacket and scarlet waist sash.

Hand on sabre hilt, he announced: 'I am Cap'n Chitterling, d'you recall? And you're the naval Johnny who cheated my troop out of takin' supper at that inn yesterday, ain't you?'

'I think that on reflection you will agree that the Sea Fencibles were there first,' Anson countered. 'Sadly we were not properly introduced when we met outside the inn. Have you come to apologise?'

The yeomanry officer's naturally ruddy features turned puce. 'How dare you! I came to demand an apology for your man's deliberate attempt to fire on my men. If I do not receive an immediate apology I will report the matter to higher authority.'

'Go ahead.' Anson shrugged. 'You could start with my divisional captain – he's over in the royal pavilion right now. Or you could complain to the Lord Lieutenant, or to the King himself for all I care. But I warn you, if you do go telling false tales you'll be making an even bigger fool of yourself than you did at the inn. Take my advice, why don't you, and go play with your troop of ploughboys.'

Chitterling reacted like the spoilt child he had been and spat out: 'Damned cheek! You have impugned my honour and I've a damned good mind to call you out!'

Anson was aware that the dafter, peacock amateur officers, who had seen no action other than the hunt, had a fondness for challenging others to duel in defence of their pretended honour, probably hoping that their adversaries would climb down. It was behaviour akin to that of playground bullies – and he had no wish to fight anyone other than the French.

With a resigned expression, he said gently: 'Look, if you are so keen to call me out, just do it. However, we are guests here of the Lord Lieutenant and in the presence of the royal family, so the timing is not brilliant.'

Chitterling wrongly took this as a climb-down and, a little too readily and with obvious relief, retorted: 'Very well, your apology is accepted.' He was taken aback when Anson took a step towards him and spat menacingly. 'If you do insist on continuing this foolishness there is a very great likelihood that I will kill you, as I have killed a good many Frenchmen.'

And staring into Chitterling's eyes, he asked venomously: 'How many men have you killed? None, I suspect. I venture that you have killed nothing but unarmed game birds and foxes. But I will be armed, with sword, pistol or whatever you care to choose, and will be aiming to kill.'

Chitterling reeled back a step at this onslaught, and stammered: 'You don't rattle me ... b-but maybe you are right in that it might be deemed dishonourable to pursue this affair here.'

Anson shrugged indifferently, and his adversary turned away muttering: 'I've marked your card. We have unfinished business and I'll deal with you when the time is right!'

Choosing to pretend he thought Chitterling was referring to a lady's dance card, he responded: 'Excellent, I'll save the first dance for you!'

His retort provoked a last snort from Chitterling, who strode off, angry but deflated, pulling his mount towards the horse lines and glancing back venomously only to see that Anson was paying him no further attention but had resumed seeing that his fencibles were still on their best behaviour.

*

The King and his entourage had dined in the magnificent tented pavilions out of sight of the rank and file and civilian hoi polloi, and partook of coffee in Lord Romney's mansion house before their carriages rumbled round the front of the building ready for departure.

The Lord Lieutenant's promised summons for Anson never came, and instead, inevitably, it was Captain Arthur Veryan St Cleer Hoare who had found his way into the royal pavilion to wallow in his sovereign's congratulations for his men's action against the privateer.

Rank upon rank of volunteers were called to attention and gave a general salute as the royal party emerged from the house and Major Kite's train of artillery commenced firing the salute as the carriages departed.

The park seethed with activity again as the detachments of volunteers marched off to their camping areas to pack up and set off home, and it was with some relief that Anson and his Seagate men hit the road back to the coast.

A message from His Majesty, cascaded to all units as they departed, thanked every participating volunteer for 'a display of those virtues and manners which distinguishes the genuine character of Englishmen.' Fagg, sitting in the first wagon with his feet dangling over the tailgate, heard it in mock amazement, muttering: 'Good fing the King didn't see Longstaff pissed as a coot then, innit!'

39

Leaving the bosun and master-at-arms to carry on with the training back at Seagate, Anson got Tom Marsh to take him home in the pony and trap for the weekend.

Among the mail awaiting him was an invitation card to the Brax Hall ball – the 'stiffy' Charlotte had promised him. Scrawled on the back he read: 'Kindly bring fellow officer.'

There was precious little choice. The social-climbing Captain Arthur Veryan St Cleer Hoare was a definite no-no, and, as he had observed before, the reputation of the impress service meant that Lieutenant Coney would be about as welcome as a fox among hens.

No problem. Anson had just the man in mind.

*

At his signal station at Fairlight, overlooking the sea on the heights east of Hastings, Amos Armstrong was pleasantly surprised when Fagg drew up in the pony and trap driven by Tom Marsh.

The bosun lowered himself gingerly groundwards and knuckled his temple in salute to the officer who had emerged to investigate the visitors announced by his moonfaced midshipman.

'Commander Armstrong, sir?'

Brushing cobwebs from the sleeve of his third best uniform jacket, the officer commanding Fairlight Semaphore Station confirmed: 'You have found him, but who, pray, are you?'

'Fagg's the name, sir, Mister Anson's bosun from the Sea Fencibles at Seagate.'

Armstrong, noting Fagg's game leg and Tom Marsh's crutches, was wondering just how effective Anson's Sea Fencible detachment could be, should push come to shove, if all were as handicapped as these two. But he was pleased at what promised to be a welcome break in his boring station routine. 'You bring a message?'

'I do, sir, but not writ down.' He tapped his forehead. 'It's in me 'ead, sir, memorised like.'

'Good man, then come inside and sup a mug of ale while you tell me. You've had a long journey.' He bade the moonfaced youngster to see to it that Tom Marsh and his pony were fed, watered and rested, and, closely followed by Fagg, ducked low inside the station doorway to avoid more trailing cobwebs.

Ale was produced and they sat at the table where the remains of a meal still waited to be cleared.

Fagg gulped down several mouthfuls of ale, wiped the back of his hand across his mouth, and launched into his message. Armstrong smiled happily as he heard the plan. He was to put on his best rig and return to Seagate in the trap, leaving Fagg in temporary charge of the station.

'But is there no word as to what it's all about?'

'I was to tell you it hinvolves ladies, hentertainment and suchlike, an' that ye'll be away for two or three days. After that the pony and trap brings yer back and orf I goes back to Seagate.'

Armstrong smiled broadly. Out of the blue had come the kind of invitation he would have given his eye teeth for – just the thing to escape the boredom of life at the signal station, even if for only a few days.

Without further debate, he hastened to make himself look presentable.

While he washed, shaved, found a clean shirt and climbed into his best uniform, he briefed Fagg on the less than onerous duties he was likely to have to perform. Once dressed, he showed him the workings of the station and entrusted the semaphore signal-book into his care. The midshipman, the two seamen and dragoon messengers were instructed to take their orders from the bosun on pain of having punishment more painful than death inflicted upon them.

Then, fore and aft hat set at a jaunty angle to match his mood, he climbed aboard the trap, calling on Tom Marsh to set a course eastwards for Seagate – and what, for a man deprived of lively company, promised to be an enjoyable adventure.

*

Liveried footmen flanked the ornamental cast-iron entrance gates to Brax Hall. The gates were hinged to tall brick pillars topped by stone pineapples, and the lime tree avenue was illuminated by flickering flames from scores of torches stuck in the ground at regular intervals.

Tom Marsh's pony and trap crunched up the gravel driveway and joined a queue of carriages dropping off guests at the wide front steps

276

where more servants wearing the green, silver-buttoned Brax livery ushered them through the open door between impressive ionic columns.

Anson and Armstrong climbed down, and inside were announced by Roach, the butler, and greeted by a line-up led by Sir Oswald and Lady Brax. Close by, stood their sons William, in extravagant yeomanry cornet's uniform, and the younger George – together introduced by their father as 'the heir and the spare'. And beside them were the three daughters, each wearing a richly-braided military-style jacket – one red, one blue and one rifle green. They clustered round their naval guests.

'Aha, ladies!' Anson named his companion and exclaimed as light-heartedly as he could manage: 'Now I can see what you meant about being in uniform when we next met! If I may venture to say, you are extremely smart ...'

Charlotte, whose bosom appeared to be making every effort to escape its jacketed confines, riposted: 'I trust you will volunteer to join our regiment, Mr Anson, or will I be forced to press you?'

The thought of being pressed by her jolted him. Consciously or not, she seemed to have the knack of discomforting him each time she opened her mouth. As Anson pondered his stammered response of 'I er, er...' it was the youngest sister, Isobel, who came to his rescue. 'Much as Jane and I would like us to be, we are of course not really a regiment, Mr Anson.'

'No,' Jane agreed, 'merely ladies expressing our patriotism through our form of dress – at present.'

He had recovered his wits enough to stutter: 'And most patriotic and ch-charming you three look.' But the next guests were moving down the line, and to his huge relief, he and Armstrong were able to escape into the ballroom.

As they accepted glasses of champagne from a footman, they were approached by a portly, young, crimson-faced yeomanry officer who pointed at him and called out, 'Good God – it's the pirate admiral!'

Anson's stomach clenched as he recognised the loud-mouth he had encountered en route to Maidstone and at the royal review.

He forced himself to give a jocular response. 'Not quite an admiral just yet, I fear, Chitterling.'

'Taken the trouble to remember who I am, eh?'

Beside Anson and Armstrong, in their plain navy frock coats, the yeomanry officer – all silver braid and buttons with red stable belt, broad stripe down his overall trousers and with spurs a-jangling – looked like a peacock next to a pair of magpies.

Acting under previous orders, Anson's sisters Elizabeth and Anne appeared and dragged a delighted Armstrong off, insisting that he join them in the dancing, leaving their brother and the yeomanry officer glaring at one another.

Chitterling prodded Anson in the ribs and crowed: 'Should have had that soldier boy who was with you flogged for firin' his musket. Frightened the damned horses!'

'It was purely accidental—'

'Damned if it was! The cretin did it on purpose – and I'll tell you, if I ever see him again he'll feel the flat of my sabre on his back. And that's just for starters.'

Anson shrugged. 'I daresay a marine who's been in as many real fights as him will be able to handle himself against a farmer on horseback.'

As soon as the words were out, he realised he had gone too far. Once again, this was neither the time nor place to provoke a public argument, and he really had better things to do than to embark on some kind of vendetta with this preening, podgy poltroon.

But it was too late. His adversary had turned a deeper shade of crimson. 'Why, you jumped up water rat! You'll pay for that remark—' He looked around to see if anyone else had heard, but there was no one close. Putting his jowly face up close to Anson, he hissed: 'If anyone had heard what you said I would have been forced to call you out, here and now. But, in deference to our hosts, I will forego that pleasure.'

'Very wise.' Anson had battened down his temper now. He fixed the peacock with an icy stare and with heavy sarcasm told him: 'Of course I am scared witless, but I am happy to oblige you at another time – and in another place.'

Once again Chitterling misread this as a climb-down and dug himself in deeper. 'I've been hearing about you, Master Anson. You're the fellow who got himself captured, broke his parole and scurried back to England when the Froggies' backs were turned, ain't you? An officer who gives his parole and then sneaks away is a poor sort of gentleman. So much for honour!'

'That is a lie. I never gave my parole. You are beginning to irritate me, and much against my better judgment I may be forced to teach you manners.' He glared icily at Chitterling whose face betrayed a hint of unease.

The duel of stares was brought to an end by the arrival of the Brax sisters.

Charlotte grabbed Anson's arm. 'I see you've made friends with Dickie Chitterling, but we cannot have you boys hiding in corners chatting about horses and boats. So we've come to drag you off to dance.'

'A pleasure Charlotte!' brayed Chitterling, relieved at this timely intervention. Taking her free arm he pulled her away from Anson and almost dragged her into the line-up of dancers, giggling as she went: 'Steady on, Dickie. I'm not one of your mares!'

In a flash, Jane was on Anson's arm and leading him into the fray. But, as he submitted to the inevitable, he caught the youngest sister Isobel's eye, read her disappointment at being left out and vowed to ask her to partner him later. He noted that although only 14 or 15 she was already showing signs of her eldest sister's voluptuousness, but he suspected her character and demeanour more matched that of Jane.

The music grew louder as the players hired from Canterbury warmed to their task on violin, double bass, flute, horn and the Brax family's expensive new Broadwood piano, and guests whirled to country dance reels and rounds.

Anson had been taught to dance passably well by his sisters and cousins as a child, but was rusty and awkward now – a hornpipe being more to his taste than a stately minuet or even a more boisterous quadrille. But with a fixed, slightly anxious expression he concentrated hard, always a half step behind, as he followed his partner's moves – praying that he would end up in the right place when the music stopped.

Eventually, after he had been led around the dance floor by both Jane and Isobel, the moment came when Charlotte Drax emerged from a noisy group of volunteer officers and tacked across the ballroom towards him.

'Now, Mr Anson, I have seen you dancing with both my sisters – twice with Jane. So now it is most definitely my turn to have you ...' And when the next dance was announced she tucked her arm through his so that her bosom squeezed against him as she led him onto the floor.

Anson was able to acquit himself without capsizing or colliding, but he was no natural dancer and gritted his teeth throughout the ordeal, raising his eyebrows in mock alarm as he passed the euphoric Commander Armstrong, currently paired with Elizabeth, her sister Anne glaring jealously from the sidelines.

Each time he crossed paths with Charlotte, she gave him a coquettish pout. It was a sultry night, and when the music stopped she again grabbed his arm and appeared to be close to swooning.

Anxiously he asked: 'Are you alright Miss, er, Charlotte?'

'I need air.' She fanned herself with her spare hand and, her arm interlocked with his, marched him out into a broad passageway and then through a side door onto a terrace.

There was something almost premeditated about the manner in which she had performed the cutting-out manoeuvre, thought Anson, and, once outside, far from being revived by the night air, she collapsed against him, cooing weakly: 'I feel so faint, please don't let me fall ...'

He clasped her tightly to keep her from falling, and she leaned her head on his chest, moaning softly: 'My buttons – they're too tight. I can't breathe.'

Charlotte was indeed breathing in short gasps and the buttons on her military-style jacket were clearly under great strain. Supporting her with his left arm, he set about freeing her top few buttons.

That mission accomplished, she murmured: 'More ...' and he happily obliged, his fingers fumbling with each remaining button until the jacket fell open, revealing only some kind of thin shift that barely covered her ample bust and diving cleavage.

Suddenly revived, she glanced up at him, smiling, and triumphantly looked down at the objects of his obvious fascination. Then she reached both arms around his neck, pulled him towards her and with lips slightly parted pressed a lingering kiss on his. Anson's hands went up to her now-freed breasts, but the sudden sound of voices close by made them both start and he pulled away from her.

Two of the older male guests had emerged from the ballroom and were chatting about the effect of the war on corn prices.

'Warm night, what?' one greeted them.

Anson stammered: 'Very, er very warm indeed ...'

'But a little cooler out here, eh?'

Charlotte muttered softly: 'Coitus interruptus!' and, as she turned away, Anson could see that she was deftly buttoning up her jacket, apparently totally recovered from her swoon.

She said loudly so that the newcomers could hear: 'I've cooled down now, Mr Anson. Perhaps you will kindly escort me back to the ballroom?'

Anson dutifully obeyed, although he was far from cool. The minx had set his blood on fire and as he led her back into the ballroom she squeezed his hand, whispered: 'We must continue the business in hand quite soon …'and made a beeline for another group of cackling volunteer officers, leaving him both elated and disturbed.

As he watched her laughing and joking with them, Jane and Isobel appeared at his side. The elder girl wagged her finger at him. 'Now that Charlotte has let you off the leash for the moment, we insist that you mark our cards, Mr Anson. I still have two spaces on my dance programme.'

'And I have three!' Isobel volunteered with a winning smile.

*

On their way back to overnight at the rectory, Armstrong, his tongue loosened by Brax champagne, chattered happily about the delightful evening he had enjoyed as the focus of the Anson sisters' attention. 'Such delightful, charming, girls, *mon vieux*!'

40

A few days later, a sealed letter, heavily scented, arrived for him at the Rose.

He opened it to read a two-line message:

'We have unfinished business. If you wish like me to resume where we left off, name the day, time and (discreet) place. Another interruption would be too maddening ...'

It was signed simply 'C' and it did not require a genius to know that this was not Chitterling inviting him to a duel, but Charlotte suggesting an assignation. And he blushed with a mixture of desire and apprehension.

*

Anson could not sleep. It was impossible to banish Charlotte's seductive message from his thoughts. He tried to think of other things, and in his mind he went back over those few sweet hours with Thérèse at the Auberge du Marin.

But always that brief encounter on the terrace came back to him. The rise and fall of her bosom, her full pouting lips, her small hand brushing his thigh and her suggestive remarks that left so little to the imagination, had captivated him.

Her obvious availability gnawed at him, yet he knew she was trouble. Of course he could arrange a tryst, but what then? As far as she was concerned, potential husbands were clearly in season. Once he succumbed, would she drag him off to the altar? His parents would be delighted for him to marry into the Brax family with their vast acreage and elevated position in so-called county society.

Squire Brax himself had given him the strongest of hints that he would be acceptable as a husband for his eldest daughter. But if he succumbed, how long would it be before the fever wore off and Charlotte became bored with his obsession with the navy and the war and offered her affections elsewhere? And there was little doubt in his mind that she was perfectly capable of that. He had noted the familiar way she had handled that brainless dandy Chitterling at the ball, and suspected she was potentially as wayward and predatory as her father was, by common repute.

It seemed he tossed and turned for hours. Would one encounter necessarily have to lead to a lasting liaison? Having captured him, would she quickly tire of the thrill of the chase and move on to her next prey? Or was there a slight desperation in her flirtatious behaviour – a need to find a suitable husband before, as her father had blatantly stated, she ran to fat like her mother?

Marriage to her, and at this time, did not attract him. A short, passionate affair did. But what had passed unnoticed at a French inn would surely be noticed here in his home county. Sam Fagg might call it 'shittin' in yer own nest'. His parents would insist that he did the right thing. Honour would be at stake.

The battle raged to and fro in his mind, but finally exhaustion overcame him and he fell into a restless sleep, dreaming fitfully of her and of fighting the ghastly Chitterling for her hand.

He awoke as dawn was breaking, pulled back the curtain at the window overlooking the street, and sat at the small oak table that served him as a desk. Charging his pen, he carefully wrote a brief note and addressed it to Miss Charlotte Brax, Brax Hall, Farthingham. It read:

'Dear Miss Brax

Should you, perhaps accompanied by your sisters, be visiting Folkestone in the coming weeks I should be honoured if you would consent to dine with me and a brother officer here at the Rose Inn which is a respectable establishment favoured by local society and which can with notice provide a good table. I have ascertained that suitable rooms for you and your sisters could be provided if it proved necessary to stay overnight.

I have the honour to be

Your humble servant

O Anson, Lieutenant, Royal Navy.'

Satisfied that should others have sight of the note, they would see that it properly observed the niceties. He was certain, too, that if Charlotte really was setting her cap at him, she would realise why he had worded his invitation so politely – and would surely find a way to elude her chaperones when the moment came.

*

Armstrong's departure for Fairlight, and Fagg's return, had heralded a period of intensive training for the detachment, and drills with the great guns, muskets, half pikes and cutlasses improved apace.

Anson told himself that if the French could invade in daylight they could equally come in darkness, so he arranged a night exercise, with the boat crews rowing towards Dungeness and practising with the carronades, albeit more dumbshow.

They rowed back at first light, and, tired after his night's work, Anson ate a large breakfast at the Rose before retiring to his room to catch up with some sleep.

He must have slept soundly for several hours until noise from the street woke him, but he remained on his bed, drifting in and out of sleep until a sudden creak of the sprung floorboard outside his room jerked him into full consciousness.

Instantly his feet were on the floor and he reached for his sword, unsheathing it with a faint rasp of steel. This might be the landlord with a message or, equally likely, it could be MacIntyre coming to search his room, unaware that anyone was there, or to kill him if he knew he was abed. Anson was, as yet, blissfully unaware of the former bosun's fate.

Stepping silently behind the door, he steeled himself as it creaked open and made a grab from behind at the figure entering in the half light. A distinctly feminine squeal and soft yielding flesh told him this was no hairy Glaswegian bosun, and as he made to let go the interloper turned in his arms and laid her head on his chest.

'Dear me, Mr Anson, I hoped you would be eager, but not that eager!'

Astonished, he looked down at Charlotte Brax, dropped his sword and stammered, 'I'm so s-sorry. Please accept my apologies. I thought you were—'

'Please don't tell me you were expecting some other young lady. You'll hurt my pride most terribly if you were!'

Still clutching her, Anson protested: 'N-no, of course not. I thought you might be a bosun I have just had to dismiss.'

She registered pretended shock. 'Now you have really insulted me – taking me for a hairy, smelly sailor! It must be this jacket.' She was wearing the same brocaded military-style creation that he had helped her unbutton so ardently on the terrace at the Brax Hall ball.

'No, no, no – the man I was expecting has a grudge, a score to settle, and when I heard the floorboard creak I thought he might be—'

'Coming to kill you? How exciting! So you don't normally greet your lady visitors in your nightshirt with your weapon unsheathed?' She made the remark sound so suggestive that he pulled away slightly in case she was referring to his growing reaction to the way she was clinging and wriggling against him.

'I, er, I assure you I don't have lady visitors—'

'Women, then?' How was it that she always had an answer and managed to give everything she said an erotic twist?

'No, no w-women either.'

She laughed. 'Your most discreet landlord kindly directed me to come straight up. I told him I was your sister!'

'Good grief!'

'So, big brother, I can feel that you like me. Are you going to show me just how pleased you are to see your little sister?' And she raised her pouting lips to be kissed.

He obliged her, gently at first, and then fiercely as passion flared. All inhibitions flown, he guided her back towards the bed and they sank down together. The buttons parted again, she hauled her skirt down, and he pulled her silk chemise over her head and fell upon her bosom, kissing and caressing feverishly.

Her small chubby hands tugged at his nightshirt. Over his head it went and, naked, they grappled one another, sinking back on the bed and melting together as they made love urgently, fiercely, greedily.

*

Temporarily spent, they lay back, his arm beneath her. She made no attempt to cover herself and through half-open eyes he studied her shapely body, bordering on becoming over-ripe. Good grief, he thought, but she was a desirable, seductive creature like no other he had known. And, as she teased him about the speed of his onslaught and broadside, he realised, too, that this was far from the first time for her.

Where, when and with whom had she learned? In the heat of the moment he had cared not.

They dozed, she aroused him again, and it was early afternoon before they dressed and made their way down to the dining room, Charlotte announcing to the landlord: 'I'm absolutely starving. Kindly bring me a beef steak, thick and rare, and the same, I think, for my brother. He's a little shrivelled in appearance, don't you think, and is in need of building up!'

With a knowing smile, the landlord touched his forehead. 'Certainly Miss, er, Anson, I'll get the cook onto it right away.'

Anson looked heavenwards with resignation, and as he led Charlotte to a table she whispered: 'Mrs Anson would sound better ...'

She chattered away throughout the meal and Anson let it all wash over him as he ate – until she mentioned that Chitterling had called upon her at Brax Hall twice already this week.

He looked up startled. 'Chitterling? What's that oaf to you?'

Charlotte smiled happily at his obvious jealousy. 'He must have fancied his chances with me after I danced with him at the ball. Oh, he's a pompous clodhopper I know, and if you give him half a chance his hands are all over you like an octopus ...'

The thought of that uncouth bucolic dandy making free with her stung Anson's pride that had been bolstered by their own feverish coupling. 'Surely you are not encouraging him?'

She hesitated, giving him an arch look. 'A spinster like me has to keep all the, shall we say, balls in the air. If I'm not married soon, everyone will assume I'm on the shelf – and Chitters' father does own an awful lot of land. Not to mention that he's been sniffing around me as if I were a prize bitch on heat!'

'Good grief! After what's just happened you can't possibly be thinking—'

'Of marrying the dreaded Chitters? He wouldn't be my first choice, but don't you sailors say any port will do in a storm?'

'But—' Anson spluttered.

'But all the buts you like. You've just sampled the goods but I haven't heard a declaration of love or a proposal of marriage from you ... yet, Master Anson.'

Mouth open, Anson recoiled as if he had been slapped around the face with a wet fish. The confounded woman was trying to force him into an instant proposal.

'I, er, er ...'

She gazed at him expectantly, lips parted in a half smile, but before he could say something he might well live to regret, the dining room door swung open and Fagg limped noisily in, coming to something passing for attention and knuckling his forehead.

'Beg pardin, sir, ma'am.' His eyes swivelled and plunged down her cleavage. ''Umble apologies fer interrupting yer dinner, but somefink's come up. There's a dragoon arrived all 'ot an' bovvered, carryin' a henvelope and he won't see no-one else but you, sir. Sorry sir.'

Charlotte's face clouded over, but Anson, hugely relieved at this last-ditch reprieve, leapt to his feet, apologised profusely to her for the interruption, and instructed Fagg to escort her back to her sisters shopping in the town while he dashed off to receive his messenger, muttering: 'Duty calls. I'll be in touch ...'

But even as he said it he knew he would be in no hurry to resume where they had just left off.

41

Once alone, he broke the seal and read the note:

Mon Vieux

Were you to pay an official (and social) call on the Officer Commanding Fairlight Semaphore Station you might learn intelligence to your advantage, and oblige your Ship and Shovel friend with the only civilised company he is likely to enjoy this whole year.

A Armstrong

Commander, Royal Navy.'

The mention of intelligence could be of great importance, and it would be fun to see Armstrong again. Not least, the timely arrival of the messenger had enabled him to escape the clutches of Charlotte Brax.

Much later, in bed – alone – that night, Anson could not get the smell and feel of her out of his mind. Back in France there had been a genuine fondness between him and Thérèse, but this was different. This was pure lust.

He could not in all honesty say that he even liked Charlotte Brax. Yet he was still overwhelmed with desire for her. What man would not be? But now that he knew that the unspeakable Chitterling was also involved with her, he realised that he was in incredibly dangerous waters, and that a continuing affair possibly leading to marriage was certain to end in tears.

*

A dawn start and a day's ride in Tom Marsh's pony and trap cleared his mind and brought Anson to Fairlight on the Downs above the small fishing port of Hastings.

The port was familiar to him from his school books as one of the Cinque Ports that had for centuries provided ships and men to fight the French, and had spawned the Royal Navy itself.

The semaphore station nearby was much as Armstrong had described it when they met at the Ship and Shovel in London the night before both were due at the Admiralty to plead in vain for sea-going appointments.

It was a small wooden building, with two main rooms and a newly added extension, that could have been taken for a poor cottage were it not for an 80-foot mast for running up flags and signal balls.

With some relief, once more the naval officer out of his natural element, he dismounted stiffly from the trap.

The captain of this land-locked ship greeted him with the warmth of a man starved of clubbable company. Pouring Anson a glass of undoubtedly smuggled claret, he asked with more than passing interest after Elizabeth and Anne, 'such charming girls, quite charming!' And Armstrong's face shone with delight when Anson produced a scented letter from Elizabeth that he had promised to safeguard for her 'til he next met his friend.

'Don't get many missives here, apart from official demands for returns of all sorts.' He sniffed the letter with an expression bordering on ecstasy, murmuring: 'I'll savour it later.'

Anson smiled knowingly. He had helped his sister draft it, conveying maidenly interest rather than the keen infatuation that had struck her when Armstrong danced with her at the Brax ball.

Sipping his wine, his friend confided: 'I did so enjoy that interlude – the ball and all. It's dire here, *mon vieux* – day after day with naught but a whining midshipman, oafish signalmen, a couple of extremely regimental dragoons who are no fun at all, and the odd dog-walker and idle gawper for company.'

'Where do you sleep?' asked Anson.

'I paid out of my own pocket to have this extra room built on. It's my private retreat.'

Dinner was what Armstrong called a ragamuffin affair – rough and ready but nevertheless wholesome mutton and potatoes, liberally washed down with more of the smuggled claret. The meal was rounded off with cheese, apparently weevil-free ship's biscuit, and a good brandy, again undoubtedly of recent French origin.

Anson, enjoying his brother officer's hospitality and the opportunity, rare since leaving his *Phryne* friends so abruptly, of sharing naval gossip with a near equal, was content to wait for Armstrong to impart his promised intelligence.

When the moment came, Armstrong was direct. 'Obviously I have received the request for information regarding our visiting French privateer.'

Anson nodded. 'I take it that's the reason for your summons, although I'd have rated it a pleasure to partake of your hospitality whether or not.'

Armstrong shouted for his midshipman, dozing in the corner, to double away and fetch the log, and the lad returned with a battered, leather-bound volume.

'When I read your letter, well, signed by Captain Hoare but I've no doubt drafted by you, I thought your privateer might be the one that took a coaster off Hastings at about that time. Didn't see it myself, so I couldn't be sure.'

Anson had heard about that incident. 'Yes, that was reported to me and it could well have been my Frenchman. But I've heard nothing since.'

'There's been no further sighting down the coast here since then, maybe because he went back to base for repairs, re-victualling or whatever. But a few days ago a gun brig with an oval sail patch was reported as having taken a merchantman off Chichester.'

Anson leaned forward expectantly. 'And have you seen her here?'

'No, not yet.' Armstrong opened the log at pages marked with slips of paper. 'But look, your letter asked about sightings of a brig with a patched sail and at the time I doubt anyone thought of looking backwards. I certainly didn't, and if I had there wouldn't have been any references to the patch because that only came about after your escapade off Folkestone.'

'So where does this lead?'

'Well, *mon vieux*, when I heard about this latest Chichester sighting, I went right back through my log and find that in the past we have recorded sightings of a similar vessel, minus patched sail.' He turned to the marked pages of the log. 'Look here, here and here.'

'You can be so exact?'

'Of course. The role here is to observe and report any enemy ship activity, semaphore it to Admiralty, and send a dragoon galloper off to report to the soldiery if a French landing is threatened.'

He tapped the book. 'As you will know, the only way to keep intelligence in any sort of order is to keep a seaman-like log. Everything we see is recorded here, and I can tell you with near certainty that your privateer passed this way heading east at least three times before your tussle with her.'

'Good grief! So how does this Chichester sighting fit in?'

'Well, I've been in contact with my wingers in the signal stations to the west – we're a sad breed with plenty of time on our hands for such whimsy – and their logs match mine.'

'How do you mean?'

'I mean that each time the privateer passed here he had first been reported off Chichester and so on. So, if I judge it correctly, and if the Frenchman is the creature of habit I believe him to be, he will pass this way again, beating easterly, sometime next week – Thursday or Friday, if I calculate correctly, picking up any small undefended coastal craft he chances upon.'

'Really?' Anson could not hide his astonishment.

'That's right. His beat appears to be from around about Chichester in the west through eastward, maybe as far as the North Foreland. He stays out of range of shore batteries, leaves anything that looks as if it could bite back well alone, and goes for the minnows.'

Anson took the proffered logbook and examined the marked entries.

'This is remarkable! Your observations are of the utmost interest to me. Although we have never learned her name, this is almost certainly the privateer that we tackled off Folkestone, and I agree that your predictions are the most likely – if our Frenchman follows his normal pattern.'

Armstrong was pleased with his friend's reaction. 'Yes, we can safely assume that unless something occurs to change the Frogs' habits, the *Égalité* will be here snapping up English coasters again towards the back end of next week.

Anson was stunned. 'Did you say *Égalité*?'

Armstrong nodded. 'That's our privateer sure enough. According to my Chichester opposite number she carries her name on her prow in red paint. The name can quite clearly be read with a good glass, and excellent examples are provided to us glorified look-outs by a grateful Admiralty. I suppose the red paint and the name are some kind of revolutionary statement.'

For a moment, Anson was distracted. His mind went back to the mole at St Valery-en-Caux and the failed attempt to cut out this very same privateer.

291

Armstrong noted his reaction. 'Clearly the name means something to you?'

'It does indeed. Now that you have confirmed the name, I find I have two scores to settle with this Frenchman – one in Normandy and another off Folkestone.'

'Well,' said Armstrong, recharging the glasses with slugs of brandy, 'let's drink to third time lucky.'

*

Back at the detachment building, Anson, still suffering from the vestiges of a hangover resulting from a convivial night at Fairlight, conferred with Fagg and Hoover. 'We three have had two unfinished encounters on account of this *Égalité* – in Normandy and now here. If we can engineer a third match, I am resolved to take her by whatever means.'

Fagg was doubtful. 'But, beggin' your pardin, sir, if we row out in them gunboats, won't the Froggie just duff us up? He won't come in range of one of the batteries again – not if he's got any sense.'

Hoover agreed. 'And without cover from the battery we'd be sitting ducks for sure.'

Anson agreed. 'Quite so, and that's why we'll be ready waiting for him next time. But we'll be looking like toothless minnows ripe for snapping up for a pike's breakfast.' He frowned at his own extravagant metaphor, wondering if he had got it quite right, but Fagg and Hoover appeared to have caught his drift.

He outlined the plan he had hatched up with Armstrong over a good many brandies at Fairlight, and gave his orders.

For once the shambolic nature of his Sea Fencibles would be a positive advantage, as would their normal callings – as fishermen, boatmen and harbour rats of all persuasions.

This would not be a time for immaculately turned-out and well-drilled man-of-war's men. Apparent sloppiness and slovenly seamanship, would, Anson hoped, lure the Frenchmen on – and into a trap.

42

His dreams were interrupted by a shake from the publican bearing a flickering candle. 'Are you awake, sir?'

A dazed nod.

'There's a galloper come for you!'

Now he was wide awake, well aware of what this must mean. 'Show him up, Mr Griggs, show him up – and leave the candle if you will.'

Griggs touched his forehead and disappeared down the creaking stairs, returning after a few minutes with a lantern and followed closely by an intelligent-looking, blue-jacketed, booted and spurred dragoon.

Throwing up a salute, he announced: 'Dragoon Dillon, sorr, 'ttached to the Fairlight station as galloper.' He handed Anson a sealed paper. 'From Commander Armstrong, sorr.'

'Landlord, I'd be obliged if you would forage your kitchens and feed Dillon here and get your ostler lad to look after his horse while I study this message. I'll be down shortly with a reply.'

When the pair had clattered off downstairs, no doubt waking the rest of the house, Anson broke the wax seal. Holding the paper close to the candle flame he read the short message, clearly written in a hurry:

'Personal for Lieutenant Anson, Royal Navy

Greetings mon vieux. *The fun begins.* Égalité *expected off Hastings Thursday early forenoon. Suggest you initiate proceedings as planned.*

Armstrong.'

*

Little negotiation was required to obtain the agreement of the master for the use of his coaster, the *Kentish Trader*.

If William Gray himself had been unwilling, which he was not, his wife would certainly have persuaded him. She alone knew how close she had come to being raped and perhaps then murdered, or at least abducted to endure a worse fate at the hands of the French privateersmen. And in her eyes Anson and his fencibles could do no wrong.

As soon as Anson broached borrowing their vessel 'to strike a blow against privateers' the Grays agreed immediately.

The couple and their crew were all keen to remain on board for whatever was in store, but Anson declined. He asked only that the most experienced of their crewmen – a grizzled veteran named Josh Crowe, who knew the coaster and her ways backwards – came along to act as sailing master.

Anson had taken immense pains with his plan, rehearsed with Armstrong during his visit to Fairlight and later with Lieutenant Coney, the impress officer at Folkestone.

It had to work. Failure could mean death for many of his men, the loss of a vessel he had borrowed without authority, and possibly both gunboats, leading to an inevitable court martial and disgrace. It was too painful to contemplate.

Crucial to the plan's success was Armstrong. By now he would have consulted his opposite numbers in the stations to the west and set up a reliable means of communication so that he would learn of *Égalité's* approach well before the privateer appeared off Hastings.

The *Kentish Trader* was to lurk off Fairlight, watching for signals from the semaphore station announcing the Frenchman's imminent arrival.

Timing would be critical. Anson had to have precise notification of the privateer's approach and then flee, enticing *Égalité* to follow. They needed to arrive off Seagate with the coaster losing sea room to the privateer but still sufficiently far ahead to avoid capture.

Then, just when *Égalité* was close enough to pounce, Anson's trap would be sprung. Yes, it would be a close-run thing and, not least, would require careful briefing if his fencibles were to get it right.

After the earlier brush with the privateer, he knew the men would do their duty, but would they remember their orders when the shot began to fly?

*

All preparations made, Anson and those selected to sail in the coaster slipped aboard singly so as to avoid drawing unnecessary attention.

Idle observers might well have taken him for the real skipper, dressed as he was in Gray's normal sea-going rig, a loose canvas smock jacket hiding his uniform and wearing a scruffy sou'wester instead of his naval fore-and-aft hat.

Crowe jocularly chivvied the four fencibles who were replacing the normal crew. In their everyday work clothing they were indistinguishable from the real thing.

Presumably out of mischievous humour, Fagg had allotted the role of female bait aboard the coaster to Handsome Smith, so nicknamed owing to his extreme ugliness.

Already he was tiring of being told: 'Your turn in the barrel tonight then, eh 'andsome?' – rising as he always did to such bawdy attempts at humour at his expense.

Anson, ever tolerant of badinage among the men, reflected that pox-pitted, whiskery, broken-nosed, cauliflower-eared, snaggle-toothed Smith was the very last man one wanted to meet in a barrel, even if that way inclined.

He only passed muster as a female with any on-lookers by keeping his back firmly seaward, hoping that the borrowed dress and bonnet would fool watchers.

The coaster's deck was littered with barrels, bales and crates that Anson hoped would appear, through a glass, to be the overflow of a sizeable, and perhaps valuable, cargo stowed below.

It was a relief to all on board when Crowe at last adjudged the tide was right, and the *Kentish Trader* was able to slip out of the harbour and tack westward against a light westerly breeze.

Off Dymchurch, they rendezvoused with a fishing smack, sailing close together until a graunch transfer was possible and a dozen fencibles carrying muskets, cutlasses, half pikes and boarding axes clambered aboard.

They were briefly welcomed by Anson, and immediately made their way down the hatch into the bowels of the coaster. So far, so good.

By late afternoon, the *Kentish Trader* was off the East Sussex coast and through his telescope Anson could clearly see Fairlight signal station some hundreds of feet above.

There was no activity other than a horse, most likely the mount of one of the dragoon messengers, grazing on the cliffs beside the station.

Having consulted Crowe, Anson gave instructions to hold station as best he could and peered below to see the hidden fencibles. 'Is all well down here, boys?'

A chorus of 'aye ayes' was countered by Shallow. 'Orlright, sir, but there ain't a lot of air and it's gonna get a might smelly down 'ere ...'

'Fair point. Take turns on deck, no more'n four at a time and keep low. If the Frogs suddenly appear we don't want 'em to get the idea we're anything other than a fat little merchantman begging to be taken as a prize. We'll keep the hatch open and as soon as they're sighted, disappear below and batten yourselves down for the chase.'

They muttered agreement.

'If we can draw them back to Seagate, we've got a nice little surprise for 'em. You can appear like jacks-in-the-box and give 'em the fright of their lives!'

*

From the signal station, Armstrong had logged the arrival of the coaster and watched her as she tacked gently to and fro, holding station. He could imagine the tension on board and hoped it would not be too long before the Frenchmen appeared on the scene.

But daylight began to fade and there was still no sign of the privateer.

On board the *Kentish Trader*, now that the only light came from a watery moon, Anson allowed everyone on deck and, after a meal of cold beef, bread and cheese, his fencibles made themselves as comfortable as they could among the crates and barrels, smoking their clay pipes and yarning.

Handsome Smith, minus bonnet and wig but still wearing his borrowed frock and large false bosom, came in for more light-hearted banter, receiving several insincere proposals – only one of them for marriage.

Anson, propped against a barrel, smiled at the repartee. He was content that the bait was set and that all was ready for springing his trap. But he was only too well aware that the Frenchman might not follow his usual pattern, or that the system to give early warning of his approach would fail. Or the weather could change and thwart his plan.

Never one to worry about things he could not change, and lulled by the motion of the coaster and the soothing sound of the sea, he dozed and finally fell asleep.

*

Up in the signal station, Armstrong fretted. Even with a pale moon, spotting and signalling was virtually impossible.

Handing the midshipman his telescope, he instructed the boy to sweep the westward horizon and sing out if he spotted a sail.

'And take care with that glass, you young cretin! Drop it again and I'll string you up as a warning to other careless middies.' Armstrong was acutely aware that he had signed personally for the 2ft- long instrument. It was fitted with achromatic lenses and had cost their Lordships two guineas, supplied under contract, according to the inscription on the brass-work, by Messrs P & J Dolland of St Paul's Churchyard, London.

Ideally, he would have obtained one of their superior 3ft models, but that would have cost him six guineas out of his own pocket. Anson had one, he knew, but then not every officer had been so lucky with prize money.

Muttering to himself about the inequalities of life and what an idiot he had been to join the navy and allow himself to be marooned ashore in such a God-forsaken spot instead of pursuing a lucrative land-based career, he took a wineglass from the cupboard.

Highway robbery, the law, banking or some equally crooked yet handsomely remunerated profession might have suited, he reflected. Resigned once again to his fate, he downed a glass of good French wine, origin unclear but highly suspect, and partook of a frugal repast of cold meat and boiled potatoes.

He checked on the yawning youth, who had nothing to report, and stood him down for the night.

For a while, Armstrong swept the sea westward with the glass, but visibility was poor and he soon gave it up as a waste of time. Nevertheless, he called the duty signal rating, bade him take a two-hour stint with the telescope, and sat in his high-backed armchair, blanket over his legs – his sole comforts in his draughty eyrie.

Reaching for a week-old copy of the *Sussex Weekly Advertiser*, he settled down to read. But fatigue and the wine took effect and his head soon began to droop. Every now and then, he jerked back to life and continued to read in fits and starts until finally a gentle snoring emanated from the depths of the armchair. For once Commander Armstrong was not 'watch-on, stop-on.'

*

It was not the sighting of a sail, but the sound of galloping hooves that alerted the duty seaman, whose eyes had become sore staring conscientiously out to sea through the glass.

He flung open the signal station door shouting: 'Sir, sir – a rider!'

Armstrong was immediately wide awake, and flung down the newspaper. 'What is it, Lloyd?'

'A horse approachin', sir, from the west!'

'Good man, load a musket just in case – and wake the others.' Smugglers, or even escaping French prisoners, were not unknown in these parts and it was sensible to take such precautions at night.

'Aye aye, sir.' Lloyd's warning shout had already woken his fellow seaman and Dragoon Hillman, but the sleepy midshipman needed a firm shake.

Outside, with his sword drawn and musket-wielding Lloyd at his side, Armstrong watched the rider approach and dismount, noting with relief the man's blue jacket and Tarleton helmet with its distinctive woollen comb.

'Dragoon Dillon. Welcome home! Do you have news?'

Dillon, who had been waiting at the Beachey Head signal station to bring back news of the privateer, drew himself to attention and saluted smartly despite the dark. 'I do, sorr. There's an urgent message for you from Beachy Head, sorr!'

'Good man. What is it?'

'Don't know 'xactly, sorr. It's written down, but they tell't me they'd seen that Frog ship you're after, a-headin' this way, sorr.'

'Excellent!' Armstrong snatched the message and called to Lloyd: 'Make sure Dillon gets some vittles.'

'Thank you kindly, sorr, but I'll see t'me horse first.'

'Of course. Then get some rest, there's a good fellow.' He turned to Dillon's fellow dragoon. 'Better get saddled up, Hillman. You've a long ride ahead of you.'

This was the trouble at night, Armstrong thought. No chance of signalling and the only way to get a message away was by dragoon messenger. Good though these specially selected, well-mounted, light cavalrymen were, single horse-power was not much good when the utmost despatch was required.

Still, there were six hours to dawn – time enough for the rider to make it to the next station at Dungeness where the gist of the warning could be signalled eastward and a fresh dragoon could carry the full message on to Seagate.

Inside the station, Armstrong opened up the message from his opposite number at Beachey Head and read:

'French privateer, a brig with patched mainsail, and of some 12 guns or more, believed to be Égalité, *reported to have taken a small coaster off Chichester and sent it away with a prize crew. Privateer then headed east. If she maintains course and speed expect her off Hastings first light tomorrow.'*

Armstrong scuttled back into the station, feverishly rummaged for pen and paper, and, after a moment's thought, added a footnote to the message he had received from Beachy Head:

'Am warning Kentish Trader *and expect her to draw the Frenchman towards Seagate arriving mid afternoon.'*

Then, he wrote a second message and signed, timed and dated both.

Outside, handing the messages to Dragoon Hillman, he ordered: 'This one's for the officer at Dungeness, asking him to make a short signal. The other is for him to send on by one of his dragoons to the Seagate Sea Fencible Detachment. Tell the officer it's life or death. Don't fail!'

Hillman saluted. 'I'll not fail, sir.' And he mounted up, turned his horse expertly and trotted off towards Kent.

Armstrong watched him until cloud blotted out the moonlight, then turned and strode purposefully into the signal station.

Minutes later a maroon rocket whooshed from the roof and sped skywards, a red streak in the gloom. Having, he hoped, captured the attention of the look-out aboard the coaster, Armstrong ordered the firing of six musket shots – the pre-arranged signal to warn Lieutenant Anson of the earliest time *Égalité* was expected to arrive in the vicinity.

Dillon, although more used to handling his cavalry carbine, supervised the firing and reloading of the station's two muskets with powder and wad only. 'It's noise we want, boys,' he told the two seamen, 'and we don't want to hurt any passing seagulls, do we now?'

There was a pause after the sixth musket shot, and then an answering rocket flew up from the coaster. It was green. Armstrong punched the air triumphantly. 'It's worked, they've got the message!'

For once, even the moon-faced midshipman was smiling. 'Go and open a couple of bottles of that good wine, my lad. Our task is over for the time being, and I reckon we all deserve a glass or two. Damned if we don't!'

Afloat, Anson assessed the situation with some satisfaction. The dragoon messenger's early warning of the privateer's appearance further west and the simple signals he and Armstrong arranged had clearly worked, proving as effective as if they had been close enough to speak.

There was plenty of time for his men to rest. A skeleton watch would suffice to hold their station and keep a look-out as best they could in the gloom.

Giving strict orders that he was to be given an immediate shake if anything occurred, he settled down himself. Tomorrow promised to be an eventful day.

43

On board *Égalité*, Capitaine Eugene Lapraik had ordered lookouts to sweep the horizon for sails. Two days earlier, they had fallen on an English coaster, ejected the crewmen and sent it with a prize crew with orders to head for the Normandy coast. If they dodged blockading English men-of-war successfully, he and all his men would be the richer.

This stretch of coast was his favourite hunting ground. There were rich pickings to be had from the busy coastal trade, especially whenever the wind blew strong from westward. When that happened, the English cruisers on station off Beachy Head would take shelter under Dungeness, leaving the field clear to privateers like him who could get among the struggling merchantmen and take their pick.

It was blowing now and, with a fast run eastward, *Égalité* would be somewhere off Hastings come first light, ready to swoop down on any unsuspecting merchantmen tacking slowly westward.

Failing that he would continue towards the Kent coast, confident that he could out-run most merchant craft heading for the shelter of the Downs. Either way he sniffed more prizes.

*

On board the *Kentish Trader*, a fencible lookout spotted a sail bearing west and gave the dozing officer a shake. 'Sail, sir! Could be the Frogs!'

Awake in a jiffy, Anson reached for his glass. It was barely light, but there was no mistaking the two-masted vessel on the horizon. The large patch in her main topsail was a dead giveaway. And, as if confirmation was needed, another red maroon was fired from the Fairlight signal station, where Armstrong, too, was awake and alert, monitoring events through his own telescope.

On board the coaster, Josh Crowe supervised the raising of the kedge anchor and running up of the canvas, a simple enough task in a small vessel like this and with plenty of spare hands. 'East, is it, sir?' he asked.

'East it is, Mr Crowe, and we'd best be quick about it if we're to race the Frenchman to Seagate!'

*

Aboard the privateer, Capitaine Lapraik's attention had been captured by the Fairlight maroon and through his glass he soon spotted the coaster that was hurriedly making sail only a mile or so away. He could clearly see the master, wearing a loose canvas smock and sou'wester.

This, he recognised, was almost certainly the small merchantman he had taken off Folkestone some time past but had been forced to abandon, with the loss of two of his men when the shore battery had found his range and put a shot through his mainsail.

Vowing to himself that his prey would not escape him again, he ordered the boy drummer to beat to quarters and the chase began, his best gunners crouching at the bow-chaser ready to put a ball across the coaster's bows as soon as the gap was narrow enough.

*

When the dragoon messenger from Dungeness clattered into the Seagate Sea Fencible building, Fagg was well prepared and knew exactly what to do. He despatched Tom Marsh with his pony and trap to summon all members of the detachment who had not sailed with Anson, and then to seek out Lieutenant Coney of the impress.

Coney had undertaken to round up enough men to crew three fishing boats to act as cover for the gunboats as they rowed out to rendezvous with the *Kentish Trader*.

All went well, and it was not long before the small flotilla of fishing boats slipped out of Seagate harbour, followed by the two gunboats, one commanded by Fagg, the second by Hoover. This time they had powder and shot.

*

By the time Dungeness faded into her wake, the privateer was visibly gaining on her prey and Anson was concerned lest he might have to heave to and strike the flag flying from the coaster's topmast before he was near enough to the reception party he had planned.

But he need not have worried. Josh Crowe knew every inch of this coast and this vessel. He needed no telling and squeezed every vestige of speed out of the *Kentish Trader*.

The gap was closing but Anson reasoned, correctly, that the captain of *Égalité* would be reluctant to sink the prize he must be confident of capturing after giving chase for a few more miles.

On they sailed, and as they neared Seagate, Anson was relieved beyond measure to see a cluster of fishing boats lying off the port. It was then that the crack of the Frenchman's bow-chaser and the whoosh of a ball ahead decided the immediate issue. He shouted to the fencibles hiding below: 'This is it, men. Stand by, but wait 'til they've boarded us.'

He turned to Crowe. 'Strike the flag, but we'll sail on to get as close as we can to those fishing boats.' Crowe nodded, the flag came fluttering down, but the sails remained taut.

More valuable yards were gained before the privateer's bow-chaser barked again and another ball splashed by. Anson shouted: 'Haul down, but lubberly – we need every yard we can make.'

The sails came down slowly and slovenly. The *Kentish Trader* gradually lost way and *Égalité* approached, backed her foretopsail, drifted closer, and bumped alongside. Grappling hooks were flung across and half a dozen armed Frenchmen leapt aboard.

From apparent docile acceptance of capture, in an instant the demeanour of the coaster's fencible crewmen changed dramatically. They produced pistols from their smocks, and Anson shouted to the men waiting below: 'Now, boys!'

The hidden fencibles erupted on deck, relieved to be free from confinement, and raring to have a go at the Frenchmen.

It took only minutes for them to overwhelm and disarm the small boarding party and cut the grappling hook ropes, freeing the *Kentish Trader* to yaw away from the privateer. As this was happening, and as if on cue, the first fencible gunboat appeared from behind the fishing boats.

It was Fagg, in the number one boat with Sampson Marsh at the carronade, who was first to manoeuvre into a position to get in a shot. Shouting to the rowers to hold her steady, he struggled to line up the gun.

But this was easier said than done. Despite the flattened oars acting as a brake, the swell and the breeze buffeted the boat this way and that. And, on board *Égalité*, some of the Frenchmen had woken up to the danger and a few armed with muskets were running to the side, kneeling and taking aim.

A crack, and the first musket ball whined overhead. Sampson silently thanked his maker. It was just as difficult for the Frenchmen to aim true in this sea as it was for the gunboat crews.

The number one boat was hit by a wave and turned sideways on to the privateer, provoking Fagg to shout: 'Stop fannying abaht and keep this effing canoe steady! Ain't you lot never rowed a' effin' boat afore?'

Several more musket balls whined past and one struck the hull beside Marsh, sending splinters flying like darts. One razored his cheek as it spun past but he ignored it. Crouching over the gun with the slow match in his hand, he cried: 'Now or never!' And at the tiller Fagg roared: 'Ship larboard oars. Starboard oars, bring her round!'

Whether by luck or judgement, somehow the rowers did what was demanded of them, and for a few seconds *Égalité's* prow swung into Marsh's view, in line with the gun.

It was enough. He shouted: 'Fire!' and the carronade erupted with a terrific shock that flung it back on its slide.

The recoil sent Sampson and the nearest oarsman sprawling, and for a moment he was unsighted and confused, the blood from the splinter slash pouring from his cheek.

But a ragged cheer from Fagg and the unaffected rowers nearest the stern told him what he so desperately wanted to know. The ball had struck the privateer to the starboard side of her bowsprit, leaving a gaping hole and sending a swarm of splinters on their deadly path, delivering mayhem and death. The biter bit.

Sampson knew only too well what devastation a carronade ball like that could cause when fired from such close range. It would have sent timber splinters flying like daggers, felling men as if they were mere skittles in an alley.

For the minute, the crew of Fagg's gunboat were as if frozen, stunned by the detonation, but the French marksmen were not and a ragged volley of musket balls screeched in, lower now, and one or two struck the woodwork.

Fagg woke to the danger. 'Heads down an' row like 'ell!' The gunboat had already swung away from the privateer, and, as the oars bit again, he pulled the tiller over and headed for the coaster where fencibles could be seen restraining the captured Frenchmen.

If Fagg's boat could get behind the bait, they would be comparatively safe. The privateer captain would not risk firing at her when half a dozen of his own men were prisoners on deck. And, if they could get alongside, the number one gunboat crew would be well placed to use the coaster as a bridge to attack *Égalité* herself.

Sampson Marsh had no chance of reloading the gun without help in this choppy sea. So for the moment, he knew, his job was done and well done at that. He grabbed a half pike – gunner turned boarder.

The three fishing boats apparently awaiting capture were ignored by the French. Capitaine Lapraik was busy sorting out the shambles on *Égalité's* gun-deck, urging his surviving gunners to get a clear aim at the gunboat. At the same time, he was preparing to grapple with the coaster again and send more boarders across to secure the prize. Too busy to take account of surrendering fishermen, it was his biggest mistake.

The second gunboat suddenly emerged from behind the fishing boats, oarsmen rowing furiously toward the larboard side of *Égalité*.

As the Frenchmen began their second attempt to secure the coaster, Hoover's boat clattered against their larboard side, and grappling irons were thrown aboard.

The French captain looked around, confused. Too late, he realised something was terribly wrong as a dozen fencibles swarmed on board led by Hoover, musket aloft, shouting: 'Follow me!'

Capitaine Lapraik took in what was happening and screamed orders to the men who had been firing at the first gunboat to turn and fire on the boarders. But other crewmen had snatched up weapons and were closing with the fencibles, preventing their comrades from firing.

For a few moments, a hand-to-hand battle raged and it seemed that the boarders would be thrown back into the sea. But now more fencibles led by Anson were preparing to swarm aboard from the coaster and the Frenchmen were about to be hard pressed on two fronts.

All eyes were on the fight and no one noticed more grappling hooks being thrown over the rails. Fagg's gunboat had arrived.

The hooks held fast, and the gunboat graunched against the brig. Fagg leaned forward, jumped for the privateer and pulled himself over with the aid of one of the ropes. He stumbled and fell face down on the deck, but was pulled roughly to his feet by Marsh, who had followed close on his heels.

A terrific din, shouting and clash of weapons came from the larboard side, but no-one confronted Anson, and more members of the *Kentish*

Trader's temporary crew, looking at their most piratical with cutlasses, pikes and tomahawks at the ready, joined him.

He threw off his smock and sou'wester, drew his sword and held it high. 'Together now, boys!' he shouted. 'Let's show these Frogs what's what!' And waving his sword he yelled: 'Charge!'

Cheering wildly, they followed him into a headlong assault on the Frenchmen who, stepping over dead and wounded comrades, were still desperately holding the earlier boarders at bay.

Capitaine Lapraik, alone on his quarterdeck, heard the yells and turned in horror to see this second wave assaulting his men from the rear. Worse, what he had thought were impotent fishing boats were now closing in, bristling with armed men – Coney, his impress men, and volunteers he had gathered from the Folkestone detachment.

Impotent, Lapraik stared wild-eyed, wondering what to do. He failed to notice that Hoover had broken away from the melee until the marine appeared at his side, bayonet-topped musket pointing at his gut.

There was nothing for it but to raise his hands in surrender.

Anson had pushed his way towards them and, anxious to avoid unnecessary bloodshed, appealed to the Frenchman to call upon his men to lay down their arms.

Capitaine Lapraik paused for a moment, then nodded. Cupping his hand to his mouth he shouted: '*Garçons, nous sommes perdu. Déposez les armes!*'

And Anson called out to the fencibles: 'Enough men! The ship is ours. No more bloodshed.'

At first a few, and then more and more of the Frenchmen threw down their weapons and stood warily eyeing the fencibles who now surrounded them.

'Pick up their weapons, men, and guard them well!'

Anson approached the French captain, who bowed slightly and offered his sword, hilt-first. Taking it, Anson looked the man in the eye, acknowledging the gesture with a nod – glad that more lives would not be lost in a futile fight to the finish.

He pointed the blade towards the deck, paused for a heartbeat or two and then slowly and carefully took it in his left hand and offered the hilt back to his adversary.

The Frenchman appeared almost overcome, and gratefully took the sword and sheathed it. '*Merci Monsieur, vous êtes très gentil.*'

'*C'est rien.*' Anson shrugged. He was not interested in collecting trophies. It was enough that the privateer had been taken without further bloodshed.

There was an awkward silence between victor and vanquished, broken by a shout from starboard. 'On deck there! Has she struck?'

It was Captain Hoare, rowed out in a borrowed boat by a few of the fencibles who, for whatever reason, had not been at the rendezvous when the alarm was raised and had missed the fight.

He clambered aboard, sword in hand, and took in the scene. 'Struck, has he?' indicating the French captain.

Anson nodded. 'Yes, it's all done and dusted.'

Hoare grinned smugly, but his expression turned to one of astonishment when he noticed the French captain still had his sword. 'Bloody hell, Anson!' he roared. 'The wretched man's still got his sword! Whatever were you thinking?'

He pointed his own blade at the Frenchman's throat and shouted. 'Your sword, *monsieur, immediatement!*'

Capitaine Lapraik shot a dismayed look at Anson, who could only shrug and mouth '*pardon,*' and, realising that he was now confronted by a senior officer, the Frenchman bowed to the inevitable, drew his sword, and handed it to the newcomer.

44

Back ashore, Captain Hoare quizzed Anson in detail about the operation and when he had heard all he sat back and folded his arms. 'Hmm. All very risky, was it not?'

'Surely war involves risk, sir?'

'Of course, of course. But you took risks that, had things gone wrong, would have impacted on me.'

'I'm afraid I don't follow, sir—'

Clearly irritated, Hoare rubbed his chin and frowned. 'Follow is what you are supposed to do. Follow me, as your superior officer. Not go dashing off risking all on such a foolhardy venture without clearing it in detail with me.'

It was Anson who was irritated now. 'But I did inform you of my plan, sir, and I cannot agree that it was foolhardy. It worked, did it not?'

'Do not presume to try my patience, Anson. You know damned well that your message informing me what of you were about would reach me after you had set off. You knew perfectly well that I could not call the whole thing off because you had already sailed. Covering your tracks after the event, why, it's the oldest trick in the navy!'

Anson said nothing. He had expected his superior to be somewhat miffed, but was nevertheless surprised that the total success of the operation had not mellowed him.

The captain wagged a finger at him. 'I, as captain of this division, must now report to their Lordships on what has occurred.'

'Of course, sir.'

'You must realise that had it gone wrong, if you had lost men, or worse, lost the coaster or even these gunboats Home Popham sets such great store by – if any of this had transpired, it would be I, yes me, who would be grovelling to the Admiralty, apologising for your cock-up. It would be me who would be facing a court martial—'

'Assuming I had been killed, sir—'

Hoare shook his head violently. 'No, no! It would be me who would have carried the can. Their Lordships would not have believed I had not agreed to the operation. And, even if they did believe that I did not know of it until after you had set off, they would have marked my card for failing to exert proper command and allowing my subordinates to do as they please. I would have been ruined Anson, ruined! I would have been drummed out or at very least have ended up permanently on the beach, losing my honour – everything.'

Anson accepted the captain had something of a point. 'But I, er we won, did we not, sir? So none of this worst-case stuff will actually apply …'

Hoare nodded slowly, emphasising his agreement, his pudgy frowning features dissolving into a sarcastic smile.

'Exactly Anson, exactly. As you so generously point out, our operation, though undoubtedly risky, was in the event a complete success. If we had lost there is no doubt whatsoever that the blame would have been laid at my door. One loses some, and wins some.' He raised his hands in an expansive, told-you-so, gesture.

'So now, my dear Anson, many times removed kin of the Anson, it will not surprise you that I will take the credit for this little win. It will compensate somewhat for the loneliness of command that one has to endure, and for the sleepless night you gave me when you sailed off on your little adventure without deigning to obtain my blessing first.'

Anson shrugged resignedly. He had not expected plaudits and laurel wreaths from this quarter.

Hoare reassured him: 'Of course you will receive an honourable mention – and your due share of the prize money I intend to wring from their Lordships from the sale of *Égalité*.'

'Prize money? D'you really think …?'

The captain had already guesstimated the value of the privateer. An eighth would go to the flag officer, and as, in effect, captain of the ship, Hoare himself would be due two-eighths, which should do more than top up his coffers.

He smirked at the thought. 'I've not yet come across a flag officer who would turn down the chance of an eighth of anything, so the admiral will most certainly support my claim. Your share should amount to a useful sum, Anson, although you'll be sharing with Coney of course, and your harbour rats will get more than enough for a giant piss-up. So everyone will be happy.'

It would certainly be a huge boost to the already sky-high morale of the men, Anson acknowledged. 'Thank you, sir. If it comes, I've no doubt the money will be most welcome. Do you require my help with your report?'

'I think not, Anson. I know enough of the affair, and, of course, it was I who accepted the French captain's surrender.'

'Dishonourably took his sword long after I had returned it when the Frenchman struck his colours to me,' thought Anson. But he was not inclined to debate the matter further. Hoare would write whatever he wanted to write, and Anson could already guess that version would paint his superior as the true begetter of the action – and the victor. So what? All those who mattered were those who were there, and they knew the reality.

'Then if you have no further need of me, I have wounded to see to and the French prisoners to hand over to the military.'

'By all means look to your men, Anson, but leave the prisoners to me. I have sent to Shorncliffe for an escort and will hand them over personally.'

Aye, and no doubt act the part of the conquering hero, thought Anson. But he held his peace, touched his hat and strode off along the Stade.

*

The wounded had been taken to a nearby pub, where the lightly injured were seated, being fussed over by their mates and a couple of wives.

Three of the more seriously hurt were laid out on tables. Crouched over one was Phineas Shrubb, and, to Anson's surprise, the apothecary's daughter Sarah was with him, scissors in hand cutting away at the wounded man's trousers.

Shrubb looked up when Anson entered. 'He's taken a musket or pistol shot in the thigh – pistol most likely.' He drew a gasp of pain from the man as he levered his leg up to peer underneath. 'You're a lucky man, brother. The ball went in, missed your bones and came out of this hole at the back. Very lucky. If it had splintered your bone I'd be reaching for a saw to take your leg off. As it is, we'll clean you up and stitch you up. You'll need to stay off it for a while and it'll smart somewhat, but you'll be almost as good as new.'

He turned to Sarah. 'Probe it to make sure no bits of those filthy trousers are stuck in the wound, douse it with spirits and sew him up.'

She nodded and picked up a large pair of tweezers. The wounded man blanched and, catching Sarah's concerned look, Anson stepped forward. 'Hobbs, isn't it?'

'That's right, sir. An' I can tell you I don't feel very lucky like the doc just said I were.'

'You'd know all about it if Mr Shrubb was taking your leg off. You've just got to bear up for a little bit longer, Hobbs. They have to make sure the wound's clean before it's stitched.'

Shrubb agreed. 'There's many a seaman's lost a limb all because a bit of his clothing was carried into the wound by a ball.'

Sarah sat beside the wounded man, tweezers at the ready.

And Fagg told Hobbs, reassuringly: 'This won't 'alf make yer eyes water.'

Hobbs grunted two words through gritted teeth of which only the 'off' was audible.

'Good man!' said Anson. 'Just try to stay still while Miss Shrubb here fishes for anything that shouldn't be there.'

'Do me best, sir.'

Phineas handed the wounded man a leather mouthpiece. 'Here, bite on this, and you two ... hold him down. The wounded man's younger brother and one of his mates took hold of his hands and shoulders as he bit on the leather, and Sarah wiped his face gently with a damp cloth and began her probing.

Shrubb turned to his next patient, who was clutching a blood-soaked cloth to his face. Pulling it carefully aside he revealed a long open slash wound from temple to jaw. 'Very nice and clean. All you'll need is a bit of needlework and you'll be almost as handsome as ever.'

Tom Hogben forced a painful smile and clutched the bloody cloth to his wound again.

'My Sarah will sort you out soon as she's finished digging for the rest of Joe Hobbs' trousers. There's no-one so quick and neat with a needle and thread.'

Ned Heale had taken a cutlass blow to his right shoulder, and another blow had severed two fingers from his left hand, which had already been bandaged and was being held up by his mate to avoid further loss of blood.

Shrubb carefully pulled off Heale's coat, which fortunately for him had blunted the blow somewhat. He revealed a bloody welt and what promised to develop into impressive bruising.

'Not bad at all,' Shrubb decided. 'We'll bandage that and strap you up. You should be good as new in a couple of weeks.'

Fagg queried: 'Gonna be a bit tricky for 'im to eat and such with both his arms in slings, ain't it Phineas?'

'True enough,' Shrubb agreed, telling Heale: 'You'll know who your real friends are in a day or two. Pity we can't sew your fingers back on for you, but I doubt that'd ever be possible in our lifetime, even supposing we could find 'em.'

Anson asked: 'Are you married Heale?'

'Dear me no, sir, but me muvver's a widder an' she'll look arter me.'

'Aye, sir,' confirmed his mate. 'I've sent fer her and she'll be 'ere presently I 'spect.'

Indicating Heale's hand, Anson sympathised. 'Very sorry that you've lost two of your fingers. Damned shame that. But we'll make sure you are looked after until you're fit enough to work again.'

Heale was philosophic. 'Could 'ave bin wuss, sir. Could 'ave bin me Saturday night finger. Now that would've bin ockered!'

Anson smiled, and he looked across at Sarah, now busily stitching Hobbs' leg, to see that her face, too, bore the merest ghost of a smile. For a strictly brought-up Baptist girl, she clearly knew more than most about the ways of the world.

Confident that the wounded were in good hands, Anson signalled Fagg to follow him and they left the pub and headed for the Bayle.

On the way, he told the bosun: 'We've been incredibly lucky. Only three men anything like badly hurt and all three likely to make a good recovery, and Sampson Marsh's cut's not too bad at all. The rest, well, scratches, bruises and bumps – that's it.'

Fagg agreed. 'If we 'adn't caught them Froggies by surprise like, and if more of 'em 'ad loaded their muskets and whatnot it could've bin annuver story altogether.'

As they made their way up the steep and winding High Street, shopkeepers and their customers stopped what they were doing to turn and stare. Everyone in the town now knew who these men were. Every inhabitant must have heard gunfire, and already the word was spreading about what would no doubt soon become known as the Battle of Seagate.

An aproned baker came to the doorway of his shop and called out: 'Beaten the Frogs 'ave you, gents?'

Anson touched his hat. 'Aye, you might say your Sea Fencibles have given them a bit of a drubbing.'

'Good on you, sir. Tryin' to invade was they?'

'Not quite. Just a bit of piracy.'

And Fagg threw in: 'We give 'em a bloody nose orlright. That lot won't bovver us no more.'

By the time they reached the fencible building, they were being followed by a small crowd of well-wishing information-seekers who were becoming increasingly difficult to fob off.

Outside the battery, a familiar figure was in conversation with the mayor and assorted portly town worthies. Anson groaned: 'I feared as much. Captain Hoare is already reporting his great victory ...'

Fagg made to comment but was stopped with a glare from Anson. It was the duty of a petty officer to acquire selective deafness whenever his superior said something insubordinate about one of his superiors.

Hoare was showing the mayor a sword. It did not require a genius to work out that this must be the one Anson had returned to the French captain, only for Hoare to snatch it back, together with his honour.

As Anson and Fagg approached, Hoare was holding forth. 'The very blade gentlemen, the very blade, no doubt encrusted with the blood of innocent English seafarers – the very blade that damned rascally Frenchman surrendered to me not an hour since!'

'Well done, sir, well done indeed!' the mayor exclaimed to assorted 'hear, hears' and 'well saids' from his fellow townsmen.

'Merely doing my duty, gentlemen. Pleased to have made this stretch of coast a little safer. One less piratical Frenchmen to interfere with trade, eh?'

Hoare spotted Anson approaching but appeared in no way fazed. With apparent generosity he told the assembled townsmen: 'Lieutenant Anson, here, played his part too gentlemen. As did all your Seagate men serving with my Sea Fencibles. Spilt a drop or two of blood, did some. But no permanent damage done, eh Anson?'

So little concern had the divisional captain shown towards the casualties, that he had marched right past them without a word or a backward look. He was keener by far to bask in the acclaim of the mayor and his hangers-on.

But Anson's face concealed his growing contempt for his superior. Instead, he touched his hat dutifully and reported formally. 'We've three men with significant wounds, sir, but Shrubb is reasonably confident they'll make a full recovery. One has lost two fingers though. And there's a dozen more with cuts and bruises. Nothing too serious.'

'How about the French?' the mayor enquired.

'We need to double-check the numbers, sir, but there are certainly 13 dead, almost all killed when one of our gunboats fired its carronade into their gun-deck.' He looked at Fagg. 'How many wounded, would you say ... a dozen?'

Fagg agreed. 'Somefink like that, sir, and round abaht 30 prisoners.'

Hoare demanded: 'Who's guarding them? For heaven's sake don't give them an opportunity to escape!'

'The wounded are being treated by two local doctors and the rest are quite reconciled to their fate, sir. Some of my most trusted men have a party of them at work bringing their dead comrades out of the ship. The rest are confined under guard awaiting the arrival of the troops you sent for from Shorncliffe to escort them to the hulks at Chatham.'

'Where is their leader?'

'Capitaine Lapraik is at liberty, having given his parole, and is helping the doctors tend his wounded men.'

'At liberty? By whose leave?'

'Mine, sir. Notwithstanding his current profession, he is a proper French naval officer, and, I believe, a man of honour. That is why I returned him his sword.'

Hoare reddened. 'Honour be damned! The man's nothing but a pirate. You may have picked it up, but he surrendered his sword to me as commander of the force that took his ship. Confine him immediately with the rest of his cut-throats. I'll not have a man like him wandering loose in Seagate frightening children and old ladies!'

The mayor nodded approvingly, and Hoare addressed the growing crowd of townsmen. 'Your worship, gentlemen, if you would care to accompany me down to the harbour, I invite you to inspect this captured privateer and the scum who crewed her.'

There was general assent, and the mayor seized the opportunity to become part of the day's triumph and ingratiate himself with his fellow townsmen by inviting all to take a glass with him after they had looked over *Égalité*.

Hoare beamed enthusiastically. 'Splendid, Mr Mayor, splendid! And you will have the pleasure of witnessing the handover of my prisoners to the military.'

Anson and Fagg slipped away and headed back to the Stade. He would have to explain to Capitaine Lapraik that, despite giving his parole, he would have to join his men under guard.

By the time Captain Hoare and his admiring and growing entourage arrived there, he had well and truly planted the seed that he fervently hoped would grow into a civic dinner in his honour, ideally highlighted by the award of a presentation sword subscribed for by the town's business community.

News of the Battle of Seagate had spread widely and crowds had gathered around the harbour area, anxious for a glimpse of the victors – and the vanquished Frenchmen.

They were rewarded with plenty of spectacle, the bringing ashore of the dead Frenchmen, whose bodies were laid out in a row on the cobbles, the arrival of a detachment of the scarlet-jacketed Cinque Ports Volunteers to take charge of the prisoners, and all climaxed by the arrival of the supposed *victor ludorum*, accompanied by the mayor and leading members of the corporation.

Ignored by the crowds, Anson, the true victor, threaded his way through the gawpers to the pub where the French casualties were being treated. At all costs he determined to make sure Capitaine Lapraik was not humiliated further by the puffed up Hoare.

45

Wearily, Anson made his way back to the Rose Inn. He had barely slept or eaten properly for many hours and was close to exhaustion.

The landlord was all smiles. 'You've been busy, so I hear, sir?'

'You could say that. I'm certainly ready for my bed, Mr Griggs. Any chance of some food? A cold plate? Anything will do.'

Griggs grinned. 'Already thought of, and as soon as thought of, fixed. You'll find a plate of cold meat and bread in your room along with a nice bottle of red.'

'Good man. Most thoughtful. I'll bid you goodnight, then.'

As Anson turned for the stairs, Griggs called: 'Oh, by the way, sir, you're bed's bin turned down and warmed for you. I daresay you'll sleep like a bebby tonight!'

Slightly puzzled at such solicitude, Anson thanked him again and climbed the steep and narrow stairs, holding the wooden banister to prevent himself stumbling. He was more fatigued than he had been since his escape from France, or even his early days in the service when mastheaded by a Spartan first lieutenant for some long-forgotten misdemeanour had drained him of all energy.

There was a dim light under his bedroom door. Griggs had even thought to leave a lighted candle for him.

But when he opened the door, he realised the reason for the landlord's knowing grin. The supper plate was on the bedside table, along with the promised wine. And by the light of the single flickering candle he could see that his bed was being warmed right enough, but not by a bedpan.

'My sailor, home from the sea. I thought you would never come!'

It was Charlotte Brax, hair loose on the pillow, her bosom straining against a tight and diaphanous nightgown.

'Good grief!' Anson could not have been more surprised if he had found one of the sea lords in his bed. Charlotte pouted. 'It would have been rather more flattering if you'd said 'heavens' instead of 'grief', dear boy.'

Anson spluttered. 'You took me aback. How on earth did you …?' But he knew the answer before he had completed the question. This formidable young lady would have no difficulty getting anywhere she wanted. 'I suppose the landlord—?'

She smiled knowingly. 'The landlord seems to have a soft spot for me. In fact I rather think he'd liked to have kept me company while I was waiting for you. Now, take off that scruffy uniform and join me in this nice warm bed.' And she patted the mattress beside her, as if smoothing a place for a pet cat.

*

Next day, Captain Hoare penned his report, written on the basis that Anson would not have sight of it. No, it would go straight to the Admiralty and by the time it was Gazetted, as he fervently hoped, it would be as gospel.

In any event, Hoare had by now convinced himself that he and he alone had master-minded the whole operation and carried it out with great personal *élan*.

He had worked out what needed to be said, and, decanter of wine beside him to ease the effort of composition, he addressed his despatch in the customary style:

'Divisional Captain To My Lord Commissioners

To inform your Lordships of the successful taking of a French privateer off the port of Seagate by gunboats of the Special Sea Fencible Detachment under my command. The privateer Égalité, of 12 guns, out of Normandy, has been a regular raider along the coasts of Kent and Sussex for some months past, boarding, taking or robbing and sinking a number of small craft and causing disruption to trade.

The operation, which I had been planning for some time in line with intelligence gathered by me from westward, was timed to coincide with the privateer's predicted appearance in the area of our Channel ports. It was carried out by two of the new gunboats currently being trialled by the said detachment under my command, and it is respectfully suggested that its success was largely due to the manoeuvrability and armament of these craft and of the determination and high level of training of my Sea Fencible crews.

The privateer which was in the act of attempting to capture a …'

He scratched his head, searching for the right word. A small coaster did not sound sufficiently important. Then he found just the word, underlined it and continued,

'...*merchantman was herself taken by surprise in a carefully planned operation, fired upon by my gunboats, boarded and taken after a stiff action following which the master of Égalité, styling himself Capitaine Lapraik, surrendered his sword to me.*'

He paused to take a swig of claret and think through what else needed to be said. Casualties, hmm. Wouldn't do to play them down. Those Whitehall warriors tend to judge an action by the amount of blood shed …

So he continued:

'*Fifteen of my men were wounded, some seriously. Of the French, some 30 were killed or wounded, and the remaining 35, including their captain, taken prisoner and handed over by me to a military detachment I summoned from Shorncliffe for escort to the Medway hulks.*'

Slight poetic license perhaps, but he could hardly be accused of exaggerating the butcher's bill. After all, the numbers could not be faulted if cuts and bruises were taken into account.

Now he would have to acknowledge some assistance from Anson, but no need to pile it on. Uppity young officers were best reminded of their place in the pecking order through the judicious use of faint praise, and Hoare was a past master at that. He took another sip of claret, dipped his nib and continued:

'*I have the honour to commend to your Lordships the steadiness and resolve of the S F and mention the support I received from Lieutenant Anson, of the Seagate Special Detachment, and Lieutenant Coney, of the Folkestone Impress Service, under my command.*'

That, he thought, would do nicely. Anson would not like it. But then he would not see it until it appeared in that official Bible, the *London Gazette*. And by then …

An apt quotation came to him, and he amused himself by reciting aloud: 'The Moving Finger writes; and, having writ, Moves on: nor all thy Piety nor Wit Shall lure it back to cancel half a Line, Nor all thy Tears wash out a Word of it.'

Not, he thought, that Anson had much piety or wit, and he was unlikely to burst into tears!

Now, a spot of prize money would come in handy – and would make him extremely popular with the men. And head money too, for the prisoners, at the going rate of £5 a head. So Hoare moved his pen on, adding:

'In view of the exceptional efforts made by the Sea Fencibles in ridding the coast of a hitherto extremely troublesome raider that had caused considerable losses to our merchant shipping, I respectfully request that your Lordships consider authorising the award of prize money and head money in this case.

I am Sir, your obedient servant
Arthur Veryan St Cleer Hoare
Captain Royal Navy.'

*

Her scent lingered on, but she was gone by the time Anson regained the land of the living. He splashed his face at the washstand and as he shaved he thought back over the encounters with *Égalité* – and with Charlotte.

Clearing up the aftermath of the battle with the privateer would be irksome but straightforward, and Boxer would be a great help with the inevitable paperwork, although no doubt the divisional captain would already have been hard at work polishing his own image at Anson's expense in the official report.

He could safely leave the physical tidying up to Fagg and Hoover, although he would make a point of visiting the wounded himself. That was a matter of duty.

And he must get a message to Armstrong at Fairlight to let him know that their plan had resulted in a highly successful outcome.

After such a victory over the French, and last night's cavorting with Charlotte Brax, he knew any man should be feeling elated. But he did not.

The contests with the Normandy privateer had given him a purpose and her capture would inevitably leave a void.

And somehow he knew that by succumbing to lust once again, he had painted himself into a tight corner.

So it was that, as he went down to breakfast under the knowing eye of the smirking publican, he felt not only a sense of anti-climax but a twinge of shame and apprehension, too.

Brooding over his eggs and bacon, his attention was grabbed by the noisy arrival of Fagg, annoyingly cheery and loud.

The bosun knuckled his forehead. 'Beg pardin for interruptin' brekfust, sir, and a good mornin' to you and all that, but there's a hurgent message what's come for you from Commodore Poporf, or whatever he calls hisself, by way of a dragoon. It ain't writ down, so I've 'ad to remember it. Wants you to drop everythin' and get yerself up to Chatham soonest. Says he's got a himportant mission for you and time is of the hessence!'

Anson waved him to a chair, and signalled the landlord to bring the bosun a plate of bacon and eggs. What, he wondered, could Commodore Home Popham want with him – and at Chatham?

This was not normal chain of command stuff, otherwise the message would surely have come through the divisional captain. So could it be something to do with the special role he was promised when appointed to the Sea Fencibles?

There was only one way to find out, and he called for the ostler to ready his horse.

Historical Note

Had HMS *Phryne* existed, the raid on the Normandy coast in an attempt to cut out a troublesome privateer could well have happened, maybe with a similar outcome. Anyone visiting St Valery-en-Caux today can see that, with its mole and sheltered inner harbour, it would have indeed been a tough nut to crack.

An Auberge du Marin does exist, although well away from the location it is given in The Normandy Privateer. It is a good place to stay, with excellent cuisine and cellar. The inn has perfectly good loos – and today's patron certainly does not use the front wall as a urinal!

Lieutenant Anson, his fellow-escapers and most of those they encounter, are, of course, entirely fictional, although based to some degree on characters the author has come across in all three services over the years. Weapons, uniforms and conditions of service may have changed dramatically since the Napoleonic era, but the cheerful, courageous, indomitable spirit and sense of humour of the British serviceman lives on.

The Sea Fencibles did exist. They were a naval militia – a kind of Dad's Navy – during the French Revolutionary and Napoleonic Wars. They were the brainchild of the peculiarly named Commodore, later Rear Admiral, Sir Home Riggs Popham, a controversial, scientifically-minded officer known to some in the service as 'a damned cunning fellow'.

The fishermen, boatmen – and no doubt smugglers – who served as Sea Fencibles were commanded by regular naval officers and given a protection against being pressed for the Royal Navy. They were paid a shilling a day for training with the great guns, muskets and pikes to protect Britain's coastline from invasion.

Although the threatened invasion never came, they were involved in a number of actions, mainly against French privateers, but assessments as to their worth and effectiveness varied considerably. They were disbanded at the Peace of Amiens, but reinstated when war broke out again in 1803, and served on until 1810, by which time all likelihood of invasion had long passed.

Hardres Minnis, Farthingham and their inhabitants are a fiction, but if they did exist you would find them among Kent's ancient manorial commons, most now enclosed, in that remote triangle of the North Downs, between Canterbury, Folkestone and Ashford.

Most of the other characters are fictitious, but Phineas Shrubb is based on a real person who was indeed a Kentish apothecary, glover, Baptist preacher and later surgeon's mate in a warship, and he did advertise his cures as described.

Similarly, Seagate is a figment of the imagination. It is near Folkestone, but is not Seabrook nor Sandgate, although it is located somewhere to the west, close to Dungeness Bay, where the Spanish Armada had planned to land troops, and Napoleon might have done had it not been for the Royal Navy.

Oliver Anson, distant kinsman many times removed of the great circumnavigator and reformer of the navy, has, as yet, not carried out any of the clandestine missions Home Popham had envisaged for him. But, in time, he, Fagg, Hoover and their oddball fencibles, will sail again.

Printed in Great Britain
by Amazon